AVALON
LOST

LIGHTYEARS TO BEFORE GO I SLEEP

LARRY GENT

ALSO BY LARRY GENT

The Benedict Forecasts
Be All That You Envy (2018)
Never Been To Mars
To Money And A TV
Bedroom Walls That Save Us (2018)

Vörissa's Catalyst Online

Patch 1.01: New Game+
Patch 1.02: Escort Mission
Patch 1.03: Corpse Run
Patch 1.04: In Another Castle
Patch 1.05: Silent Protagonist

LIGHTYEARS
TO BEFORE
GO I SLEEP

LARRY GENT

Published in Canada by Midnight Reading Publishing, Ottawa

Gent, Larry, 1983-, Author.
      Lightyears To Go Before I Sleep: Avalon Lost / Larry Gent
ISBN: 978-0-9959515-0-1
Ebook ISBN: 978-0-9959515-1-8
Copyright © 2017 Larry Gent

Cover Design: Hampton Lamoureux

Midnight Reading Publishing
511 Brittany Drive
Ottawa, Ontario
K1K 0S1

To my loving wife, Valérie Gent.

You are my stern manager, my drink waitress, my kitten wrangler, my dial-a-distraction and my #1 fan. You've always been there for me and I can never properly show how much that means to me.

Thank you.

I love you.

You are my RL Perfect Ten!

AVALON
LOST

The day humans took to the stars, they discovered many things. They learned they were not alone, they learned that the galaxy was full of new races and they learned that many beings didn't like humans at all.

When a war resulted in Earth become uninhabitable, humanity had no option but to build three of the biggest ships ever seen - each the size of a small state - and live on them as they sailed the stars. They built the *Argyre*, the *Mag Mell*, and the *Avalon*.

Humanity's enemies destroyed the *Argyre*.

The *Mag Mell* made a jump into warp and was never seen from again.

Only the *Avalon* remains.

Legally designated a 'floating planet', the *Avalon* is a city in a ship and the crown jewel of the Human Endurance Fleet. It floats through the stars acting as the home planet for all of humanity until they can find a suitable replacement. Because even amongst the stars everybody needs a place they can call home.

Welcome to the *Avalon*.

CHAPTER ONE
8 days until Pherca Moon Invasion

Captain Agrima Cantor eagerly turned the page as she read, her eyes engrossed in the ongoing events that unfolded between the covers. Books were available dominantly on datapad, digital forms of the bricks they once used to be. Yet for those lucky enough to have experienced it nothing compared to reading a book the way they were always meant, pristine ink on strong pages all bound together with a reinforced hardcover. She leaned back in her chair, her legs resting on her desk as her right hand dropped to the furry body that rested in her lap. Her fingers scratched the feline behind his ears, her fingers motions quickly garnering approving purr. In the days past she never had time to read, let alone to read and finish a book during working hours, but life had changed for the Captain. She no longer had the same lifestyle she once did.

A beep from her console pulled Cantor from her vivid world of fantasy and back into reality. She closed the book, dropped it on the table and keyed in her security code. Practice allowed her to do all of this without disturbing the high overlord that slept in her lap. The captain groaned as she read over the bulletin.

She reached to her lap and guided the jet black cat to the floor. "Sorry, Cinders, but its work time." The cat landed gracefully on the floor, circling around the chair. He watched and waited for his pet, the human Captain, to rise from the chair - *his* chair - and put on her uniform jacket before leaping back into the now vacant spot. He curled up into a ball, his eyes following her as his human pet exited his office.

Captain Cantor exited her ready room onto the bridge, her demeanour changing the moment she fell upon her staff's eyes. On her own she was allowed to relax, on the bridge she had to project confidence. Out on the bridge she was in charge. Her word was the law and all of her crew needed to see strength and leadership in her actions.

"The away team is returning," she barked. The officer on duty rose from the main chair and approached the helmsmen. "Inform docking and prepare for their landing. Unless the good Doctor Tsia says different we will being moving onto the next designated sector."

A small purple alien, humanoid but significantly smaller, looked up from the science console with a concerned look. "Be they safe?" Cantor replied with a nod as she took her chair. The science officer clapped her hands together and looked to the heavens. "Blessed be the *Spellsong*."

Cantor rolled her eyes and rubbed the bridge of her nose. The alien was Hera'sun and the best damned science officer to man at that station, alien or human. Cantor had done a lot to keep Hera'sun on her crew, fighting off reassignment orders from HEF and recall notices from Hera'sun's own species, the Monastica, but having her as the science officer meant dealing with her and her racially strong religious beliefs. To the Monastica everything was a blessing, and everything required thanks. Even the most trivial aspects of their life, the end of a day, a good meal or a pleasant smile needed them to clap their hands in praise.

The ship's shuttle and crew was returning with nothing to show for it. It was expected, the mission being an archaeological survey of recently discovered ruins on numerous dead planets but after each returning from each mission with little to no new data, it became harder and harder to care. Cantor and her crew would do this mission to the very best that their skills allowed but it still seemed like a waste of resources.

Cantor took her chair and pulled her keypad close. Habit dictated that when Cantor sat at her chair that the first thing she did was check the ship's readings and sensor scans. The numbers on her screen were identical to those it displayed six hours earlier: the ship, the *Mojave Desert*, was fighting fit and this region of space was beyond empty. It was dead space, filled with planets long since abandoned and long since deceased.

The planet they currently orbited was just another

dead rock, one more celestial body scratched off an ever shortening list; another planet not suitable for home. There were standing orders for every human vessel: search for a new home. It wasn't a complicated directive - the search for a planet to replace the Earth that was lost - but the practice was difficult. There existed thousands of planets in the Milky Way galaxy but not many left to choose from. Hundreds of planets were spoken for, belonging and inhabited by the hundreds of sentient races that existed out there. Humans were not the first species to take to the stars and when they got there, they didn't make friends easily. With every good planet taken and most of the rest dead or inhabitable, humans were left with no option but to carry on sailing the stars, searching every every rock for somewhere to call home.

But for now, alone in the dead of space, Captain Cantor was assigned a babysitter mission. Most captains would be insulted to be on such a mission but for her it was a saving grace, the lifesaver for her naval career. Transferred off of the *C.S.S Molokai*, Cantor was pulled from combat; something that had needed to be done.

Cantor looked at her clock; the shuttle should be on board now. She pushed her keypad away and rose from her chair. "OOD," she ordered, using the officer on duty's acronym, "Plot a course for the next sector and warm up the sub-light engines. We launch on my command. OOD take the chair, and await my comm."

Cantor ducked through the doorway and made her was down the hall. The *Mojave Desert* was a much smaller ship then she was used to, her last beauty was a frontline battleship, but she could make it from *Mojave*'s bow to stern in twenty minutes, ten if she double-timed it. This ship and its weapons battery was a fraction of what she was used to but it was more then she needed. Weapons didn't make a captain great, tactics did. The *Mojave* wouldn't be frontline fighting but she could still protect herself when needed.

She reached the docking bay just as the away-team started to strip the life suits off their tired bodies. The away team was small, her Chief of Security Lieutenant Commander Harold Morrison and one of his security team, Petty Officer 2nd Class Marcus Branford, her shuttle pilot Sub-Lieutenant Denver Cole, Hera'sun's mate and archaeologist Nurem'sun, and the civilian team lead, and scholar in charge of the mission, Dr. Bristol Tsia.

Cantor crossed her arms and watched her team. "Status reports please, Lieutenant."

"Aye, ma'am," Morrison's accent was thick; the kind that made ma'am sound like mom. It was a classical accent, traditional to the upper levels of *Avalon*. "No injuries, no damage, no threat. Everybody is five by five."

"Bravo Zulu, Lieutenant." Cantor looked over at the human archaeologist. "Dr. Tsia, what did you find?"

"Just more markings on more fallen walls," Tsia replied. She had many long days worth of study and review ahead of her, all with the hopes of deciphering the ruins and drawing historical conclusions of the past but none of that meant anything to the captain. "We're done here and can move on to the next sector whenever you're ready, Captain."

Cantor reached for the wall-mounted communication unit and dialled the bridge. The hum of the sublights powering on echoed through the ship as she gave the order to move.

Tsia pulled off her helmet and scratched the back of her head with an ecstatic sigh. It never failed, when she knew she couldn't scratch was the moment she really had to and being stuck in a space suit as she walked a planet with no air defiantly qualified.

Tsia was a conundrum of a woman, the aftermath of two worlds. She looked mostly human; a lithe body, firm, toned muscles, and limber legs, but for those who looked closely there were notable differences. Her light blue hair was easy to overlook, a colour easily replicated through artificial means, but the true difference lay in her eyes. The irises were a deep and hypnotic violet, an unnatural colour for humans which seemed to draw a person in and ensnared their gaze. The deeper one stared into her eyes, the more the colours seemed to swirl and twist like a kaleidoscope. It wasn't human but neither was her father. Doctor Bristol Tsia was an example of a growing trend and one that not all humans agreed with. She was of the part of the genesis of the Neo-Humans, one of the first of the inter-species offspring.

Bristol's mother was human - she was open about

this - but nobody really knew what race her father was. It was a big mystery and not one that Dr. Tsia enjoyed speaking on.

"Alright, Doctor Tsia,"Cantor said as she released the comm. button. "File your survey reports into the system and begin the preparations for the next sector and planets. Morrison and Cole: the XO will need your reports as well."

Morrison gave the Captain a snap confirmation as she exited the docking bay. Petty Officer Branford collected firearms from the military and civilians alike.

Admiral Richard Golden frowned as he looked at the orders before him. They didn't make sense but there they were, staring him directly in the face. As he re-read the orders for the fifth time his mind retreated to his military classes from his youth, retreated to a question he was asked by his professor.

What is the difference between an officer and an NCO? The class filled with answers of responsibility and duty but one student, one of the few officer candidates to be risen from the ranks of NCO, gave an answer unlike anybody else in the class.

"An NCO's duty is to obey orders; an officer's is to question those that don't make sense."

The orders before Admiral Golden didn't make any sense and neither did the person who gave them. He didn't look important, dressed in a long grey trench coat, military boots, black slacks and a white t-shirt. Yet he designated as Codename: Keepsake. The Admiral knew nothing about him, aparently nobody did. His file was virtually empty. It held nothing about him, nothing about his military career and nothing about his past. It just had instructions. There were detailed regulations about what he could and could not do and the 'could not' section was almost non-existent. The Keepsake protocol seemed to give him a temporary rank with near limitless power, authority and jurisdiction but never for long.

Before today, the Admiral had never seen or heard of the Keepsake protocol but here it stood, in human form, requesting access to another protocol he'd never heard of: the Fragarach protocol.

"Are you sure of this?" the admiral asked again. The admiral did not know what the protocol did; he was willing to admit that because nobody knew. The Fragarach protocol had existed within the *Avalon* system since the ship's creation and in all that time it had never been accessed and never been altered and yet the Keepsake wanted to do both. The only thing anybody knew about the protocol was that it was set in place to protect the *Avalon* in the event of a great disaster and that the file had an attached clock, slowly ticking downwards. The file wasn't to be opened until the timer reach zero. "It is almost fifty years too early."

The Keepsake paced frantically in the admiral's office, his hands by his face and his two middle fingers bouncing up and down like they were fanning him.

"I know; I know; I know; everything been sped up. It makes no sense. This is not the way things are supposed to happen. The program's wrong but it is never wrong, which mean someone is changing the program, but who, and why, and how?"

Golden watched in amazement as the Keepsake erratically paced around the room, touching anything and everything as he tried to explain. His speech was quick, erratic and randomly changed in pitch. "Me and Wiki, Wiki and I, we both have it figured out. We have worked on the math and we have watched the waves of space. Now is the time, the *Avalon* will come under great disaster and you need to the Fragarach protocol."

"What is the disaster?"

"I can't tell you, I am not allowed," the Keepsake made a loud and slightly disturbing irritated sound, "I don't even know if what I am doing now is allowed. To be honest I don't even know if the disaster is the same. Why don't people ever listen to me? Just activate the project; I gave you the master code, so just do it."

The admiral sighed. "Fine, but you really need to tell me the truth about who you are."

"No, I really, really do not, Admiral."

With an final deep breath the Admiral pulled his console close and booted up the program. It took two biometric scans, vocal recognition software and a typed-in code to activate. As the program started the Admiral found himself eagerly waiting to see what lay within. He wanted to see what was worth all the trouble.

The screen blinked with a map. It wasn't anything important, just a small sector in space and a blinking dot. It was located in what was *technically* known space but that was being generous. It was an empty sector of known space void of planets, moons or even a star. The program showed where this dot had been and where it was planning on going. The admiral stared in disbelief.

The Fragarach protocol was a tracking program for a single ship.

"What is this crap?" he asked, angry and disappointed. "How is this dot supposed to help us?"

"You need to send your closest ship to that dot, now! Well, you were suppose to send a ship there yesterday by the new program calculations but we will chalk that error up to me. I have a lot of errors under my belt but I can always use more."

The admiral just shook his head as he keyed up a log of all human ships, military and civilian. He wanted to send one of his biggest ships, or his flag ship. He wanted to make sure this dot, whatever the hell it was, did not fall into any other races' hands but all of the ships were days or weeks away; all except for one. He brought up the ships information and smiled. He didn't like the size of this ship or it armaments, but he did like the captain. The admiral grabbed his comm-unit and called his assistant.

"I need you to get long range communications up. Call the *Mojave Desert* and get me Captain Agrima Cantor. I have new orders for her."

CHAPTER TWO
8 Days until Pherca Moon Inva---
24 hours until attack on Kiron Po ---

ERROR: DATE UNKNOWN

"The dreams, they always started the same way. They start off pleasant enough," the soldier whispered. "They start off like we are now. Both of us are in bed, I have my arms around you, holding your body tight against mine. I can feel the warmness of your bare skin against my breasts, I can feel your heart beat, slowly and steady, uncaring for the horrors that the dawn will bring but that was always you. You could fall asleep easily and sleep through anything. You didn't let stress get between you and whatever it is you see when you sleep.

"It doesn't work like that for me. I am cursed with the thoughts of every mission, every detail and every person. The first time this happened, the real time, you fell asleep almost instantly. I stayed awake for nearly four hours before I finally fell asleep to the sound of your breathing.

"Now I don't want to close my eyes because I know what will happen. It happens every single time, my eyelids will close and things change. The world will become fuzzy, like static in a movie and when I open my eyes I'll be outside. I will have to give that speech again - I hate that speech now - and then it begins. Those creatures will attack us, wave after wave, and I will fight. It's all I know how to do: fight. I will fight with everything I've got but they won't stop or slow down. I will fight and I will lose. They say I won; the hero of The Last Stand at Kiron Port but I didn't win. Humanity won that battle; I lost it. I lost my friends, I lost my family and I lost you. I lost everything and now I have to relive it, night after night, year after year. I think I died that day, died in the explosion and the bombings and this is my punishment for a life of murder. This is my own personal hell.

"I can feel it, my body's tired, and it wants to sleep but I know what will happen if I do. I am going to wake up, and I am going to have to watch you die." The solider, Allana Guiver felt her eyelids get heavy, her eyelashes pulling down until it happened. Her eyes fell closed.

When her eyes opened Allana found herself where she always did, standing before a docking door with the love of her life trapped on the other side. Tenuvah Sheppard: a long blonde haired woman with green eyes and a need to heal. She was a doctor, a woman sworn to do no harm.

"What are you doing, Allana? Let me out!" Tenuvah screamed, jamming the keypad over and over, each press getting a depressing error beep. She gave up, resorting to smashing her fist against the steel, tears rolling down her cheeks. "Let me out. Don't do this to me."

"Get on the ship and get out of here." Allana's pistol dropped from her hand. She pressed her hand on the transparent steel. "I need you to live; I need you to continue being my Perfect Ten."

The doctor cried, dropping to her knees. "I hate that name so much."

"I know you do, babe," Allana laughed, her eyes already tearing up. "But you need to go and be safe, you need to go and help people. I am going to go and make sure you get there and, for god's sake, please listen this time. Please!"

He found her in a corner of a side room, crying softly. Master Corporal Christian Tribal was the only person that could approach her like this. No one else even dared. She was Major Allana Guiver: the legendary soldier. She had led thousands of soldiers into battle and taken on hundreds of missions. To everybody else, she was relentless warrior and an unwavering figure of strength but he never saw her that way. It wasn't that he was special or had a connection to the Major. It was just that he understood that beneath the legend lay a woman, one as frightened and scared as the rest of them.

They were on a suicide mission. Every fighting man and woman on that rock understood that and they all had accepted it but Allana had less chance than any to get out. She would be the first on the field and the last to retreat. She wouldn't leave until every last breathing person on that Port made it out. So while a part of her was happy she sent the Doctor away, Tribal understood that she'd basically said her final goodbyes to the women she loved.

"Major." It was only a single word, he rarely said much, but it carried with it the strength she needed. She looked up at the young sniper. Others could have their faith in her tested by seeing the Major like this, but for Tribal, it only strengthen it.

Without another word he offered her his hand. With a sniffle and sounds that seemed like the cross between a grunt and a cough, she took the hand and climbed to her feet. The sniper handed her a battle rifle and nodded.

She nodded back, and with a deep breath, proclaimed "Let's go be heroes."

"It doesn't matter where you're from," Allana began. She stood triumphantly atop the table, her military voice booming across the entire base. This was the speech, the speech she had given time and time again and the speech she now loathed. It had worked so well the first time but repeating those same words, over and over for all of eternity, had soured the words in her mouth. "I don't care what country you're from, what colony, what ship, what platoon, what division or even what room because as of right now you are all in Guiver's Battalion and you belong to me.

"We have one mission and one mission only: to get the civilians off this port. The Navy pilots are going to fly escort so that leaves us with no air support. So we do this the old fashion way. We will man every cannon, every AA gun and every turret on that wall. Everyone who can hold a weapon will hold one because those four legged, spine-backed bastards are going to descend from the valley with everything they've got and we have to keep them at bay. We will not falter; we will not fail. We are Guiver's Battalion and we do not lose. We will hold the line and we will prevail.

"We are getting our friends and family off this planet and there is not a damn thing that those aliens can do about it. We have a chance to end this war today and to save a whole lot of people. So we will fight and we will win. Do you understand?"

A loud *yes, ma'am* filled the air. This was enough for the Major but the Master Warrant Officer wanted more. He needed more. "Oi! The Major said do ye understan'?"

The major cracked a smiled as a deafening *yes, ma'am* drowned out all other sound. That was Brian McCree, her Master Warrant Officer. MWO McCree was infantry, born, bred and raised. There was no other trade for him. He was a gruff man, tough as nails and deadly with a gun, any gun. He was a highlander or a Teuchter as he called it. He spoke in a tongue that half the time she couldn't understand and the other half she didn't want to. But he was loyal and he was deadly.

"Everybody grab a gun and get on the wall," Guiver barked, "and we will send these godless bastards to the depth of hell."

"Da."It was a chilling Russian accent made scarier when one saw the man who spoke it. He was Sergeant Piotr Budian and he was the battalion's explosives expert. "Guns are secure, my Major."

"Man the AA." Guiver glanced over at the young man with a grin on his face: Corporal Jamie Diswal. "Kid, you five by five?"

"Hell, ma'am," He laughed. "Fighting without twenty-five kilos on my back? This'll be a walk in the cake."

Diswal was the signals operator; he normally fought with a massive radio strapped to his back. The kid was young, full of piss and vinegar and he was never more than two steps away from having a good time. Sadly the kid never had a mind for sayings or proverbs. "Where's your lucky bowler?"

With a twirl, Diswal drantically placed his hat atop his head. "Safe and sound, right where it belongs. It ain't going to do much in my bag now is it?"

Guiver just smirked. The kid's eternally positive attitude was infectious. "Take the right end, keep them off the wall."

Every time the battle repeated it went the same way, no matter what she tried and no matter how she altered her plan, she never could deviate from what had happened. She relived it, time and time, the exact same day, the exact same horror. It played out like a scripted show. Guiver took to the wall with her rifle in hand and looked out on the valley below. The Arau Pau, an alien race that looked like a hunched over human with an exposed spinal cord, stormed forward on all fours with guns mounted on their backs. They charged up the hill with an unmatched animalistic carnage. The Major leveled her weapon and let out a war cry. She opened fire.

The mounted gunfire ripped through the vanguard like a hot knife through butter. The bolts cleaving through skin and tearing off limbs, but the Arau Pau keep charging. The alien menace climbed the hill, fighting their way up to the walled spaceport. Christian tried to cull the herd, his sniper bolt slamming through skull after skull and as the Teuchter gunned them down with a steady hand, but they never stopped. They sent air attacks and Sergeant Budian shot them out of the sky but they never stopped. They sent para-troopers raining down from above and the Major picked them off before they reached the ground, but they never stopped. They just kept on coming.

They sent suicidal warriors strapped with explosive to breach the wall while others climbed over their fallen cohorts in an effort to scale. Guiver's Battalion put down each that approached with a bolt to the chest or caught them in an explosion but Guiver's men couldn't hold out forever. The Arau Pau just kept coming.

The first to fall was Budian, crushed by a chunk of falling debris. Allana cringed inside but fought onwards. Christian was next, shot from behind by a lone paratrooper lucky enough to make it within the walls. Allana died inside but did what Christian would have wanted and kept on fighting. When the wall was breeched and everybody fell back, the Major met her opposite; an Arau Pau Warmaster. It was stronger than the others, faster than most and grown with a greater urge to kill then any human was used to.

It knifed the Warrant Officer to death instantly, a blade cutting across his neck mid way through a leap. McCree's fallen body an afterthought as it tore onwards. The Warmaster ignored everybody else as he sprinted for Allana and pounced, its powerful clawed hands tearing her rifle in two. The Major's memories of wrestling the Warmaster were vivid, the vile smell of its breath, the feel of its harsh armoured skin against her fists, the pain of his returning strikes crippling her body and the coldness of the blade's steel as it was thrust deep into her lower stomach. But the memory that was most vivid in her mind was the combination of joy and fear Allana felt when the echo of a gunshot filled her ear.

A bolt tore the Warmaster's shoulder, then another, then a third. Allana kicked the beast off of her, drawing her pistol and firing a pair of her own deep into its chest. Allana scrambled to her feet and looked to her savoir.

The love of Allana's life, Tenuvah Sheppard, stood

behind her holding a pistol, her hands shaking. The first time it happened Allana felt regret that a woman who swore never to harm another soul had broken her vow in order to save Allana. The Major never thought herself worthy of such a sacrifice but she was still happy to see Tenuvah standing there. The horror came next, the moment she feared every time the dream restarted. Time seemed to slow as a burst of fire went off and four bolts tore through Sheppard's body. Allana knew it was four, it was always four. It was always to the same place and always at the same exact moment. No matter what the Major tried, no matter how she varied her battle plan it always happened the same way: Tenuvah died and Allana became an empty husk of a body. Each time it she was forced to experience her true love's death Allana's soul died a little more.

Allana closed her eyes, ready for death but when she opened them she found herself back in bed, holding a sleeping Tenuvah close. Allana cried. She knew things couldn't change, she knew what would happen and she knew had no choice.

She had to restart the day all over again.

"The dreams, they always started the same way. They start off pleasant enough," Allana whispered.

CHAPTER THREE
8 days until Pherca Moon Invasion

"A long time ago," Nurem'sun began, sitting at the head of the galley table. His wife sat to his right and numerous of the crew sat with them, hanging off of his every word. "Our planet was in dire straits. We were not the people we are now; we didn't have the racial religious guidance, we did not have the peace that holds us together; we were simply chaos.

"Our people were separated into colonies, hundreds of colonies, much like your countries, and nobody got along. So we fought. For eons we were driven by war. It manipulated our governments, swayed our people and was the strongest influence on our economy. We grew our science to build better guns, we improved our medicine to keep our fighters alive longer and we learned industry so we could build faster.

"Then the inevitable happened, we split the atom. The translation is iffy but our people called it the Bang Age. It sounds horrible in your tongue but the meaning is accurate. We rained nukes down upon each other, flooding our planet with fire and death. There are always casualties in war but our planet was quickly becoming the largest one."

Cantor watched, doing her best to hide her enjoyment of the story. She was not well versed in xeno-culture and xeno-religion but the basics were taught in officer training. The Monastic were one of humanity's closest, if not only, allies so all officers were taught as much about them as possible, mainly how not to accidentally cause a political issue. She knew this story, the origin of their governmental standing, but knowing the story and hearing it spoken by one so versed and charismatic was entirely different.

"At the moment of our end, the instant before we destroyed ourselves, our salvation came." He continued between sips of the large drink that sat before him. Nurem'sun was an archaeologist, he enjoyed telling a story and he was good at it. The problem was when you got him going sometimes it was hard to get him to stop. "On that day our race changed. It came from the heavens, on the day of the last battle of the last war, three purple lights appeared in the night sky together in a triangle and shone over the world."

Nurem'sun's little hands move energetically as he told his story, his eyes wide and his face vivid, like a teacher telling a story to a room full of eager children. "Our guns stopped working and our urge to kill vanished. For three days not a single gunshot fired and not a bomb dropped, instead we looked to the heavens and waited."

"Waited for what?" Nurem'sun smiled at the young pilot's eagerness. Cole clung desperately to every word the Monastic spoke, taking it all in. Cole was a young man, twenty-three, and a pilot whose skills were nothing short of making him a prodigy. He was new to the universe, a child becoming a man, and this was his first deep space posting. For Cole this was everything he enlisted into the navy for. He wanted to see the far reaches of space, he wanted to work with new races and he wanted to learn all he could about the verse. For a storytelling archaeologist, Cole was the perfect audience: attentive and eager to learn.

"We waited for a sign, any sign." With a dramatic wave of his hands he continued with his telling of history. "For decades a small group of philosophers, or cowards as they were known at the time, declared that the only way that the war would end would be if something drastic occurred that shook the world. These lights were that drastic event.

"On the third day, everything changed. Every radio, video-screen and holo-tube lit up and began broadcasting. It started with medical instructions, details on how to heal our wounded, followed by specs for an energy system unlike what we could ever come up with. There were details on energy propulsion, space travel and even the instructions to the gate system. All of this was light years ahead of what we could understand, let alone build, but it gave us hope.

"For two days the transmissions continued, uninterrupted, and then, as it mysteriously as it came, it vanished back into the black. The lights spent only five days in orbit but it had shaken my people to its core. None of the Monastic factions could understand the information; it was well beyond even the greatest of minds. So they gathered together, the best and brightest, each working together to understand the information, each planning on betraying the other the moment it all made sense, but as the months turned to years, the tensions died and science became our goal.

"My people debated for years about it, debating the meaning of its appearance but it came to an agreed idea. That it was the sign, a precursor for peace and prosperity. For some it became a divine sign, a religious calling. It wasn't long until a church built up around the visitor, people worshipping it for the peace it brought and the advancements it gave us."

Cole stared in disbelief, "An entire church based around a one-time sighting? You mean it never died down? The loyalty and faith, even as the generations passed?"

"It died down, youth tends to bring naysayers. But it happened two more times in our history, each at a moment of a great need, the same three lights, the same three day wait, and the same two days transmission of nothing but social, medical and technological advancements. After the third time it became evident. Those lights, which we later learned was called the

Spellsong, had become our savoir. It was an idea that spread planet wide, encompassing the majority of our race in a single religious belief."

"So your entire planet follows the same religion?" Cole was astonished, "Earth never could have that, even now on the *Avalon*, we have dozens of religions, most of which I have never heard of or even understand."

"But let me ask you this, Sub-Lieutenant Denver Cole," Nurem'sun asked with a laugh. "Have any of your religious figures come down to save your entire race? Have they ever made themselves known?"

Cole shook his head, "but doesn't the need of proof contradict the meaning of faith?"

Cantor laughed, the chuckle slipping past her lips. A religious zealot versus a hometown Christian; as much as she wanted to watch the racial debate a beep from the galley wall's comm. unit called for her attention.

"Go ahead," Agrima answered as the galley went quiet. The OOD on the other end quickly replied.

"Ma'am, I have an urgent message incoming for you on Priority One channels from the home bird farm."

Cantor rubbed her eyes, wincing internally as she did. Priority One channels meant trouble. They were the channels reserved for Navy admirals and presidential orders; nothing else. If they were contacting her in this region of space then something was wrong. "Transfer the call to my cabin, I'll take it there."

The captain took off running. It didn't take long to cross the corvette but every second longer it took meant that the admiral or, god forbid, the president spent waiting on her. She reached her room faster then she thought humanly possible and slid behind her desk. She brought up the view-screen and keyed in her Captain's code. Each starship captain had two special codes, the first was for the Black Box, a device that would track the *Avalon* anywhere in space, and the second was for Priority One channels.

The screen came to life with the image of Admiral Richard Golden, the military commander of the *Avalon* and second highest ranking position in all of humanity's armed forces. Cantor snapped her body firm. "Admiral, this is an unexpected honour. What can I do for you, sir?"

The man looked tired and distraught, the weight of a recent decision resting on his eyes. "It's been a while, Agrima. How have you been keeping yourself?"

"Good, sir."

"Any relapse?"

"No sir, I am fighting form, sir." She was getting nervous. She had known Richard for years; it was their friendship that had gotten her this command instead of a forced retirement. She owed him a great deal. "Richard, what's wrong?"

"I have a change of orders for you. I have sent your communications officer coordinates. I need you to immediately change course and head to the new location. There you will rendezvous with a ship, we're assuming it's a ship; you will rendezvous with something there.

You'll know what it is when you see it. Whatever it is, get it and bring it back home to the Bird Farm."

"Sir, what of my standing orders? What of the civilians?"

"This supersedes all orders, Agrima."

"Richard...Dick, what is it? What will I find?"

The admiral laughed a sad and tired laugh, one filled with disbelieve. "I'm sorry, Agrima, but I have no bloody clue."

Both were quiet as they stared at each other, each officer thousands of light years away but looking each at each other through a screen. The admiral looked worried. "Agrima, you are the closest. I wouldn't ask you if I had another choice. I wouldn't want you to put you in this position but this is most likely going to result in a guns hot scenario."

Guns hot; that mean a fire fight, a space battle. That meant combat. Her eyes went wide. "I'll take care of it, Dick, I promise you."

"I know you will Agrima." The admiral's social defences fell, his face showing relief for but a brief moment, before returning to normal. "You always come through for me."

Cantor fixed her greying hair, pulling her beret over the entire mess as she entered the bridge. She had a rule when she entered the bridge: walk tall and look proper. It was only a personal rule but it meant a lot to her. If she looked like she deserved to lead, then others would follow and now she needed them to follow.

She began speaking the moment her foot hit the floor, her feet walking her to her chair. "Communications: Did you get the coordinates?"

"Aye, ma'am, uploading them now."

"Very good. Call the XO to the bridge. Helmsmen: what is the time frame to get to our destination?"

"It would take four hours to get to the gate and three days in warp."

"Spin up the drives and make course at top speed." She didn't wait for the reply; instead she took her seat and pivoted her keypad close. She pulled up the ships status on screen and reviewed its combat readiness. Her shields and weapons were functional and her engines primed for battle but what forced her hesitation was her crew. It was not that she doubted their skill, her crew was trained for any combat situations, but for the last three months they'd been posted out in the black, alone and with no contact. Isolation for that long had effects on the human mind and readiness. Combat drills could help reignite their combat readiness which left only her readiness to worry about. It had only been a year since she had been removed from the front line, since she had seen combat. HEF's medical has sanctioned her for duty but deep down she knew that she was nowhere close.

"You rang?" Cantor looked up to the bridge door. The entering officer was her executive officer, her second in command. "ODD: you have the bridge. Commander I would like a word with you in my ready room."

The Commander followed his Captain into her ready-room, closing the door behind him. The ready room was a small office adjacent to the bridge reserved for the ship's Captain to sit and work while her ship sailed the black seas. The ship's executive officer, or the XO as the navy called them, had his own office, but it was never as nice as this.

The Commander raised an eyebrow as his Captain, without a word, handed him a datapad. The file was coded classified and, because of such, security locked. He thumbed in his code, the hand-held computer reading his biometrics as it verified the clearance. It wasn't long before his name and photo flashed upon the small screen.

Commander Francis Somers.

He looked at the stranger who existed in the old photo. This mysterious being was a younger man then him, his hair red instead of grey, his eyes crisp instead of being a walking path for crows and his looks youthful instead of tired. It was moments like those that reminded Somers that he was old, moments when the image of him in his youth now looked like a stranger.

The file unlocked and Somers gave it a read, pushing up his glasses as they slid down his nose. He couldn't believe what he was reading. He had never heard of Fragarach Protocol, chances were no Commander had, but it seemed unbelievable. A protocol built into the *Avalon* system and, somehow, into Humanity's governmental system that would somehow lead humanity to victory. It sounded farfetched, it sounded fictional and it sounded like a bad science fiction film, but there it was in front of him, authenticated and coded.

"This is..." His voice trailed off in disbelief. He rubbed the top of his head, an area now void of hair, "I don't know what to say, Agrima. We're looking for a space messiah or a powerful uber-weapon? This is beyond weird."

Cantor gave a small snort. "I know, Frank, but apparently this is real. According to the Admiral when we get to our destination, whatever it is that's there, it's going to light up that area of space like a nova."

"And every salvager, pirate and enemy Humanity has will be drawn to it like a moth to the flame." His captain just nodded as he finished her sentence. He looked back at the pad, he knew what coming next and he knew why she was worried. "That is a long trek to the gate to have to do alone and under fire."

"We have three days till we drop out of warp; I need my ship ready."

"She will repel all attackers, Agrima. The crew and this fine lady will not let you down." Somers reassured.

Cantor held up her hand as she continued her list. "I'll need shields and weapons primed and ready when we pull out. I want sub-lights to be spun up, have Morrison assemble a boarding party and have a shuttle prepared."

"I'll take care of it."

Cantor walked over to her chair, but instead of

taking a seat she stood behind it, grasping the handmade seat by the back. She squeezed the leather tightly, her knuckles going white as her nerves tried to get the better of her. She looked up at her second in command. "I will need you on the bridge beside me when we re-establish normality. When the fighting starts, I'll need you there in case..."

Somers just nodded as her voice trailed off and her gazed dropped. He gently rapped the table thrice with his hand, the sudden noise pulling her attention back. "It's my job to make the captain look good, ma'am; I'll be there."

CHAPTER FOUR
5 days until Pherca Moon Invasion

The darkness of space lit up as the *Mojave Desert* tore out of warp, the sub-light engines spinning up as the ship achieved normality. All of the crew on board were abuzz; after three days of preparation they were anxious to get to work.

Petty Officer Branford stood before his team, each dressed in black with a tactical vest built to absorb some of the damage from gunfire. He encouraged his small five-man team, reviewing with them the objectives as each re-checked their rifles and pistols. Branford slapped in his magazine and after a small pistol spin, returned it to his waist holster.

Sub-Lieutenant Cole finished his pre-check on his shuttle and began to power-up the small transport craft, opening the rear hatch to allow the boarding party in.

On the bridge Cantor exited her ready room, her uniform proper and her beret set upon her done-up hair. The XO stood up as she entered and walked forward, standing behind the helmsmen. "Report." Her tone was brisk; her nerves and insecurities hidden beneath military bravado.

"We have clear space, ma'am." Somers explained, leaning down to double check what he read off the ship's scanner. He pushed up his glasses and wrinkled his nose. "No ships, no planets, no asteroids and no floating pods. There is nothing."

"Commander: do a double check on our location and begin a wide scan."

"We are scanning the area to confirm our position as we speak," he explained as he pushed up his glasses. "We're comparing stars and planets. Hell, we are even looking for the North Star."

"Incoming: We have an exit gate forming."

Space lit up with the bright colour of the warp as an exit gate formed. A large ship tore through the gate into normal space. Cantor glanced at her screen and studied the ship's build. It was unlike anything she was familiar with, its design so contrasting to the human norm. Humanity was very traditional with their ship's design, a main rectangular section with two smaller compartments acting as wings, which closely resembled the catamarans of Earth old. But this unknown ship had a design vastly different. It was a single hull, curved like a human U, with both ends at the bow and the engines coming from the broad side of the stern.

"What can you read, Hera'sun?" Cantor was optimistic, but cautious. This could be what she was here to find or it could be a trap. She worried that it was a new enemy ship but deep down she thought it unlikely. It lacked the solid lines of the Kobolds or the rugged feel of the Arau Pau.

"Our scanners are being bounced back, nothing is working." The small science officer frantically worked, trying different scanning methods on varying wave lengths, but with the same effect each time. Her scans were proving useless. "I have an energy spike coming from the ship. This might be a weapon."

"Brace for impact." Cantor and Somers dropped into their command chairs, specially designed seats that protected them during an attack.

No attack came.

Three beams fired from the alien ship but they never reached the Mojave. The rays of light stopped halfway between the two ships and hovered in space, each purple ray identical to the one before it. To the humans it looked like three purple glowing dots in space, together which formed a triangle; a glowing, purple triangle.

Cantor hesitated, debating whether or not to rise from her chair. She looked over at her science officer, a quizzical look on her face. "What was that?"

Hera'sun gave no answer; instead she just stared at the screen in disbelief. This was a purple triangle in space. This was the fourth coming.

She dropped to her knees and began to sing, the bridge filling with her beautiful voice and confusion from the rest. Hera'sun ignored their looks and their judging stares and kept singing, pausing only to begin to bow. As her lips pulled away from the floor she continued her song, loudly and with great pride.

Somers tried to get his science officer's attention but the devote Monastic would not be budged until her prayers were completed.

"Leave her. Take the station," Cantor ordered. She wasn't a religious woman but she understood. This was the returning of Christ. This was reincarnation of Buddha. Somers rose from his seat and moved toward the abandoned console to man it. The XO looked over the reading, over what Hera'sun had previously tried, and began to continue where she left off, altering the scan methods until something worked.

"This isn't a weapon," he explained. "It's a transmitting device but the power output is way off the chart, much higher than anything I've ever seen."

Lieutenant Commander Harold Morrison looked up from his tactical station. He wasn't normally a tactical officer but on a ship this size the job normally fell to the chief of security. "What is it? What are we all looking at, ma'am?"

"I think we are looking at the *Spellsong*." Cantor answered, not believing her own words.

"Blessed be the *Spellsong*!" Hera'sun cried out, her praise briefly interrupting her song.

"I have scans."

Hera'sun abruptly stopped singing and jumped to her feet. She scrambled over to her station, climbing to her seat and began to review the data with her XO. She was not one to take her religious practises lightly but they would have to wait. Now was the time for science. Scanning the divine vessel had to be handled carefully. "How did you get past their blocks?"

"I didn't," The XO pointed to the read-out, pushing up his glasses as he did. "Whatever was blocking our scanner just stopped. The data is pouring in. I've got no life signs, no weapons and read-outs on technology that I can't even begin to understand."

"One life sign," the little one corrected. "It's faint, but I have one life sign. It appears to be in a cryo state of stasis. Ma'am, there is somebody alive over there."

Cole steered his shuttle across the night, departing from the *Mojave*'s small docking bay and making its way to the much larger Spellsong. The shuttle slowly flew alongside the hull, scanning the ship from a closer range and transmitting its findings back to the *Mojave*. The *Spellsong*'s hull was built from an alloy that the scanners couldn't identity, a purple metal that seemed to eternally ripple like a rock dropped in a pond.

"What do you think, Lieutenant?" Branford climbed into the cockpit as Cole looked over his scanners.

Cole shook his head. "I'm not showing anything new, PO, but I have located a docking bay on the ship's starboard side."

"How are we going to get in?"

Cole spun the shuttle during his approach, aligning it in space with the *Spellsong*, before flying alongside the hull. Cole came to a halt, hovering off the starboard side. "I'll try to hack into the network and open the gate but if that doesn't work we burn through the hull."

Cole began his cyber assault on the ship's system, his ship's antennae searching for a network. All ships, despite origin and race, needed a vessel wide network. The linked system would keep the power flowing, the life support active and provided a working regularity. This system was normally on a highly secure and encrypted wireless network. The universal acceptance and adoption of the wireless network led to an entirely new method of ship combat. The larger ships, or specially fitted starfighters, would attempt to hack into the opposing ship's network during combat, a practise that created an entirely new post on the bridge, and interfere with the ship's system by uploading viruses, remotely disabling shields, or even altering or hindering targeting systems. Cyber warfare and network defence was a defining trait in the HEF Uprising, a major chapter in the failed Kobold Unification, one that, along with the Human-Monastic alliance, led to the downfall of the Kobold Empire.

The shuttle bay door opened and Cole's shuttle began its docking procedures, the *Spellsong* pulling in the smaller transport ship.

"What the hell?" Cole looked down at his system as the *Spellsong* shuttle bay doors opened. It didn't make sense; he hadn't found a network, let alone had the time to crack its securities, break the encryption and open the doors. The ship had done it on its own. "I didn't do anything, Branford. Be careful."

The Petty Officer nodded as he opened the cockpit's weapon box and handed Cole a pistol. "Wilco; we'll be on channel two, so keep an open line and watch your six."

Cole ejected the energy magazine, pulled back on the receiver, before replacing the mag with a slap. He pulled back on the pistol's hammer and thumbed on the safety. "I'm not reading any operational life support."

Branford grabbed his respirator system and pulled on his mask. "We are entering no life support; gravity boots and air mask are a go."

The shuttle docked and the crew readied themselves, Cole sealed and pressurized the cockpit, protecting him from vacuum, and the crew opened the back hatch. They exited the shuttle with their rifles at the ready, the boarding party moving as an organized mass, moving like a line of army ants, each sailor covering the other as they moved across the docking bay.

Hera'sun fidgeted in her chair, she was anxious and nervous. It had been an hour since the team had departed and no response as of yet; it wasn't abnormal it was just annoying. She needed an update, she needed answers. She requested to be on the away team numerous times, only to be rejected each time by the captain. She understood the reasoning, the *Spellsong* was an unsecure location and she didn't have the combat training needed to board it, but on the inside she was broken. This was the icon of her religion, her race's divine savoir, and she was not allowed to board it, to see it firsthand.

Cantor sat in her chair, her demeanour seemed calm and collected, but on the inside she was nothing but tension. Her keypad was pivoted over by her chair and it clacked away as she searched the HEF database for anything it had on the Monastic religion. She had Nurem'sun reviewing his historical text and the Monastic sacred text, a book they called the Kerratum. If what floated in space before her was the sacred ship of the Monastic religion she wanted her experts to be fully versed in the sacred writing.

"I have an incoming ship on the warp sensors."

Cantor pushed the keyboard away and stood up. Many captains preferred to remain seated in a ship battle; some even relaxed during a skirmish. When she was an XO, her former captain would drink tea during combat. She was of a different school of thought. For Cantor a battle required her to stand and to remain standing until the last shot was fired. A battle was not an easy thing for any crew to deal with, it was stressful and a single mistake could cost upwards of hundreds of lives, so for Cantor if they were to be on edge then so would she, the added bonus that standing and moving kept her blood pumping and her attention on the happenings.

"Is the beacon functioning?" The communications officer gave a naval aye in reply. The beacon was interstellar law; on any salvage or emergency stalls a transmission had to be broadcasted, much like the emergency blinkers on a hovercar. The beacon would broadcast a repeated message, claiming the area as protected or neutral ground depending on the situation, and for this situation the beacon claimed this salvage as HEF territory.

Cantor watched as an exit gate formed and the bright, but familiar, colours of warp poured out into the blackness of space.

"All hands prepare." Cantor's hands shook but she barely noticed, her heart raced and her breath drew short, but it never registered. "Come about to face the gate. Morrison: open all gun ports and target the incoming ship with all front batteries, I want all remaining batteries lock and loaded and scanning for other exit gates."

"Aye, ma'am," Morrison replied; his fingers moving faster than Cantor could keep up. The lieutenant-commander checked the targeting system as plates on the hull opened and a dozen rail guns and a pair of energy cannons emerged from within their metallic cover.

"Begin loading the cannons," Somers barked. It was a figure of speech, a verbal relic of a time long since past even when humans still roamed the Earth and ships still sailed the seas. The cannons never needed to be loaded, they were energy based weapon that accumulate massive amounts of energy and fired it out in a single blast. These days the order was little more than slang that meant power up the guns.

Somers and Cantor both knew that the odds were the ship that came out of warp would be bigger and stronger and in a fair fight would easily tear them apart, rivet by rivet, but he was not in the mood for a fair fight. For Somers there was a saying, rooted deep within Earth's history and human lore, a saying so old that its origins were lost, but its meaning was never forgotten.

Han shot first.

"We have a ship entering normality." Morrison's guns pivoted on the outside of the hull, all barrels pointing at the exit gate and the dark blue ship that tore out of warp. "It's a Kobold ship, blue flight and medium size."

Cantor's body just froze. Try as she might she couldn't convince her lungs to draw air. She was not ready for a battle in any form. She knew it, Richard knew it and Frank knew it. This went double for a skirmish against a Kobold ship. Kobolds were a humanoid race, half the size of men and covered in scales. They were merciless warlords who lived in monstrous clans. They once had a powerful empire with lesser races like the Javihorn and the Teeliquin at their command. When their lust for power tossed the entirety of the known verse into a war that the Kobolds couldn't win, their empire crumbled. The Kobolds were a sliver of their former grandeur but they were still dangerous. Cantor hated the Kobolds as most humans did. She fought in the war and had lost many friends and shipmates to their foolish greed and blamed each loss squarely on the then Kobold emperor. It was true that she gained a great deal of promotions during war time, moving from lieutenant-commander to captain in only five years, but that was not the way she wanted to move up the ranks.

"They have shield powering up, gun-ports opening and I am beginning to track weapons build up," Morrison called out.

The Kobolds came out of warp with their guns at the ready. They didn't bother to scan or open communications, they just came to fight. Somers scowled. The Kobolds had to have been in warp, scanning this sector of normal space while Cantor and her crew had been docking and securing the alien ship. From warp they saw the *Spellsong* and they wanted it.

"Put all targeted batteries at fifty percent and open fire," Somers said, pushing his glasses up his nose. The rail guns opened up, firing volley after volley of energy bolts, the massive dual barrels recoiling backwards with every shot. The bolts smashed against the Kobold's shields, round after round, punishing the ships and weakening its safeguard.

"I have no deviation in their course; shield damage is minimal and their weapons continue to charge." The laws of warp space were different than in normality. A ship could travel faster and longer in half the time but not without cost. Energy weapons were useless and projectiles would just end up back in real space. When a ship re-entered normality in a combat scenario the first thing they had to do was load the cannons.

"So much for the warning shot." Frank looked at his Captain. She was near catatonic, her body frozen. Frank would have preferred the go-ahead to escalate but he was the XO. Without the Captain giving orders it was his responsibility.

"Take off the training wheels. I want all guns to full power, target the ship with all available batteries and fire at will." An additional four guns rotated on the hull, targeting the Kobold ship, and began to open fire. Frank watched on screen as all the guns barraged the shield. He walked over to Morrison's console, the tactical command station, and began to watch the tactical read out. He was waiting for a spike in the Kobold energy level, waiting for a shield blip. "Cannon one: fire!"

The main cannon lit up as a massive energy ball fired outward, crashing into the blue dragon ship, the shields cracking briefly, flashing before them like static on a screen before returning to normal.

Hera'sun peaked up excitedly with a clap. "Blessed be. I've violated their network, and uploaded a virus. Their targeting systems are offline. They are unable to shoot back."

Frank smirked. They gotten the upper hand only be being prepared and being sneaky but it was only a momentary advantage. Viruses were not what they used to be, a small program that could cripple an entire network singlehandedly. They had evolved and so had network security and anti-virus software. In combat a virus, like the one Hera'sun had uploaded, would be little more than a temporary distraction but a distraction, even a temporary one, could turn an entire battle.

Frank looked up at the bridge crew, glancing back occasionally at the tactical screen. "Comms: keep on the lookout for a white flag. Helms: If they get guns back online prepare to move us between them and the Spellsong. We'll take the damage before she does. Tactical: start re-loading the first cannon and prepare to fire the second."

Air returned to Cantor's lungs as her body thawed. Like a stiff axle her arm creaked and popped as she finally moved it. Her heart race and her arms twitched but she stared down the Kobold ship. Most ships were like a Rorschach test; you could look at one and see a different shape or creature. Some looked at human ships and saw vast birds; Monastica ships looked like unfurled armadillos and Zineris ships, with their reinforced plated hulls, looked like metallic turtles floating through the endless black sea but when human eyes fell upon the Kobold's ship they found them remarkably similar to mythical dragons.

The Kobold ship was still bearing down upon them, their speed and angle never changing. Somers' smirk quickly faded. If they wanted to play chicken they would play but the difference was the *Mojave* had her guns.

"Fire second cannon." A second ball of blue energy shot forward, passing the dozens of energy round volleys that accompanied it, and crashed into the shields, the blow shattering the protective barrier like a pane of glass.

"Enemy shields are down."

The guns kept firing, the bolts now crashing against the hide of the unprotected dragon. Sparks and small fires ignited, the small pockets of oxygen beneath the hull acting as an oxidizer for the flame until it quickly became extinguished by the vacuum of space. The dragon began to turn away from the battle, its sub-light engines igniting brighter as it took off.

"They're turning tail," Morrison called out.

"Cease fire." Frank stepped away from the tactical console, moving across the bridge as he returned to his chair, but didn't sit down. "Keep the dragon ship targeted. I want cannon one to remain loaded."

"Open up a channel to shuttle one," Cantor said, her first words since the Kobolds' arrival. "XO: get me an update."

The communication officer gave an affirmative aye as he worked the system, opening a direct line to the shuttle. "This is Cole, go ahead."

"Do we have an open line with the boarding party?"

The line went silent save for the sound of clicking keys, "Boarding party has been patched in."

"Branford here."

"We have just had an encounter from a blue dragon ship," Somers began, "We have repelled them but they are still in the area. How much time does you and your team require Petty Officer?"

"Actually, Captain, I think we are just about done here."

"Already?" Frank was surprised. This was an alien ship and they already had the ship secure.

"The operating system is insanely simple; it adapts to your requirements and predicts your needs. We have the life support and gravity operating, we have the ship communications booting up and we have a docking system operational. You can land the ship on the top of the Spellsong and not only could you board through the docking corridors but from a quick glance you could mount this baby and ride her all the way home."

"And not call her the next morning," Somers joked. "Any idea what race it belongs to or what language is the system in?" Somers felt no shame admitting that Hera'sun's curiosity was wearing off on him. With each passing moment he was growing more and more desperate to know more about this legendary ship.

"Not sure on the race," Branford explained. "The language was unlike anything our translators had seen but after a couple minutes the ship's computers and screens all started randomly using English text."

"English?" Hera'sun was confused, she didn't know that term.

Frank looked back and quietly responded. "That's the Human prime tongue. English is the old Earth name for the language." He turned back to view screen and the open communication line. "What about the life form aboard the ship?"

"We found a cryo-pod and have it secured but we are not touching it. I am advising a hull-hull docking with the Spellsong and send across a tech team and a medical team to check out the popsicle. I'd also want the bookworms."

"The archaeologists?"

"Yes, captain," Branford explained. "We are still working with a guess and check system here, perhaps the civilians can decipher something here that we can't."

Cantor retired to her ready room and stood before her mirror. She stared at her reflection but hated who stared back. She used to be a battle hardened Captain. She'd flown ships into hostile space and even participated in the Elbe Siege but here she was shivering like a seaman recruit in their first skirmish. Was this all she was destined for, to spend the rest of her life as a washed up Captain too afraid to pull the trigger? Perhaps this was it; this was the time to do what she dreaded most. Perhaps it was time to retire. Agrima was thirty-eight years old when she made Captain; an age while young in peace time was not uncommon in war. She was a forty-seven year old woman now. Her hair was greying, her bones were creaking and she was still single. She was a career military lady, something she never regretted, but it did leave her with little else to do when her career ended. She may not have been born or bred for the stars but by the time the Navy finished with her there was no replacement for the starlit heavens.

There were other possibilities. She could sign onto a shipping line company, captain a freighter ship and run supplies from one end of the black to the other. Shipping companies loved captains like her; they jumped to recruit skilled members of the Navy of any rank but a sailor at her rank, or even somebody at Frank's, they'd pay big bucks to pull them away from the armed forces. She'd have her own ship again, she'd have a loyal crew but it wouldn't be the same. It wouldn't be HEF.

There were also the corporations. Just like the shipping lines they were always scooping up skilled pilots and captains. Fortune 500 companies like Universal Crops Growth were always bidding for the best. They had their own private military and company fleets. It would be closer to the HEF, more of a military setting, but chances are they wouldn't offer her a position. They needed fighting fit and she was significantly less. Aside from being a yacht captain for some rich family or a freighter captain she was running out of options.

CHAPTER FIVE
5 days until Pherca Moon Invasion

Dr. Bristol Tsia sat behind the alien console, her books and handheld spread across the dashboard as she focused on the alien screens. She had been working for hours but she was officially getting nowhere. The ship's automatic translator had converted nearly the entire Spellsong database into Human Prime but she still needed reference points for all of the text. Every lead she had would bring a brief hope of light into eyes but would quickly flicker out. They all happened the same way; she'd thumbed down a list, pause and then review her notes. She'd smile for a second and eagerly read on only to eventually find that one fact or tidbit of history that proved the last half-hour's work fruitless. She'd groan, curse and start all over again only to find herself exactly where she was thirty minutes ago, nowhere closer to an answer.

"Got anything?" The voice startled her, causing a jump in her chair. She tried to catch her breath as Lieutenant-Commander Harold Morrison leaned in.

"Any development?"

"Caliste esti." It was a French curse from an old Earth, one of the few languages to survive the First Jump. "You scared me, Harold."

"Sorry, Doc, but you got anything?" Morrison was a dark haired man with narrow eyes and a full navy beard. Bristol had seen many men like him before, career-lifers with the spark vanishing from their eyes. Morrison was in his forties and still a Lieutenant-Commander, he had the ambitions to climb higher but at his age he'd come to the soul-crushing reality that it wasn't going to happen.

Tsia pulled up her books and handhelds close and began to bring up what she found. "I have found so much confusing tech and writings. There are verbal commands, adaptive weapons and Nurem'sun thinks he found something about a teleporter or transporter system."

"Is that even possible?"

"Nurem'sun says its theoretically possible but Hera'sun says it isn't," Tsia explained, "and I'm not insane enough to get inbetween that married couple."

Morrison smirked. "Tell me about these verbal commands."

"I have come across a series of command level codes. They are verbal commands with directives for enemy, superior, caretaker and friend."

"This is a verbally run ship?"

"That's the peculiar part, from what the science team discovered this ship does have a verbal command structure built in but these codes are not built into the ship." She grabbed her handheld and with her thumbs brought up the command code, "Look at this one. 'Himinsan-Terra'na-Dovitama'."

"What does it mean?"

"Um...so far I think it means we are friends, stand down now. That's not a ship command, hell I don't know what system would need such a command. I had the science team trace back these codes; they say that they are tied into a remote system, the améliorer system."

"Améliorer?"

"It's French; it roughly means improvement, or growth."

The Commander looked confused. "So the ship is improving itself?"

"No clue, big guy."

Morrison stood up, scratching his chin as looked at the doctor. "Alright, keep at it."

Morrison looked at his chronometer and yawned. He had been on *Spellsong* for four hours now. It hadn't taken the team long to perform a docking, the *Mojave Desert* now sat atop the alien ship. They even discovered that the system could do a rudimentary link, giving the *Mojave*'s helmsmen basic control over the *Spellsong*'s steering and engines. With that they were off, on their way to return to gate so they could make the jump into warp and start the long run home.

The gates were essential for space travel; they

allowed access to a sub-space region known as the warp. The warp allowed ships to travel great distances in space in a short amount of time. It wasn't faster than light travel but it was as close as any known race was ever going to get. Warp was a weird region of the universe and a lesson in opposites. It seemed to exist for the sole purpose of ship travel but contained enough force to eject any ship that entered it. No ship except for the largest and most powerful, mainly the gate builders, could enter the warp without a gate but exiting from the sub-space region was easy. The warp constantly tried to eject ships, forcing pilots to learn how to sail the warp winds, but this ejecting force meant that a ship could come out of the warp wherever a pilot wanted. Entry was still limited entry by a gate.

Each race had a different name for the gates. The humans referred to the astral gateways as the Trent-Gates, named after the human man to discover them: Professor Samuel Trent. The first human gate was built outside Earth's orbit. It was weak compared to current standards and at that time humans knew very little of warp. This meant that the furthest humans could get was the dwarf planet Pluto and its moon Charon. It wasn't until a mysterious glitch, and a discovery by Professor Trent, that humans learned the gates could do more. With more power and more warp experiments humans found freedom from the Sol system and access to the rest of the Milky Way.

Those events lead to the creation of the biggest

human ships of its time, the Pervian class ships, and a historical leap through the gate. It would be forever known as the First Great Jump, the travel through warp with fifteen thousand souls looking to see what lay beyond the veil of night.

Morrison vacant gaze fell to a cry for his command. He was the ranking officer aboard the *Spellsong*, he was in charge of the four teams aboard and he hadn't had a moment pause since he got here. He had been running from squad to squad, first to the science team who were examining the engines, the computers, life support and other systems. Then to tactical who were trying to determine if this ship could defend itself if needed. The archaeological teams were doing their best to decipher the ancient unknown dialogue and scriptures, seeing what help they could give to the others, and then there was medical. Medical had the task of examining the frozen soul stuck aboard this ship: the Popsicle.

This vessel was little more than a ghost ship, dark and void of any life, the plot of a slasher film. It was a classic story where a team of soldiers and numerous oddly placed nude teenagers find a drifting ship and nobody makes it off alive, especially not the nude ones. The teenagers always seemed to die in the worst ways. For once in his life Morrison was glad of his age and that his clothes were firmly in place.

He waved over medical as he approached. "Okay, give me the report."

Acting Sub-Lieutenant Brea Mallory looked over her glasses at her superior officer. She was the *Mojave*'s chief of medical staff. For a larger ship the position would normally be held by an older officer and one of higher rank, but for smaller ships a skilled medical officer of a lower rank proved sufficient.

"With the science bunch and my team of medics." The term team was pushing it, she had five on the ship normally and only one stayed aboard the *Mojave*. "We have examined the cryo-chamber. The chamber is in perfect working order. The woman in there is fine but some of the cryo-chamber's backup systems seemed to have malfunctioned."

In a slasher film the soulless killer always emerged from a broken cryo-chamber. "Malfunctioned how?" His voice cracked briefly, enough to catch a curious look of Brea. Morrison coughed as he tried to cover a blush. He was way to old to be afraid of slasher films.

"Well to be honest we are not sure what it does but it seemed to have taken gunfire damage." She flipped through pages on her handheld. "The chamber has a cerebral linkup, which at first I thought was to monitor the brain for damage but it barely has an analytical reader. Instead it has a writing function, or did."

"Did?"

"Yeah, the writing function seems to have been corrupted or broken. Now it doesn't write; it just displays."

"Writing? Displaying? And all of this is occurring in

her brain?" Morrison was confused, "is this sort of this possible?"

"Science squad seems to think so but it's hard to tell."

Hera'sun looked up from behind the unknown system attached to the cryo-chamber. "The theory behind it is sound; a system of implanting knowledge directly into the brain but nobody has ever come up with how to do this."

"So this woman has been learning while she's been frozen?" The doctor nodded. This plot was getting worse. Morrison frowned as he made a decision. Any and all slasher films were being removed from his vid-queue the moment he got back to his room. Morrison looked over at the science officer. "How are you holding up?"

Hera'sun wrinkled her nosed as she worked. "I am torn, Lieutenant-Commander. I am a lady of science, a woman of learning and advancement, but here I sit in the greatest artifact of my religion. I want to look at this like I would with other new technology but my devotion, my beliefs, make it very difficult."

"And what of your mate?"

"Nurem'sun?" She snorted, "that arrogant not-a-real-topic-of-study archaeologist mate of mine is like... how does your kind say it? He is like a bull in a candy shop?"

Morrison wanted to laugh but knew it to be undiplomatic; instead he took to cough to cover his amusement. Mallory was not held by the same hesitation of her superior, she burst out laughing almost immediately. Hera'sun eyed them both curiously. "I made an error in the saying didn't I?"

"Yes, but we won't take offence." Morrison smiled, "our children aren't cows, well most of them anyways." Hera'sun stood quietly, looking at her handheld as she translated the words and looked up their meaning. For a moment she looked horrified, finally aware of the meaning of the insult she just inadvertently spoken, but eventually took to joining in on jubilation.

"Forgive me," The words escaped between fits of laughter, "Your human sayings are so difficult to comprehend at times."

"Then don't study the South." Morrison regained his composure, "medically how soon can we unfreeze her?"

Mallory scratched her head, "Thirty minutes sir, maybe less."

"Make it happen."

"The dreams, they always started the same way. They start off pleasant enough," the soldier whispered. "They start off like we are now. Both of us are in bed, I have my arms around you, holding your body tight against mine. I can feel the warmness of your bare skin against my breasts, I can feel your heart beat, slowly and steady, uncaring for the horrors that the dawn will bring but that was always you. You could fall asleep easily and sleep through anything. You didn't let stress get between you and whatever it is you see when you sleep.

"It doesn't work like that for me. I am cursed with the thoughts of every mission, every detail and every person. The first time this happened, the real time, you fell asleep almost instantly. I stayed awake for nearly four hours before I finally fell asleep to the sound of your breathing.

"Now I don't want to close my eyes because I know what will happen. It happens every single time, my eyelids will close and things change. The world will become fuzzy, like static in a movie and when I open my eyes I'll be outside. I will have to give that speech again - I hate that speech now - and then it begins. Those creatures will attack us, wave after wave, and I will fight. It's all I know how to do: fight. I will fight with everything I've got but they won't stop or slow down. I will fight and I will lose. They say I won; the hero of The Last Stand at Kiron Port but I didn't win. Humanity won that battle, I lost. I lost my friends, I lost my family, and I lost you. I lost everything and now I have to relive it, night after night, year after year. I think I died that day, died in the explosion and the bombings and this is my punishment for a life of murder. This is my own personal hell.

"I can feel it, my body's tired, and it wants to sleep, but I know what will happen if I do. I am going to wake u, and I am going to have to watch you die." The solider,

Allana Guiver felt her eyelids get heavy, her eyelashes pulling down until it happened. Her eyes fell closed but for the first time, in a long time, when she opened them she was surprised. Every time her eyes opened she found herself standing in front of the docking door, watching Tenuvah Sheppard go, but this time she was somewhere different, somewhere new.

Lieutenant-Commander Harold Morrison stood in the cryo-room, watching as the teams scramble about. The science team prepared the chamber for extraction while the medical observed the life signs.

"Marines: on me." The remaining military huddled around him, listening as he spoke. "We have command permission to bring her out of sleep, so I need you guys to prepare the room. I want all doors sealed and all possible personnel armed. She will be dangerous; the killers always are on the ghost ships."

Petty Officer Marcus Branford stared in disbelief. "Um sir? The killers?"

Morrison frowned. That last bit wasn't meant to be out loud. "Never mind; I want all weapons armed and ready. If this is bad we need to drop it here. For all we know this is a prison ship."

"How dare you!" The outcry was sudden and unexpected. Morrison spun around to see a very angry science officer. Crap. "It is no such--"

This couldn't go on, Morrison cut her off. "Stow it! We're playing this safe instead of sorry."

Bristol watched all of this and frowned. She wanted to know what lay behind frozen glass, what person from the past stood before them, but this was ridiculous. Anybody coming out of cryo would be tired and stiff, like a man waking up from a long deep sleep. Chances were they be suffering from atrophy. How much threat could the sleeping woman pose?

"Branford you take point. I want Campbell on your left and Thibodeau on your right." Morrison pointed with his hand as he directed his team, "Keiser and Winters: both of you are on this side of the door. Mallory: I want you and your team armed. Keep one in here with you and send the other three outside the room. If you guys fall I want available medical to be able to patch us up."

"Aye aye, sir." With a wave she chose her two, and double checked her gun.

"Good. I want all civilians out of the room and all remaining security to form a choke-hold outside the door." Morrison pointed to a Master Seaman Taro Mori. "Mori: take the slug-throwers and secure them outside this room." They had found them in a gun rack beside the slumbering woman. Old firearms, which fired bullets not bolts, kept in perfect condition. The last thing Morrison wanted was for the killer to awaken and to be armed with a good ol' fashion slug-throwers.

"Sir, is this really necessary?" Bristol questioned.

"You have your orders."

Bristol wanted to fight and argue, she wanted to

contest the orders, but she couldn't. The secondary security team, and the relief medics, escorted her out. She watched as the sailors sealed the door, locking her out from the most important archaeological event of this decade. She kicked the wall with a yell, the sailors looking up curiously at her. Their attention lasted only a few seconds before they returned to work. The three sailors and two medics worked quickly as they set up their defences. The boarding party had locked and secured all the doors in the hallways. If the frozen woman made it past the room she'd be forced down a long hallway and directly into the ambush. The sailors and medics would be at the end of the hallway, each with a SMG or military issue pistol; they would use the corners as cover and aim down the hall. If the popsicle made it to them she wasn't making it past.

"Follow me." Bristol Tsia looked down at her colleague, at the Monastica with the wicked grin. "I have an idea."

"Oh no, no, no you don't." Hera'sun's eyes went wide. She knew that look, she had seen that look numerous times during their twelve year relationship and each time she saw it Nurem'sun got into trouble.

He pulled both of his ladies down the hall, past the navel choke point, and into a room filled with screens and keypads. "I was doing a search on some of their systems, helping the tech-heads with their search, when I came across a monitoring sub-routine. It will take some clickity-clack from a science officer but we can wire this room to monitor the extraction."

Her head had started shaking halfway through his explanation and it just gained speed the more he spoke. She loved her mate but that man brought with him loads of trials and tribulation, sometimes she wondered if it was more than he was worth. "No, no, no. Why would we do this?"

"Just think Kirsh'sha," Bristol blinked in surprise, Kirsh'sha was an example of a Monastica spousal nickname, a very intimate nickname that was not supposed to be said before an audience. "Think of the historical event I am missing, the paper I could publish, the novel I could publish. Think of....."

"You could have published dozens of papers. You just hate writing," she snapped. "You hate all paperwork and I haven't seen you touch your novel in seven years."

He was running out of arguments and Hera'sun was not being swayed. Bristol didn't like to get between couples but she really wanted to see the thawing. She hesitantly added fuel to the fire. "The science."

"Yes, exactly. Think of the science-y stuff you're missing." He flashed his mate a smile and inside she cringed. She was doing what the humans called swooning. That smile had won her over numerous times. He'd convinced her to join the scientific academy to allow them both to become academics, during the war he convinced her to enlist into the Diplomatic Corps. to become what the human's called spies, and he'd convinced her to become his mate, all with that damned smirk of his.

With an exasperated sigh she shook her head. Why did she fall for that damned smirk each time? She tuned to the keypad and frantically began typing. "Fine, but I am placing all of the blame on you when, not if, but when this goes wrong."

Tsia watched them as they worked together, the two bickering, pausing only to correcting each other, and then returning to the bickering again. It was love, in any definition of the word, on any planet, with any race, it was love and Bristol was jealous.

She hadn't been with anyone in years, an event that was a large factor in her taking this mission. Her parents wanted her to meet someone, to find a nice partner and settle down. Her parents didn't care that she favoured the company of women, nobody did anymore, they just wanted her to be happy and they wanted grandkids. Science could help provide Tsia with the later; the former she had to do on her own. There was a time in humanity's history that people had a problem with same-sex marriages and unions but when humanity dropped to forty-four million people, 0.64% of previous population, people stopped caring. There were more important things to worry about.

She wanted love, who didn't? But she had been burned in the past when it came to love, most times metaphorically but in the case of her last relationship, literally. When her last serious relationship ended with her in the hospital, getting treated for second degree burns, she became a little weary. Yet even at the end, and after she was healed and back on her feet, despite her shyness and hesitance, she still wanted to be loved. All humans wanted to be loved, all races did.

"Blessed be. I have it!" Nurem'sun boasted.

"You did not, I did it. The *Spellsong* guided me." Hera'sun corrected.

Regardless of who accomplished the task, the large screens lit with colour as the cameras captured every movement and action within the room and displayed it before the three. Hera'sun hid her smile as she watched the screens. Truth was she desperately wanted to see the thawing. This was the *Spellsong*, the Savior of her people and the symbol of her god. Whoever this woman was she was clearly the Avatar of the *Spellsong*. She was witnessing what would make the new chapter in the Kerratum first hand. Nurem'sum glanced at his mate and smiled. His hand quietly reached across and took hold of hers. Her stern face finally gave away to the faintest of smiles. They were watching events unfold – together.

Morrison stood behind the room, his handheld in his hand and gun on his belt. He checked the last few details before attaching the computer to his belt. He tapped the comm unit in his ear and began to give the final orders. "Team Two: are you ready?"

The reply came over the open communication's line. "The choke point is prepared, sir, and we're locked and loaded." Hera'sun tapped a few keys, calling up the cameras in hall, and a second screen filled with the images of the choke point. She could see the pilot, Sub-Lieutenant Cole joining the sailors, a pistol in his hand.

"Sub-Lieutenant Mallory, are you and your medics ready?"

The doctor, at the sound of her name, looked over her glasses at her superior officer; she looked back down at her handheld for a final verification. "All set here, sir."

"Good. Take position." She dropped her handheld on the metallic table and drew her pistol, giving it the once over while things were still calm. With her medics armed, and her own gun ready she gave Morrison a nod.

"Good. *Mojave Desert*: this is Boarding One," Morrison said across the comms. "Do you copy?"

"This is *Mojave Desert*," Commander Somers voice carried over the line. "We copy. We have audio and visual all at five by five. You may proceed."

"Aye, sir. Team Two: Seal the doors." Bristol watched as the doors slammed shut, the mechanism locking and the room becoming its own prison.

"*Mojave Desert*," Morrison stood straighter as he gave his final speech. His feet stood shoulder width apart and his hands rested behind his back. "This is Lieutenant-Commander Harold Morrison requesting permission to begin extraction of Unknown One."

"This is *Mojave Actual*," Captain's Cantor's voice boomed. Her voice never lost its commanding presence over a comm line. "You are authorized to extract."

"Aye, ma'am, very good." His right foot shifted back and his right hand fell to his pistol on his belt. He put a slight bend into his knee. "Petty Officer."

Branford nodded. "Weapons at the ready!" The order was loud and said in manner that made the words slur together but nobody misheard what he said. Morrison drew his gun, Branford level his shotgun, Thibodeau raised her rifle, the butt pressed into her shoulder, Campbell gripped his SMG with both hands and leveled in before his eyes, and Mallory, along with her medic team, raised their pistols. The medics glanced between the life signs screens and the cryo-pod; they had to make sure the woman survived the defrosting.

Petty Officer Branford stepped forward, his shotgun pointed at the pod, and he reached for the door to open it, to bring the frozen passenger into the new world.

Danger!

Her eyes shot open and her mind raced. The ice that surrounded her body melt into water and drained out the bottom of the pod. Every inch of her body twitched, moving like a surge of electricity had just been shot through it. Confusion swept over her; she didn't know where she was. When she opened her eyes she expected to be in front of the docking door but she wasn't even on Kiron Port. Major Allana Guiver had no clue where she was but she was certain of one thing. She was cold.

Under attack!

She tried to move her body but found it unresponsive. She willed them to move but got nothing. It was like waking up when her limbs were still asleep. She needed to focus and think rationally. She needed to figure out where she was and wha ---

Repel all boarders!

Her brain spun. She couldn't think straight. There were thoughts screaming in her head like an internal alarm clock. Her brain repeated one message over and over; her attempts to focus doing little else but fracturing the message. With a growl she just stopped.

Danger! Ship under attack! Repel all boarders!

It was an activation code. The moments those words clearly passed through her mind a spasm went through her body, every nerve and muscle twitching at once, her once tired and weak muscles had been abruptly awoken as a large injection of adrenalin shot through her. Her body was now as ready as her mind and she had just as much control over it.

The visor over her eyes, a small piece of electronics that were like small glasses without the temple arms, activated and began to feed her information. First was the ship's status: boarded and docked with a Human Endurance Fleet vessel called the *Mojave Desert*. What in God's name was the Human Endurance Fleet?

Next came the immediate room, the glasses lit up with intel every person in the room. It started with name and rank followed quickly by their weapons and their training. The ship had been listening in on the open communication lines and even tapped into the docked ship's computer. The intel flashed before her eyes, moving faster than she could possibly read. But despite her human limitations all it took was the brief moment it took for the data to flash and Major Allana Guiver knew it all. Correction: whatever was controlling her body knew everything it needed. The boarders had already lost; they just didn't know it yet.

She glanced forward, the visors acting as a heads up display, and saw Petty Officer 2nd Class Marcus Branford reaching for the door. For the first time in centuries Major Allana Guiver moved.

"Oh my god," the medic cried out, her voice muffled through the glass. The glasses zeroed in on her and brought up her profile: Acting Sub-Lieutenant Brea Mallory – Chief Medical Officer of the *Mojave Desert*. "She's awake!"

"She's awa..." Branford never got to finish his surprised exclamation. Allana grabbed two levers in the pod and pulled down. Like the escape pod in a star fighter, the cyro's door shot off, shooting forwards at a breakneck speed and crashing into the surprised Petty Officer. Both door and man crashed to the ground, the impact sending his shotgun sliding across the floor.

A massive amount of mist and dry ice poured into the room, quickly obscuring everybody's vision. The system knew Guiver was outnumbered and calculated that by giving her concealment her odds of success would greatly increase.

Allana, or whatever was controlling her, dashed out of the upright pod and ducked to her right, Morrison's left. She grabbed the SMG barrel and with all of her strength pushed it back into Leading Seamen Devin Campbell. It was a small weapon, without a long base that pressed into his shoulder. Without the extra support the push slammed the butt of his weapon into his nose. After a satisfying crunch she pulled the weapon free with her left hand and struck the vulnerable neck with her right. The large black man gasped for air. Allana stepped into the body, putting her legs before his and grabbing the back of his neck. With a judo throw, using leverage and strength, Campbell tripped over her leg and crumpled to the floor.

Target down. Danger remain: Attack!

Allana was like a passenger in her own body, watching her arms and legs move like a TV show she had no control over. She couldn't even change the channel to something better. But Allana fought any way she could, throwing her will at her body but having as much effect as an egg against a brick wall.

Contact: 3 meters and closing behind you. Attack!

She pivoted behind her, swinging the stolen SMG by its barrel and knocking Able Seamen Viviane Thibodeau's rifle barrel downward as she fired. The burst of three bolts burned into the deck instead of Allana, an outcome that despite her lack of control she greatly preferred. The AS' medical record flashed on her glasses and Guiver struck; she slammed the SMG into Thibodeau's left knee, striking a joint that had been injured a month prior. Thibodeau, a marine, fought back the scream as her leg buckled. She tried to limp backward but Guiver struck again, this time to the side of her skull.

Target down. Threat remains. Attack!

With an upward glance she spotted the medical officer levelling a pistol at her. The gathered intelligence flashed in a fraction of a second. She was Acting Sub-Lieutenant Brea Mallory, MD. She was a medical doctor and therefore someone who cherished saving life instead of taking it. Even as a trained solider she would hesitate before firing, a hesitation that would cost her.

Medical Personnel – non-lethal only. Attack!

Allana was glad her body wouldn't kill the doc but she didn't want to die either. Instead her body lobbed the SMG at the doctor's face. It was human instinct to protect their eyes and rightfully so. It wasn't a bad instinct, merely a survival one and one that could be exploited. As if like clockwork Acting Sub-Lieutenant Mallory raised her hands to deflect the thrown weapon, pointing her gun away from Allana as a result.

Threat remains. Eliminate Threat! Attack!

Her body stepped forward and kicked. It was a powerful frontal kick, one of the strongest attacks in any human based martial arts but one of the easiest to see coming. The foot slammed into the Mallory's chest, a pair of ribs snapping under the strike, and sent her crashing backwards over the metallic table. Mallory fell to the ground in pain, taking one of her medics with her.

The mist was beginning to fade, the mere seconds of distraction it granted expiring. Her eyes fell upon Chief of Security Lieutenant Commander Harold Morrison in the distance, a military grade officer pistol in his hand.

Gun – target promoted to immediate threat. Evade!

Her body dove into a forward somersault, her hand grabbing Mallory's discarded pistol as she rolled. Allana rolled to her feet, narrowly missing the Lt.'s gunfire, and levelled her pistol at Lieutenant-Commander Morrison.

Firearm obtained. Return fire! Attack!

She screamed internally as her iron sights lined up on Morrison's forehead. So far her body hadn't killed anyone and she wasn't going to allow it to start now. Allana summoned every bit of strength she could muster and threw it behind her will.

Stop!

She tilted her wrist and fired twice, both bolts burning into his shoulder. She did it! She stopped whatever it was that controlled her from killing. She didn't have full control but she was getting there.

Two threats remain. Attack!

Her body dashed forward, her pistol now looking at the young man her glasses identified as Ordinary Seamen Jacob Winters. She squeezed the trigger thrice as she ran, her bolts ripping through leg, shoulder and arm. With each shot she threw her will behind it. She was not going to feel guilty over a death she had no control over. She was not going to add another name to the list.

A bolt slammed into her side and every nerve in her body and brain screeched like a banshee. She'd just been shot; Allana struggle to keep what control she had from fading away. A second bolt slammed into her and sent her spinning to the ground. What semblance of control she'd wrestled away now slipped between her fingers as her pistol turned to return fire. The sights fell on Keiser's forehead and her finger squeezed the trigger.

No!

The bolt snapped his head back and sent Keiser crashing to the floor. Allana internally screamed. The kid didn't need to die. She climbed to her feet. Why? Why did he have to die? This was another one, another life she failed to save; another name to add to the long list. She was tired of this, of all of it but here she was, fighting again, and for wh —

A fist struck her face and sent her back to the floor. Branford had climbed back to his feet and charged her. Allana's back hit the floor with a thud but her leg kicked out at the PO. He stepped back to avoid the kick. Allana could see the debate in his eyes as she rolled to her feet. He wanted to draw his pistol, every solider did, but this PO didn't. He knew how to fight which meant that he knew that in close combat a firearm belonged to whoever wanted it more and right now she doubted anybody on this ship wanted his pistol more than her. He threw a punch as she approached him but Allana blocking the fist with the butt of her pistol. She saw him wince as bone met steel. He screamed as he stepped back, shaking his hand as if it was wet. She watched as he eyed her, his gaze watching as she shifted her feet, changing stances. Training told her that in a close quarters combat she was best to just holster the pistol and fight but all she wore was a bright blue skin-tight one piece. Instead she ejected the magazine and cleared the chamber before dropping the pistol at her feet.

He attacked quickly, his foot moving faster than most could follow. She blocked the first kick with her arm and regretted it instantly. Behind that speed was strength and power and her arm stung the moment the foot made contact. The instant his foot returned to the deck his fist followed, punching in a combination with blurring speed. Allana marvelled how her body knew where the next punch was going, how she knew where the next punch was going. Her body dodged and blocked and even back-stepped, if by instinct, to avoid a roundhouse kick, one she would have never seen coming and barely saw save for the wind passing by her nose.

This was Savate, a kickboxing martial art that originated in France back on old Earth but she had never trained in it; hell she had never even been to France but somehow she knew it. Her limbs acted on their own, her muscles knowing where to go and when, blocking incoming punches and striking his face and chin when she had a chance.

She saw her opening, a wild punch coming for her

face. Allana stepped back, her stance changed again as she switched forms. She grabbed the incoming fist and as spun. It was Kinomichi, another style from France, and for those who watched she seemed like she was dancing, twirling herself and her opponent on the dance floor. The truth was much different; she was using Branford's ki, and redirecting it away from her.

Allana kept spinning; striking at Branford exposed side when possible, until she stuck her legs before his and sent him tumbling to the ground. As his frame collided with the steel bottom she pounced, her hand grabbing his head and clutching it tightly. Her body was going to snap his neck. Despite her brain still reeling from the shot, she tried again, forcing all of her strength and her will in one place.

No!

Her arms shifted and wrapped around his neck. Her body tightened its grip and squeezed the lungs until no air could enter. Seconds later Branford passed out. Allana internally sighed in relief.

Immediate threats dealt with. Recalculate. Two potential remain.

Allana knew there was one more medic unaccounted for, he had simply fallen over, and Doc Mallory was still conscious. She pulled Branford's pistol from his belt and cautiously searched the room. The battle replayed on her glasses, moving it at 20x speed. She paused the replay when the medic came on screen; he was out cold on the floor, knocked out when Mallory crashed into him. That left only Doc Mallory.

One potential threat remains.

"We are here to help." Mallory crawled along the floor, clutching her chest. She spoke with a pained voice, each word causing her misery. "Please stand down."

Allana wanted to ask who they were and why they were here but as she tried to speak only one response came out. "Confirm command code now." She tried again, over and over, but each time she could only produce the same response. It was like her dreams; she wanted to alter the events on Kiron Port but no matter how hard she tried it always came out the same. "Confirm command code now."

Professor Bristol Tsia gasped as she watched. This woman was a ruthless killer. Seeing a sole woman take out an entire crew was something straight out of a movie. She moved like a choreographed fight scene. She dodged gunfire, blocked punches and ducked under kicks. She was a deadly warrior but somehow she was still beautiful, twisting and dancing like a ballerina.

"Teviak!" Numm'sun cursed. The woman had rearmed herself from the discarded weapon and was moving to the door. He grabbed the radio and called out to the remaining sailors. "The woman has cleared the room and heading for the door. She's on her way to you."

Hera'sun eyed her mate's partner. Tsia was watching the screen muttering quietly. "What is on your mind?"

"Confirm command code now."She muttered louder, "The popsicle, she keeps repeating those words over and over. Why?"

"She's like a robot," Hera'sun suggested, "or a computer looking for a password."

"Yeah but where do we type it in?" her mate asked. "Or do we just yell it loud enough."

Tsia's eyes went wide. She knew what that meant. "I need to get in there."

Hera'sun looked scared. "What? Why?"

"I know the code." The science officer narrowed her eyes. Her mate trusted this human to Via'ln Triangle and back. She should do the same. She just nodded as she grabbed her mate's radio. "Master Seaman Taro Mori, this is Hera'sun. I need you to let the civilian in."

"No can do, ma'am." Mori called out. "She's coming right for us. I cannot let a ---"

"Command Code Order." Hera'sun scrunched her face. She hated pulling rank and rarely did so. She glanced at Tsia. "Go."

Bristol exited the computer room and bolted down the hallway. She reached the cryo-bay door just as it opened. The female soldier stood before her, powerful and unmoving but with a hint of fragility, and stared at her. "Wait! Don't shoot!"

The lady soldier raised an eyebrow at the desperate beg. She opened her mouth and gave the same reply as always. "Confirm command code now."

She only had one try at this. "Himinsan-Terra'na-

Dovitama."

The solider blinked at Bristol, the weapon lowering. "Command confirmed. Allies on board."

Bristol let out a sigh of relief, it had worked. She screamed in surprise as the lady soldier suddenly stepped forward only to fall to the floor. Bristol looked down at the woman. Whoever she was, she had just single handily taken out seven armed sailors without a weapon of her own, and now she lay on the cold deck, unconscious.

CHAPTER SIX
4 days until Pherca Moon Invasion

Captain Agrima Cantor had no clue how to write her report. She watched the event unfold on the main viewer, the Mojave picking up the *Spellsong's* camera feed, but she still couldn't believe it and neither would the Admiral. A single unarmed marine, awake for mere seconds, had disabled an entire heavily armed security team; put three of her crew into the med bay, including her chief of medical staff, and all without being severely injured. Was this soldier that good or was her crew in need of serious training? The truth probably lay somewhere in between the two.

She sat at the ship conference table, her chair seated at the head, while she looked over her command staff. Her XO was present, as was the injured Brea Mallory, the humiliated Lieutenant Commander Morrison and the confused Hera'sun. Because of her quick thinking and expertise in human history Doctor Bristol Tsia was invited to join the meeting.

"First and foremost do we have any idea of who

she is?" With so many unanswered questions Cantor figured this would be the best place to start.

Acting Sub-Lieutenant Brea Mallory answered first. She turned in her chair to face the Captain, wincing in pain as her ribs moved. "Her prints and DNA aren't coming up in the *Avalon's* database for anything in the past fifty years. I'm digging deeper but that will take a while."

"The *Spellsong's* databases refer to the Avatar as little else but the Major, the Human or the Great Soldier. We have no proper name to work by," Hera'sun explained."We did discover a single reference to the *Greatest Sufferer of the War*."

"The Avatar?" Morrison asked with a raised eyebrow.

Hera'sun nodded eagerly. "This human is the deliberate descendant of the *Spellsong*, she is our Avatar." The science officer clapped her hands together. "If I was to put this into human familiar terms, and I apologize for generalizations, but this is the beginning of our New Testament."

Bristol's ears twitched as she listened. She pulled her handheld closer and quickly began to type with her thumbs. The *Greatest Sufferer of the War*; she'd heard that saying years upon years ago back in university. It was in a history class from some old professor - some old *tenured* professor - who liked to question every norm that history had established. But what class was it? She racked her brain as she tried to remember.

"I will keep translating the database to see if I can find anything else."

"Alright; what about security?" Cantor turned to her chief of security.

"I have Branford and his men assembled," Morrison began. "I have two guards at her door round the clock. They will be making sure she doesn't leave. We know this one is military and we know this one is dangerous but my men will make sure that the pretty little thing is locked down."

Something in her brain triggered as Cantor chastised Morrison. Pretty little thing; she knew that phrase, the professor used to call her that all the time. He was a perverted old man, always wanting the young students to join him after class. The students always made fun of him while marvelling at his success rate. She smirked as her memories quickly formed. They called him Professor Hard-on, mainly because of his sexual attitude but also because it rhymed with his last name, Gardon. Professor Clark Gardon; that was the old pervert's name. Bristol feverishly began to pull up his published historical books and began to scan the text for the term *Greatest Sufferer of the War*.

"What about *Spellsong's* security?" the science officer asked.

"We've called in HEF backup but they won't be here for three days at least," Cantor explained. She glanced at Hera'sun "But your government, despite being five days away said they'll be here in two."

The little science officer just smirked. "They will push every gear on every engine to make this pilgrimage."

"What of our space Jane Doe's medical status?" Cantor interrupted.

The conversation came back around to the injured Doctor Mallory. "She is in perfect health, and if I had to guess, better then when she went in."

"How is that possible, would not her muscles weaken and tire after years of unused?" Hera'sun asked. Cryo-preservation was rare but her people had experimented with the idea.

"Yes, but there was a series of secondary systems installed into the chamber. The first was a series of nano-sized robots that operated within her body. These nanobots, which are far beyond known sicence, had two separate functions. The first was combat readiness. In the event of the ship being attacked they wanted a way to repel boarders at a moment's notice. The nanobots would keep Jane Doe's body ready to fight, as we saw earlier. However, to fully come out of cryo sleep takes hours, long enough to reboot your brain and body. It's like waking up from a deep sleep. Speeding this up is, as far as we knew, would be impossible so the nanobots found another way around it. They could wake up the portions of her body needed to fight almost instantly, the portion of the brain that works on instinct and reaction, and the muscles."

"But how did they not suffer from atrophy?"

Mallory gave the crew a devious smirk. "That's the

part I love. The nanobots used stimulation and massage of the muscles to keep them in fighting form. The muscles never suffered from atrophy because the small robots in her body made it so they never slept. Her body has been switching between sleep and awake for, God knows how long."

Hera'sun eyes went wide. "This is amazing. It's a simple solution but still so technically advanced. Blessed Be."

"But if you have a fighter operating on instinct, awoken by the computer I assume, how does it tell friend from foe?" Somers spoke up for the first time, his curiosity peaked.

"It can't."

"So she attacked us because we tripped some sort of security system and the only reason we stopped was because of the command codes that Doctor Tsia discovered." Morrison spoke without waiting, it finally made sense. At the sound of her name Bristol looked up from her handheld computer, suddenly aware she had no clue what the group was talking about. The captain frowned at her briefly before returning to the conversation at hand.

"What what was the second function, Doctor Mallory?"

The Doctor looked over at her Captain as she spoke, "Training, ma'am. That cerebral unit we found was placing her mind into an instructional simulation. Her mind was in a hyper-advanced version of those old virtual reality systems. From what we could decipher she was being trained in martial arts forms, advanced weapon tactics, battle strategies and military manoeuvres. She was being filled with a thousand and one ways to kill. Whoever froze her wanted her ready to fight a war."

"Yeah, but most of that is based on muscles memory, combat fighting, weapon usage. How good is knowing kung fu in your mind going to be if your body doesn't remember learning it?" Morrison's question came from years upon years of military training. Turning his body from the flabby slab it was as a teenage into the lead fighting machine he was now.

"The nanobots took care of that. When they stimulated the muscles to keep her body in fighting form, they would stimulate them in to mimic a punch, a kick or even reloading a weapon. So they basically taught muscle memory to the body." Mallory leaned back in her chair, a smile on her face despite the pain in her chest. This was a medical astonishment. She was already thinking about the papers she could publish in the medical community. She was eyeing the promotion, the possibilities. If her eyes could change forms, like they did in cartoons, hers would be massive stars.

Morrison leaned forward in his chair, a concerned look on his face. "I would be ignoring my job if I didn't bring this up but didn't the cerebral device malfunction?"

Hera'sun nodded. She tapped on her handheld and changed the display screen in the conference room.

"The device was built to train her to be an Avatar of war. It malfunctioned due to what we can only assume was gunfire - obviously not ours. It started reading her memories and replaying a certain memory over and over again. It had to build an extensive simulation based on her thoughts and memories." She paused as she looked for an example. "It is like if we were trapped in this meeting forever. You would try to change the conversation, say something different, but no matter what you did it would always end up in the same way. In order for the simulation to accurately portray that it would build vast character simulation on each of us."

"So whatever Jane Doe's memory is, she has been living it for eons?" Cantor asked.

"Probably closer to four hundred years." Everybody in the room turned toward the voice that hadn't spoken a word the entire meeting. "I think I know who she is."

Bristol quickly thumbed her handheld, sending a pair of images to the main screen. The first was of the medical photo Mallory took of the woman that slept in the med bay, the second was a military photo of a legendary historical hero. The photos were identical.

"Her name is Major Allana Guiver. She is the hero of Kiron Port, the legendary soldier and in the words of my old pervert professor, the *Greatest Sufferer of the War*." Bristol thumbed the two photos and brought up her military record. She started to read out the highlights. "She was PPCLI; true blooded, old fashion infantry. She enlisted, was assigned to the PPCLI nine months before the first jump and the Crisium Concord." When Arau Pau attacked, the nations of Earth unified their military forces and became the Earth Defence Initiative. This was signified by the Crisium Concord. "In the five years of war she went on more mission than any other soldier. She shot up the ranks, got a field commission and even got her own command, Guiver's Battalion."

Mallory drummed on the table as she looked over her glasses. "I had to learn about that at the academy, every officer did. Her battalion preformed more attacks on Arau Pau soil, hell they even boarded and secured an Arau Pau star cruiser. That battalion is a legend." Her face scrunched up. "Didn't she die on another mission?"

"I thought that was made up for that movie."

"Christ, if that's who she was before she went in," Morrison asked. "What did the pod make her? What will she be like now that she's out?"

The room went quiet. Bristol thumbed her handheld, the military file on the screen changing into an image of Kiron Port. She coughed to break the silence and pressed forward. "None of that even counts for what went on here, the last stand of human kind and the great Arau Pau blitz. This is the memory I think she's been playing over and over."

Morrison nodded. "It makes sense that she would choose her greatest victory."

"No, she chose her greatest loss." Somers spoke again, his words once again drawing the crew's attention. "It was probably an instinctual thing; the first thing that pops into your head is the worst possible thing. History says that battle is a great win for humanity but for her it wasn't."

Bristol nodded. "She lost everything at that battle. She lost her senior staff, most of which were close friends of hers, she lost most of her battalion and she lost the woman she loved.".

"She'd already lost her family before that," Somers quietly added.

Hera'sun head dropped as she spoke softly. "Wow; can you imagine living the worst day of your life over and over, everyday for nearly four hundred years?"

The room went quiet as each person thought the same thing, of the worse day of their lives and then reliving it for an eternity. The silence seemed to stretch until Morrison spoke up. "So what do we do with her, ma'am?"

The Captain sipped her coffee as all eyes turned towards her. "Get her up and on her feet. We have a week until we hit the bird farm, I want her up to date on all current weapons we have on the ship and any and all relevant information about..." She paused as she tried to work out what to say next. "Get her up to date on the verse."

"Are you sure about that, ma'am? She could be considered a security risk," Morrison reminded.

"I don't think we could stop her if we tried. Besides, whatever she was frozen for we want to make sure she's ready for it."

Major Allana Guiver was alone in her room. She sat on her bunk and stared at the grey wall. Allana expected a lot of things to change in four hundred years, the culture, the technology and verse she'd live in but as she stared at the grey walls of the human navy's ship she found a drop of comfort knowing that walls were the exact same military grey that they had always been. Out of all the things to survive Earth, out of all the things humanity could have taken with it to the stars, somebody decided that the recipe for military grey paint was crucial. She could have found it comical if it weren't so depressing.

The executive officer assigned her a small room. Commander Francis Somers. She repeated the name out loud. She grabbed the datapad on her desk and held it awkwardly in her hand. They looked like the smartphones from Earth but without any of the buttons. With a simple blink the screen came to life. She looked at the names of the ship's staff. There were so many new names she had to learn. She'd read somewhere that a mind could only remember so many names. If that was true, then her mind was all filled up with her list.

The ships chief medical officer, Acting Sub-Lieutenant Brea Mallory, taught her how to use the datapad after the medical examination. Allana had been examined more times then she could count but never had it been as awkward as this. Turns out when a soldier cracks a doctor's ribs in the middle of a battle, things get uncomfortable when a day later said doctor has to see that same soldier naked. After she woke, it had taken a while for Guiver to remember everything that happened on the *Spellsong*: assaulting the *Mojave Desert's* crew, harming some and injuring others. But when it came back so did that unmistakable feeling of guilt.

Aside from cracking two of Brea Mallory's ribs with a kick, Allana learned the severity of her bestowed injuries. She gave one medic a concussion, broken the nose of an unlucky Leading Seamen, brutally beaten the Petty Officer and shot three men. There was more for her guilt list, as if it didn't have enough shit on it. At least she didn't kill anyone.

Human guns don't kill humans.

Allana stared out the porthole watching the stars fly by. It was a lot to take in. It had been four hundred years since the Kiron Port, four hundred years since her life collapsed. She had a chance to rebuild it but she wasn't off to a good start.

She expected so much to change in the future but humanity still had no planet to call their own, the races of the verse still viewed humans as brutal warmongering pariahs and human could do little else in the universal economy than be guns for hire. You can give it a new coat of paint, switch up the tires and install a spanking new radio but it'll still be that same ol' car.

The door opened behind her but Allana didn't move. Using the reflection in the ship's window she watched as Petty Officer Marcus Branford walked into her room.

Branford was in his thirties, blond hair, blue eyes and was a decently looking man, but sadly his left eye was black, his bottom lip was fat and his face cut. Most of that was her fault.

"Follow me." Allana finally turned around. She wanted to apologize to him but instead she raised a quizzical eyebrow. He was a sailor, a lifelong military man who lived and breathed combat, and he had just been badly humiliated. She could tell he resented her and that he wanted another crack at her to prove his worth, but it wasn't gone to happen. He knew that and irritated him.

"Where are we going, PO?"

"I have been ordered to upgrade your weapon clearance. We're going to the firing range."

Allana followed the PO throughout the *Mojave's* narrow hallways, stepping over the knee knockers and ducking through the short doors. They walked for ten minutes, Branford stopping every couple of minutes to point out a defining location or aspect of the ship. He showed her the galley, the mess, the bridge ladder and even the heads, all before opening a large door and stepping into the ship's firing range.

It was a long thin room, perfect for distance shooting. An energy bolt could never burn through a ship's hull, only weapons fired from a ship or a fighter had the firepower capable to do that. Branford secured the door, locked it, and flipped on the 'in-use' sign. He walked over to Allana.

"Alright, according to military record, you are Allana Guiver and you have never officially resigned or have been removed from the military roster. Before the dissolve of the Earth Defence Initiative you were recruited and transferred over into the Human Endurance Fleet as a member of its army. As of this moment you are returning to active duty roster of the HEF, assigned to the *Mojave Desert* under the command of Captain Agrima Cantor. Please consider this you official welcome back, Major." His tone was official, the naval non-commissioned officer making sure he crossed every T and dotted every I, but it was drenched in heavy dose of apathy. He shook his head in disbelief. "According to the HEF database you are the last human soldier in the verse."

Allana couldn't help but release a small laugh. She was always a Major, always a soldier, she never had a chance to be anything else, and it seemed that fate was trying its best to make sure she never got the chance.

"Alright, time to go over firearms. Rule One: Humans cannot kill humans. This means that any human-made firearm will not kill a human. It will hurt like hell and fry your brain but as long as your physiology is human, you'll wake up the next morning. It'll feel like your hangover fucked a migraine but at least you'll wake up." Branford paused to let what he said sink in. It was a big change from her time, the ability to kill taken from her gun. "These guns will kill any other race, so remember that."

Allana let her hand run over the combat rifles, Hexco manufactured and custom built for the human soldier. Allana could feel the combination of metal and plastic beneath her fingers, the grooves of the pistol grip, the ridges of the barrel and the coldness of the steel. The weapon felt familiar, like a part of her had been missing. Back in the early days, before war broke out due to humanity's mistake, Allana used to find some comfort in a shooting range. The warming feel of a cold weapon and the burst of power as she riddled a target with bullets, but now, after all she'd done, that feeling wasn't there anymore.

She picked up the P7 carbine rifle and delicately held it in her hands. They looked liked the weapons of her time, just evolved. It felt familiar in her hands, like a missing limb. She studied the weapon carefully, hushing the PO as he tried to speak. She named each part in her head as her eyes passed over it; butt-stock, trigger guard, ejection port, safety, forward grip, sights, muzzle, barrel. It was like listing her graduating class. She picked up the magazine and gave it a glance. Instead of the familiar sight of neatly stacked NATO rounds she saw machinery and glowing red lights. "Ammunition?"

He had kept quiet, allowing this woman to inspect the weapon, but it was a slow process. All this could have been over and done with if he'd just let her explain.

"That magazine is a portable energy storage unit. It gives you thirty energy bolts to fire." Thirty rounds. That was the magic number, just like in her day.

She slapped in a magazine, drew the first round into the chamber and slammed on the go button for the firing range. Her targets appeared as holograms, blue virtual figures of faceless forms. Allana thumbed off the safety, switched the firearm to single fire and, with a squeeze of the trigger, fired her first shot. The bolt tore down the range hitting the first target square between its assumed eyes. She squeezed again and again, her weapon firing bolt after bolt at increasing speed, each round downing a target. After all her sleep her aim was no longer as it used to be, somehow it was better. The nanobots had improved her firing techniques, what little it needed, and effectively made her a better killer.

Someone was taking the choice away from her.

Allana switched the rifle to burst and then to fully automatic, each time her aim only proving better then what she remembered. With the rifle complete she moved through the remainder of the guns, from the pistol and SMG, to the sniper rifle and shotgun, each weapon proving to be just like the last. Each was a weapon, evolved forms of the weapons of her past, were tools she'd never seen or touched but she used them like she had spent the last century practising.

Allana put down the last weapon and looked at her hands. What else had they put into her head? First it was Savate and Kinomichi, then command codes to render her floor-bound like a drunken college girl but now they had improved her killing skills.

Someone was really taking the choice away from

her.

Branford stared at her, his look of amazement hidden beneath the contempt he held for her. As a Marine he was impressed, he had never seen a Marine or sailor do that good on a range. Branford was often quoted as being one of the best; it was why he was assigned to the Mojave Desert and this mission. The upper brass wanted someone to do a lot with very little. They wanted someone with great skill to be able to successfully defend himself, the ship and the civilians. But here she stood, the legend herself and she was living up to the hype. What was he compared to her?

"What's next, PO?"

"Major Allana Guiver reporting as requested, ma'am." Allana stood at attention in the doorway of Cantor's ready room. She had been escorted onto the bridge by Branford and from there to the Captain's ready room by the *Mojave Desert*'s Chief of Security Lieutenant-Commander Harold Morrison. She repeated the name in her mind, over and over.

Cantor nodded and offered her a seat. As the Major sat down across the table from the Captain, the door opened and the ships executive officer, Commander Francis Somers, followed by a young sailor, walked in and took a seat beside her. The Captain forced a smile as her steward placed a sandwich and a drink before each of them. She waited for her steward to depart before speaking.

"Thank you for joining us, Frank." She began, getting a nod from her second in command. "I wanted this sit down between us three so we could talk things out between us. I have been on the priority channel with Admiral Richard Golden, the ranking admiral of the navy, and he is ordering us back to the bird farm at top speed,"

Allana snorted, the navy had the most ridiculous names for things, the army had their own terms and slang, but nothing as lame as bird farm for a docking ship. "Until then you are to be put on active duty and are temporarily assigned to me and my ship."

"Yes, Captain, the PO told me such," Allana replied as she reached for a cup. She took the warm glass into her hand and brought it to her lips. Coffee; how she missed coffee. "But I'll be honest, ma'am. After everything I've been through, I just want go outside."

"You wish to quit?" Frank asked, making no attempt to hide his surprise. Outside was slang for the civilian world. If the stories were true, Allana had literally been frozen in time to be humanity's savior and now that she had been thawed she no longer wished to serve. "How can--"

Cantor quickly interrupted her XO, cutting him off mid sentence with a small chuckle. "I understand, Major, but to be honest: that's way above my pay-grade. I'm not one to pass the buck but that sounds a lot like Admiral Golden's problem to me. I can't take you off active duty, but he can. So until then..."

Allana nodded as the Captain's answer drifted off. Deep down she already knew the answer, but she still had to ask. "So what are my duties?"

"Frank, if you would." The captain delegated as she started in on her sandwich.

"Your assignment is to bring yourself up to fighting form," he explained. "You have already gone through weapons training; to be honest we expected that to take a hell of a lot longer. Now we want you to sit with a tutor and take a crash course in present day...well, everything. They'll go over the *Avalon* and current humanity culture, universal politics, who we like and who we don't, and a quick blip on the last four hundred years. It sounds like a lot but we have a week until we reach the bird farm and we're not going to let it go to waste."

Allana nodded. "Who will be tutoring me? One of the military boys?"

Cantor shook her head."No, Major, we have something special for you. We have a pair of civilian historical bookworms for you to work with. Their current mission has been temporarily scrapped so might as well keep them busy--"

"Before the civilians start whining," Allana finished with a chuckle. Civilian bookworms; Allana rolled her eyes as she sighed. Civilian academics had a tendency to go on and on, droning on until their voice blended with the background noise. They were so unlike military teacher who got to the point quickly and yelled at you if you couldn't keep up. It was the military way.

"Tomorrow morning you'll perform PT with the marines then you'll report to the civies." Cantor placed her cup on the saucer and returned both to the table. She smiled at the pair that sat across from her. "Are you finding it difficult to adapt?"

Allana quietly ate her sandwich, unsure of how to answer. She looked around the room, glimpsing at the paintings on the wall, the statues and trinkets that rested on the desks and tables, and the small couch. Nothing looked the same any more. The paintings weren't done in oil or liquid based paint anymore, instead the artist used coloured lasers to paint the canvas. The trinkets weren't human artifacts but archaeological and artistic sculptures from foreign culture and the furniture wasn't made with wood, or even that fake wood the used during the war, this was some new substance she had never seen before, a mix of plastic and some alien material.

"Everything is so different from the world I knew. The ships are unlike anything we had, there are aliens that actually like humans now and things aren't even close to what I call normal." The only thing that did make her smile was the black ball of fur that sat curled up on the couch. "But then I see a cat on a navy ship and things seem a little closer to what I once knew."

Cantor gave Allana a small chuckle. "A cat on a naval ship is a tradition, it have been that way since the first Trent-Gate."

"Ever since a cat saved an entire crew after they

encounter some rare space virus."Allana laughed, "they must still tell that story then?"

"They never stopped," Franked laughed.

Allana looked back at the cat. Tenuvah was a cat person. She used to love them. "What about dogs? Do they still exist? I was always more of a dog person."

CHAPTER SEVEN
4 days until Pherca Moon Invasion

In the depth of space, night-time was little more than a matter of perspective. There was no sun to light up the sky, no white clouds and no blue skies. All that existed was the endless black and the sprinkle of starlight on the curtain of the universe. On a ship like the *Mojave* day and night existed as little more than numbers on a clock. The crew worked on something called *Avalon* standard time, something she wasn't familiar with yet, but all she knew was this was night-time and most people were asleep. She was tired of sleeping, she'd slept enough.

Allana grabbed a pair of armless glasses off of her dresser and slid it into her shirt pocket. She was wearing black navy pants and a blue navy work shirt. She never looked good in navy blues, never, but that was the only uniform they had. Allana exited her quarters and made for the docking door. A small alien female came around the corner, her face beaming. She clapped her hands together and pointed them to the heavens.

"Oh blessed be! I have found you. I have been

meaning to introduce myself. I am Hera'sun, science officer of the *Mojave Desert*."

Allana smiled and offered her hand to the small scientist. "I am Major Allana Guiver of the Earth Defence Initiative." She snorted. "No wait, that's not true anymore, is it? I guess I'm now part of the Human Endurance Fleet."

It still sounded weird to Allana. For all but nine months of her military career she was part of the Earth Defence Initiative and now without a choice in the matter, she belonged to somebody else. Apparently now she didn't fight to defend earth from space, but to help humanity endure it.

"Oh, it is very, very nice to meet you, Major Guiver."

"So you're a Monastica correct?" Hera'sun nodded her head eagerly, "And you guys worship the ship or something? I'm sorry, I am still learning about you."

"We worship the fact that our God sent us the ship." Hera'sun corrected. "Do you follow a religion?"

"I was raised Roman Catholic but it's been a long time since my last confession and that was before the freezing."

"Well our belief is much like how Christians pray to God, the Virgin Mary or baby Jesus. We believe in our God as our almighty, the *Spellsong* as our people's Savoir and very soon our Avatar."

It made sense. Allana was not one to question religion; it wasn't for her so she didn't partake. It was hard to find solace in religion when she did little else but kill. Most religions didn't look too kindly on the same-sex marriages either - at least they didn't in her day. She didn't want to be vain but curiosity over took her. "So I ask in the least rude way I could come up with but what does that make me?"

"Christianity, as far as I know of it, has no comparison but Hinduism does." Hera'sun's eyes went wide with excitement. "I am here; I witnessed your arrival so I have been given a monumental honour to suggest a term for you, something that could be put into our Sixth testament. So I am going with the term Avatar."

"So your people are going to worship me? That's not a good idea." Allana scrunched up her face. She didn't like the idea of people worshipping her. "The last thing anybody needs is to follow my way of life as an example. I am not exactly the lesson that needs to be taught."

"Modesty: what a divine trait."

"You're the science officer right?" Hera'sun nodded. "How does a woman of science believe so heavily in religion? Those two tend to fight more the two hungry pit bulls over a t-bone.

Hera'sun opened her mouth and closed it several times as she tried to translate this unknown patter. Human saying were an oddity at best. "One does not preclude the other. Our believe states that science is part of God's will. It's like playing a video game; did you era have video games?" Allana just nodded. "Well for the game to work the programmers construct a world, then they create the physics in the world. The programmer then has to put challenges in to test you, to better your skills and let you level up, get bonuses, and become stronger. Finally you are plucked down in the middle of the game. It's a simplistic analogy but we view it existence the same way. Our creator manifested the universe, manifested the physics and the laws we live by and then plopped us down within it. Science is reward for our trials, a perk after we all have levelled up. They are not enemies, they are allies. We found you by means of science but that science is little more than our creator's will."

"I think you've officially shot passed this old soldier's philosophical limit for the day, ma'am, but you have given me something that's going to require a lot more thought. In meantime perhaps you can help me?" The Monastic raised her eyes eagerly. "I need to get to the *Spellsong*. Can you show me the way?"

"It would be my pleasure."

Petty Officer Branford did his best to remain hidden as he carefully watched the popsicle crossing onto the Spellsong, the little science officer trailing her like a lovesick puppy. The *Spellsong* was off limits to all members unless accompanied by one of Cantor's senior staff or science squad. Branford quietly followed.

Allana stopped at the cryo-chamber and ran her hands along the inside. She could feel the groove her body made, the feel of the material against her skin and the cushioned rest that existed for her head. The pod was hell but she missed it. Things made sense in there, she fought and she killed and then she did it all over. Out here she was a mess. Out here she didn't know up from down, she didn't know left from right and, worse of all, she didn't know who she was.

She stepped away from the pod and over to the cerebral device. The busted machine had stuck her in a living hell. She knelt down and stared at the small hole in the side. It was the entry burn of an energy bolt, similar to the ones she fired not hours earlier; one shot was all it took to throw her into a digital hell. Her memory was still fuzzy, Doc Mallory said they would come back slowly, but the unit took damage when an alien ship tried to board the *Spellsong* and she was awakened, for no more than two hours, to repel the attackers. That was the extent of her memories lately, a series of battle flashbacks; the horrific highlights on some sport channel.

She withdrew the armless glasses from her pocket and placed it into a small groove. The glasses and the machine lit up as the two connected. The glasses were the same she wore when she was frozen, the same ones that put her mind into a virtual world and ones that, when the upload finished, would do so again. She watched in silence as the machine blinked and whirred to life, the small screen signalling a massive data transfer. When the transferred completed she returned the glasses to her chest pocket and the room returned to silence. She crossed the chamber and knelt before a floor panel. She waved her hand across the floor tile, a small sensor reading her hand, and a hidden door slid open. Allana grabbed a green duffle bag from the revealed compartment. This was it, the last few things she owned in the verse. A set of clothes, she assumed, that were horrifically out of date, a couple memorable trinkets from her life, battle worn that they were, and a couple weapons, now most likely considered antiques and horribly obsolete. People called her a living legend, one of humanity's greatest soldiers from history, but what legend had everything she owned in a green duffle bag that was older than she was?

Allana stood upright, closing the door with her foot, and walked out of the room. The ship buzzed as she passed. It lit up the moment she stepped aboard the *Spellsong* and now as she stepped off, rejoining Hera'sun, it seemed to shut off.

Alone and back in her room, Allana lay down on the bed. Her back was pressed against the linen and she stared at the ceiling. With her unopened bag safely stowed beneath her bunk Allana took a deep breath and withdrew the glasses. She whispered to herself as she balanced the armless glasses on her nose. "I'm coming."

With a double-tap on the top of the nose bridge the lens flared to life. Allan watched as her cabin's walls, the entire ship and all of space dripped down to the floor, like water on a wall, and melted away. In its place stood the lush jungles of Anya Caw, the Arau Pau's nursery planet, and dozens of cloth tents. Allana had spent nine months stationed on this planet on the hell hole of a posting, living towering trees and fighting off the ferocious predators. This planet served as a classroom as Allana, teaching her what Vietnam vets knew first hand: jungle warfare. Each week she led another mission inwards, getting further and further; never knowing when the next step would trigger another ridiculous trap or walk into an ambush of psychotic nursemaids and overprotective den mothers. Every day there was a mission in futility; hiding and fighting only to discover that their hard won victories were little else but what the Arau Pau let them win. Yet what was hell for most held a special place in Allana's heart.

This was the first time she could control the simulation since she was frozen almost four hundred years ago. Four centuries of experiencing what others wished of her, four centuries of doing whatever the hell they told her to. Now that she was fully awake and completely aware she had complete control and she'd chosen this violent hell hole for a reason.

Allana knew which tent was hers but she avoided it, instead she walked towards the personal tents of the medic staff. She pushed one open and saw her lying on her cot, covered only by a thin blanket. She was a dark skinned woman, with jet black hair, brown eyes and tender lips.

"This is what you choose?" The doctor laughed in disbelief, the blanket cascading down her body with each chuckle. "Don't get me wrong, I am flattered but you can be anywhere you want, anywhere in all of creation, hell, you can be in places that creation can't touch and you choose here."

Allana stepped beneath the big net and began to undress, stripping the green combat suit off her aroused flesh. "Why wouldn't I? We spent so many happy hours in this cot right here together. You were my hope in a jungle that had none."

"Well you do know how to make a girl blush and if you can get me to blush then you are doing something right." Allana laughed as she peeled the final piece of clothing off her own body. The now bare Allana stepped closer to the cot and leaned in slowly. The medic rose to meet her, anticipating a kiss but Allan had something else planned. She grabbed the blanket and sharply pulled it, yanking it clean off the surprised medic. The doctor squealed in protest, citing such arguments as cruelty and jerkiness as she fought to regain the blanket. Allana watched her medic squirm, her medical hands desperately trying to wrestle control of the prized cloth away but the soldier would have none of it.

Allana eventually gave in and descended upon the bed, the blanket fluttering slowly behind her. The cloth eventually covered the two women as they held on another. The medic seductively whispered, "I'm glad you're here."

"So am I, babe, I missed you." Allana replied. "I love you, Tenuvah, I really do."

Allana was never one to love-and-leave but as soon as she and Tenuvah finished up the world dissolved again, replaced by the chaotic sounds of Jupiter Station. The space station, which floated in orbit around its namesake planet, was a floating city that acted as a military port. Deafening explosions ripped through the floating city and the populace descended into chaos.

"Really, ma'am?" Corporal Jamie Diswal, a redheaded kid barely aging twenty, called out over the thunderous Arau Pau gunfire. "Ain't no place better in the verse then this for us to be having a little chat?"

The pair crouched by a building corner as the alien stormed the city, their vanguard ripping through the unexpected law enforcement like bullets through a glass pane window. Allana pointed to a pair of fallen cops. "What can I say, kid, every path has its puddle."

"I don't think that saying's correct, ma'am."

Allana signal the kid forward and bolted for two members of the Jupiter PD. They slid in alongside the corpses and quickly rifled through the bodies, each grabbing a pistol and all the ammo they could carry. Armed, the pair bolted for cover. Allana had chosen the Jupiter Invasion, when the Arau Pau slipped past the human fleet and launch a direct attack on the space station. The attack caught the military off guard and placed Allana and Diswal miles away from military base with no hope of regrouping.

"Penny for whatever the hell you thinking 'bout?"

"Damn it, kid, I think that's the closest you've ever gotten to a correct saying and you're not even real." Allana and the kid popped up from cover, their police issued pistols roaring to life as they opened fire on an encroaching Arau Pau platoon. Their accuracy was deadly, the kid's almost better then hers; damn farm boys and their guns. Each ground-pounder needed only two shots, at most, to fall. "I'm awake, finally, in a world I don't know anymore. We have no planet, no home, nearly no allies and no hope. I'm free and they want me to fight. They don't even know against what but all I want is to go outside."

The pair dashed across the street, dodging gunfire, and leapt through a glass display and into a clothing store. It was the kid's idea, if memory served her, no time for cover fire and hostiles closing in on them fast. He was quick on his feet and always smiling. Before the attack he was just some off-duty corporal who happened to be nearby when the invasion started. After the window trick she decided he was hers. She had him switched to her platoon, despite the list of infractions his record held. The kid was on his feet a fraction of a second after her, his pistol up and firing as the moved to the rear exit. The kid paused, grabbed a black bowler hat off the rack and plopped it down on his head; a perfect fit.

"That's not the problem, ma'am. You just think it

is." He ejected his magazine and slipped in a fresh one. "You're just lost. What you need is something to hold onto. Your green bag is full of stuff from the past, from your old life with me and the gang, but you need to start a new bag. Never forget us," He smirked and ran his fingers across the brim of his hat. "Especially me with me good looks, but you can't hold onto to us forever. A lad like me self, I can't be tied down to just one woman. It ain't fair to the rest of verse's women now is it?"

She looked at him, her mouth forming the words that now lived in history. She couldn't change these words, her mind wouldn't let her. These words were like a definition. When her brain looked up Corporal Jamie Diswal in her mental dictionary the definition was this very conversation.

"What are you doing with that hat?"

"I'm think it be me new lucky hat," Diswal said with a toothy grin.

"What happened to your old lucky hat?"

"Burnt in a fire; I think its luck ran out."

"So you're keeping that one?"

"You know what they say, ma'am, a penny earned is like two in the bush!"

Allana just shook her head. "That's not how it goes."

Jupiter stationed melted away as reality returned. Allana took off the glasses and put them on her shelf. Diswal and Tenuvah weren't real, she knew that, but somehow this helped. She pulled her green bag out from underneath and pulled open the zipper. She remembered little from when she packed this but what she did recollect hurt. She recalled the emotion she felt putting something in to remind her of everybody she held dear, from a trinket to something special. She pulled out a black bowler and placed on her dresser. It wasn't Jamie's, his burnt up with the rest of Kiron Port, it was new one she bought him for his memorial. Deep in the bottom of the bag was a red box, no bigger than a man's wallet. She paused for a moment, her mind wondering if men even used wallets anymore, but ignored the errant thought as she cracked the seal and opened the box. Inside was an engagement ring. It didn't have a diamond on top like the classical ring, an impractical setting for a soldier; instead it looked like a wedding band made from white gold with diamonds set in.

With tears in her eyes Allana ran the ring between her fingers. "I miss you, Ten," she whimpered. "I miss you."

CHAPTER EIGHT
3 days until Pherca Moon Invasion

Morning, or whatever it was that passed as morning deep amongst the stars, came not just like clockwork but only as clockwork. It came with Allana on her feet doing the most natural and basic thing a soldier could do: physical training. She trained with the marines, running a continuous loop around the ship before eventually retiring to a weight room. She started in the rear, feeling stiff and tired now that her body was under her own command again, but quickly caught up. With each lap she did she could feel the joints loosening up. She found her muscles remembering what they did best and falling back on old graces. Before long she was sprinting alongside the youngest.

The workout felt familiar, morning PT was the basis of the military. It brought her a small piece of mind. Running was never her favourite thing, she much preferred team sports, but it had become something soothing to her, something familiar.

Once the marines hit the weight room Allana cornered

the heavy bag and gave it a playful jab. The synthesized material felt thick and sturdy against her fist. She jabbed with her right a second time and a third before striking the bag with a powerful left. Her body responded to the punch, the familiar feeling rippling through her body. Allana shifted her stance and punched again, assaulting the bag with a barrage of blows.

Boxing; her dad taught her growing up in high school; the sweet science. He taught his little girl how to defend herself, how to knock the block off of some boy when they got to grabby. It proved useful in war but lacked the need in high school. Word got around very quickly about her lifestyle.

"Such a shame, like losing Helen of Troy to the other side." One overly poetic boy in high school commented on her coming out with those very words. She never thought of herself as overly pretty. She was rugged and tough, a farm girl of sorts. At the time she thanked the boy and said that they would always remain friends, she probably killed him with that line, but as she looked back she had to wonder if the Trojan War would have happened if Helen of Troy had been a lesbian.

Her leg slammed into the side of the bag with a spine shattering kick. In a blur her foot echoed the kick twice more before her entire body pivoted and struck the heavy bag with a powerful back-kick.

Taekwondo. She enrolled in a dojo shortly after battle school. She wanted to learn how to make her entire body a weapon and not just her fists. Her sensei, her teacher, was a tall man with energy to spare. He encouraged every student with the energy and zeal of a twelve year old.

"And then bam! You've kicked him through this wall and into the next."

The bag jostled with each kick she fired at it. Her stance shifted and she moved in closer, her knees and elbows striking the thick material as she switched to the infantry grade close-quarters combat style.

Boxing, taekwondo and CQC; those were the three styles she knew before jumping into the freezer, whatever she knew now was a crap shoot. She closed her eyes, briefly, and let her mind calm itself and muscle memory to take over. She shifted into savate then into kinomichi, those two weren't as big of a surprise as they were a couple days ago, but when she slid into Muay Thai then Pi Gua she found her body moving in ways she knew nothing of.

She came to a halt, her chest heaving at the intense workout and looked at her arms. She knew nothing about Pi Gua, she hadn't even heard of it before today, but there it sat, all the lessons and all the facts, in her brain. What else could her body do now? She couldn't help but smile as her eyes fell on her palm. I know it like the back of my hand. It was a common saying back in her day. Now she didn't even know what the back of her hand could do.

"Ma'am?" The voice snapped her out of the reverie. She eyed the tall black man who stood before him. It was one of the soldiers from her thawing. Names were still absent but the bandage over the nose was a dead giveaway.

"Yes?" She scrambled to find the name.

"It's Campbell, ma'am," he offered.

"Right, Leading Seamen Devin Campbell." She frowned. "I'm real sorry about the nose."

He shrugged. "If the marines were safe everybody would do it." She chuckled. "How about giving me a chance to get even, ma'am? I'd love a chance to spar with you."

She opened her mouth to turn him down, the last she wanted was some enlisted man trying to make a name for him by taking the supposed legendary soldier down, but she never got the chance before he spoke again.

"Since being on ship I rarely get to spar with somebody new. I don't want to grow complacent," he explained. "Sparring is one of the most important parts of Jeet Kune Do. Sparring against superior foes makes us better fighters. I don't see anybody better than the you. Besides I'd kick my own ass if I miss the chance to spar with the legend."

She couldn't help but smirk. She liked this guy.

Bristol watched as Nurem'sun pushed away from the table, putting his palms into his eyes, yawning and stretching in the chair. The pair of them had been assigned to teach the Major about the verse and bring her up to speed as much as defrosted humanly possible.

Nurem'sun turned around and spotted Bristol. His eyes went wide as his face battled exhaustion with excitement. He leaped from his chair and scuttled over to her.

"This woman is a machine! She is a computer!" He exclaimed happily, "we have gone four hours straight and she is just absorbing it. I swear I am just installing it into her mind. Do you know she's not even tired yet?"

Bristol looked over at the redhead soldier as she stood up. She could only see the back of the Major's head, her crimson locks stopping just below her ears, as the soldier walked to the edge of the table for food and drink. She was wearing naval uniform, black slacks with a dark blue working shirt.

"What did you go over?"

Nurem'sun clapped his hands together rapidly. "Oh, it was brilliant fun. She wanted to go over humanity and the post war aftermath. That ended up taking no time at all, so she wanted to know about us, my people, and that made me very excited."

"Did she mention what she wanted to do next?"

"She wants to learn about the Kobold Unification and current human situation." Nurem'sun explained, "she's done some reading but want a more comprehensible rundown."

Bristol grabbed her handheld from her pocket and thumbed the screen. Her thumbs typed quickly as she searched the computer for her files. "Okay, I have the stuff she asked for. I'll give it a quick re-read to make sure I am ready while she eats."

Bristol's long-time archaeological partner froze for a moment as he stared up at her. A nefarious smile crossed his face. The exhaustion from his voice vanished as a sarcastic playful tone filled the void. "Wait a second; are you not Doctor Bristol Tsia?"

Bristol was confused. "Nurem'sun, what are you doing?"

"Answer the question. Are you Doctor Bristol Tsia?"

"You know I am."

"Well I am confused, because I heard Doctor Bristol Tsia was an expert in human history. I heard that her area of expertise was in the human post-stellar exploration era. I heard that she knew everything like the back of her hand, that she was an expert in the field."

"Nurem'sun, what are you doing?" The Monastica scrunched his face as he jokingly glared at her. Bristol rolled her eyes. "Yes, that is my area of expertise and I wouldn't be in this ridiculous field if it wasn't for you."

"Then why would this expert need to re-read all of her material?" Nurem'sun's face exploded with a sinister smile, a sign he was about to do something evil or wicked, or at least something Tsia really didn't like. "You really haven't had a chance to meet the Major have you?"

The little archaeologist called the Major over with a smile. Bristol watched as the soldier turned around. She had already seen all of Allana's features between the medical documents and historical files but meeting her face to face for the first time was completely different. All of her characteristics seemed more vibrant. Her red satin hair, her shamrock green eyes and her pale tender lips came together in a vivacious package.

Bristol brushed the hanging blue bangs from her face, hooking the strands of hair behind her ear. Her right hand hovered by her ear, twirling her hair in circles and wrapping it around her finger. Nurem'sun elbowed her leg. She looked down at the smiling little archaeologist as he spun his two index fingers in exaggerated circles. She looked confused at first but suddenly realised what he was hinting at.

She was twirling her hair like a fourteen year old girl.

"So, you're the woman who could stop me cold. You know I have had the toughest and strongest of this universe's bads try to stop me, and it turns out that the cutest thing can do it with a word." Bristol smiled and started blushing. The Major offered her hand. "I'm Allana."

Bristol took the offered hand and gave it a shake. She admired the delicacy of her touch, and the warmth of her skin. "Bristol, Bristol Tsia."

"Oh don't be modest, partner," Nurem'sun giggled. "You are Doctor Bristol Tsia."

She felt Allana's hand tense slightly as they shook. "A doctor, that is really impressive. Are you a medical doctor?"

"No, I have a doctorate in human history." Bristol

released the soldier's hand and smiled. "As soon as you're done eating we will begin."

Allana nodded and returned to her meal, munching away while Bristol prepared her notes. She found it difficult to prepare, her gaze wandering away from the handheld and over to the legend that sat beside her. Allana was a rough and tough soldier, with sensual lissom body, built for war and combat, but Bristol wondered how deep that soldier's exterior of hers ran. She'd read the stories, she was a woman who had taken a lover, or seven, before settling down with Tenuvah Sheppard (or whatever facsimile of *settling down* the legendary soldier took). So somewhere deep within all that that rough and tough existed something soft and gentle, or once did.

After the final bite the two began, Bristol's lesson starting with the background story of the Kobolds and their clan based power empire system. The Kobolds were simple to summarize, a conquering race separated into dozens of smaller clans. The strongest clan then claimed dominance over the rest and their leader became the Emperor. The Kobolds became more difficult and complex when one examined the clan differences and politics. Their Empire spanned the stars and consumed numerous lesser races beneath their command like the Javihorn and the Teeliquin. Things changed when the last great Emperor took the throne. He wanted a greater legacy and decided that he needed more planets to have it. The conquest started slowly, taking small moons and planets, before launching an all out attack on the Kiltvyu systems.

While many individuals volunteered to fight, Humanity as a race avoided the war. The human governments were desperate to change their universal reputation from warmongering savages. But when the Kobolds began to attack HEF supplies ships, humanity was left with no choice but to fight.

"Is it true what I read?" the Major asked. "That the war ended because of one human war criminal?"

Tsia frowned. "There were many factors to the Kobold defeat. They over-stretch their resources, they pushed too hard near the end and they didn't expect the rebellion from several smaller nations that proved quite costly," she explained. "But yeah, one major factor was how one pilot held an entire civilian ship hostage. He forced the Kobold fleet out of the Hanari system and into an ambush. The Kobold flight was wiped out."

Tsia squirmed uncomfortably in her chair. "It was a dark day for humanity. Ever since we hit the stars mankind has been viewed as little more than warmongering savages. This did little to help our cause."

"What happened to the pilot?"

"He was Special Forces, so he was secretly tried as a war criminal and after that nobody knows. Hell, nobody knows who he, or the rest of Samurai Squadron, really were." The more things changed the more they stayed the same. And with that they moved on, jumping back and forth through history like a fictional time traveller.

Allana carefully followed Bristol's teachings, her lesson were vibrant and precise lacking the eternal tangents that normally came with civilian teaching. When she was assigned this class she expected a pair of long winded know-it-all, but what she got was an energetic and passionate alien story teller, and a hypnotically seductive woman.

Allana blinked in surprise at her own thoughts. She couldn't be thinking that about the doctor, she couldn't be thinking of any woman that way. It was disrespectful; it was wrong. Allana admitted to herself she was real fortunate to be on a ship manned by intelligent and beautiful women. The Acting Sub-Lieutenant Brea Mallory was incredibly attractive, Doctor Bristol Tsia was stunning, and even Captain Agrima Cantor was a fine looking woman for her age but they were all off limits, everybody was.

Allana looked back at the handheld. "What the hell is that?"

Bristol looked at the picture that held Allana's attention and frowned. "That is the Planet *Avalon*."

"Bullshit. That cannot be the *Avalon*; that looks like a pile of space trash," Allana shook her head. "I was there when the *Avalon* came off the line. She was a thing of beauty. She is a simple rectangular ship, but she glimmers like the stars, shines like the sun, and floats like the crystal clear rivers of northern Ontario. This looks like a wet bar of soap somebody dropped in the trash. There's crap all over it. What the hell happened to her?"

Bristol typed everything the Major spoke. There wasn't a soul alive that was around when the big three launched, except for this woman who sat before her. This was a new perspective on a historical event.

"The *Avalon* needed repairs and humans needed more room. The fleet expected to find a planet relatively soon, they discovered the Arau Pau home world almost instantly, but the known verse was vastly different then what we expected." Bristol explained, "So the *Avalon* became a generation ship. We salvaged old ships, attached hulls and compartments onto the *Avalon's*, and made the ship bigger as we needed."

Allana just shook her head. She was not a ship enthusiast like some of the guys she knew - used to know - but she liked the Avalon. "The *Avalon* was one of three identical ships. I know that we lost the Argyre in the war, but what happened to the *Mag Mell*?"

Bristol shrugged. "It's lost. The remaining sisters and their captains decided to make a jump through warp to whatever relay destination they were going to use, but when the *Avalon* came out of warp the *Mag Mell* was nowhere to be found. The *Avalon* waited at the rendezvous point for an entire month while the HED sent search parties out to as many realistic locations as possible, but she was never found. According to history the *Mag Mell* jumped into warp and never made it back to normality. Its official status is MIA."

"Forty-four million people vanishing in a matter

of hours. Time has not been generous to the likes of human-kind." Allana suddenly paused as she replayed the conversation in her head. "Did you say Planet *Avalon*?"

Tsia just nodded. "The *Avalon* is legally a rogue planet." She snickered at the Major look of pure confusion. "After the Arau Pau-Human War, humanity was left with no planet to call their own, this you know." Allana nodded. "The rest of the races declared us savages and wanted to try us for war crimes."

Allana nodded again. The Arua Pau-Human War ended without any winners. Humanity lost their home world and a massive chunk of their populace and the Arau Pau were essentially wiped out. Their numbers were so few that most didn't expect their species to survive and if they did their bloodline was going to be wrought due to incest.

"A team of human lawyers set out to defend themselves from these allegations and eventually came up with one solid defence. Each law required a person to be of a home planet. Humans didn't have that. It was a clever defence to say the least.

"Humanity was left with a radiated planet and no world to call home. The interplanetary governmental organization known as the League of Races decreed that the humans needed to be held to the same rules and regulations as the rest of the known governments but the writings on which the League of Races and its laws were built upon required a home planet. Without a planet the humans would become exempt to a great majority of their laws."

Tsia explained how for the first time in the history of the known verse a ship was deemed a rogue planet. The *Avalon* became the human's home world, a legally defined planet floating through space, and subject to all planetary laws and regulations.

It came with a great number of benefits, protection from invaders, admittance into the University of Universal Peace, and declaration of humans under the Sentient Rights Act, but it came with unforeseen circumstance. The *Avalon* was now held by the same planetary regulation that all other were, this meant that citizens of the known verse, from any other planet, moon or colony could immigrate to the *Avalon*, and even apply to be a citizens. The *Avalon's* government set to work, building a series of immigration laws and utilizing a points system by which citizenship was granted. It then decided that all citizens of the *Avalon*, of the Human Endurance Fleet, would be known as Mankind, the term human reserved for the species itself. There were very few aliens who lived on the *Avalon*, six thousand on a ship of forty-four million, most of which were here as ambassadors, government staff, or on a work visa. There were very few who immigrated there and even less who became one of Mankind.

Tsia went quiet and Allana understood why. It seemed like a romantic theory, the last of humanity drifting through the stars to find a new home, but both of them knew the truth; humanity couldn't last like this for long. Mankind needed a home and soon or they would become little more than the nothingness that they sailed.

Cantor stirred at a knock on her door. She looked up surprised. She signalled the guest to enter. Cantor lowered her data-pad as Major Allana Guiver walked in. With a wave of her hand she offered the seat across the table.

"It's late, Major Guiver," Cantor inquired. "What can I do for you?" Allana took a seat and cleared her voice.

"I would like to ask you a couple questions Captain," Allana began, her tone and words were cautious and slow. "Most are just questions that I need a military answer for but some may be a little personal in nature."

Cantor placed her hands on the table and took in a deep breath. She understood the need for a military opinion on history. Most military members tended to think the same way; it was an aftermath of the training. From day one in basic training each military recruit was taught to think, look, move and act in a certain way: the military way.

"You deserve as much, Major. So what's on your mind?" Allana deserved a lot more than a couple answers.

"From my readings I know how the human race feeds itself," Allana began. "We rent small habitable planets and moons from our allies and we farm them but why doesn't the *Avalon* have a hydroponics farm?"

"The *Avalon* does," Cantor explained, "but it's nowhere near large enough to feed the entire race."

"So if the *Avalon* and humanity have no resources of its own, nothing to export, how do we gain the money to rent space?"

"Some xenobiologist say that each race has an affinity for one thing. They each have one aspect that makes their race superior to the countless other. It is not a wildly accepted theory but it is an academic one." Cantor explained. She didn't like what she was about to say but it was a reality she couldn't avoid. "So if that theory holds true then we are forced to ask the question. What is it that humanity does better than anybody else? The answer is killing; humans are better at killing than any other race.

"Humanity has become a military power for hire. It didn't start this way; we sort of descended into it. Humans are called in to patrol areas, deal with terrorist cell or colony uprisings and basically clean up a foreign government's dirty laundry.

"We do this legally through the League of Races. Humanity had become their peace keepers, the clean-up crew and their assassins. It started out with the most noble of intentions, a way to redeem our name in the aftermath of our sordid history, but different leaders have different agendas and the idea has sadly become corrupted."

Allana leaned back, rubbing her temple with her

hand. She didn't know how to respond. She was filled with a mixing pot of emotions. She felt anger and disappointment in humanity coupled with relief and gratefulness for the League's generosity. It took a while before she could answer, before she could reply. The words slipped through her lips quietly. "So we fight the wars nobody else wants to?"

"That about sums it up." The Captain sat up in her chair. "Humanity does a lot of good, mind you. We've settled civil wars and we've quelled terrorist uprisings. Two years ago we were sent into Homodole VII, a planet that housed the – an alien race called the Wei'nul; there are two major faction of on that planets and they'd been feuding for years. They come to a peace after many, many years but it's a highly unstable peace. One of their sleeper cell programs, I can't remember whose side it belonged to, got a false signal and activated. The LOR requested HEF aid and we dealt with the bio-upgraded soldiers."

Augments; after battle school she was assigned to 3rd Battalion of the PPCLI. Eleven days after being posted the augment rebellion began. All across North America, illegally modified humans tried to overthrow their governments and Allana fought against them. She was just a green grunt back then, fighting with unrefined skills and no instincts. The rebellion was a frightening chapter in human history, a lesson in the horrors of technology and scientific ethics. Somehow knowing that others races had made similar errors in their history made humans seems not so barbaric.

"That answers a number of questions," Allana explained. "I was reading over the military transcripts of some of the Marines on board. There seemed to be a great deal of combat and action for a time of peace. Now I know why."

"You're reading military docs on your time off? Why not read a book or watch some vids or films. We have thousands of movies and episodes on board."

Allana just scoffed. "When I left my – time – I was watching a show called *The Citadel*. Ever heard of it?" Cantor shook her head. "It was a fantasy show based off of a series of books. It was about this kingdom and the five nations that fought to rule it. I was in season four and it was just getting good. So what do I do? Do I try and find the show and watch how it ends? Or do I find a new show? If so, where do I start? What are the *do not misses* of this era? Hell, will I understand the films? Will I even get any of the references?"

Cantor stared at the Major for moment before shrugging her shoulders and nodding. The solider had a point. "So military docs it is. Well as a ranking officer you have this privilege." Cantor knew what came next. It wasn't an easy subject to approach but at least the Major was doing so with tact. "So who else's file did you read?"

"I read yours, Captain. You were a top notch naval captain during the war. Now you're on a dump posting, no offence. What happened? I went looking into your file but it has all been redacted."

"You were right, this is personal." Cantor forced a half-hearted smile on her face, "At least you warned me." She stood up from her comfortable Captain's chair and walked to the small fridge in the corner. She pulled it open and withdrew a bottle of water for and the Major. A quick toss sent the bottle flying through the air and into the nimble hands of the legendary soldier.

"It's a difficult matter and a private one," Cantor explained as she opened her bottle. Allana tried to apologize but the Captain waved her quiet. "We are counting on you to save the world or some such nonsense, the least you can do is be safe in the knowledge that you can count on me."

Allana twisted open her water and took a deep drink. She watched as Agrima paced nervously in her office, sipping her water not out of thirst but out of a need to fiddle. Finally the Captain spoke. "I made captain early on in the last war; I was the XO of a ship and took over when my Captain died. The crew knew the chain of command so they followed me without question. Assuming command of a ship is a difficult task in peace time but in war is a whole other fish. During the battle its fine, the crew obeys orders or the ship goes down, but when the shooting stops that's when they question you. I survived them and I survived the war."

Agrima never talked to anybody about this. There were doctors and mental health professionals she's spoken to but outside of the shrinks no one understood.

Allana was different. She'd seen battle, she'd made combat decisions and been forced to live with the circumstances. She'd sent people to their death. She understood the burdens of command.

"I hate to say it but peace drove me crazy, there was no excitement and no adrenalin. I volunteered to go on any mission they needed but I never once put my crew in unnecessary risk or made a bad order. My decisions didn't all turn out perfectly but they were always the best choice in a bad situation; until Tali'mar.

"My ship was the C.S.S. *Molokai* and I was patrolling in the outer layers of Monastic space. We were on the hunt for a small pocket of Herosian terrorist. Intel had put them in the sector training their men. We searched each planet in that system, thirty-two in total, looking for them. We finally gained a lead when we landed on a semi-barren world of Tali'mar.

"Our energy reading put them in the north-east hemisphere of the planet. We sent Recon platoon to investigate and they came back with a positive ID on the enemy base camp. They were doing it all there, drugs, slaves and weapons. It was the illegal trifecta to fund their operations. So I made my call and sent ground forces to assault the base while the Molokai would entrap any escaping ships as they left orbit. It didn't go as planned.

"The ground forces were over-powered and massacred, the slaves were all executed, and any starfighters I sent in for air support were shot down by hidden AA-guns. It was a disaster. Turns out they were trying to construct their own Trent-Gate. They wanted to enter the warp without the policing that came with public gates. After they were found, they threatened to activate it on the planet."

A Trent-Gate had never been activated on a planet. Some scientist believed that the gravity of the warp combined with a planets own gravity would simply rip the world in two. Doomsday theorist predicted a much worse scenario.

"I ended up opening fire on the base from orbit costing what few innocent lives were left and the possibility of any information on other Herosian cells."

Allana didn't know how to respond. The Captain had probably killed hundreds with a single command but she would have saved hundreds of thousands. The math made the choice look easy but people weren't numbers.

"A military investigation proved that despite the outcome I acted within approved methods. Truth was they were wrong. I could have waited for reinforcements, I could have authorized a black-ops incursion, I could have even requested a long-run sting operation but I chose the direct approach.

"I was put back on duty but I started questioning all my choices and it got my people killed. The Herosian cells came after me directly. They attacked my men on leave, they interfered with missions, and they intercepted transmission and even warned others who

I was pursuing. Then they cashed in all their chips and assaulted the *Molokai* directly. After an explosion on the bridge I froze. The ship almost went down if it were not for the help of the Koonai, a nearby Monastic ship.

"I was shell shocked and taken off duty. They thought I was better but the next combat situation I froze again. I was about to be forcefully retired when I saved by an Admiral, a friend of mine. He put me here, far away from battle to help salvage what's left of my career. Far away so I can just play captain until I fade away into the darkness of space and age."

"I think you need to stop then."

Agrima gave a small chuckle. "Honestly, I've been thinking the exact same thing; that it's time for me to stop and retire."

"I beg your pardon, ma'am but that's not what I meant at all," Allana corrected. "What I meant was you need to stop playing captain and actually be a captain."

Agrima froze partway through sipping her beverage. "Excuse me?"

"I don't how the corps is today but during the first war they had a belief drilled into them. A marine was a marine for life." Allana shook her head. "Marines were a bunch of well dressed pretty boys but for all their posturing they got dedication right. You can't stop being who you really are. It's the same for a captain, no matter how short or how long you're actually a captain, you are a captain for life."

Agrima returned to her seat and sat down. "It's not

as easy as that, Major. I'm not in the same fighting form that I once was. Back in the war I could lead a fleet of ships in certain death and not bat an eye, now I can barely do a firing exercise without clamming up."

"I've been there, my Battalion's superior has been there; thousands of other have been there as well. You have to plow through it. You have to become something stronger. I know this isn't the answer you want, it's not all wrapped up, but it's the truth. You either become stronger or quit and I don't think quitting in you." Allana rose to her feet to meet the captain's level.

"I have - had - a friend, a Master Warrant Officer. He told me when you stop worrying about battle is when you have to start being worried 'If fighting stops getting to ya'-"

"Then fighting's already gotten to you." Cantor finished.

"Your crew has the upmost trust in you Captain; all you need to do is be worth of it."

CHAPTER NINE
3 days until Pherca Moon Invasion

He sat alone in his shuttle, huddled in the darkest corner he could find. He placed himself as far away as he could from both the cockpit and a working light as possible. This was where he always sat, where he always suffered. He sat on the floor hugging his legs, his knees pressed against his face. His entire body shook violently and he couldn't decide what to do. He saw the possibilities, he could sit there and suffer, he could get up and inject himself with the much needed medicine, he could return to bed and try and sleep it off or he could toss himself in an airlock and then hit eject. He could clearly see all these options but he couldn't know which the right solution was and which would be wrong, although he had a feeling that the airlock solution would fall under the wrong category.

His was running out of time, in more ways than he cared to admit. He needed to get home.

"Are you still playing battery operated boyfriend?" The arrogant voice asked over the shuttle's speakers.

He took a deep breath and concentrated. If he tried, if he really concentrated, he could end the shakes for now but it would only serve as a temporary solution. His shakes would be return; they always returned. They never seemed to go away for long and they wouldn't, not until he got home. He crossed his legs and began to concentrate. He thought about home, the crystal cities made of glass, the interstellar walkways and the vast beauties of the Quil Tarra system. With a couple deep breaths he began to calm down, his heartbeat returning to normal and his shakes slowing until they eventually stopped.

He looked down at his hand, the sole quivering limb, and clenched a fist tightly. The hand wouldn't stop trembling but it would have to do. He marched to the ship's bow, grabbing his long grey trench coat on the way up, spinning it onto his arms and back.

He stepped into his cockpit and looked at the dancing holo-man on his ship's dashboard. It stopped and looked up at his pilot. The hologram, known as Wiki, opened its digital mouth to speak. "Why are you single with twitches like that? Shouldn't the fems be all over a man like you?"

He glared at Wiki and frowned. The digital being was his only friend in the known verses, the only one who could follow him on his travels, but it was a rude arrogant piece of intelligence. "Cat form – Now!"

Wiki looked crushed. "Keeps, come on, that was a joke. Don't make me go cat."

"I said now."

The digital human grumbled as all of his limbs were pulled inwards, Wiki temporarily becoming a black blob before new limbs and body emerged in the form of a Earth cat. "There; you happy? You know I hate this form."

"Then watch what you say." He was the Keepsake, the ruler and pilot of the *X-35 Blackwing* combat shuttle and future hero of the universe, if he could ever get back there. "Okay, what do you got, Mr. Kitty?"

The cat grumbled as it approached the controls of his digital world. Lines of codes fused together, forming lines of string that shot across Wiki's world, thousands of strings moved at one, filling the digital world like a spider's web or a fishermen's net. To the Keepsake it looked like chaos but to Wiki is was pedestrian. With his feline paws he swatted at the string, pushing lines together and knocking other threads from the sky. Wiki purred as he pawed at digital space, a loathsome involuntary act that came with this form, and operated the computer in a manner in which only he could. "The revised pattern is starting. They will emerge from the warp and rain down hell upon humanity. They bring with them the fury of the ages and the fear that drives them."

"Cut the theatrics," Keepsake mumbled. "This is still too early; we have to figure out why this is happening." Wiki took the newly compiled strings of data, formed together in a ball of twine and swatted it against the wall.

The data vanished from Wiki's world and appeared on Keeps' screen.

"But it has to happen, Keeps," Wiki mewed. He choose a random spot before him, pawed at it till it was ready and, after circling it twice, curled up in a ball and lay down. "Everything rests on this war."

"A lot of people are going to die in the meantime." The Keepsake touched the holographic screen that floated before him and watched the ball unroll, the data pouring out on his screen.

A long time ago, or yet to come, he fought for humanity, fought to protect them. He had lined up with any and all that could fight and together they stood against the Evolved, ready to fight and willing to die. He wanted to say that he lined up alongside the best, the brightest, the strongest and the fastest but they had died out long ago. He lined up with whoever was left.

But that was so long ago, so far in his past that it had yet to have happened for everybody else. He had changed a lot since then, his motivations and responsibilities, but deep down he was the same person. He had to look after the weak, he had to save the people but he couldn't just focus on humanity and its descendents anymore; he had to look after much more. He had to look after everybody. Here, there and everywhere, they now all belonged to him. But letting go of humanity was not easy. He wasn't human himself, not like those upon the *Avalon*, but he was close enough. He was a Fondrian and he had to be their savior.

For days on end the Keepsake barely left the cockpit. He sat in his captain's chair as Wiki piloted the Blackwing, keeping the small vessel within the *Avalon*'s shadow. Keeps watched his holographic screen and studied the information as it poured in. He kept his eyes peeled to the live feed from the news networks, the contact readings from HEF ships and the fleet wide communications. He had access to more information than any human alive, or soon to be, and none of it was good and none of it was helpful. It was like attending an all-you-could-eat cheeseburger buffet while being on a diet.

The aliens descended upon humanity like locust on the farmer's crops. They were the Viatos and they were here for war. Their starfighters tore from the warp across human airspace. The Keepsake watched as diamond shaped starfighters engaged the elite HEF squadron orbiting the Nova Teer system and destroyed each in the dark abyss of space. He never blinked as a pair of human frigates were forced out of hyperspace over the icecaps of Hertacle 4 and were quickly overpowered and destroyed, all by a single alien corvette.

"Why are you watching this, Keeps? Why are you torturing yourself?" Wiki asked. Finally allowed to return to a form he enjoyed, the avatar was back to walking around his digital world as a humanoid, his hands keeping active by rolling a small coin over his fingers. The Keepsake looked over at his digital companion. The AI was always a snide and arrogant personality but he cared about his pilot. They existed as a symbiosis, Keepsake could not get home without the AI, and Wiki had no power or purpose without the traveller.

"I have to, Wiki. Somebody does. What happens here has to be remembered and you and I both known it never will. This war will just be forgotten, everything here will be forgotten." Keeps stretched, his bones creaking as he moved. "Besides, somebody is changing the game, somebody is changing the rules."

The holoscreen beeped as a small corner of his map expanded. The pilot read over the new information, his eyes darting back and forth between Wiki's compiled data and the sensor readings from the far corners of space. "It's happening again."

Wiki raised an eyebrow curiously. He flipped his coin into the endless white world that surrounded him. The coin melted into the invisible wall, the silver dot growing until it became a massive television. He watched the news on the screen and studied the information. The report spoke of the unknown aliens striking all over human controlled space, downing dozens of human ships, and razing numerous farming colonies. Their latest target had been the farming planet Carnfell deep in Therorian space. The planet was attacked by a single ship and met little resistance.

"Why weren't HEF ships there?" The Keepsake began to get anxious. His hands began to shake and his mind began to race. Nothing made sense right now, events that were crucial to this war were not happening as they did in the past, or were happening as they were supposed to. "So if the big fight isn't happening there where will it be happening?"

Wiki frowned. "I don't know, Keeps. Things keep changing and even I can't keep track of it all."

Captain William Belmont sipped his tea silently as he sat in his customized raised chair, looking up from his cup as he looked out upon the large bridge. He was the commanding officer of the HEF cruiser C.S.S. *Italy*, one of the largest ships in the human navy. While large in size, the *Italy* was not the capital ship of the navy; that right was reserved for the C.S.S. *Ireland*. Captain Belmont had always wanted to captain the Ireland, a posting that unofficially put him next in line to captain the Avalon, but as more time passed it was beginning to *look* like he would never get it. He was fine with that, or at least that is what he tried to convince himself each night. Command of the *Italy* meant an eventual planet on his epaulet, the icon that signified the rank of Admiral, but it did put the *Avalon* just a hair's breadth out of reach.

While everybody in HEF served the *Avalon*, only the best and most skill candidates got to serve as her immediate crew. These were the sailors that steered her across the stars, the ones that fired up her engines and those who armed her weapons. Being assigned to the *Avalon*'s crew was the dream appointment and none more so then the role of captain. There was no official regulation that said the captain had to come from the *Ireland*, any sailor who met the requirements could qualify, instead it was more of an unspoken tradition. So while Belmont officially still had a shot he wasn't holding his breath.

"Sir, we have incoming ships from warp."

Captain Belmont raised his eyebrow. He keyed his console and looked over the scheduled events. They were not scheduled to rendezvous with any ally ship, they had been ordered to return to *Avalon* space at maximum speed. They received the order three hours ago and were booking across Livorian space as fast as her sub-light engines could move her. Belmont's eyes fell to the officer on duty. The senior officer stood at his console, a large three part computer that looked like a politician's podium. The board was green as his fingers danced around the keys. Belmont didn't need to interfere yet, this was well within the OOD's abilities.

"Shields up and weapons powered." The OOD wasted no time. HEF had been ambushed from warp all across known space and the *Italy* would not be next. "All hands to battle stations. Target the exit tear with all available batteries."

Belmont nodded in approval at the command. He looked up at the main view screen and waited anxiously. Space exploded with the rainbow of space as an unknown ship emerged. It was a simple design, shaped like a large spike or stake with dozens of diamond shaped fins attached to each side. The ship accelerated and flew directly at the *Italy*.

"All weapons target the ship and fire."

Captain Belmont put his cup down and intervened. The OOD's actions were not wrong, they just weren't the most efficient course of action. "Belay that. Helmsmen: I want evasive manoeuvres. Do not let that ship get close to my girl. Tactical: Open fire with the energy cannons but stagger the blast. I want all remainder of the batteries targeting those fins. Lock onto as many as possible. Communications: I want our status updates and sensor reading being sent out on Priority One channels every forty five seconds. Anything you find or scan about these aliens gets put in the updates. I don't care how mundane."

The cannons fired, the balls of energy crashing against the ship. The bolts never made it to the hull but instead collided with the wall of forward shields. The shields rippled as blast after blast collided against it, barely a moments rest between each shot.

The OOD looked away from his podium and back at his Captain. "Sir, if we ignore the propulsion fins and target their forward shields we can break through their protection and target the hull directly."

"Those aren't propulsion fins," Captain Belmont was man who disliked being unprepared. This unknown threat had assaulted HEF ships across the verse. Belmont had been reviewing whatever material the other ships had collected. What little data the HEF had on circled around the diamond shaped starfighters. As if on cue, the diamond fins began to fall off the alien ship like dominoes, spinning as they cleared the ship and turning towards the *Italy*. "They are starfighters. All batteries open fire."

The *Italy*'s gun fired the surrounding space filling with bolt of energy. The system screens of both tactical and the OOD lit up with the battle. They showed the Italy's energy bolts crashing into the alien starfighters but felling few of them. The diamond fighters returned fire. Each shot smashed against the Italy's defences, plummeted the shields until the defensive barrier fell. With the shields down the starfighters began to swarm, flying headfirst towards the *Italy*. Each starfighter crashed into the side of the *Italy*'s hull, but not a single one exploded, instead they stabbed into the HEF ship like darts on a board.

"Sir, we have multiple hull breaches."

Captain Belmont jumped from his chair, his hand knocking his precious cup of tea from his chair. He approached the OOD's podium and began to bark orders. "Ready the marines and arm every available soldier. Tell each of them to get to repel alien boarders. OOD: seal the bridge."

The OOD gave an approving grunt and keyed in the Captains orders. The door to the bridge slammed shut and locked as a pair of steel crossbeams slid across the door, securing it from the inside. All around the bridge several hidden compartments opened up revealing dozens of hidden guns. Each sailor grabbed one. A pair of marines each grabbed a rifle and took point at the door. Captain Belmont returned to his chair and drew a pistol of his own. He slid a clip into the firearm and tucked the weapon into the back of his pants. Walking over to the marines he grabbed the third rifle.

"Rien va passer a travers nous, Capitaine." French marines rarely spoke English. They never saw the point. Some found it a hassle but the French marines were some of *Avalon*'s best, so they dealt with it. The marines had just promised Belmont that nobody would get by them, and the Captain believed them. He knew they would die before they let a single alien onto this bridge.

Belmont turned to his crew. He ordered the aliens on his screens and watched, getting angrier with each passing moment, as they moved through the Italy like a virus. These grey alien humanoids, these ungodly husks, ripped their way towards the bridge. They were grey beings with throbbing veins, opaque skin and weapons and miscellaneous tech grafted to their bare skin. Their main weapon, a plank looking rifle, were bolted to their right arms, their back up firearm, an E-shaped pistol, was kept in a chest cavity. They looked like hideous burn victims desperately clutching to life.

His men fought valiantly but died quickly; these aliens would launch themselves at large groups, huddle in corners and sacrifice themselves with no hesitations. They fought with unorthodox tactics. His men just couldn't adapt quick enough.

The flames of a console erupting caught the Captain's attention. "OOD? What's going on?"

The OOD moved from one console to another, glancing back to his captain when he got a chance. "We are dead in the water, sir. We have no control of sublights."

"Alright switch." Belmont tossed his rifle towards the OOD and took position at the commander's podium. The computer instantly recognized him and began lighting up and routing second and third tier system to his console. The OOD cocked the rifle and moved to the bridge door. "Comms: Have we gotten any transmission from them? Any demands for us to surrender?"

"Nothing."

"Fine. I want those priority one updates going out every five seconds, send out anything and everything. Gunners: abandon all starfighters and target the main ship. Fire at will, use everything we've got and do not stop. I am rerouting all power from navigations to you. Everybody else, grab your guns and get to the doors."

"Ils sont a la porte." The aliens had reached the door. The marines each opened a small gun port into the narrow hallway and filled it with their barrels. The OOD quickly organized the bridge crew into a defensible position, each taking cover behind a console or chair.

"For the *Avalon*," The OOD whispered as the sounds of energy bolts slammed against the steel door. The French marines looked at each other and smirked. The two sailors looked back down the sights of their rifles.

"Pour l'*Avalon*." The barrels of the French rifles erupted in burst of fire. The guns would pause, for a brief moment, only to adjust their angle and fire again. The bridge crew watched nervously on the screens as the marines gunned down team after team of invaders, the energy bolts burning through their disgusting hides as pieces of skin fell off with each shot.

Belmont did his best to ignore the wave of fire against the reinforced door, the crashing sound growing to deafening level. Instead his eyes and fingers worked together as he routed the ship's remaining energy to the guns. Engines were now offline, as were navigational systems, emergency control and over half of the ship's life support systems.

Belmont's screens began to flicker as the ship's sensor began to register numerous energy spikes from within the alien cruiser. The unending volleys of fire from the *Italy*'s weapons had finally taken their toll on their hull and bright burst of light the ship exploded.

They were killable, and that was important.

Happy as he was there still was nothing to cheer about. The foreign ship didn't exploded but instead separated into dozens of smaller ships like a puzzle falling apart in mid air. Each piece, at the moment their disassembly, ignited their sub-lights and began to retreat.

The science officer's voice was panicked and scared. "We have multiple incoming warp signatures, about a dozen or so. I think we're about to hit with their reinforcements."

As the seconds passed the illusion of survival seemed to dissolve away. He routed control of all batteries to his podium and began to target as many warp tears as possible but instead of a swarm of incoming ships the disassembled pods began their retreat.

"Th...they opened their own warp gates." Belmont looked over at his stunned science officer. Both looked stunned. "That is not possible, sir. No ship that size can open one gate into the warp let alone a dozen."

"Send this info immediately. The Avalon needs to know." Belmont hands shook. This was not some trivial detail about humanity's attackers; this was a rewrite of the laws of the universe. This was on par with rewriting gravity, ignoring laws of motion, and abandoning the basic laws of physics. This fact was a game changer.

"The door's about to fall, sir." Belmont looked over at the OOD, the scared officer running to take the place of a fallen French marine. This was the end, they could not make their stand any longer, and as the captain he had one final thing to do. Belmont knelt before the command podium. Resting now at eye level was a small compartment that held the most important device on the ship.

The black box.

The black box was the most crucial device in *Avalon* security. It allowed any HEF ship to enter *Avalon* space unhindered an unescorted. The black box allowed for high-level priority channels to function and most importantly it gave a real-time update to all HEF ships of the Avalon's current position. The *Avalon* was a fully functional ship and it never stayed in one place for very long. The black box made sure all humans had a way home.

Each captain's orders were different because each ship's mission was different, but each of them shared two distinct directives. The first was to search for a vacant planet on which humans could call their own; the second was no captain could let the security of the black box be compromised by any alien race, not friend and certainly not foe.

Belmont flipped a small switch and stepped back. The box ignited in a bright flame as the phosphorous melted the sophisticated interior. Belmont raised his right arm to protect his eyes from the light. When it came to the black box every captain knew that it was better to be safe than sorry.

Belmont drew his pistol from the back of his pants and cocked the weapon. He pulled back the hammer and levelled the barrel at the bridge door. He knew this was the end for him, yet his hand never shook and his courage never wavered. His eyes narrowed as he stared down the gun iron sights.

With a final explosive burst the intruders broke through the blast door, the blast sending the final French marine to his death as the frail alien corpses advanced onto the bridge like a swarm of locusts. Belmont squeezed the trigger and as his pistol's first shot led the wave of oncoming fire from the bridge crew only a single thought crossed his mind.

I guess I'm not getting those planets.

The Keepsake slammed his open palm against his chair arm rest and let out a loud angry yell. This was not supposed to happen; the *Italy* was not supposed to fall. The *Italy* was meant to be crucial, it was suppose to turn the tide in the war but instead he has just watch it sink.

Wiki looked up at his pilot. This was killing him; forced to watch thousands of lives die, having the ability to stop it but not being allowed to interfere. It got harder each time it happened, each war he was forced to live through, but this time was different. This time somebody was doing what he could not.

Somebody was tipping the scales in their favour.

The Keepsake abruptly stood up and moved to his main console. Any sense of humour, anger or anxiety was absent on his face, instead there was only a determined look with a small scowl. Despite the narrowed eyes Wiki could still see the look of resolute. It was a look he had seen a couple times before and he never relished the chaos that follows.

"Keeps, what are you doing?" Wiki was a synthetic entity, the evolutionary descendent of the artificial intelligence, and he wasn't much for fear. There seemed no need for it most times but when the Keepsakes got that look Wiki got afraid and for good reason. "That look...I know that look. I know that look means trouble,

I know that look means broken rules and I know that look mean a whole whopping load of chaos."

Keeps hunched over his console and began typing, his fingers pressing the holographic keys. Wiki watched as the holographic screen began to search the spatial sectors.

"Things should have been moving in a straight line, things should have been going according to plan. Things should be happening the way they already happened." Wiki knew what would happen next. This was an excited and determined Keepsake. This was the Keepsake that made ridiculous goals, impossible promises and ludicrous actions. "Somebody is altering things, somebody is cheating."

Wiki was scared. Between him and the Keepsake, they had the ability to change history, to bring down entire nations or save a collapsing society but neither of them were allowed to. It was forbidden, but when the Keepsake got this way, when he said to hell with the rules things changed, big things.

"What are you doing, Keeps?"

The pilot moved back to his chair, his fingers resuming their rapid typing only this time on the second holo-computer. "I am intercepting all HEF priority one channel, something that's impossible unless you're us, and then I am duplicating all messages, sending the copied along the original course and rerouting the original to a position of my choosing."

Keeps darted back to ship's console at the sound of

a beep. His fingers typing quickly as he began to direct the transmissions. Wiki shook his head. "You can't do this."

"The hell I can't. I know I'm not allowed to stop things so instead I'm going to arm my side with knowledge so they can better prepare themselves."

"Changes are bad, Keeps. You know this; too many changes and we can't go home."

"There are millions out there that can't go home," Keeps snapped. "Are we really more important than them?"

"They're already dead to us, everybody is," Wiki argued.

"Look at the *Italy*," he snapped. "Look at that ship and tell me they were already dead?"

For a moment, Wiki said nothing. His next words were soft spoken. "It is against the rules."

"The game switched to rugby and I don't like losing."

"What are you talking about?"

Keep looked back at the screen that housed Wiki's digital universe and gave the SE a wicked smirk. "What I mean is we were playing soccer but somebody just decided to pick up the ball and run with it."

CHAPTER TEN
2 days until Pherca Moon Invasion

He saw them coming, the pair of them. He had tried to avoid them, to trick them, to get past staunch security but it was inevitable. His attackers had trapped him and they were going to finish him off. Walking away wasn't an option, it never was, that simply left fighting onwards and dealing with the cards that life dealt. The pair got real close, clutching their weapons tightly as they advanced. One held back in defence as the other approached at full speed. The attacker turned his shoulder at the last moment and slammed his victim against the wall.

The roar of the crowd was deafening.

The puck slid away from the victim as he crumbled to the ground, the second attacker scooping it up with his stick and skating away. The lead attacker pushed off on his left foot and skated away to join his partner leaving the lone defenseman in a pile on the ice.

Allana screamed as she slammed both fists on the glass. "Get up! Go after them! Don't take that! Come on!"

The Oiler defenseman climbed to his feet shook the cobwebs loose and skated after Calgary's wingmen. Allana cheered him on. She returned to her chair and looked beside her at the laughing doctor. Tenuvah Sheppard just shook her head, her blond hair tied tightly in a bun.

"Calm down, Anna," Tenuvah said between laughs. "It's just a game."

Allana shook her head. Tenuvah was the only other woman in this verse or the next, aside from her grandma, that had permission to call her Anna. "Have we just met, Ten? Have we not been introduced before? You know I love hockey and you know I love the Oilers."

"As long as they don't play the Sens?" Tenuvah teased; her sinister smile growing as she pitted the Major's two hockey loves in a hypothetical battle.

"Hey, that's not fair." The Major defended, the smile never leaving her face. "I was born and bred a Sens girl."

"I know, I know, but since you were posted here you never get to cheer for Ottawa and since you seem stuck here you might as well cheer local." Tenuvah had heard this speech over and over but she never minded the reruns. Allana always gave this speech with such conviction and joy that it was always nice hearing it. "It's a silly sport anyways. Who plays a game on ice? Now soccer; that's a sport."

"No sticks, no body armour and no razor sharp blades, are you sure it's even a sport?" Allana laughed as she debated, jumped up suddenly and cheering as the two players dropped their gloves and began to fight. "Punch him in the kidney!"

For a brief moment the two hockey players became gladiators in an ancient arena, fighting for their lanista and the crowds, combating for the glory and fame. The two pairs of fist flung violently as they scrapped, grappling and using their strength to punish the each other, all while paying customers watched. The battle ended quickly with the Oiler center having his jersey pulled over his head, several punches to his gut, then being tossed to the ice.

Allana once more took her anger out on the glass before her. She looked over at her date with disappointed eyes. Allana pinched the shoulders of her jersey, identical to the fallen Oiler, and pulled it out to better display it. "I go and spend good money on his jersey, his specifically, just because I like him." She released her pinch, the shirt falling back over her fit form. "The least he could do is learn how to take a punch. Hell, I'll go over to his house and pummel him myself till he learns."

Tenuvah laughed at the thought, mainly because she'd actually do it if it meant a better season for her favourite player. She loved when Allan got excited for the things she cared about. She found it cute and damned it if her excitement wasn't contagious. Allana continued her excited rant.

"Anything as long as he learns not to fold like a shirt..." Allana began to drift off as her search for a witty simile, "in an automatic folding machine."

Tenuvah raised an eyebrow. "Not your best line."

Allana burst out laughing. Her joke was horrible. It was pathetic and well beneath her. "Yeah I know. I came out strong but began to slack off." Allana turned back to her team and resumed yelling. "Like these guys. Damn it, I hate losing and we're losing so badly tonight."

Tenuvah pulled the major back to her chair. "Then why relive this date? You don't get to see the end of the game, you get pulled away for work and your proxy team gets beaten as bad as the Leafs do."

"Nobody gets beaten as bad as the Leafs do; it's impossible." Allana looked her date in the eyes, her gaze lost in the Doctor's sparkling emerald. "Later on in this date, or in the real one, I get an urgent call from work and I have to leave. It turns out to be some stupid readiness drill or something, but when I try to apologize and beg forgiveness you just look at me and tell me that you understand. You tell me that you will always be here for me and you will always wait for me because you love me.

"This date was the first time you told me you loved me, and I was in such a rush to leave that I didn't realize it until I was half-way back to the base."

Tenuvah gave a smile, not the soft one that normally preceded a blush but more of smile of success. She had deciphered the mystery that was this visit. "So tell me about her."

Allana's gaze returned to the game, her eyes

following the black puck on the bright white ice. "Who?"

"You're not feeling guilty are you? It's okay. Tell me about her."

The Major's gaze never left the ice, not even as she started speaking. "She's a doctor, like you, but not of medicine. She's an archaeologist, a history buff bookworm. She reminds me a lot of you. You are both smart, strong women. You do what you believe in despite what people tell you, and you're both quick on your feet."

"She sounds nice. You attracted to her?"

"She's hot as hell; it's hard not to be, but her eyes. They grab you and won't let go. The colours seemed to move and change as you watch them. She's the girl with kaleidoscope eyes."

"Beatles reference -- wow. You must really like her." Tenuvah reach over to her Anna and gently held her chin. She turned the major's face towards her. "It's okay. You are allowed to be with her or anybody else you want. You don't have to feel guilty."

"I'm not ready yet. "

"Liar," Tenuvah said with a smirk. "You and I both know that you're ready. I know what you've been thinking remember. All those years in the pod, all those years hooked up to the computer, I know every thought that ran through you mind. I know that you're stalling and I know why. I know why you're still clinging to me."

Allana pulled away. She didn't want to talk about

this, about Dr. Tsia or the future. She just wanted to worry about the past, to live in it, to relish the simpler time of her life. "I'm no---,"

"You're not wearing the ring." Tenuvah interrupted. "I proposed to you, and you wore the ring for a long, long time. You don't wear it anymore. You don't even wear it around your neck."

"I...I..." Allana stuttered. "I'm sorr--."

"Don't you even finish that sentence," Tenuvah scolded with a smile. "You have nothing to apologize for."

Her comm unit rang and Allana reached for it. She looked at the name even though she knew who it was. The screen read CFB Edmonton; work was calling. She answered the phone and endured the brief conversation. A patient Tenuvah waited for the call to end.

"Who dares call you during a game?"

When she chose this date she expected the ending dialogue to be the same. Those words no longer belonged to Tenuvah, real or simulation, they no longer belonged to Allana. Those words belonged to history, to her memories.

"I am so sorry. I know this is your only night off this week but I have to go. Please forgive me?"

"It's okay. Normally it's me cancelling the dates."

"Can you wait until I get back to finish our date?"

"Oh, Anna, I will always be here for you and I will always wait for you because I love you." The words soothed her soul and warmed her heart. In a relationship filled with heartbreak and loss this was one of her favourite moments, but nothing beat Allana's response.

"That's great, really. I'm sorry but I got to go." It was a smooth response that would have earn respect from Casanova. Allana left the Rexall Place arena in a hurry, reliving the date as best she could, it wasn't until she stepped foot outside the busy building things changed. As she opened the door she wasn't greeted by the city of Edmonton, instead it was the C.S.S *Prince Caspian*, a freighter ship with a breached hull, floating towards the EDI fleet. Allana was dressed in a thick white atmosphere suit and carried a modified assault rifle specially designed for zero-g use. Her breathing echoed in her helmet as she sluggishly moved through the ships interior. Every soldier, sailor and marine went through zero-g combat training but Guiver hated it; a bulky suit, poor mobility and a touch of claustrophobia, none of it was appealing.

"It's behind this door." Sergeant Piotr Budian marched behind her, his firm Russian body and worn features protected in the same type of suit as the Major was. Allana silently nodded and grab the emergency door release. With gloved fingers she counted down from three and as the final finger fell she pulled hard on the release. The door shot open and Budian stormed the room with Guiver close behind.

The pair stormed the *Caspian*'s engine room with the guns at the ready. The room was empty, just like the first time, save for a massive bomb strapped to the sublights. Allana's memories came rushing back. The Arau Pau had boarded a civilian ship, killed the crew, stolen the supplies, then strapped a bomb to the engines and launched it at the fleet. Budian and she had to board the ship and defuse the bomb before it took the ship, and the fleet, with it.

"Why the hell did I choose this memory to talk?"

"Of all the insane missions we ever took this one was my favourite, my Major." Budian strapped his rifle to his back and knelt down by the bomb. He began to poke at it with his tools. "An insane plot, a horrible bomb and the fate of our entire fleet at the touch of my fingers; this is heaven. I told this story to the pretty ladies so many times and damn near every time it ended up with that woman bunking with me."

Allana rolled her eyes, mainly out of habit. She couldn't fault him for his womanizing ways. Back before she settled down with the good doctor she was just as bad, sometimes worse. More than once they had competed for the same girl. "Our success here was a major story all across the system. This was the mission that made me – us – a household name. The media made us heroes."

"After this mission monogamy, let alone marriage, was no longer a possibility." He laughed. "To be the woman who tamed a hero. They all leapt at the chance. I gave each the possibility but the odds were much against them."

"So why even fool yourself with the pretext of

marriage?"

Budian started ripping out wires. "Because deep down I believe in one true love, in happily ever after but I didn't live long enough to find her. Is it any coincidence that we talk of true love, my Major?"

"I never could put one past you could I?"

"Da." Budian tossed a random piece behind him as he dug deeper into the device. "The good Doc gave you the go ahead, so what's the problem?"

"Tenuvah was my happily ever after, my OTP," Guiver admitted. "I was ready to pack it in, retire and live happily ever after with her. Have dozens of kids, grow old and make her life miserable the entire time."

"Nothing says love like making each other miserable."

"Miserable Love," Allana laughed. "And then war did the only thing it's meant to do, it took our loved ones from us. I lost her and you. I lost the kid and the mute. I lost the highlander. I lost everything. But as I look back I know that deep down, I was happy. Friends, family and the love of a good woman with a touch of excitement to keep me from being bored; there is nothing more I could have asked for. I had my one true love, many didn't get that chance. So do I deserve another?"

"Bomb defused and with three hours to go. Damn I'm good." Budian stood up and stretched. He wasn't boasting about his skills, he was just stating facts. He was Guiver's demolition expert and he was that good. He looked at her and snickered. "So the *Spellsong* has been reading the *Mojave's* computers. It's learning so very much about this new era of yours. Did you know that Space Hollywood made a movie about this mission?"

"Space Hollywood?"

"It's my nickname for the human cinematic companies," he explained with a shrug. "In the film we have to shoot through a bunch of monkey-men to get here and we don't defuse the bomb until the last second."

"Some tropes never die, do they?"

"We spend the entire movie thinking about our lives, our mistakes and of loves lost. They even make up a Russian woman for my love interest, a long-lost girl I messed up with." He shrugged as he plopped down on the floor. "Truth is the movie was more a love story then an action or war flick. It talked about how hard it is to love a military man or woman; how the spouses make the true sacrifices. But deep down, if the love is true, it is all worth it; every last sacrifice and fight."

"This is relevant, how?" Allana asked. She paused for the briefest moment before interjecting a second question. "Was my actress hot?"

Piotr Budian let out a bellowing laugh. "Very much so, my Major; she was indeed a looker." He pointed to the wall. "Outside that hull is the EDI's fleet. There are tens of thousands of troops waiting to go boots down and start fighting; each of them not knowing if they will make it back to their loved ones but still they fight."

She understood. "Love is what keeps us going. Love

is why people fight."

"And despite all the war, my Major, love holds the universe together," Budian finished. "Never flinch away from love."

She stood not knowing what to say. Eventually she spoke. "I know I'm not speaking to the real you, I'm speaking to what my memory remembers of you so anything you say to me is just what my mind thinks you would have said, but I have to ask you a question." He raised an eyebrow. "Why is it always *my Major*?"

He flashed a smile, a brilliantly charming smile that made most women weak in the knees. "I know that I am a dog yapping at completely the wrong tree; I came to terms with that fact centuries ago but despite that I have looked out for you, I have always stood by your side and I have always followed you to the pits of hell. That's what made you my Major. But more so then anything else I have always loved you, my Major. I cannot be with you, rules prevent it, regulations forbid it and above all else fate decided against it a long time ago, but here I am, head over heels in love with a woman I cannot have."

She had suspected that for years but always held the respect for the sergeant never to bring it up. But to hear it out loud, even in this digital world, was heartbreaking and uplifting all at the same time.

Then he burst out laughing.

"That line was used in our movie. It won the pretty boy actor who played me an endless legion of sappy young female fans. The man was forever type-casted as the pretty boy romantic lead. He did a couple movies as me, I apparently got my own spin-off film series, and he even played a brooding vampire character a couple times but he is always known as the man who played me." Budian laughed again. "I am good at four things in this verse; getting women, defusing bombs, appealing to girls as one of history's most helpless romantics and ruining the career of any pretty boy who tries to play me. All in all, I say that's a decent life's work."

She wandered the ships halls, lost and bored, as she figured out what to do next. Between sleep, study and training she was driving herself mad. She needed something to do. She tried a game or two on her handheld but found nothing to hold her attention. Deciding to eat, despite not being hungry, she headed towards the galley. She was half-way there when the sound of a stadium of fans echoed down the hallway followed by the angry disappointed scream of a fan.

She knew that scream. She used to make that scream. It was a sports fan scream.

Allana found her pace picking up slightly as she moved towards the sound. She found herself in the recreation room staring at a massive future-space TV with some sporting event playing on the screen. She watched for a moment, edging herself to the couch, as she tried to figure out what the game was.

Sitting on the couch, happily watching the game, sat the young pilot. He turned around, sensing someone behind him, and was surprised to see her standing there. He stiffened up his body and sat at attention. "Can I help you, ma'am?"

"Relax, kid," she said as she nodded to the television. "What is this?"

"Hockey."

Her face lit up. It didn't look like hockey; there was no ice, no skates or overly zealous announcer in weird clothing, but somehow she got the feeling. "It's not ice hockey, that's for sure. Tell me about it."

He gave her a smile. "The playing field has no gravity. You put two teams in the field and you have to get the puck and put it in the opposite goal." The goals were at the top and bottom of the room and each had floating goalies. The puck looked the same but the sticks were closer to lacrosse sticks from her day.

"They say when we took to the stars some kids found an empty compartment, nailed down two goals, and then just shut-off the gravity to the compartment," the pilot explained. "And that's how hockey was born. Well, this version at least."

Allana watched as the forward winger pushed off the wall and passed the puck to the forward who one-timed it towards the net. The goalie spun and deflected the puck sideways. It was interesting, zero-g lacrosse, but despite the name it didn't have---

Allana's eyes went wide as a defence goon smashed the winger into the wall with a diving tackle. The winger spun, grabbed the defensemen and tossed him into wall beside right him. Seconds later a fist fight broke out.

Ok, she thought, *this might be hockey.*

The pilot offered his hand. "I'm Denver Cole."

She took the hand and shook it. "Sub-Lieutenant?" he nodded. "It's a pleasure, Cole."

"Denver, ma'am, please." He corrected. "My Daddy used to say that last names are only for working hours. If you drink together or watch a game together, you use first names like regular folk."

Allana laughed loudly. She loved it. "Denver it is. Call me Allana."

CHAPTER ELEVEN
Invasion Day

Two days passed quickly as Allana quickly fell into a routine, the soldier finding comfort in habit. She'd start the day with tears, then morning PT with the marines, lessons with the civilians, lunch, more studying, a stern solitary brooding session followed by reading mission reports and operation testimony before retiring to tears and bed. She wasn't usually an emotional woman but according to the good doctor the aftermath of such a long cryosleep was her chemical balance was all out of order which meant her emotions were being amplified. She'd be right as rain in a couple days, with the help of the doctor's meds, but until then she was having a hard time keeping her sorrows bottled up.

Perhaps that wasn't a bad thing. Psychologically speaking she'd been bottling her emotions for so long. It almost felt like forever. It wasn't intentional, it just happened. In war she lost people, it was almost the definition of war, so she'd harden herself, every solider did. They'd pretend they didn't want to know the new recruit's names and when the inevitable gunshot or explosion, or half a dozen other methods, finally separated a warrior from their friend all that was left to do was toughen up and bottle it deep down inside. It was the only way to push forward and survive. Now her body was rebelling. She'd bottle too much for too long and it was all coming out.

Brian, Christian, Jamie, Tenuvah and dozens upon dozens of other names floated out, each one lost to the various wars and battles. That was all her history was, that was all she was. She was a grim reaper walking through the endless black with nothing but death surrounding her.

A knock on the door caught her attention. She let her sobs die down to nothing by sniffles as she pulled on a shirt and answered. Standing outside her cabin was the little alien science officer. The Monastica smiled at her and offered a tray of fruit and toast and a glass of juice.

"Good morning, my Avatar," she cheerfully interjected. "Blessed be the arrival of another morning."

Hera'sun carefully brushed past the Major and delicately placed the tray on her nightstand. "The captain needs you as soon as possible in her ready room. I noticed you missed breakfast. Adapting to a new..." She chewed on her lip as she searched for the right word. "...a new timezone can be difficult. So I brought you something to eat while you get ready."

Guiver grabbed a small berry; something that looked like three blueberries fused together, and popped it into her mouth. She expected a soft taste but got a juicy crunch much like an apple. She eyed the science officer and forced a smile. "Thanks, Hera'sun."

"You should throw some water on you face and join us quickly. Things are developing."

Allana entered Captain Cantor's ready room to find all eyes upon her. Every senior officer on the *Mojave* was already there and waiting. She looked around confused; trying to deduce what was wrong by the looks on each of their faces. It had been a while since Allana had been on active duty, let alone serving on a naval ship, and she assumed she had forgotten a great many things but she did remember that when all senior officers were called into one room that something big was happening. "Major Guiver reporting as requested, Captain."

Cantor waved for the Major to sit down as she handed the Major a tablet computer which came to life as the Captain began to type on her own handheld. "In the last twelve hours HEF ships have come under fire from an unknown alien race or races. We're looking at ADVA beings with ADVA tech." A translation blinked on her screen. ADVA meant advanced. "Twenty-three minutes ago we received a series of priority one transmissions."

Again her screen blinked to life. Priority one transmissions were highly important transmission that went from ships directly to the *Avalon*. They were deemed impossible to be rerouted. Despite those facts, the messages had been rerouted directly at the *Mojave Desert*.

"We verified the transponder codes and security markings. Other than a series of rerouting commands and a single anomaly they check out. These transmissions are from the *Italy*."

"What was the anomaly, ma'am?" Lt. Commander Morrison had learned a long time ago not to trust anomalies. The captain clicked her handheld, each tablet lit up with the anomaly on their screen. It was a single message, text only, that had with it a simple explanation that in truth brought up more question then answers.

Thought you might need this information. – K :)

"Who is God's name is K?" Morrison asked. Allana just sat quietly and listened. She was trying to play catch up.

"I have no clue, Lieutenant, but the anomaly was registered to a ship called the *X-35 Blackwing*. She isn't HEF but she has a black box which makes her a HEF ally."

Somers fingers danced over his tablet as he listened. He was searching through the HEF registry, both civilian and military but was coming up empty. "There no such ship in the HEF fleet. This is some sort of..."

"*X-35 Blackwing* is a covert ship whose call sign is listed under the executive branch beneath the EDI Prime Minister's shuttle *Malus One*." Everybody in the room turn towards the interrupting voice. Allana blinked rapidly as she realized that everybody was looking at her.

Somers' fingers resumed their search, his tablet linking with the *Avalon*'s database and scanning his bio-signature for verification. Cantor was the first to speak. "How did you know that?"

"That ship's call sign existed back in my time, back in the war." She stammered her words for a brief moment before correcting herself. "The first war. I had a mission involving the *X-35 Blackwing* in a support role." All of this new history and knowledge was playing havoc on her speech pattern.

Somers' fingers came to a halt with a final exaggerated keystroke. Each tablet screen in the room flickered as the XO shared the information he had to the ship. The file had very little information on it, lacking the ships design plans, schematics and capabilities. All that existed was a series of jurisdictions, ranks and seemingly limitless power in the command structure.

Allana looked up at the group. "I take it this isn't normal for the HEF?"

For the first time since the meeting started Hera'sun spoke. "No, my Avatar, as far as I know there is nothing like it within your organization."

Allana politely nodded at the Monastic science officer. The Avatar name was cute at first but it was starting to wear a little thin. "So what was in the message anyways? What did the *Italy*, or this K, send us?"

Cantor typed on her handheld, sharing the contents of the transmissions with the tablets in the room. "It has all sensor data, ships readings, video recordings, tactical observations and any other data they collected during their encounter with this unknown alien race."

"Blessed be the Great One. They sent us all we need to know to protect the *Spellsong*."

"No, it's more than that," Somers interjected. His voice didn't have the excitement that the Monastic did. His tone was that of a man who has seen the poor hand he had been dealt and had accepted his fate. "They sent us everything we need to know to fight them. Everything we need to know to go to war."

The room went silent.

Each person let the XO's last words roll around in their head. Morrison interrupted the silence. "But why us? It was directed at the *Avalon*, at HEF's military command. So why go through all the trouble of sending it to us?"

"Because of Guiver," Somers said quietly. "Somebody wants her ready to fight."

"And I don't plan to lose," Cantor declared. "Hera'sun, start pouring through the readings. Look for any scientific knowledge that can be gained from it. Morrison and Somers will begin examining the battle and begin devising some tactical manoeuvres. Make sure you share what you've got with Cole." Cantor looked over at the Major. "Start watching how they fight. I want you to know --"

A message from the bridge abruptly interrupted the captain. "We have an urgent sector wide SOS incoming."

Cantor gave the message a read, the severity of the SOS clear on her face. "What else do you have?"

"The message was sent out on all channels, including via Priority One, but have stopped. They are being jammed, ma'am."

Canor thanked her officer and closed down the line. She looked at her senior officers and their anxious eyes. With a deep and heavy breath she spoke. "As of fifteen minutes ago the unknown aliens have attacked the Pherca moon."

The senior officers gasped in surprise but Allana just looked confused. "What is the importance of the Pherca moon?"

"The Pherca moon is a farming moon. Its habitable celestial body owned by another race. It is not big enough to support all of humanity but its big enough to grow a lot of food," Somers explained. "There are dozens of farming moons that the HEF rents from other species. We put small cities up and we harvest crops and food for humanity."

"How many humans are on that farming colony?"

Somers shook his head. "Just over a million and a half."

"What is HEF plan for mobilization?"

Somers shook his head. "The HEF fleet is at best fifteen hours out. The moon isn't defenceless. They can hold out for a while but not long."

"We're closest aren't we?" The words came out of her lips but she already knew the answer. She was always closest or the bravest and the best equipped. Fate had an annoying habit of making it so it had to be her doing the fighting.

"We are the closest but our mission is to get the *Spellsong* and the Major back to the *Avalon*."

"We could release the *Spellsong*, Captain." Hera'sun suggested. "We have a Monastic ship on route to meet with us as we speak. We equip it with a beacon; release the ship into warp space. The warp tides will push it out into normality; the Monastic ship will find it and escort it to a rendezvous point of our choosing after we save the people on that moon we get it back."

"We can't save everyone," Cantor injected. It was a somber thought but a needed one. "We could be there in six hours. Assuming we can get a team dirtside and safely get us out of gun's reach, that gives us optimistically ten hours on the ground." Cantor glanced at Morrison. "What can we realistically expect a team of marines to be able to do in that time that cannot wait?"

Morrison rubbed his chin as he leaned back in his chair. "Assuming we get ships off the ground and safely into the air we can get six hundred souls out in a civilian cruiser, twenty-five to fifty in a freighter or corvette and if we sardine them in, we can get thirty to forty on a shuttle but they have to get to a battleship or cruiser soon; shuttles are short-range at best. Six ships means 3600 people."

"These aliens will have had eight hours on the moon," Allana rationalized. "What will their foothold be like then?"

Morrison nodded as he exhaled slowly. Cantor looked over at Somers, both eyes met and they each thought the same thing. This was a shit storm and they were flying right into the middle of it. "I'll contact *Avalon* and propose this to them and wait for the green light. In the meantime we get ready for an attack. We get the ship fighting fit while Somers and Morrison prepare Branford to lead the landing party."

"I'll lead it, Captain."

Cantor shook her head at the Major. "That's not happening, Guiver. My mission is to protect you, not send you into battle."

"I am going." This was not insubordination, this was not arguing, this was a fact and Allana needed the Captain to know it. One point five million lives hung in the balance. Allana wasn't sure what she was ready to fight for in this new future of hers but one point five millions lives seemed like a good reason to start. "I am the ranking officer in ground combat, I have more experience in extraction and siege battles and this is what I do, ma'am. I fight; it's what I'm made for. I am not sitting this one out."

Reality vanished and Guiver found herself lying on her back, strapped to a gurney and being pushed down a hospital hallway as she bled from the chest. Above her, remarkably moving alongside, were three doctors including the stunning form that was Doctor Tenuvah

Sheppard.

"You're an idiot!" Allana looked up at the heavenly form that was her one true love and all she saw was a pissed off face looking down at her. "Seriously, what in the hell possess you to relive this moment?"

Allana opened her mouth to speak but the doctor shook her head. "See, the jungle planet I get, we spent that entire deployment between the sheets. I enjoyed that. The hockey game, I get that too, I told you I loved you but what the hell are you doing here? You've got a gaping chest wound, you're bleeding out and I'm not even sure you'll make it. So why, why are you choosing this moment to talk to me?"

"I wanted to see you one last time."

"Oh?"

"I'm going planet side into battle and if I don't come—"

"Stop it!" The firm commands of stern Tenuvah always soothed Allana. Perhaps it was because Ten would talk to her in a manner that most wouldn't dare to. Perhaps it was as a medical woman she was a voice of reason nine times out of ten. Perhaps it was because despite all the horrors the Arau Pau had thrown at her, Angry-Tenuvah was still the scariest thing Allana had ever seen. "I told you we don't do this. We hug, we kiss, we say goodbyes but we never do this. We never do the *if I don't see you again* bit. It was our rule. If you can't handle the rule then give up this meaningful relationship and go back to the endless stream of floozies."

"You know I always did enjoy the floozies. A different woman each night had it pluses."

Tenuvah scowled and slapped the Major on her chest wound, the blow causing insurmountable pain. Ten looked at the other doctors. "She needed immediate CPR."

"This isn't what I wanted in the way of response," the Major winced.

"Bullshit!" Allana looked up with a confused gaze. "This is exactly what you wanted. You wanted my loving-stern voice snapping at you or else you wouldn't have allowed it to happen. You control this VR remember, not me. Anything that happens here happened because you allowed it to. Hell, part of me thinks you want me to smack you upside the head." Tenuvah smacked her open palm against the back of Allana's head. "See, I was right again."

"I didn't come here for abu—" She stopped in mid sentence as Ten pointed to her open palm. "I came here because I'm going into battle – again – and I'm scared."

"I know, babe." Her voice had changed. She wasn't stern anymore, simply caring and kind, a soothing combination. "I've been reading the mission reports. This isn't anything you can't handle. You've survived worse. This is what you do, you save people."

"But I always had a reason to fight," Allana injected. "I fought to save the people I loved, I fought to protect my friends, my family and I fought so you didn't have to Ten. I don't have you anymore. Now I am going to fight to protect people I don't know, for a race I no longer belong to and for a verse that frankly I have no right being in."

"What about her?"

"Who?"

Ten pointed once more to her open palm. "I will smack you again if you don't smarten up. I'm talking about Doctor Bristol Tsia."

"She means nothing—" Tenuvah arched her hand back. "She doesn't! I mean...I don't know if she does. She's smart, she sexy – oh god is she sexy!"

"I've noticed, babe."

"But she's not you."

"She never will be. I'm not asking her to be and neither should you." The doctor explained, "she will always be her, nothing more. She's not my replacement, she's not my substitute; instead she is somebody completely different and original. You like her – you obviously have a type – and you're allowed to peruse her. It might be only a fling, it might be more. Who knows? But you're allowed to live your life."

Allana just stared at the ceiling.

"You need to look at your world, small as it is right now, but you do have anchors to this timeline. You have friends on this ship, the big black guy you've been sparring with and the pilot you've been hanging out with. You have family, the Monastic couple."

"They're not family, I'm just some religious figure to them."

"Really? Then tell me why Hera'sun shows up every morning to check up on you? Why does Nurem'sun help guide you through this modern world you seem so lost in? They think of you as family now. You may not realize it but they've kind of adopted you into their circle."

Those words just hung in the air.

"Then we get to the girls. Seriously, how do you always find yourself knee deep in women? You make most men jealous with your appeal."

"That's an exaggeration."

"Really? You haven't been flirting with both Doctor Tsia and Doctor Mallory?" Ten accused. "There is no denying it; you have a type."

For the first time since this vision started Allana let out a smirk. Doctors, why was it always doctors?

"Do you remember how we got engaged?"

Tenuvah smiled. "Of course; you came into my emergency room on a stretcher bleeding from the chest – this memory. Except you were passed out by now and I worked feverishly to save your life. A couple hours later a nurse came into my office and handed me a small box and a letter. The box held a ring and a letter written to me. It was your *if I don't make it* letter. You said you wanted to marry me and were building up the courage to ask. So I took the decision out of your hands. I was there when you awoke and the first words you heard from me were will you marry me? Is that the engagement you meant?"

"We have other engagements?" Allana laughed. "Yes, that engagement. I loved you so much when I awoke. You did for me what I couldn't do. I tired four or five times to propose but I never had the courage. What if you had said no? I always regretted not asking it myself."

Allana blinked twice and her bindings disappeared. She climbed off the gurney and knelt on the floor, pulling the ring from her pocket and holding it open. "Doctor Tenuvah Sheppard, my Perfect Ten, will you make me the happiest woman in this verse and the next by marrying me?"

She watched as Tenuvah's face exploded with a big smile, a tear sliding down her cheek. She covered her mouth with her hand. She nodded whimpering the word yes over and over. She took the ring and slid it on her finger. She pulled Allana, still bleeding, to her feet and held her head delicately. The Major closed her eyes as their lips pressed against one another.

When her eyes opened Allana found herself not in the arm of the woman she loved but instead in the firing range aboard the EDI's battleship *Nova Holme*. The ship was the flagship of the EDI fleet, a massive carrier for the human forces and the makeshift home for the Major during the war. Accompanying her in the firing range was the Teuchter, her highlander.

For a moment she had forgotten she still wore her glasses, for a moment she had forgotten she was still in Neverland but seeing the rough and gruff Master

Warrant Officer Brian McCree standing before her reminded her where she was.

"Wull ye look at ye, lassie. Prim and proper but without ye stoat in yer step?" The old soldier stretched his neck as he looked around. "I ain't yer first foot but be I yer last?"

Talking with McCree was always difficult. He was Scottish through and through and sometimes a little too much Scottish for her. Hell, sometimes he was too Scottish for the Scots. The man looked expectantly at her, asking if he was the last one she spoke to. She shook her head. "I haven't talked to Master Corporal Tribal yet."

"Ye nev'r chat to the silent b'y, ye just chat at'm." He wasn't wrong. Tribal was quiet kid, he never said more than he had to, if that.

"How be Tenuvah? She still got the stoat in her bosom? She be a bonnie lass that I'd bring to the scratcher and I'd leave me breeks at hame." A wicked and perverse look spread across his face and waggle took over his eyebrows. She always had to slowly translate what the highlander said to fully understand the meaning but that grin of his told her she'd be better off leaving that last phase as it was.

"Stop being a thrawn auld Jimmy." He was a lecherous old man and she ordered him to stop.

"The lassie be learning the lingo," he said with a whoop and a laugh. "So what be all the stramash? The Stushie?"

She looked over at the guns, real or fake she didn't

want to touch them. "They need me to fight again. They need me to kill." She scoffed at herself. "And I volunteered this time, just like the time before that and the one before that. I can't say no to battle if it means saving people in trouble and I am fine with that."

"So what be the problem, lassie?"

"I was frozen for some important task but I don't know for what. I want to be here for something peace related or something that would help the future but when I wake up after a long cold dream I find they only need me for war, they only need me to kill. Past, present or future all I am is a soldier, a killing machine. I don't want to be a fighter anymore. I want to be done with it."

McCree looked over at his superior officer with a half smile. He grabbed a chair and sat down. "I ever tell ye aboot me first fecht? I be so nervous I boaked all over me foxhole. Me frein tried blether to keep my calm, but talking never helps.

"When the rammy began I realized something. I be a soldier, it's not all I be but it is what I be. I can be a soldier because I like to fecht and I like to kill or I can be a soldier because I know it be for helping those wha need it."

Allana looked over at him and smiled at him. The highlander was older then her, or at least he used to be. She didn't know anymore how to calculate her own age; did frozen time count? The highlander that stood before her wasn't based on math, he was based on her memories of him, and the thought of the grizzled solider she knew as a young child vomiting on the battlefield brought a laugh to her lips.

"It be the same for you hen. Ye be a soldier, it's not all ye be but it is what ye be."

He was right; he always was when it came to war and fighting. She would have to choose for herself if she wanted to be a fighter for fighting sake, or a fighter because the world - no that term was obsolete now – a fighter because the universe needed fighters to protect them.

"Look at it this way lassie. They be getting into all sort of fecht without ye up till now. So whitever this be they must be in wee sort of trauchle to thaw ye oot. They ain't thaw ye oot for them lizards nay them fecht with the aliens whatsits. This be big lassie."

"Now go have a dram and have one for me." The lecherous look, wicked smirk and eye waggle all returned at once. "I'm gonna stay here and think of your hen all drookit. Give me a shot with her, I'd make her a fair puggle."

Once again her mind decided not to translate that, for the sake of her sanity.

She looked the old warrior in his eyes and smiled. "Haud yer wheesht ye scunner."

He erupted with laughter. "I be loving ye and the lingo hen, loving it."

The MWO vanished as Allana slowly removed the glasses as did the Nova Holme, the hospital and

Tenvuvah. The past returned to exactly where it belonged, far beyond Allana's reach.

She carefully placed the glasses on her desk and climbed out of her chair. She grabbed her green bag and unzipped it once again. She rooted through the bag till she found a long black weapon, a special weapon given to her by the old soldier himself. It was a black cutlass knife, or a sgian-dubh as the highlanders called it. It was thirty-five centimetres from tip to butt and had a curved wavy blade. It was a gift he'd given her many years ago; near identical to the one he wore, the one he lost on Kiron Port.

"Every highlander wore one in secret," McCree had told her when he gave it to her. "But no one ever lied about having one."

The definition perfectly fit the life of a soldier. Every super-power kept their special soldiers a secret but none would ever say they didn't have any.

Captain Agrima Cantor stood in the Mojave Desert's galley, surrounded by the ship's crew. Dozens of eyes stared at her, each nervous and expecting some encouragement from their commander, from their Captain. With a final deep breath for support she pressed down onto her handheld and brought a large screen alive with an image of the Pherca moon.

"The Pherca moon is under attack and the people down there need our help." She began slowly, her speech picking up speed as she went on. "There are five ships on their way but the first of which will not be here for eight hours. The people down there don't have eight hours.

With a few clicks on her handheld the screen zoomed into the three ships and the two HEF ships surrounding the planet. The Captain continued. "These are the Viatos. They are an alien race of unknown origin. They have attacked several HEF ships and now are targeting our food. The Viatos began by attacking the HEF ships in orbit around Pherca. Now they have landed their ground forces dirtside and currently taking a foothold. Reports say they've been battling the local marines and private military employees but they have our sailors heavily outnumbered.

"At this point retaking the planet is no longer an option. The alien ground forces, or husks as we're referring to them, have disabled the sentry systems and secured almost all key strategic positions save for Paick Starport. As of ten minutes ago the starport are still under HEF support. Civilians are flooding to the starport but we have no way of getting ships into orbit. The Viatos have the air filled with starfighters."

Morrison raised his hand. The Captain gave him a nod. "Where are we getting this recent intel, ma'am?"

"A news reporter called Sera Gamble." The Captain answered, "She is a tricky one. I don't know how she is getting past the alien jamming signals but she is broadcasting us updates. She also reports that the two HEF ship orbiting the moon, the *Norway* and the

Marseille, are heavily damaged and may even be dead in the water. So this will be us going in, alone."

Murmurs rippled across the room as the weight of the Captain's words echoed within each of them.

"The *Mojave Desert* will come out of warp and eject the shuttle. The *Mojave* will provide cover until you get your boots on the ground. Then we rabbit. We cannot engage the ships in a fair fight let alone two against one. The ground forces - callsign: Bungee - will be led by Major Allana Guiver."

Petty Officer Marcus Branford scowled as the Major rose to her feet. What the hell were they doing giving her command? What the hell were they doing putting her in the field? When he was assigned to *Mojave* he was given command of all marines aboard. He was supposed to report to Morrison, not to a woman who just stepped out of the freezer. Her skills, knowledge and training were out of date. She had no business being out there.

He rubbed his neck, still sore nearly a week later, and quietly debated with himself. Was he lashing out at her for logical reasons or was it more ego based? He tried to remove himself from the situation, like he'd done many times since she came aboard, and take a look at things from a logical viewpoint and every time his training came back screaming. She was a risk and he didn't want to be there when somebody got killed because of it.

Standing at the front of the room Allana cleared he throat as she touched her tablet. The large screen changed to the moon's surface before zooming in on the starport.

"We will have two primary objectives. The first will be to make our way to the starport and secure it. We'll need these to extract the civilians. The second objective will be too locate and reactivate the automatic sentry guns. They'll clear the skies. Anybody have any experience with a sentry system or similar computer system?"

Only a single soldier raised her hand. Major Guiver looked past the legions of lowered hands until he spotted the volunteer.

Dr. Bristol Tsia.

Allana came to a single undeniable conclusion: fate hated her. She looked away and scanned the rest of the *Mojave*'s crew. "Anybody?"

Bristol hated being ignored. She spoke up. "I can get the system on line."

Major Guiver looked back at the doctor and shook her head. "I'm not taking a civilian into battle."

"I fought in the war. I can handle a mission like this."

Fate *really* hated her.

Allana shook her head. She wouldn't allow it, she couldn't allow it. "I don't care. Our duty is to protect civilians, not send them on missions."

Bristol hated a great many things but above all else she hated being coddled. "With a couple soldiers we could secure it and I will get it back on. So unless while you were a popsicle they taught you how to reactive a fully automated sentry gun system that operates a seven level sensor system strengthened with a HEF friend or foe codec encryption readers then you need me."

The room went quiet as the two eyed each other. Doctor Tsia was normally a friendly, non-confrontational person but here she was snapping back at the Major. Allana just frowned. Military men and women would never talk back to a superior officer, especially not in a manner like this. She never minded discussion or suggestions but that was always done in a respectful manner. It was all part of the rules. Civilians didn't have to follow those rules. She was a major in the army, the last true soldier in the entire universe. She demanded deference and she needed compliance. So why did she always fall for a women that wouldn't listen to her?

It scared the Major that she obviously had a type. It scared her more how right Tenuvah always was. What scared her most was how she didn't understand a single word of that techno-babble the doctor had just given her.

Her and fate were going to have words, this Allana promised the verse.

"Fine you're with Bungee." Allana reluctantly agreed, turning her head towards the petty officer. "Branford: make sure she gets a weapon so she can play soldier."

Bristol glared at the thawed solider, her eyes narrowing in anger. The soldier that stood before her was a specimen of beauty, a strong hero and war-bred fighter beauty but she was also an arrogant sod. Bristol knew the limits of her own skills. She'd run mission in battlefields like Pherca dozens of time during the war. It came with the job. Yet in the eyes of the Major she was nothing more than a civilian who'd get in the way.

The military were always like this. They thought that they were here to protect the civilians from all threats - foreign and domestic - and most importantly to protect civilians from themselves. They were doing their job but Bristol hated the mentality and attitude that came with it. If you hired people to protect you weren't allowed to be angry when they actually did it.

With a few stroke of the keys Major Guiver brought up the automatic sentry guns. "Nova Kingston has dozens of sentry guns that to regulate the skies. They operate on a multi-linking system. You can take down one and the rest will still be active."

The screen changed to an identical building only smaller in size. "This system doesn't have a centralized hub or anything, making it impossible to take down the guns unless you go at it one by one. According to Hera'sun the system is completely offline. She doesn't know how it's happening; it shouldn't be possible by your future tech – present tech.

"We will land on the planet and proceed upwards. We'll try to land as close as possible but their fighters have a dominating control over the sky. We'll punch our way through the city to the nearest gun." The gun flashed on the map, "and see what we can find from there. If we need to split up Ensemble will depart from

Bungee and secure the tower. The rest of us do what we can to get the civilians to the ships and get them off planet."

She looked around the galley, all the eyes staring at her. "Any questions?"

The captain stepped forward and thanked the major, disabling the large screen with a touch of her handheld.

"Those people are relying on us to save them and we will not let them down. You have your orders and you have your assignments. We launch in an hour. Be ready."

Branford chased after Lieutenant-Commander Morrison as the meeting came to an end. He called out for the *Mojave*'s head of security. Morrison slowed his step and turned his head back. "What can I do for you, Branford?"

"I have a concern, sir." The PO carefully chose his words. "With all due respect I think we've made a mistake in our planning."

Morrison came to a full stop. "You've got my attention. Make it quick."

"I should be running this mission not Major Guiver," he explained. "She's untrained, she unqualified and she was just removed from cyro-sleep not even a week ago."

"You cleared her. You qualified her on all weapons and equipment that the HEF uses in a mission like this."

"But that's all theory, sir. She's been frozen for four hundred years while being hooked up to a broken dream machine. For all we know the moment she sees battle she'll freeze and get everybody killed."

"That's why you're 2IC on the ground."

"Sir, this is a mista—."

"Enough." Morrison shook his head. "I heard you; I understand. Your conern has been noticed. However, this is her mission; deal with it. Get your boots on the ground and keep eyes on her. If things go to hell deal with it. That's what you do."

The moment Allana reached her quarters she went straight for her green duffle bag. She withdrew the dagger and placed it on her bed. She'd have a blade on her but it wouldn't be this one. What she was going to use were a simple pair of black combat boots. The most important piece of equipment that any soldier could have was their footwear. Good pair of boots normally got overlooked but a poor pair could result in the death of a soldier.

She held the familiar footwear in her hands. The boots were the perfect analogy for her. They were a little stiff from a lack of use and long-term storage but they would hold up. The boots were always reliable. Guiver gently worked the material with her hands. They were black boots built from waterproof leather with nylon side panels which improved ventilation and comfort. The ankle guards and shin straps had taken numerous kinds of damage, scratches, burns and cuts but they still held together. To some the idea of taking up valuable storage space just to bring a pair of boots would seem ludicrous but for Allana the thought of going into battle without them seemed crazier.

Allana reached under her bed and grabbed a large green trunk by the handle and pulled it out. She flipped off the guards and lifted open the cover. She looked down at the futuristic battle armour that lay before her. The armour was modular in design, built to be worn with as little as just the vest or assembled with multiple attachments to act as full-body armour that could pressurize to withstand the vacuum of space.

Allana pulled off the disturbingly blue naval work shirt, the guppy colours seemed wrong on her body, and reached around her back to unclasp her bra. She tossed both onto her bunk and pulled open the dresser in her room. When they gave her the room they gave her some clothes as well. A majority of it didn't fit right, some of it was altered so it wouldn't fall off, and the remainder was lucky fits from the hand-offs she got from the ladies and guys of the ship.

Allana grabbed a sports bra and started to pull it over her naked torso. The sports bra was a perfect fit, as luck would have it she was the same size as the good Doctor Brea Mallory. A thought crossed the Major's mind as she dressed. Here she was with another doctor's undergarments pressed against her naked flesh. It was always doctors.

She had a type.

A small coo caught startled the soldier's attention

and instincts took over. Allana spun towards the door, snatching the dagger from the bed, the blade nearly jumping from the sheath into her hand. Doctor Bristol Tsia stood in Allan's doorway, her eyes unable to leave the woman's body. She was at a loss for words. She didn't mean to startle the woman, she only want to talk to her but there she was standing in her room undressed. Allana broke the tension as she lowered her weapon.

"It's not polite to stare."

Bristol quickly looked away, not wanting to stare like a fourteen year old boy. "I—I'm sorry. I didn't mean to intrude."

"In or out."

Bristol raised an eyebrow in confusion before remembering that she stood in the open doorway. Bristol stepped in and gently closed the door behind her.

"I didn't mean to be rude but the door was open."

"I thought I closed that."

Bristol put her weight behind the door and gave it a sturdy shove, stopping only at the sound of a loud click. "These doors on the old ships need a good push to make sure."

Allana returned the dagger to its leather home and dropped both on the bed. She started to look for her shirt. Bristol eyed the dagger, remembering the speed at which the soldier had wielded it. Bristol always thought she was fast but her eyes could barely keep up with the Major's hands.

"What do you want?" She questioned as she pulled

a thin black t-shirt over her head. Bristol watched as the smooth skin vanished beneath the fabric. "Or are you just here for the show?"

"I wanted to talk to you about the briefing."

"I figured as much. Spit it out." Allana undid her belt and lowered her pants, stepping out of her clothes. Bristol's words escaped her as she became stunned at the disrobing soldier. She was used to women disrobing before her; it was the desired outcome when one pursued the ladies in a romantic manner. But seeing the Major's body was a heavenly and horrifying sight at the same time. Allana had a magnificent body akin to an Amazon or sports star. It was firm and toned but it was also covered with cuts, tears and the scars of bullet holes and stab wounds. It was like a classic painting torn and faded through mishandling. Allana snapped her fingers to grab her attention. "I need to get ready so says what you have to or get out."

"You cannot talk to me the way you did. I am fully trained and can take care of myself." A sudden burst of confidence and strength empowered Bristol's words; she felt the sudden need to prove herself before the soldier, to show that she was as tough as the Major was.

Allana shook her head as she pulled on a black pair of combat pants over her well shaped legs. She fastened the belt and reached for her boots. "Have you ever been on a battlefield?"

Bristol frowned. "I have, numerous times; never as a marine but as an operative."

Guiver looked over, a glimmer of confusion resting in her eyes. "What are you, Bristol?"

"I am one of the Nivican," she explained quietly. "It was a joint organization between the Monastic and the HEF that took educated people and gave them advanced training from both governments so they could act as –." Her voice trailed off as she searched for the right words.

"You're a spook." It all began to fall into place. "I get it now. You were probably plucked from university, good grades and a high aptitude in the desired areas would have caught their attention, and you were recruited into spy school."

"It was a program they started when war looked inevitable." Bristol confirmed. "I met Nurem'sun after training and we were assigned as partners."

"Did they close the program after the war ended?"

"No, it still runs. Nurem'sun and I decided to leave. He wanted to spend more time with his mate and I didn't want to do these missions without him. I returned to school and got my doctorate."

"So you've been on missions before but you've always had to Indiana Jones your way through things."

"Indiana Jones?" Was that a name or a verb?

Allana carried on, ignoring the interruption. "You fly by the seat of your pants and make things up as you go along. You only have you, your partner and the hot chick that got accidentally wound up in everything to worry about. The battlefield is completely different. You aren't killing because it's down you him or you. You walk out on that battlefield to kill. There is no other way to argue it."

Allana grabbed the battle armour's vest piece and slide over her head. She tightened the waist straps. "I just wanted you to know what you're getting into."

The doctor brushed her hair back behind her ears and smiled. "That's sweet and all but you don't have to look after me. This is a whole new world for you, a whole new verse. I have to look after you."

Allana slide her issued knife into a chest sheath on the vest. She gave it a final adjustment and made for her quarter's door. She paused before the archaeologist and gave her a smile. "Sports bra and underwear haven't changed; the navy is still full of themselves, war still exists and I am still needed to *kill for peace*. Trust me when I say things haven't changed that much."

Major Allana Guiver stood in the docking bay watching her troops. Each marine carefully inspected their weapons and checked their equipment as they prepped themselves for the fight. Everybody prepped for battle their own way, some remained solemn and quiet, like her and Campbell, others psyched themselves up with slaps and chants but the few who had yet to see combat just seemed scared. Allana had never gone into battle with sailors but she had with US Marines. They were a grandstanding bunch, tough and tall, but they were a tough as nail group. Yet despite their skills, back in the day any solider worth their salt preferred to rely on soldiers. They were the green-camo wearing red-blooded soldiers that trained the same way so they could fight the army way. The army turned kids into adults. They made heart-breakers and life-takers. They made bad-ass bastards that people could rely on in their time of need.Even today she wanted the same thing, to be able to rely on those she trained alongside, but that wasn't happening anymore, it might not ever happen again.

She was the last soldier alive.

She was also way too young to be saying back in the day. She'd caught her herself saying it ever since she awoke. She knew she was technically older than the ship and her entire crew but she had made a decision: time under ice didn't count.

"You shouldn't be going on this mission." Branford voice was low, just a hair's length above a whisper, but she heard it clearly. "You know this, I know this. You're painfully unqualified, untrained and untested. You're just a ticking time bomb and you're going to get somebody killed."

Allana didn't look back; she couldn't be seen arguing with her 2IC just minutes before the mission. Instead she just looked forward, keeping her eyes on her troops.

"You decide to bring this to me now?" Her harsh whisper seamed with anger. "If you have a problem with me step off this mission. I can do it without you. I rather not do this without your skills but I cannot have someone who will question my command watching my back."

"I'm not going anywhere. I have to be there when you screw up, mostly to keep everybody from getting killed but partly just to watch you fail."

Allana spun around and grab his vest. She yanked him close, her face, hidden from everyone but him, scowled as her hands feigned a vest inspection. She whispered quickly.

"Is your ego so fucking thin that you're willing to risk the mission just to see me fail? Are you still pissed about what happened on the *Spellsong*? Is that it? Fine! You make sure you and everybody on this squad makes it back and I'll give you your shot at me. You can try to beat the living shit out of me if it will make you feel better but until then you take every inch of rage and loathing you feel for me and you stow it so fucking deep inside you and get *my* troops ready. Is that clear, Petty Officer?"

He glared at her and nodded. "Yes, ma'am."

Allana shoved him back, releasing him. She grabbed her firearms, sliding her pistol into its holster and clipping the rifle to her vest. She carefully stowed her grenades in her vest as she watched Branford go person to person, checking their gear.

"They want you to say something."

Allana looked for the voice, a young female sailor stood in front of her and handed her extra ammunition. She recognized the young sailor; she had beaten her face in on the Spellsong. "Able Seamen Viviane Thibodeau right?"

"Oui, madame." Thibodeau was only twenty-four years old. She had blond hair, brown eyes and the kind of attitude and skill needed for a knock-down-drag-out firefight.

Allana accepted the extra clips and slid them into her vest. "You are on Ensemble right?"

"Oui, madame. I am the ranking sailor."

"Good. You make sure the civilian doesn't do anything crazy."

Thibodeau laughed. "It will be a difficult task. She tends to be energetic."

"Yeah, I get that feeling," she said with a smirk. "By the way, been meaning to ask, what's with all the French?"

"It's part of my regiment tradition," she explained. "Every Marine in my regiment is taught French and we mostly only speak it. I speak English here because I'm the only one from my regiment aboard."

"What regiment?"

"Nous somme les Marines 141 HEF: Les Van Doos."

"Where did you get that name?" Allana couldn't believe her ears. She recognized that name. The Van Doos was an anglicized pronunciation of the first two syllables of vingt-deuxième, the 22nd in French. "You know back in my da— er— the Canadian Forces had a French infantry regiment called the Royal 22 Regiment. Everybody called them the Van Doos."

Thibodeau just nodded. "When the HEF was born,

all of the marines regiments were formed from different marine and infantry regiments across the Earth that was. Ours, one of the few French ones to survive, was born from the Canada's Royal 22nd." She laughed briefly, realizing how rehearsed her voice had sounded just there. "That history lesson is crammed down every OS's throat the moment they enter battle school."

"Every marine regiment has a similar history," Campbell explained. "I'm from the 99 HEF Satellite Jaegers: Island Hoppers; born from the Royal Irish Regiment."

"PO Branford and I are from 150 HEF Marines," Keiser boasted, "Devil Dogs! We're part of the biggest marine division in the entire HEF. Origin: 5th Marine Regiment, United States Marine Corp."

"124 HEF Marines," Winters added, "Wolfhounds; Royal Irish Regiment."

One by one each of the ship's twenty marines, minus those guarding the Spellsong, listed off their regiment and origin. Many came from division in groups of two but as each spoke Allana saw descendents of the military history of Earth standing before her. The Earth she knew, and its military might, no longer existed but the spirit of the EDI, the Canadian Forces and all the armies she fought alongside in the first war carried on. It gave her a glimmer of hope, an anticipation that her regiments, the Princess Patricia's Canadian Light Infantry, still existed, in one form or another, amongst the HEF.

"As I live and breathe," Allana look at the waiting

sailors. They were looking at her now, every one of them, each expecting something from her. She nodded their way. "Why do they care what I say?"

"You are a soldier, you are a legend. We all had to study you in history," Thibodeau explained. "Besides they are following you into battle. They are scared. Anything you say will rile them up."

"You are famous for your speeches, Allana," Dr. Tsia added. Thibodeau handed the civilian some extra clips. "Every one of your big speeches has been recorded through history. Some were probably taken out of context or some details were overlooked but the only way people know you is through how history remembers you."

"They know their jobs. They'll be fine."

Bristol's eyes narrowed. "Fine then I'll do it." She turned towards the soldiers and loudly cleared her voice. "It doesn't matter where you're from."

Allana recognized the speech immediately. She *hated* that speech. She had spoken those words over and over until it haunted her. This was not the time for this speech or any other. "Doctor, stop."

Bristol ignored the Major and continued. "We don't care what level you're from, what colony, what ship, what platoon, what division, or even what room because as of right now you are all in Guiver's Battalion and you belong to her."

She had enough. I said stop!"

All the heads in the docking bay looked over at

her. They were all watching her, expecting her to say something. She had to speak now. "You're all trained for this. We move as a squad and nobody goes off alone. If we find a PMG or marine whose in fighting form pull him in to your squad and keep pushing. We're getting these people off that moon. Now load up and keep calm. Your training will kick in."

"That wasn't the most poetic or graceful but it worked." Tsia chuckled as she climbed aboard the shuttle.

Thibodeau shook her head. "And I have to guard that one; quelle chance." Allana laughed. "Major, what's a PMG?"

"It stands for a mercenary who works for a private military. Private Military Goon. Why what do you call them now?" Allana asked.

"Soldiers."

"Yeah, that's not going to fly," the Major said shaking her head.

CHAPTER TWELVE
Pherca Moon Invasion +6:00 hours

Captain Agrima Cantor anxiously rubbed her left hand with her right. She was nervous and rightfully so. This was not opening fire to scare away a dragon ship, this was full on battle. She was diving into a shit storm, outgunned and outnumbered and was doing so willingly. It had been five years since the Kobold Unification, since the last war. She lost a lot during the war and more in the years that followed. When Richard saved her career she was never suppose to see combat again, not until she was ready, but as the old saying went life's what happens when you're busy making plans.

"Ma'am, we are ready to launch the attack."

Commander Somers spoke up. "What about the guns?"

"The gun will have enough emergency energy loaded in them to fire two full volleys of blaster fire the moment we get out of warp instead of waiting for it to power up," Morrison explained. "The problem is it'll overload the guns and leave us without active weapons for ninety seconds."

"Ninety seconds is a long time."

"Aye, sir. I'll do what I can with shields to keep us up but we'll just have to keep moving."

Ninety seconds; it felt like an eternity in a firefight, people could die, ships could explode and an entire war could change in ninety seconds.

"Anything on the channels?"

"We have a transmission from the Viatos, sir, its being broadcast as a warning for all ships."

Somers looked over at his communications agent and nodded. "Play it."

"To all incoming ships: We are the Viatos and we control this airspace. Surrender now or be wiped out."

The communications officer stopped the message as it began to repeat. "That was in English, the translation matrix didn't even need to run that message. It just keeps repeating over and over in English."

Somers looked back over to Morrison. "Is Cole and the shuttle ready?" The tactical office replied with a nod. Somers looked over at his Captain and asked the question she was dreading. "We are ready, ma'am. Do we have permission to launch the attack?"

Captain Cantor dialled in on her chair computer, the system opening the ship wide intercom. "This is the Captain speaking. All hands to battle stations, we are commencing the rescue mission. I repeat: all hands to battle stations."

Captain Agrima Cantor switched off her intercom.

She rose from her chair to her feet, her shaking hands hidden behind her back. It was time. She looked at the helmsmen. "Bring us out of warp."

The *Mojave Desert* tore out of warp and spun in space as it dodged the *Marseille*'s still hull, skipping across the atmosphere, and flew towards the *Norway*. Coming out this was insanely dangerous. A ship exited warp at high speeds and if a ship's pilot didn't have the necessary skills to combat a planet's gravity then they could easily lose control and crash into the celestial body. It was a risky move that the HEF avoided during regular circumstances. They were, however, light-years away from regular circumstances.

A regulation exit would have forced the *Mojave* through a gauntlet of Viatos ship fire, a plan their shields and hull could not survive, but this alternative exit put them between the Viatos and the moon.

The *Mojave* spun as Viatos fire filled the eternal midnight of space. Alien bolts crashed against the HEF's shield as others blew past, missing the human hull by mere meters. Enemy fire staggered, pausing for a moment, as the *Mojave* ejected a pair of pods from its stern, each exploding in a burst of bright energy.

Like a gunslinger waiting to draw his pistol, Denver Cole's fingers itched to grab his controls. He stared at the red light, waiting for it inevitable change. He hadn't been able to fly in a while. He had piloted the shuttle to and from a planet or from ship to ship, but that wasn't flying. Flying was when you sat on the edge of your seat trying to pull off the dumbest and wildest moves possible. It was when you lived by your split-second decision and acted on instinct. Flying was where everything was on the line and you never had a moments doubt. That was what Cole was born to do, what he excelled at. It was what he lived for and what got him in trouble. He was assigned to the *Mojave* as punishment, away from all the real flying. Now they needed him to be bad again.

The light flashed green and he slammed on the gas. The *Mojave Desert* ejected the shuttle and Cole fired up the thrusters and sped towards the surface. The gun ports on the *Mojave Desert* opened all over the ship as the guns emerged. With Lt. Commander Morrison at the control they fired a full volley downwards at the planet. The ship rained blaster fire from above, ripping through the unlucky diamond starfighters that were in its path and clearing the landing zone of troops.

Cole piloted the shuttle downward, spiralling down around the *Mojave*'s zone of fire. Cole's left hand gently clutched the joystick as the fingers on his right hands danced over the key on the console. Cole smirked as the targeting system locked onto the nearest diamond fighter, his fingers gently squeezing the trigger. A burst of fire shot out from the shuttle's cannons, ripping through the wings of the unlucky starfighter. It fell from the sky but Cole had already forgotten about it and moved on, focusing instead on the entire squadron. He open fired blindly, hitting as many diamond fighters as possible, not enough to deal any real damage but just enough to get their attention. Cole steered away from the landing zone as six fighters took after him.

Bungee squad sat quietly in the shuttle's rear, strapped into their chairs, as the shuttle violently shook during its risky descent. Tsia nudged Allana and with a nod of her head pointed towards Ordinary Seamen Winters. The young marine twitched in his chair, his breathing loud and heavy. Allana knew what the kid was thinking; it was the same that most soldiers and marines thought on their first drop: fear. Fear of dying on the ground, fear of being shot out of the sky and fear of being shot in space

"You should calm him down." Tsia suggested.

"Nope. They're marines; they don't do calm." She glanced to the back. "Branford: deal with him."

"Winters!"

"PO?" The OS sheepishly asked.

"Marines hymn: Go!"

The kid didn't even stammer. His lips opened and his lungs started belting out the words. They came clear and practised, as they'd been sung dozens of time before – even for an OS as himself.

From the Halls of Montezuma,
To the shores of Karoface;
We fight our planet's battles

In the air, on land, and space;
First to fight for right and freedom
And to keep our honor clean:
We are proud to claim the title
Of the H.E.F Marine.

Thibodeau joined in quickly, beating Campbell by
a fraction of a second, and the rest by a mere heartbeat.
Tsia looked on in awe as the entire shuttle, save for the
preoccupied pilot, the unfrozen solider and the civilian,
sang in perfect timing.

Our flag's unfurled to every breeze
From dawn to setting sun;
We have fought in every clime and place
Where we could take a gun;
In the forests of savage lands
And in sunny tropic scenes;
You will find us always on the job
The H.E.F Marines.

Here's health to you and to our Corps
Which we are proud to serve;
In many a strife we've fought for life
And never lost our nerve;
In the black they sail on
Protecting the Heaven's scenes;
They will find the 'verse is guarded
By H.E.F Marines.

Allana just smiled. Past, present or even here in the future, the one thing that never seemed to change was the marines. They were big, they were tough and they were full of themselves. Luckily for them they were always able to back it up.

The large numbers on the shuttle dash quickly counted down; thirty seconds and counting. Cole had attracted a large amount of hostile attention, more then he could handle on his own, and if he couldn't time this right he and every person he carried with him would be brutally massacred by enemy fire. The shuttle rocked as the blaster fire crashed against its stern.

Twenty-One seconds.

With his free hand Cole's fingers began to dance along the control board's keys. He didn't need to look at what he typed, hours of practise had drilled into his head where each key was and what they did. With a twist of his fingers Cole began to adjust the shuttle's shield strength, focusing the majority of defence's strength to the back to protect his rear.

Seventeen seconds.

The shuttle bobbed and weaved as enemy fire flew past, bolts scraping across the steel taking with it the paint. He twisted in the air, shot upwards, and even barrel rolled sideways. Cole could feel the shuttle's hull creak and moan as he pushed it to its limits. It wasn't a starfighter; it wasn't even a combat shuttle. It was little more than a taxi; chances were high that taxis were more durable.

Eight seconds.

Cole pushed down on the control stick and the shuttle obeyed. With the full strength of the engines behind it the ship dived, spiralling downwards as it sped towards the ground.

Five seconds.

The diamond fighters barely hesitated as they dove after Cole. They were built for speed and created for war. They were able to perform these manoeuvres without difficulties and had no trouble keeping up with him but that's what Cole was counting on.

Cole watched the clock as the ground sped towards him; he had to time this right. He pulled up on his stick and levelled the shuttle with the ground. Cole fired the afterburners and rocketed towards the landing zone.

Two seconds.

The diamonds fighters spun and twisted in the air, moving like a leaves on the wind, as they turned after the HEF shuttle. They were a second and a half behind him but closing fast. Cole sped forward, the rear shields at maximum and the thrusters at full. With a final burst of speed the shuttle crossed over the landing zone. Cole glanced at the clock.

Zero.

Cole smiled.

The gun aboard the *Mojave* spun as they opened up with the second volley. The sky opened up as red rain once again poured down onto the landing zone, the ship bound weapons cleaving through the diamond fighters trailing the human shuttle.

The steel hulls of the alien starfighter crumpled on contact with the fiery rain and crashed to the ground. The ruptured ships skipping along the planet like a stone on water until they came to their inevitable stop.

Cole brought the shuttle down low and flew towards the city, slowing down and coming to halt as they found a clear patch of dirt to land on. Major Guiver unbuckled her harness and grabbed her rifle.

"Okay, grab your gear. Remember to watch your firing zones and keep your eyes peeled," Allana yelled over the engine's roar. She clipped the rifle sling to her chest. "Do not fall behind and do not slow down. Stay together and trust your training. You keep saying you are marines. Now its time to act like it. Let's move"

The shuttled lowered till it was nearly touching the ground, it wasn't all the way down but close enough for the Major. With a final encouraging whoop Allana leapt out off the deck. Her boots hit the ground with a firm thud, dust flowing up on impact. This wasn't the hull of a ship or concrete; this was good old fashion dirt and grass beneath her feet. For the first time in a very long time Major Allana Guiver was planetside.

CHAPTER THIRTEEN
Pherca Moon Invasion +6:15 hours

High above the Pherca Moon, the spinning guns of the *Mojave Legend* slowed to a halt. Ninety seconds began now.

Lieutenant-Commander Harold Morrison hands suddenly felt heavy and useless. Until the guns powered back up, he was out of the fight. All he could do was watch and wait. Truth was his fingers were already dancing across the keys, scanning for target, studying their movements, and allowing his targeting reticules to fall on their fast moving hulls, but without his guns it all felt meaningless. The moment his gun flashed on he'd be ready but until then it was like hockey without a puck.

Ninety seconds was a long time.

Commander Somers stumbled as he walked across the bridge, the ship rocking with every bolt that crashed against the hull, his portable screen bombarding him with data. A command screen, much the like the captain had by her chair, had the potential to receive data from all active stations but most commanders didn't bring it up. That much data was more than any person could absorb and process, so he never looked at it unless necessary, instead all he had was immediate threats, shield status, and an estimated countdown until his guns were back online. The rest of the data he would leave to his well trained and trusted crew.

The *Mojave* pulled in behind the wreckage of its fallen big sister, the Norway, and turtle. They were a target if they kept moving but here, beneath the wreckage of the fallen battleship, they hopefully had a moments cover while they awaited their guns.

Like an explosion of energy her heart suddenly sped up, beating what felt like a thousand beats per second, her breathing was short and laboured, and her head started to spin. Captain Agrima Cantor stood straight, frozen in fear. This was a battle she could not win; she didn't even have a chance. She was outnumbered and outgunned. She was going to die and she was going to take her ship, her crew, and more innocent marines with her.

He legs buckled and she collapsed into her chair. She looked at Somers from the corner of her eye, the XO moving around the bridge barking orders. He had Hera'sun scanning the Viatos networks, Morrison keeping the shields up and booting up the guns, and had helmsmen plotting escape vectors. The *Mojave* needed to punch a hole through the aliens and get to the gate and Somers was the man who was going to do just that. Cantor was once a good captain, one of the best. She even had a real shot at taking the *Avalon*'s big chair, or so she'd be told, but then she broke and couldn't be fixed.

"They've stopped firing," Morrison cried out, "It's like they don't want to shoot the dead ships."

"We caught a blessing now sta---."

"Diamond fighters incoming."

"Keep our shields up," Somers yelled, "Disrupt their targeting or someth---."

His voice faded into the background as her mind became inwardly focused on one fact. They were not shooting at the dead ships. Try as she might to move on, to direct her limited attention to something else, her mind wouldn't allow her. It was as if her subconscious mind had figured something out that her conscious mind had not. She grabbed her command screen and flicked through the data, pulling up Hera'sun's scans of the Norway and Marseille.

"Guns are up."

"Open fire: All guns. Take out those diamond fighters." Somers yelled, "They have us pinned."

He had the target plotted in ready and waiting so that the moment it was ready he could get back into the fight. The barrels lit up with energy as Morrison slammed the fire button, pressing it down as hard as possible. The computer didn't care how hard the button was pressed but he still found it comforting.

Somers yelled orders across the bridge and crew

replied the stuttered cries of response. Aye after aye as the sailors went to work, Hera'sun wasn't a HEF sailor but she was a navy girl. She understood the traditions, in principle, her own navy had them as well but she couldn't let the traditional response slip by her lips, her attention was on her station.

She was the ship's science officer and because of such she had the greater station. She sat at a booth, with four screens, three keyboards and two mice surrounding her. Each flowed with information, random tidbits of data. She was working quickly, multitasking between her two major tasks. The first was the simplest. She had to scan the two HEF ships, and any Viatos vessels their scan could pierce, and pass the data through the system, sending it to the tactical, engineering and of course the command screens, the data to the command screens as it came in. The second proved more difficult. She had to breach the Viatos network.

Breaching the system proved easier then she expected but making sense of it was not. Her scenes filled with data, numbers and figures, three dimensional representations of network building blocks and billions of lines of pure raw code. As a Monastic she could take in data easier than a human could, they were a race that grew from the immediate need for science, but even for her it was overwhelming. The Viatos ships were unlike anything she'd seen and her scanners were overflowing with information. She had written subroutines into her station to group the data, flag irregularities and important figures and file it as needed but the incoming data was still enormous.

One of her many screens beep as the processor began to sort through the incoming readings of the alien ships. She gave the first data-burst a quick scan. It was a technical scanning of the alien energy weapons. With a flick of her finger she sent it over to the tactical station. With this information Morrison could realign the shields and help keep the ship afloat a little longer. Morrison would get a great deal of calculations and information from her readings from which he'd get possible targets, enemy defence capabilities, and energy build-up readings that could act as firing tells.

With a flick of her finger she sent it on her way, filed in the tactical systems and no longer her problem, her focus returning to the Viatos networks. She was trying to launch a cyber attack, to dump a virus in their system that hindered firing like she did with Kobold ships a day earlier, but she was coming up with nothing.

Her wireless receivers were defiantly finding numerous wireless networks but they didn't make any sense. The encryption was almost non-existent, what little protection it held was ancient at best, but what seemed like the first silver lining turned out to be more confusing then helpful. The networks were beyond what Hera'sun thought possible. They were using technology that had more to do with the Warp then it did with wifi networks and used math that didn't make sense. It was like a computer built at its core around a fact that 2+2 =

5; it was inconceivable.

Somers watched as the guns ripped through the diamond fighters, the one-man ships vanishing in debris of metal and gunfire, but that still left the problem of getting to the gate. He was hesitating, waiting for inspiration to give him that idea he needed for a valiant escape but it wasn't coming. He looked back at his screen but found nothing new.

Hera'sun hated to admit it but she couldn't make head or tails of the Viatos' wireless network. It nagged at her brain, it angered her. She had spent her life training to be the foremost science officer in not just the Monastic fleet but in all of the HEF-Monastic alliance. She let out a low curse as she slapped the desk before her. She silently prayed for forgiveness for her foul language. "I cannot decipher the network, sir."

"Leave it then. I want you to divert all your attention to assaulting their sensors." Somers shook his head. "See if you can confuse them."

Hera'sun did as she was ordered. Using false signals and decoy bursts of energy she would assault their sensors with faulty reading. Their tactical officer, assuming the Viatos ships were anything like their own, would be bombarded with reading of weapons fire and star fighters that were not there. The HEF called them ghosts. The Monastic had always praised the humans for their clever nicknames for mundane things. They were never happy with simply naming something once, they had to name it over and over, and then make a clever humorous name to wrap it all together. She often wondered what her own race would be like if it had such whimsy.

"There was a stagger in their gunfire earlier, what caused that?" Somers asked, to nobody directly instead to any who had an idea.

"That's when I fired the chaff missiles, sir." In the Major's time Chaff was a radar countermeasure involving spreading a cloud of small, thin pieces of aluminium, metalized glass fibre or plastic, which either appeared as a cluster of secondary targets on radar screens or swamps their screens with multiple returns. Modern versions had a similar effect but did so by firing a missile filled with dozens of micro-transmitters that broadcast thousands of similar signals each. "It slowed them down for a bit."

Their voices filled the background, like music while studying back in her academy days, but as Somers and the bridge talked Cantor examined the damage done to the *Norway* and *Marseille*. The ships were mostly intact. They seemed to have taken major damage to the life support systems and had a couple major hull breaches but they seemed to be fully operational. She hypothesized that the Viatos did what they could to kill all the human crew but left the ship as it was.

The ship was fully operational.

"Helmsmen: get ready to bolt; tactical: chaffs on my command," Somers ordered. "On my mark we go. Get our guns ready, we're shooting our way out."

"Belay that order." And just like that she was back. Her heart beat slowed to normal, her breathing levelled out and her body was able to move. She thumbed on the radio. "Armoury: is our chaff count is three hundred?"

"More or less, ma'am," the voice replied through the speakers.

"We're going to need all three hundred of them. Grab who you need. We will be loading and firing the entire volley."

Cantor thumbed to another channel and spoke again. "Engineering: power down my sublights, then spin them back up."

"Ma'am?"

"You heard me. Go!"

"Cantor?" The XO asked in disbelief, "What are you doing? I'd advise against--."

I've stopped pretending to be a captain she thought, and I've started being one.

"Hera'sun: I need all your attention on securing our network. We'll be at our weakest." Cantor climbed from her chair, back on her feet where a Captain belonged, and addressed her bridge. "Morrison: How long of a stagger did the chaff give us?"

"Hard to say, ma'am. We dove behind cover very quickly. Maybe a minute tops?"

"Start firing our chaffs out. No more than a minute between each one but vary it up. Get the computer on that. In the meantime you have full leeway with the gun. Take out any diamond fighter that comes at us and if the Viatos ships try to circle around, unload everything, cannons and all, into their face."

"Yes, ma'am."

Cantor handed her screen to Somers as she headed toward the helms. "Frank, I need you plot a firing solution. Target the Viatos engines so they cannot give chase."

"But our guns are already firing."

"Not ours," Cantor corrected; she pointed to the lifeless forms of the *Norway* and the *Marseille* floating in space, "Theirs."

The concept hit Somers like an asteroid at warp. The *Norway* was a battleship and the *Marseille* was as destroyer. They both had a hell of a lot more firepower then the *Mojave* did. He looked at the Captain's screen. She had used her HEF captains code to reactive the two seemingly dead ships, commanding it through the wifi and was slowly powering up their systems.

"That's why you shut ours down," he murmured, "and why you are launching chaffs. You're covering their power build-up with our own."

It was brilliant. Normally that tactic wouldn't work; you couldn't hide one energy signature with another, let alone two, but with the chaffs essentially blurring the lines together a sensor could never tell the difference.

Somers looked up at Cantor in a new light. She was bent over the helm plotting a course of action with the helmsmen, her mind already two steps ahead. Her hands still shook but at least she was on her feet. This was the captain he'd heard so much about. She was smart, clever, and knew her ship inside and out. He almost wished he could have seen her with an entire battleship or fleet at her disposal instead of a lone corvette.

"Sublights are spinning fast."

Cantor grabbed Somers command screen and wiped the board clean with a swipe of her hand. With her own screen, and her captain codes, safely in Somers' hands she used his, one by one she pulled up each station and made sure they were green. She pulled up the chaff firing subroutine and increased its speed. What once fired chaff every forty-five to sixty seconds would now do so every fifteen to thirty. The armoury would be scrambling but better a few moments of hell then no more moments ever.

"Hera'sun: you need to give them everything you've got; anything to slow them down." The little Monastica nodded. Cantor turned to her XO. "You ready?"

He nodded. Cantor thumbed on her radio. "Engineering: I'm going to need maximum burn."

The *Mojave*'s engines flared up as the ship bolted out from behind cover. The forward guns came about to the smaller Viatos ship, a frigate Cantor assumed, and opened fire, the cannons ripping through the midnight like glowing a ball of death. It crashed against the frigate's shields and splattered, like eggs on a brick wall. The *Mojave*'s twin cannons alternated fire, slamming ball after ball of weapon's fire against the alien defense barrier, as the gun unleashed an unending fury of brightly coloured energy bolts into the space between them. The *Mojave*'s engines burned brightly as they rocketed across the moon's airspace.

Hera'sun's fingers moved like a blur. The battle sounds falling behind the rapid click of her system's keys. She was throwing every trick she knew at the Viatos, filling their sensors with ghost ships, illusionary planets, phantom starfighters and good old fashion static. She didn't know how effective her attempts were, their systems could be miles above their own and could easily ignore such rudimentary feints, but until she knew better she'd keep trying.

Cantor looked down at her command screen. The frigate was manoeuvring towards her. The alien frigate, which looked as mangled as their ground forces, opens up their guns, unloading all barrels onto the escaping ship. Some shots went wide, other missed completely and some guns seems to spin or twitch as they fought to lock on, a side effect of the constant barrage of chaff littering the heavens, but most seem to find the Mojave just fine. The bolts, crashing against the shields, sounded like the endless rain an aluminum roof, a constant twang that resonated throughout the ship. The bigger of the two vessels, the cruiser, stood guard at the Trent-gate blocking their exit.

"Morrison: All guns on the cruise," she ordered. She looked at her XO with a wicked grin. "Hit the bug guy with everything our sisters have to offer."

All gun turned on their axels, moving away from the

frigate and aiming at the large cruise. Like dozens of stars lighting up for the first time the guns sparkled as they opened fire, pouring volley after volley of energy bolts into the larger ship. From behind, like creature rising from the grave, the two dead ships came to alive and opened fire; the *Marseille* pumping an ungodly amount of rounds into space and the *Norway* attacking with the full might of an HEF battleship. The frigate called off its pursuit, pulling away and circling back towards the *Norway*, its guns opening fire on the dead ship, but the cruiser panicked. As the weapons fire tore through its shields and collided with its hull the cruiser started to run, pulling away from the gate and retreating into space, but Cantor's surprise has already taken its toll. The ship had barely cleared the gate when it came to a halt.

"I'm reading familiar energy signatures," Hera'sun cried out. Her sensors were lighting up in the same fashion the Italy's were. "It's going to detonate!"

"Get us out of here!"

The Trent-gate roared to life in a flurry of colours as it tore open a hole in reality. The *Mojave* entered the alternate reality of warp, crossing over as the cruiser fell apart. It separated into dozens of smaller ships before roared alive and rocketed away. Cantor stood firm until the midnight of space vanished and all that was left were the prismatic colours of warp. She thumbed on the radio and started broadcast across the ship.

"This is the captain," she said carefully. "You may

stand down. We are secure in the warp. Split into readiness shift. We're holding position for eight hours until the fleet arrives. We may not retake the moon tonight but if any ship can get off that planet it's our duty to make sure they get home."

She thumbed off the radio and finally allowed herself to sit. She had her soldiers on the ground and she'd left them there. It was dangerous and it was risky but it was undeniably the right choice. Her marines had a chance to do some good, to save some lives on the planet; she just had to make sure that when they were done, she was there to get them back.

CHAPTER FOURTEEN
Pherca Moon Invasion +6:45 hours

Her boots hit the ground with a firm thud, dust flowing up on impact. This wasn't the hull of a ship or concrete; this was good old fashion dirt and grass beneath her feet. For the first time in a very long time, Major Allana Guiver was planetside. It wasn't Earth, far from it, but for now it would do.

Her firearm snapped up to her shoulder. The Hexco P7 carbine rifle was new to her but it felt familiar. She moved on instinct, carefully honed after countless battles, as she scanned the landing zone for hostile contact. Even above the humming roar of the shuttle the echo of fire fights could be heard on the horizon. The battle would reach them, an inevitable fact the further inwards she moved, but she didn't want to be ambushed, she didn't want to be surprised.

One by one Bungee squad stepped off the shuttle, their weapons up scanning the rooftops and windows, alley and streets. The last Marine called out as he stepped off the shuttle. Guiver clicked on her comms and radioed back to the shuttle. "Pigeon this is Bungee Actual. We are all clear. Get out of here and stay low."

"Roger that Actual."

"Keep your IFF offline." Guiver ordered. "Actual out."

The wind picked up as the shuttle powered up its thrusters, with a roar it took off, soaring up above the ground. Its pilot, Sub-Lieutenant Cole, kept it at building height. Without fire support open air was the most dangerous place. Cole would have to find a place to hide. The shuttle soared off, swerving through buildings like a suicidal game of bowling where if you hit the pins you died. Guiver reached for her watch and stared the timer.

"Eight hours and counting, countdown starts now." Guiver gave her platoon, the first she'd commanded in a couple lifetimes, a look. She cocked her head slightly, the familiar mass of her helmet weighing on her neck. "We have two clicks to the first sentry gun so we got to get moving. Branford: take us out."

"Thibodeau's taking point and Campbell pull up the rear." His orders came quick and concise. "Link up specs."

Allana reached up to glasses she wore on her face and thumbed them on. A flurry of data flashed before her eyes; she saw area maps, platoon locations and estimated ammunition counts for each weapon. Each member of Bungee wore these glasses, the Marines standard TBC-65 combat-specs. They enacted heads-up display of ally forces, estimated enemy locations, GPS maps, waypoint guidance system and even targeting assistance. They linked into the radios and if need be they could call down intel from a ship above. The glasses were new to Allana but the concept was not. They existed back in her day but the system was a great deal larger and part of a helmet. She held up her right fist, her thumb becoming the moveable pointer, and she began to move the data around. She closed the weather app; she didn't need that, and minimized the ammo count. She shrunk the map, moving it to the top corner, and disabled the platoon tracker. She could reactivate any of these functions with a simple thought and a blink of the eye. It felt like owning a new computer and changing the settings, she wanted it set up just the way she liked it.

There she was saying it again. She had to stop with all that back in her day.

"Take us out Thibodeau." As the platoon moved the sentry gun's coordinates appeared the map, the guidance system calculating and appropriate route.

Guiver watched the buildings as Bungee marched into Nova Kingston. There were skyscrapers with dozens of floors, streets lined with cars and stores on each block. She smirked as she saw a hole in the wall dry cleaners with a sign written in script she couldn't read. The Pherca Moon wasn't Earth but it was damn close facsimile.

Guiver cradled her rifle as she walked, most of the platoon did, but with each sound they heard, the echo of a gunshot or otherwise, their weapons would jump to their shoulders and the platoon would leap to action. They'd drop to one knee, move to cover and scan for a threat. They were not soldiers, there weren't any soldiers left in the verse, they were Marines. They were the infantry backbone of the humanity's naval fleet and they were good, damn good. They knew how to move, they knew how to fight and they knew how to work as a team but somehow despite all that they didn't feel like the army

Major Allana Guiver: the last solider in the verse.

As they walked through the streets the damage was incredible. The attack had been carefully coordinated, the ships firing on the city first from orbit then attacking with their waves of diamond shaped starfighters. Buildings were broken and busted, scarred with burn marks of alien gunfire. All that happened before the Viatos launched their ground attack, before they invaded with their infantry.

Thibodeau's French accent came across the radio. "Objective in sight."

Guiver ran up to the front, crouching beside Thibodeau. The AS pointed to the black skyscraper ahead. It was a daunting black building with few windows. It didn't glimmer in the sun like the glass exterior of the high class skyscrapers; it was a black monolith meant to look to scary. High atop the menacing structure was a quad-cannon turret bigger than most starfighters. It had barrels three meters long and as wide as a man.

"You see anything?"

Thibodeau shook her head. "Non. I haven't seen any patrols or civilians."

Guiver waved up Branford and whispered her plan. She put Branford with Campbell and the civilian in the rear while she took the rest in to clear the building. The PO nodded and scurried back. Guiver rose to her feet and leaded her team forwards.

There is that moment when a platoon commander leads her units inwards, where they cross that patch of land between a nice convenient area full of cover into an open patch with nowhere to hide. It's a moment where even the most experienced soldiers find themselves holding their breath, and for those so inclined, praying. While in an open patch if the enemy opened fire there was no surviving.

Guiver pressed against the sentry tower and exhaled a breath she didn't even realize she was holding. She signalled for a door breach and quickly took position. Thibodeau pushed her rifle around her back, the weapon still hanging from the sling around her neck, and pulled out her datapad. With a couple taps she had her lock picking app running. She waved the pad over the keypad and smirked as the electronic tumblers fell into place. Using her fingers she counted down from three. As the final finger fell Thibodeau punched the door key. The door open and Guiver stormed in.

Guiver led the way like she always did. Her rifle was the first one in and the others followed. They entered the ground floor in a single file but fanned out like a deck of cards being dealt. One by one they would peel off from the line and ducked into a side room, checking it for hostiles and aliens. With each room secure they called out clear as loudly and sharply as possible. In minutes the entire base floor was checked and the elevator secured. Guiver called in Branford and led Bungee up, riding the elevator to the roof, to the guns. As the doors opened onto the Sentry roof Guiver pointed to the gun's targeting computers.

"Okay, Doctor, get it working." Doctor Bristol Tsia nodded as she dashed to the console.

The sentry guns were a multi-linking defence system spread out across the moon. A hostile could take one of the dozens of guns down and the rest could still operate; at least that was the plan. Somehow the Viatos had taken down the entire system without destroying a single one and it was Guiver's job to get them up and running. They were years upon years beyond anything she was familiar with but that's why she the Doctor here. If it was up to her she would have left the civilian on the ship, safe and sound, but she had no other choice.

"Hostiles in sight." Major Guiver clicked her comm. and dashed to the ledge of the balcony. Leading Seamen Devin Campbell knelt by the buildings edge, a sniper rifle in his arms, as he aimed downwards. She pulled a pair of binoculars from her vest and gazed down upon the approaching threat.

Her magnified vision fell on the two grey humanoid forms that acted as the Viatos infantry. They were designated as husks but they looked like abomination of nature with weary eyes. "Just the two?"

"Just the two." Campbell repeated.

"Can't let them call for backup." Guiver explained. "Drop them both."

The rifle gave a loud crack and two blocks away, walking on the street below, a husk dropped to the ground, the top of its skull missing. Its partner's skull followed suit as a second crack dissipated into an echo.

"Sierra Hotel, Campbell." Guiver congratulated. She paused, cocked her head slightly, and eyed the long ranged rifle. "Where the hell did you get a sniper rifle?"

He pointed to the far door. "Each sentry gun has a small armoury within it. These guns are secure military points. You could lock down and hold out for a while in one of these buildings."

Guiver walked over to the armoury and shoved the door open. Campbell wasn't lying. This room was filled with grenades, explosives, ammunition and a wall full of hanging weapons. It was like Christmas for gun nuts. "Load up." She called out, "Make sure you have grenades, plastic explosives and lots of ammo."

One by one Bungee platoon came into the room, doing as she did and pocketed ammo and explosives into their vests and belts. Guiver still had a long way between here and the Paick Starport, they would need every round and every bomb to get there. He put her hand up as Campbell starting loading up on sniper rounds. "You're keeping the sniper rifle?"

"Ditching the P7 for it and a grabbing a SMG, ma'am."

"Are you any good with it?" Having a sniper would be beneficial as long as they knew what they were doing.

"Aye." Leading Seaman Devin Campbell was big man with dark skin and muscles in places where most people barely had skin. He was a walking tank who looked frightening while unarmed and just plain terrifying holding a firearm. "I'll do you proud, ma'am."

"It's not a virus," Bristol called out. "The guns are just being jammed."

Guiver reached up and clapped Campbell on the shoulder before crossing the floor towards the civilian doctor. "Explain."

Bristol looked at the solider as she approached. She pointed to her datapad with her finger. "We thought the sentry system had been shut down with a virus but every gun is up and running. They can't target anything because their sensory system is being blocked."

"Can you fix it?"

"I can fix this one, it'll only take five minutes, but the rest will still be offline."

"So we'd have to go gun to gun to fix them all?" Branford asked

Bristol just shook her head. "I'm tracing the blocking signal to its starting point." She pointed to a second sentry gun on the display. "We stop it there and the signal will stop broadcasting. The guns will fire normally."

"Until they lock them down again," Guiver frowned. She glanced at the Petty Officer. "How many starfighters could a gun like this take out before they blow it up?"

"Ten, fifteen maybe but all it takes is one lucky shot from the Viatos and this gun goes down."

"Leave this gun then. We'll head to the origin gun and turn them all on at once." Her map came alive as it calculated the best route. The next gun was three clicks away. "All right, ramblers. Let's get ramblin'."

Ten minutes later, and two blocks passed the headless infantry, Thibodeau led Bungee platoon into a small residential area. There was no suburbia on the Pherca moon, at least not like there used to be on Earth, the closest thing they had look like big city duplexes or small apartment buildings pressed together. Thibodeau pointed to a parking garage. "We can probably find a ride in there. It'll cut down on this walking."

Guiver tried to keep her attention on Thibodeau, slowly creeping to the parking's entrance, but found her notice pulled by the distortion in her combat specs. In the top left corner the line, normally flat, was bouncing like child's line graph as static came in through her comms. With a frustrated grunt she thumbed off the specs completely. She'd look at them later, when they weren't trying to clear a potential deathtrap.

"What's wrong?" Tsia asked. Guiver looked at the

civilian doctor and shook her head. She opened her moth to answer; she spoke the words but Bristol couldn't hear a single one, she only heard the explosion. A ball of fire ignited by the parking entrance and pitched Thibodeau into the air, flying backwards. They appeared next, the Viatos infantry high atop the buildings with their weapons aimed down at Bungee.

Then they opened fire.

CHAPTER FIFTEEN
Pherca Moon Invasion +7:15 hours

The moment she saw the husks with their green glowing eyes her mind started racing. Dr. Bristol Tsia had been in a firefight before - she had been in a couple - but never like this, never as part of a unit. But before the first solution percolated in her mind she felt the weight of Guiver's body on her, pushing her out of the way and tackling her into the side of a car. Tsia was quick on her feet but the Major was quicker.

Bungee unit dove for cover as the alien energy bolts rained down from above. Each bolt scorched the pavement as it made contact, leaving little but a burnt black mark. Guiver rolled onto her back, her rifle in her hand, and fired across the street. Her bolts shot upwards, moving in bursts of three, and up towards the roof. As her burst ripped through the grey body Guiver rolled to her feet, her rifle pivoting toward a second target, its barrel roaring to life as she fired another burst. Guiver's practised eyes quickly scanned the battlefield. Thibodeau lay on the ground, the explosion having pitched her backwards into the air, while the rest of Bungee was scattered and forced behind whatever cover they could find, returning fire whenever possible. Experience had taught Guiver that there was only two ways to survive an ambush; the first was to just avoid it, the second was to react fast. Avoiding a fight had never worked for Guiver but being fast was the Major's forte.

"Branford: I need an exit," she bellowed between burst of fire. "Campbell: get Thibodeau. Everybody else: covering fire!"

Bungee rose as one, the barrels of every weapon lighting up as they fired upwards. Nobody wanted to be on lower ground in a firefight but if it was unavoidable then all that was left was to push them back until they couldn't see you anymore. The HEF fire ripped through two husks and forced the rest back. Branford grabbed a grenade from his belt, popped the pin and lobbed it onto the roof. "Frag out."

Debris rained down above as the grenade detonated. Campbell, with his rifle slung over his shoulder, drew his SMG and bolted toward the French Marine. The SMG, a dual-handle JVC-DC9, roared to life with a squeeze of the finger. He was doing the dangerous work, bolting across the open field in a firefight, but Campbell never thought twice. Thibodeau was down and she needed help. He slid in beside her, his DC9 never budged as he checked her pulse. She was unconscious but her pulse was still strong. He grabbed her by her armpits and pulled, dragging her across the street to cover.

"Over here! I have an exit." Guiver spun her head around to the screaming solider. OS Winters was standing before an apartment building with its door blown open.

"Smoke out." The barrel of Guiver's P7 paused for the briefest moment as Guiver pulled a smoke grenade from her belt, popped the pin and lobbed it into the street. Smoke poured from the green canisters and rose into the air. "Retreat!"

One by one the squad, under cover of smoke, made a dash for the door. Guiver waited by the door until the last marine entered. It was Guiver's rule. She was the first one off the shuttle and the last one on it. She called out Branford's name as she stepped inside.

"The floor is clear." He reported, "I have Keiser by the stairs, Winters by the door and Tsia getting Thibodeau on her feet."

"We've got two minutes tops. We need a way out of here." Guiver pulled out her datapad. She needed a full map, more than her specs could show at once. "They'll be tracking us in no time. Where does that leave us?"

"It means open streets are too dangerous right now."

"We could building-hop." Guiver glanced up at the young seaman by the door, a skinny blonde hair kid who looked sixteen but was actually twenty-three years old. His name was Ordinary Seaman Jacob Winters. He had one of those eternally young faces that made people jealous. "I grew up here, ma'am. There are pedways that connect everything – indoor corridors that move from building to building. Damage aside, it's almost possible to move from one side of downtown to the other without stepping outside."

Guiver eyed Branford. "It'll slow us down but until we can shake those husks it will keep us out of sight from those patrols."

"Sounds like a plan."

It never ceased to amaze Bristol how the men and women of the military acted alongside one another. A week ago none of them had met Major Allana Guiver, she was just another name in another history book, but here she was moving with them through the city building as a cohesive unit. They rarely needed to talk but they always knew where to move, how to act, and what to do. It was the military way. They taught each marine the same way so that no matter what division they come from, what unit, platoon or squad, they would all fight the same.

Tsia was trained to think on her feet in a firefight situation and she was trained to survive at all cost. The marines underwent similar training but hers greatly differed. Sailors were trained to survive as a unit; she was trained to survive on her own.

Winters held up his hand and the platoon came to a halt. The platoon had just exited another apartment building and cut across the street into a small alleyway. Guiver put the kid in lead, he grew up here and he knew the streets. He was able to lead the platoon with a greater ease then those relying on a map. He waved up the Major and pointed out. Two more husks with weary eyes marched along the parallel street.

"Anything else?" Winters just shook his head. Guiver look back at the PO. "Branford: silent kill."

Petty Officer Marcus Branford grumbled quietly. Branford spoke without words, moving his team with hand gestures. He put Keiser on the rear, Campbell and Thibodeau on cover, and took Winters with him. He led the younger sailor out onto the street, slinging his rifle over his shoulder as he quietly drew his pistol with his right hand and knife with his left. Winters mimicked his PO, his hands reversed. Marcus eyed the kid as his hands shook. Killing anything from a distance was difficult enough on a man's consciousness, doing it up close and personal was an entirely different matter. The pair struck as they got close, Branford's kill was neat and clean, the husk never felt it, but the kid's knife dove in wrong. The husk's body twitch as he withdrew the knife and plunged it back in. Guiver's radio filled with static as the line in the top corner bounced rapidly. She flicked off her specs as the Branford and Winters dragged their body's back into the alley.

"Drag them here," she whispered. "Doctor: front and center."

Tsia eyed the dead bodies carefully as she crept up. They were grey humanoid forms, thin and frail, who were eternally naked. Each body had thick veins that popped out from beneath their skin like wires wrapped around a corpse. Their bodies were void of any hair on their head, back or above their eyes. These creatures looked like naked burn victims with futuristic weapons.

"So what do you make of this, Tenuva?" Guiver whispered to the ghost of the past. She glanced at Bristol. "So what do you think, doctor?

"You know I'm not *that* kind of doctor, right?" Tsia explained as she knelt beside the body, her hands running over the sickly grey skin.

"Yeah I know but you have more book learning then the rest of us," Guiver said in a mocking tone.

"I'm seeing no sex organs but there's metal plates and equipment grafted to their skins." Branford pointed out, "And look at this rifle."

It looked like a plank of wood, flat and long, that was grafted to their right arms. The barrels were built into the end. The husks held the barrels vertically to fire-from-the-hip and horizontally to aim down the sights. It had a forward grip, adjustable scopes and small grenade launcher on the bottom.

"There isn't any magazine port. They have no way to reload." Branford pressed a small button on the plank rifle and stepped back as the weapon fell off the arm. "They don't reload, they just drop the weapon."

"That's nothing, look at the chest." Guiver pointed at two thin flaps on the center of the chest. She delicately grabbed them and pulled them apart to reveal a chest cavity. These creatures has no heart or lungs where most species did, instead they had an interior holster for an E-shaped pistol. Branford withdrew the pistol and quietly examined the weapon.

"Crap, we may a problem," Tsia cursed. "Look at their shoulders. They have an internal radio system. The PO nicked it when he killed his."

"Isn't that a good thing?"

"It is but the OS is left-handed, his blade hit the wrong shoulder," Guiver explained. "Depending on how quickly they can send out their location they may already know where we..."

"Contact: 400 meters." Campbell's words cut the science experiment short as Bungee squad scrambled for their weapons. The snap of the rifle echoed through the air. "Five remaining."

Thibodeau's rifle roared to life as she fired burst after burst into the incoming platoon. Guiver sent Branford to the rear and took Winters to the front. The duo slid in behind an abandoned car and beside the French marine. Guiver stared down her scope. A platoon of five husks, six to start, with glowing green eyes was moving down the street towards them.

Guiver glanced at Winters. "Which way?" The kid pointed at the building across the street. Guiver waved up the rest of the team. "Get ready to move."

Guiver and Thibodeau popped up from cover and laid down suppressing fire as Winters and Branford ran across the street. In military science, suppressive fire was area denial fire that degrades the performance of an enemy force. In short, suppression fire was to stop or prevent the enemy from observing, shooting or moving on their position. Every military that Guiver had ever faced, be they human, augments or even the savage Arau Pau, reacted the same way to suppression fire. They ducked for cover, took pot shots and tried to lay down suppression fire of their own as they try to advance. The husks, however, seemed to be playing by different rules. Two husks took partial cover and opened fire on the car, two more bolted down the street in a zigzag fashion while the fifth dropped into a prone position and started snapping off shots.

Guiver and company ducked down as gunfire past over their head. She glanced over at Branford, secure on the other side, and saw the same confused look in his eyes. The husks' tactics were asinine. They barely cared about friendly fire, they charged head-first into gunfire. They weren't afraid; they didn't fear death and they barely utilized military tactics.

"Deuxieme vague;" Thibodeau called out. Guiver pointed at Tsia and Keiser as Thibodeau signaled Campbell for a long shot. Everybody clutched their weapons tightly as they wait for the signal. "Allons-y!"

It took only four seconds between Guiver's signal and Thibodeau's but it felt like three long agonizing minutes. At the French marine signal she, Campbell and Guiver popped up from beneath cover and resumed their covering fire, their rounds filling the street in a storm of energy bolts. Keiser bolted first, his head kept low as he dashed across the street. Tsia scrambled after him. From the corner of her eye she could see one of the sprinting husks taking a bolt to the shoulder. It did little more than flinch and keep on running. The hard contact of the building wall snapped her focus back where it belonged. She slammed into the door frame, her stolen attention causing her to pull slightly to the right. She spun around, her pistol sights lining up on a husk sprinter. Despite it being nearly five years since she aimed a weapon at another living creature she didn't hesitate. The pistol's slide snapped back three times as she fired, placing two bolts in the husk's chest and one in its neck.

Branford grabbed her shoulder and pulled her into the building. "Floor's clear; head towards Winters."

Campbell's rifle loudly snapped as a bolt travelled from the front to the rear of the prone husk's skull. The make-shift sniper shifted his aim and snapped off another pair of rounds, dropping one of the cover-bound husks. "They're closing in. We need to move."

Thibodeau dropped behind the car and quickly reached for her pocket. "We'll need some cover, un petite detonation." She fished out a small bundle of plastic explosive and slapped it against the car. She slid in the primer and nodded. "Prêt!"

"Go!" Guiver's rifle lit up as she filled the street with more energy bolt. Branford emerged from the building, using the doorway as cover, and laid down some covering fire of his own as Thibodeau and Campbell bolted across the street. The Major waited untill they were half way across before sprinting after them. "Blow it!"

Thibodeau slid into the building, ripping the detonator from her pocket and slammed down the trigger. The car vanished in a ball of flame, sending debris flying everywhere. Guiver felt the heat at her back as she ran. The explosion would cause everybody to hesitate, even for the briefest moment and that gave the major enough time to scramble to safety.

"Keep going," she bellowed as she sprinted into the building, quickly moving from one end to the other. "Winters: take us out."

What few husks they left alive would be right behind them and with reinforcements. In their position they were sitting ducks; they had to move.

"Incoming message," Keiser called out.

Guiver turned up her radio. They had only gotten four blocks away from their latest ambush. "Who is it from?"

"Don't know, ma'am."

Guiver opened the line to respond. "This is Bungee Actual: go ahead."

"Bungee Actual I have an SOS transmission from Black Helo. They are under heavy fire and their retreat is being blocked by sniper fire. They are in need of assistance." The voice was that of a confident woman, someone who was scared but was keeping things in control. "Sending you coordinate and conformation."

"Identify yourself." Whoever this was they could be sending Bungee platoon into yet another ambush.

"I've got no official codename, Bungee," The voice replied with the briefest chuckle, "But people have been calling me Newshound. My identification is being sent with the packet."

"Got the data. Hold position, Newshound." Guiver flicked off her mic. The data flashed on her glasses. Black Helo was a HEF platoon and they were only three blocks away. They'd have to double time it to get there in time but it was doable. Guiver scrolled down the message until she saw the pretty young face of a brunette reporter. Major couldn't help but smirk. Were all futuristic women this good looking?

"It's Sarah Gamble," Branford murmured. "She's that reporter lady feeding the HEF ships intel."

"She's clever that one," Guiver replied. She looked at Branford and got just a nod in return. She flicked her radio back on."Newshound, this is Bungee Actual. We're on route. We'll be there in four minutes."

"Roger that. Rerouting Black Helo transmission to you now."

The radio came alive the coordinating calls of the HEF platoon, the background filled with the sounds of battle.

"Bungee Actual out." Guiver turned to her platoon.

"Let's move; double time!" The platoon took off in a run, Branford's eyes darting across his spec screens as they ran. With a flick of his thumb the data flew from his glasses to the Major's. She gave it a quick read before nodding. "Perfect. We're going with that plan. I don't know about you but I'm really looking forward to ambushing them for once."

Branford let our a small smirk. "It's about time we agree on something."

CHAPTER SIXTEEN
Pherca Moon Invasion +7:15 hours

LS Campbell pumped his legs as he bolted down the street as fast as he could move. OS Keiser struggled to keep up. They held their weapons close to their chests as they moved, circling around the firefight. Keiser called out directions as Campbell scanned the rooftops. He was looking for a perch, a building high enough to overlook the battle with a clear view of the trapped platoon's flank, and a floor sturdy enough to shoot from.

"Here." Devin looked up at the apartment building and ran for the entrance, the steel mechanical doors opening automatically as he approached. "Upstairs! Move!"

The sailors abandoned the elevator for the stairs; the mechanical lift was a deathtrap in an attack. To make matters worse, despite the little damage the building had taken in the initial Viatos bombing, the power grid was still shaky at best. For all they knew a stiff breeze could knock out the power and trap them inside. Devin groaned as he looked up. This was going to be a hard run.

Devin and Lief took the stairs two at a time as they floors passed by, they could feel their legs burn, their muscles aching for them to slow down and stop but their friends were counting on them and they would not let them down. They stopped at the ninth floor door and took their positions. They needed to move through the halls swiftly but safely. Devin slung his rifle over his shoulder and drew the small SMG. He grabbed the door handle as Leif took a step back, his rifle aimed square at the door. He nodded at the LS.

LS Campbell pushed open the door and OS Keiser went through it, his eyes looked down the sights of the rifle, his head and the barrel moving together, shifting as one. He looked behind him, then forward, scanning each corner, door, and even checking the ceiling. Once he was satisfied that it was safe did he give the signal with a crisp, loud, clear yelp.

Devin came in behind and gently tap Keiser on the shoulder, a sign to press onward and move forwards, and the pair quickly crosses the hallway, briefly stopping at each door to check for occupants. The floor was empty, the building one of the first evacuated when the attacks started. Chances were many were just trapped somewhere else, maybe somewhere safer maybe not but at that moment all that mattered to LS Campbell was that he wouldn't be jumped while he tried to aim.

The locked door at the end of the hall forced them to a halt but not to a stop. The pair took up the positions at the door, this time switching places. Keiser stood by the wall while Campbell aimed down at the door. Keiser drew a small cylinder from his chest pocket and pressed the red button. A long thin spike snapped out. It was a door spike, a skeleton key for the new age. When the doors went electronic so did the battering ram. Keiser slammed the spike into the door panel and waited for the red button to light up. As the crimson key came alive so did the pair of sailors. The door slid open, just like on the doors before, and the pair moved in, searching each room and corner to make sure it was safe.

With the apartment locked down, and the door secured, Devin bolted for the bedroom window. The majority of the windows glass was gone, the panes shattered on the first hit.Devin smashed out the rest as he took position. He pulled a table by the window and drew the rifle from his back, flipping out a pair of small legs for the barrel to rest on. "Grab you binoculars and start scanning for that damn shooter."

PO Branford kept his rifle up as he moved through the street, his barrel watching for husks. Thibodeau mimicked her superior as she covered his rear. He pointed to a small corner store, his voice crossing over his radio. He only whispered but she heard him in her ear loud and clearly. "We'll cut through that store."

"Roger that."

The pair crossed the street and up to the store's door. It was a bridging corner store, one that had a door on either side of the building. You could enter on one street and exit on the parallel one. he two silently entered the store and moved to the other side, their rifles taking aim at the unsuspecting husks waiting outside.

Major Allana Guiver waited and listened. They were a couple of buildings down from the Viatos platoon. She could hear the gunfire that held the HEF soldier in their place yet she impatiently waited. She had split Bungee into three groups, one to the rooftops to take out the snipers, one to circle around and flank the husks, and her group, consisting of Winters, herself, and the civilian. She eyed the civilian woman with concern. She had proven herself on the field, her aim with her pistol remarkable to say the least, but she worried about her going into an attack.

She waved her forward. "When we move forward I need you to keep behind us. You'll keep our rears covered." Tsia just nodded.

Guiver glanced down at her watch. She had 45 seconds until they attacked; she just prayed they were all in position.

"I got eyes on the sniper." It didn't take long for Keiser to find the shooter. He called out the coordinates and distance, Campbell adjusting his scope and sights as he locked onto the building across the open streets. "Something weird about these guys though."

Devin peered through the scope, the magic eyepiece

that allowed him to look past the street, across the open air and deep into the far off apartment. He could see the Viatos sniper as it shot down onto the city street, he could see each movement the grey-skin made, each twitch of the nerves and how each blink momentarily caused his eyes to stop glowing green. When Devin looked through this magic eyepiece allowed him to see the hostile sniper as if they shared the same room.

"Okay, I have eyes on them. What's the big deal?"

"Look behind him, look at his spotter."

Devin adjusted his scope ever so slightly, peering behind the sniper. When he looked up the grey-skin he understood. The spotter looked like the rest of the Viatos but the similarities ended there. They alien hostiles they had come across were swift, skilled dexterous fighters. They rarely missed, rarely moved without a purpose and when they did they had no fear. Most distinctly of all they all had green glowing eyes.

This one's eyes were grey.

The spotter didn't move like the others. They were sluggish and slow; each step they took was if they were stumbling across the world like an undead horde. Devin reached up to the scope and pressed a small red button. He was recording everything his scope saw. Major Guiver would want to see this and so would the science officer, the captain, and hell even military intelligence would want to see this.

Devin brought the scope back to the sniper and gently squeezed the trigger. The barrel exploded with a shot. By the time the Viatos heard the gunshot the energy bolt had already ripped into the sniper's neck and clear out the other end. The sniper dropped to the floor, its glowing eyes staring directly at Campbell before instantly shutting off. The sniper's body shook violently as it died but Campbell didn't even pause to watch. He adjusted his scope to look back at the spotter.

The eyes of the spotter came to life, the irises exploding with light as if a grenade detonated within its grey skull. The spotter didn't hesitate or even bother to look for Devin. It spun its rifle directly at him and fired. The alien bolt tore past his face, his head still intact by the grace of a few inches. Devin dove for the floor

"Get down!" Campbell's caveat was a waste of breath as the second shot cut into OS Keiser's shoulder; the speed of the bolt spun him to the floor, the wooden planks letting a heavy thud at the speed of his fall.

Campbell grabbed his rifle off the floor and ran for the door; he wasn't abandoning his fire team partner, he was trying to save him. Campbell couldn't shoot from the same window; the spotter would easily pick him off. He needed another vantage point, he needed another window. He paused by the living room window and clumsily aimed. It wasn't the most ideal angle to shoot from but this wasn't the most ideal position. It only took him one and a half seconds to raises his riffle, look down the scope and once again find his target.Campbell looked in horror as the Viatos spotter had adjusted its own scope and was looking down at him.

It was a race to see who could squeeze the trigger faster. They were two cowboys duelling at high noon, each reaching for their six-shooter and each looking to fire faster and truer than the other. Campbell shot first, his bolt ring into the spotter's leg and forcing him to the ground. It wasn't a clear shot or even a kill shot but it was enough to keep the Viatos from shooting.

Campbell tried to get a second shot to confirm the kill but the spotter had fallen below the window line and out of his reach. He lowered his gun with a scowl, every bone told him to get over there and finish the job but his training said otherwise. The spotter would radio, if he hadn't already, and he was about to be swarmed. He needed to get Keiser and he needed to move. Campbell returned his rifle back and went to retrieve the injured OS. He hoisted the injured sailor up and the pair clumsily moved to the exit.

Time was up.

Guiver rose to her feet and moved forward, Winters and Tsia closely following. When they were in throwing ranged the Major grabbed a grenade. "Frag out!"

They each grabbed a fragment grenade from their belts, pulled the pins, and lobbed them down the street. The pineapples, an old nicknames for the frag grenades, bounced along the pavement until their fuse ran out. Then they detonated. The explosions were loud and scary, sent shrapnel everywhere and, because they were unexpected, caused a great deal of chaos.

Guiver and Winters opened fire, their rifle rounds tearing easily tearing through the grey bodies. The two military warriors were quick with their fingers, squeezing off rounds in burst of three as one target after another quickly fell. Seven grey-skins fell at the skill of their HEF weapons. Tsia wished she could have added to their numbers but with only her pistol she was out of range from where they started. It would have been pure luck if she hit anything and she needed to save the ammo.

Thibodeau watched as the husks spun and opened fire on their HEF attackers. She had them in her sights, her fingers aching to squeeze the trigger, but she waited for the order.

"Almost there," Branford whispered. He was waiting for them to advance on the Major, to pull away from Black Helo. "Now!"

Her finger clamped down and her rifle roared to life. The glass door provided little resistance as the bolts ripped through the pane and into the husks. The Viatos fell, the alien infantry lacking even the smallest chance to retaliate or evade as the bolts tore through their skulls and spines. Thibodeau dropped one, switched to another and dropped it. There was no hesitation in the French marine's fire and no gap in her grouping. She just fired small, tightly packed bursts of death.

The HEF ducked behind cover as the alien fire ripped

past them. Guiver waited for a pause before popping back up. Her enhanced aim proved helpful as she ripped through the Viatos' skulls using shots that once proved difficult. Black Helo was still trapped behind a set of dumpsters, using wreckage for cover and quickly running short on ammo. Guiver knew this fact as did the Viatos platoon.

Tsia saw it first, the Viatos husk with its rifle raised. It was firing like the rest the only difference was it had paused to take aim. She could see the plank-rifle glow brighter as the green eyed husk aimed at Allana. She didn't think; she just acted. Tsia bolted for the Major, catching her in a tackle and throwing both of them to the side, hitting the ground with a thud. The husk's shot hit where the Major had been standing and detonated in a powerful explosion. The blast pitched Tsia and the Major them further away, their bodies skipping across the ground like stone across a lake.

"What the hell?" Allana cried out.

"Grenade launcher."

"Thanks," Allana whispered. For a moment time seemed to stand still, the lithe body of Doctor Bristol Tsia pressed against her own, the warmth flowing between them. The Major felt her hand rise up the doctor's thigh, her body tingling at the touch. "I...uh..."

Doctors, why did it always have to be doctors?

Tsia rolled off of Allana and grabbed her pistol. "I'll cover you." She scrambled to her feet and levelled her weapon at the approaching husks. The slide snapped back as she fired. Tsia didn't fire like the military, the pistol firmly secured in both hands, instead she fire with a single hand, using her other to brace herself when needed. Her accuracy was impressive, fine tuned after intensive training and the hell that was the war. Tsia could never hold her own against the likes of the Major but she'd give the Viatos a run for her money.

The roar of Branford's rifle paused as instinct kicked in, that sixth sense that trained soldiers seem to develop, that moment where they seem to know danger is upon them. Branford pivoted behind him, his rifle moving with him, as instinct told him to check his six but his internal alarm signalled a second too late as the swinging end of the plank-rifle smashed across his face. The PO crumpled to the floor to the husk's attack. Thibodeau spun around to aid her superior but caught the striking foot of a husk in her chest. She stumbled backwards and crashed onto the floor. They were reinforcements, a pair of husks that had flanked them from behind.

Branford was back on his feet faster than Thibodeau's eyes could follow, his foot striking at the alien leg. The limb buckled and the alien dropped down. Branford drew his pistol and popped two rounds into the second husk, one bolt burning the grey-skinned neck and the second through its glowing right eye.

The first husk climbed back to its feet. Its plank-rifle snapped against Branford's arm. The blow caused the PO arms to flare in pain. The husk struck again, this time with its fist, and struck into Branford exposed side. He winced as the alien fist connected, these creatures were stronger then he expect, their frail frame carefully hiding their true power.His body was sore, a fact he blamed on Major Guiver's cryo-awakening. The husk struck once more with his rifle but this time the PO was ready for him. He caught the plank in his hands, his palms stinging for the catch, but he didn't let go. The husk didn't hesitate; it just grabbed his arm, pressed the ejector, and watched as the rifle fell off its arm.

Thibodeau scrambled to her feet and grabbed her rifle. She watched the two sailors, human and aliens, fought. It could all be over with a single shot from her rifle but without a clear shot the fight had a better chance of ending to friendly fire.

"Secure Black Helo," Branford cried out, his arm trapped in an alien arm lock as the grey knee slammed into his side. "Go!" Ignoring every urge she obeyed. She turned away from the knock-down scrap and moved for the door.

Two more grenades bounced along the pavement and exploded, their fragments riddling the grey flesh with steel and stone shrapnel. sia pistol snapped off round after round, the sounds of gunfire pushing out like an unending echo, as she pushed forward alongside Winters and Guiver. Thibodeau flanked from the other side, her staggering gunfire cutting off their retreat.

Branford smirked as he twisted the grey arm, pinned it behind the creatures back and slammed the surprising firm body against the surprising frail wall. Branford was breathing heavily, this scrap proving more difficult than he expected. "What the hell are you?" He asked between strained breathes.

"We are the marching force for your salvation; the cleansing grasp that will raise you from perdition." It spoke perfect English with a hollow voice that seemed to echo itself. "We have looked into the depth of hell and came out the other side."

"That's the same bullshit the Kobolds sang," Branford spat. "Here to raise us and save us from our own savagery. You war mongering filth are all the same and you'll face the same fate that every enemy of the HEF has. You'll be crushed beneath our boots."

"We are the *Avalon*'s shadow, we are here to save it but you will not be there to see it." Branford opened his mouth to speak, to cuss out the beaten, but paused as the husk's body began hum, its vein turning bright red and glowing brighter. "Do you have a god, sailor? You're about to meet him."

Thibodeau fell another husk as she bolted towards the trapped platoon; her sights moving from one grey-skinned abomination to another. She pushed herself further and faster, muttering French encouragements to herself. Her years of training guided her body's action, firing as she moved. She ducked behind cover as the husks returned fire, their attention torn between her and Guiver's squad, the husk warriors cut off from their reinforcements and dying quickly.

She peeked up from her cover, attacking with a burst of three, and she scanned the area. She could see the alleyway, with the dumpsters and the discarded car, and she could see the trapped platoon behind it. Only a handful of husk lay between them. The AS thumbed on her radio. The long-range transmissions were being jammed by the Viatos invaders but a short-range communication, a burst transmission, might be able break through. "Black Helo this is Bungee come in."

Her rifle snapped another burst as she repeated her call. She glanced in their direction again, looking for any hint that they were still alive. She saw the delayed fire of a single gun from behind the makeshift barrier. There was at least one fighter left alive. She called out again over radio, her transmission falling on assumed deaf ears.

She popped up again, her rifle roaring once more, as she moved forward. Shards of glass, razor sharp droplets of rain, filled the air as the storefront glass was torn apart by a thundering explosion. Instinct kicked in and Thibodeau dropped to her knees and pivoted back. Her eyes widened as the cornerstone vanished in a ball of fire.

Guiver and Tsia dropped to their knees as the explosion echoed down the street. Guiver cursed loudly as Viatos guns followed shortly after. The few husks that remained used the human hesitation to lay down as much suppression fire as possible. They desperately wanted to retreat but that was proving to be impossible. This left no other choice but punching they're way out.

Guiver's eyes closed. A familiar feeling of guilt returned to her. Lying in the street was OS Winters; the young sailor's face missing. Where his baby blue eyes once rested was little more than bloody entry wound of a blaster bolt.

Ordinary Seaman Jacob Winters; another name added to the ever growing list.

Guiver's bottom lip quivered as she gathered what strength she had left. "We're ending this. We're going now," she yelled. The two women popped up and opened fire. From across the street Thibodeau did the same, the lone gun from behind the dumpsters joining in for a last hurrah. Seconds later it ended, the last of the husks fell, their low numbers unable to withstand the barrage of HEF gunfire.

Thibodeau was the first past the barrier, her eyes falling on the Latino marine covering the alleyway. Several fallen bodies lay around him. The marine spoke quickly. "Pick-up ammo and move down the alley. Your sniper just gave us an exit."

Black Helo hadn't been able to retreat due to Viatos sniper fire but Campbell and Keiser had solved that problem. Thibodeau nodded, scooped up as many mags as she could carry, and bolted down the alley. Tsia was next and after hearing the same speech she bolted the same way. Guiver was last, like usual, and gave the unknown marine a once over. "You the last?" Guiver nodded. "Grab what you can and follow me."

They moved swiftly through the city blocks. Stealth wasn't an option. Black Helo and Bungee needed to put as much distance in between them and the last firefight. Bristol has been in fire fights but this was nothing like what she had gone through. Her firefights were adrenalin filled encounters, flying by the seat of her pants, improvising a plan as she went along and most times barely making it out.

This was just nerve racking.

It wasn't when the shooting started that bothered her; one gunfight was essentially identical to the next. What she found so disconcerting was the wait between the fights. It was nothing but silence, a cold uneasy hand on her shoulder teasing her of the chaos to come, of the death that would soon leap out at her. The gap didn't bother the marines; they found solace in humour and jokes.

Every sailor was trained to fight, trained to pick up a gun and know how and when to shoot it, but a Marines' training went beyond that. Not only were their bodies molded for combat but so were their minds. They trained every day, all day to become better marines. They did fire drills, they were fired upon and they ran miles upon miles of ship every single morning.

Marines were a breed all on their own.

Bristol wasn't a marine, she was just following them. LS Campbell led the group away. He had an exit in mind and Guiver thought it best to follow. Bristol found herself impressed by the Major's actions. She was a trained leader but had no problem following a subordinate in a battlefield situation.

Campbell led them to a corner street and brought to the platoon to a halt. He took Guiver and Keiser with him and ordered the rest to stay. The three bolted across the street, picked the door's lock with a spike and vanished within. Minutes later and Campbell re-emerged and waved the rest in.

They had secured a small deli, locking down and barricading all exits except for the one they came in by. Guiver rested her weapon against the wall and removed her combat specs, tossing them on the table. Anger fumed through her as she paced across the room. She flipped a table with a roar and a pitched a glass at the wall.

Petty Officer Marcus Branford: another name for the list.

Anger wasn't helping. She forced herself to steady her breathing, to focus her mind. Anger just clouded issues; anger got people killed. With her rage checked and breathing back to normal levels she turned to the group.

"Who's ranking here?" A male raised his hand. She

could see the sweat on his dark black hair and on his ever tiring face. "Give me the rundown."

"Master Seaman Alex Reid of the 126 Marines, ma'am. We were to secure the North and Twelfth intersection but we were booking it back to HQ. They ordered a full recall." Alex's tone was a mix. He was tired and worn but still desperate to show how grateful he was for the save. Reid pointed from the AS to the LS as he talked. "Able Seaman Tanya Clay: she is the biggest, bad-ass ever. She'll knock you on your ass and you won't get up. Trust me. He's Leading Seaman Sal Gregory, our combat medic. Anything else Lieutenant-Commander?"

"No, that's good. Campbell: ammo check. Thibodeau: make sure all specs are linked up. Gregory: look at Keiser. He took a round earlier; make sure he's okay; when you done that do a once over on Thibodeau," Guiver ordered, pointing out each person. "She caught the dull end of an explosion earlier and I want to make sure she's okay. One more thing." Alex raised an eyebrow quizzically, "Don't call me Lieutenant-Commander again. I'm not a sailor, I'm a soldier. I'm Major Allana Guiver."

Reid snickered. Guiver raised a quizzical eyebrow. "It's just funny. Your parents name you after the legendary soldier and you grew up to be a fighter."

"I wasn't named after her. I am her," she explained. Reid gave a confused look. "I am *that* Allana Guiver."

"We pulled her out of cryo-sleep ourselves," Thibodeau explained with a smile. The French marine turned to Campbell. "I told you that we'd have to explain it to the very first people we met."

Campbell rolled his eyes as he moved from sailor to sailor. He did a weapons check and ammo count, and began to evenly distribute the resources to both squads.

"You're her? But how?" Reid asked.

"Does it matter?" Guiver asked. Reid shook his head.

Thibodeau collected the combat specs from Black Helo and started to link them up to the Bungee's while the medic knelt by Keiser and started to examine his shoulder.

"Clay and Tsia; you two see if you two can rustle up any food and drink," Allana finished. "Reid: you're with me. Campbell and Thibodeau, join me when you done."

Bristol stretched out her arms and her back as she watched Allana sit down with the MS. The Major had pulled out a data-pad and was pointing at the screen and discussing it contents. Clay slapped her back as the two walked into the kitchen. They cracked opened the fridge, raided the cupboards, and emptied the drawers. They exited the kitchen a couple moments later with armfuls of food. he doctor beamed as she listed off what they found. "We have lots of bread, sliced sandwich meats, mayonnaise, chips, some apples and juice, water and coke to drink."

"Coca-cola?" Allana asked in disbelief. Bristol just nodded. "Wow, I never thought it would still exist. After the first war they have the ingredients let alone a place to manufacture it."

"Well they do now. I think they built their own ship or something to make it on. The Coca-Cola Company is still one of the biggest human owned companies. The aliens hated us when we introduced them to the stuff."

Allana rushed over to the table and picked up the cold red can, the moisture cooling her hands. She smiled as she looked over the familiar white writing. This was a blast from her past, a sliver of what once was. She popped open the can and smiled at the familiar sounds. She sniffed it for a moment before closing her eyes and sipping the cool carbonated liquid. She could feel the bubbles roll past her tongue and down her throat, the rich syrupy taste sending a shiver to the back of her neck that quickly spread across her body. Allana let out a small moan and had a look on her face reserved only for orgasmic pleasure. For that briefest of moments Allana was home and she was happy. She lazily opened her eyes.

The entire platoon was staring at her.

She laughed at their confused looks and gave the only reply she could think of. "It's been four hundred years since my last one. That's a hell of a withdrawal."

She took another sip and looked back at Bristol. "So what, did Pepsi survive as well?"

The doctor looked baffled. "What the hell is Pepsi?"

Allana couldn't help but laugh. Here she was in the middle of a warzone, fighting for not only for her life and the well being of her platoon but for the lives of the entire moon, and only one thing came to mind. The words broke through the laughter. "It looks like the future isn't that bad after all."

CHAPTER SEVENTEEN
Pherca Moon Invasion +9:30 hours

Master Seaman Reid led the troops through the streets. The loss of Winters meant the loss of his home-grown farm-boy knowledge but picking up the remnants of Black Halo filled that void and added more man power to Guiver's fold. She'd gained three men but lost two. With every life she lost it was hard not to let the negative thoughts out of her head. She couldn't let all this grief overtake her; there would be time for that later. Right now she needed to focus on making sure nobody else joined the list of name she could never forget.

The Major fiddled with her specs, her hands fumbling the interface like a senior on a computer. She groaned slightly; after four hundred years in cryo sleep she was a senior on a computer. Campbell's video flashed up on her glasses and she watched them as they walked. When it ended she restarted it, lopping it over and over as she scrutinized each frame.

What were these aliens? Their eyes glowed, but only some of the time, they shared knowledge but without speaking, and they had weapons grafted to their skin. Were they a hive mind race? Things didn't add up. Her only experience with a hive mind was when the augments tried to create their own using a roaming wifi network but even with their low-tech response they still reacted faster than the Viatos husk did. Could they be a people of religious zealots? They moved fearlessly and detonated their bodies for their cause yet spouted none of the religious rhetoric.

Despite all indication to the contrary they weren't a warrior race. They had radios built into their shoulders, weapons grafted to their skin, and their epidermal wires laced with explosives but they were not warriors. They didn't move like soldiers, they didn't act like combatants, instead they moved like they had a distance from their bodies. Like nothing they did really mattered to them.

A low static began to crawl into her ear as the thin line in the top left corner resumed its erratic bouncing. She sneered, to no one in particular, and shook her head. There were many things she loved about the military, the life, the honour, and the duty, but the fact that their gear was made by the lowest bidder always bugged her.

"Major, up front!" Thibodeau call out over the static. "You need to see this."

Allana passed the platoon as she crept up alongside Thibodeau and Bristol. They were crossing a major intersection using the safety of an overpass. She ducked down behind the steel guard and looked down at the street below. Marching towards them, unaware of the

HEF eyes staring down at them, was a platoon of Viatos ground troops and it numbered in the forties.

"Jesus," she murmured quietly. The Major's hand snapped up and she quickly signed out her orders. Her fingers dance and her hand bounced and spun as she put Reid, Thibodeau and Keiser on the rear, Clay and Tsia in the front with her and Campbell on his scope ready to take down anything that look dangerous. But with a slow wave of her open palm she told them not to fire. They had the high position but forty versus eight still seemed like idiotic odds.

Allana withdrew her binoculars and looked down at the oncoming platoon. The grey-skins marched in military step, each right foot hitting the pavement at the exact moment, each arm swinging together. This was parade marching in the middle of a battle zone. This was insane at best and suicidal at worst.

"Campbell: check the eyes."

Campbell moved his scope past the first line, then the second and the third. He peered at their eyes. He nodded at the Major. Their eyes weren't glowing green like the ones they encountered in the past; they were still like the spotters were, before it came alive. "No glow, ma'am"

"To hell with this," Clay cursed. She slung the rifle on her back and drew a thumper. "We could take this platoon out quickly."

The thumper was a military weapon that fired anti-personnel burst of energy. It was a military grade grenade launcher without all the shrapnel. "Stow that weapon seaman! We'd be dead in an instant," Allana hissed. This marine chick was crazy.

"Major, you need eyes on the rear of platoon."

Allana adjusted her handheld lenses, moving up the lines of ground troops before stopping on something new. The platoon was taking orders from what was obviously a commander. Where the grey-skins were lean horrifying looking creatures, the commander was a seven foot humanoid whose blue skin was covered by an armoured power suit with a domed helmet similar to the armour marines wore in zero-atmosphere combat.

Allana ordered her troops to stay hidden and waited for the enemy platoon to pass beneath them. She was afraid to move, afraid to breathe, afraid that any noise would alert the soldier beneath her. It was a difficult task to wait and see when the enemy marched passed beneath, knowing that with each step they lost what little advantage they had.

Guiver celebrated the passing of the Viatos platoon with large sigh and silently thanking whatever other worldly force was looking out for her. Whoever, or whatever, it was it that was looking over her obviously like soldiers but still hadn't made up its mind on her personally.

She slouched down. Frail blue bodies in a powersuit leading a platoon of husks; whatever ideas she had about the Viatos just flew out the window.

Able Seamen Tanya Clay carefully clutched her rifle as she moved through the city's mall, ducking past the fallen rubble as they moved through the damaged interior of the food court. Major Guiver was launching a strike on the sentry tower and had sent her and Campbell to find higher ground.

The Major was taking Reid, Keiser and Gregory through the tower's front door, Thibodeau and Tsia were going through the back while Campbell and her rained hell down from above. Clay and Campbell climbed up a small staircase and entered a reinforced pedway that crossed the street into the mall's sister building. It looked over the entrance of the Windfall Tower, a large twenty story building that held the sentry gun high atop its rooftop. The two marines crouched down below the glass and scurried like mice across the floor, stopping roughly halfway through. Campbell withdrew the sniper rifle from his back while Clay flipped open a small panel and began to fiddle with the circuitry that lay beneath.

"So you're a sniper," Clay mocked as she drew her knife from her belt. She carefully began to strip the wires as she talked. "What the hell are you doing on the *Mojave*? Snipers stay within the corps, not put out on babysitting missions on ships."

Her question was crass, rude and bordered on insubordination but Campbell just rolled his eyes. "I'm not official just good with a long gun. I never took sniper school, I turned it down."

"I get it, you couldn't handle it." Campbell barely knew the woman and she barely knew him but she seemed to have no problem mocking him. "Not everybody can cut it."

Campbell looked over at Clay, his tolerance of her quickly dropping. "I'm a spacer, I belong amongst the stars not ground-pounding. So instead I went boarding party."

Boarding party were the brave - or psychotic - souls who would breach an enemy ship and try to disable it from within. Boarding party missions were dangerous; they had a high chance of being caught, killed or being trapped on the enemy ship when any number of horrible things happened.

The whirring sound of an engine filled the small hallway as the glass walls began to retract. The doors pulled back, giving them each a two foot opening from which to shoot from before stabbing her knife deep into the panel to stop the entire process. She laid her knife and her rifle on the ground beside her and pulled the thumper from her back. With a pistol style grip in each hand she cocked the weapon and primed the first grenade.

"Today you're playing sniper not boarding party," Clay sneered. "Try to keep up, big guy."

"That's *Leading Seaman* big guy," Campbell sternly corrected. "Get eyes on the target."

Clay gently placed the thumper beside her rifle and grabbed her binoculars. Campbell stared down at the husk platoon that guarded the door. They stood in formation, three lines of five, with five others marching around. They numbered twenty to Bungee's eight. Campbell moved his cross-hair from one husk to the other. He scanned the eyes. Two sets glowed green, the rest were dull.

They were in position and had their targets. Now all they had to do was wait for Guiver and her team to be ready. All that was left was his curiosity. "So how do you know so much about sniper school Clay? You're not one yourself."

Neither bothered to look away from their magnifying lenses as they spoke, they just kept their targets locked in their gaze. "No, not yet but I have been accepted. I was to be transferred there next week. I was going to master the training and become a first rate sniper, just like my brother."

"Where is he stationed?"

Clay normal bravado drained away as the topic changed. Her brother was not an easy topic, she tried to act tough and brave but sorrow was always difficult to overcome. "KIA."

The double click came over the radio gave them the go ahead, the simple signal acting as the key to free them from their bonds. "We're a go."

Clay demeanour changed. Energy and excitement flowed through her, transforming her into eager child. She grabbed her thumper and smirked. Campbell lined his shot and exhaled as his finger wrapped around the trigger. He gave it a squeeze, never a pull, and the first round fired off. The first grey-skin dropped instantly, the green light in his eyes instantly vanishing.

Campbell altered his aim slightly, placing the cross-hairs over the skull of a second husk and a heartbeat later and it joined the first with a bolt through its body.

"Go, Clay, go!"

"Boom-di-adda; boom-di-adda!" Clay spun up from her cover, angled her thumper upward and fired. The grenade was lobbed forward, crossing the streets below in a wide arc before landing in the middle of the formation and detonating, sending bodies flying.

Only a dozen within the formation survived, the others became fractured messes. The survivors climbed to their feet and instantly changed. All twelve husks moved at once, their chins jumping up and light exploded from their eyes. It was like the spark within the bodies had suddenly awaken and everything changed when they did. Every grey-skin - those guarding the door, the survivors and those on patrol - now had the familiar green light pouring from their eyes. They didn't know where he and Clay were but the LS didn't expect it would take them long to find out. The grey-skins turned as a platoon and returned fire.

Guiver gave her a radio a double-click and waited for the chaos. Seconds later explosions echoed through the streets as Clay's grenades rained down. She rose to her feet and bolted forward, her rifle roaring to life. Reid,

Keiser and Gregory were close behind, their weapons flaring to life as Bungee mowed down any grey-skin unlucky enough to move before their sights.

The husks scattered and returned fire, a pair spraying rounds as they charged Allana's group, while others ducked for cover and took aim. The four held their ground, using the fallen debris of crumbled building as cover; Gregory and Keiser filled the street with weapons fire as Reid picked off the two sprinters and Guiver aimed for the husks behind cover. With the husk's attention split between her group and Campbell's, Guiver gave her static filled radio another two clicks.

Able Seamen Thibodeau and Doctor Bristol Tsia dashed from building to building as they circled around to Windfall Tower. Thibodeau brought the Doctor to a stop at the tower's corner and peered at the tower's main door. She could see the ongoing firefight, the echoes of Campbell's rifle as a grey-skin snapped back while Guiver's weapon riddled the closest alien with blaster bolts. It took every ounce of willpower Thibodeau had to stop herself from raising her rifle, aiming at the nearest space zombie and filling it with blaster holes. She had to sneak around back.

Two more clicks came over the radio and the two bolted. They circled around until they reached the flat wall that acted as the tower's rear. All this moving as a unit, coordinated assaults, and infantry based combat was unlike anything Tsia had ever done. During the war she was sent on many missions but there were all done solo or with a partner. She was never an infantry woman. But breaking into a building, hacking into a massive super computer and shooting her way out, this was her comfort zone. It wasn't a highly populated comfort zone but it was hers. She was a simply woman with simple taste. She liked spending her nights buried in book and, occasional when the naughty urge arose, she infiltrated an enemy base and blew stuff up.

"Set the charge," Tsia pulled a small square patch of plastic explosives from her back and pressed it against the wall. She backed away from the wall and withdrew a detonator from her vest.

With a small chuckle as she pressed down on the trigger. "Fire in the hole."

It wasn't a big explosion with wild tongues of flames licking out into the air, instead it was a controlled explosion, a shape charge, designed to punch a small hole in the tower's wall while leaving the building's integrity intact. Tsia felt an orgasmic shiver roll down her back. She knew it wasn't the healthiest reaction to an explosion but she also knew she wasn't the healthiest women.

Thibodeau climbed through the hole and Tsia followed, returning her pistol to her hand. The pair quickly moved through the hallway, checking each room as they passed. They passed through the building's interiors. Windfall's long hallways were a maze but the pair navigated their way through and arrived at the tower's entrance. Thibodeau and Tsia took cover twenty-five meters back from the door and levelled their weapon directly at it. Bungee's assault would push the husks back into the building. The Viatos would use the tower as cover and protection as they awaited back-up. That push would send them directly into the line of sight of Thibodeay and Tsia. Movement caught the doctor's eye and pulled her gaze. A simple whisper from AS gave her permission to check it out.

Tsia saw them before they saw her, a pair of husks crouched by a pair of small screens. They were watching security feed and calling out positions of Guiver's men. She didn't hesitate, she just pulled the trigger. Two bolts ripped through the first husk and two more through the second. Both bodies violently shook as the light vanished from their eyes and the last breathes crawled out from their grey lungs. These creatures were horrific in life and carried the tradition over to death.

Tsia spun and bolted for the entrance. Her gun wasn't silenced; the gunshot would have set off every security alarm in the building; if there were any husk in the interior they all knew she was here.

"You good?" Thibodeau asked. Tsia just nodded at the marine, "Good. Cover my back."

They came through the front door, backing in as their plank-rifles fired into the street and directly into Thibodeau's line of sight. Their grey-skinned backs, with thick black wire protruding from the spine and wrapping around the body like a coil of wire, were the perfect target for any marine. Thibodeau flipped the weapon to fully-automatic and just let it rip. Bungee was running low on ammunition but she couldn't be frugal now. She was in an enemy stronghold. This was the go big or go home moment.

Tsia watched the hallways as Thibodeau fired; she could hear the scampering of padded alien feet approaching and she readied herself. She saw the rifle before the skin, her pistol snapping off rounds the moment they came into view. They were charging her in pairs or trips and she was dropping them like pins before spinning to a new direction and starting again. Spot, shoot, kill and repeat, always repeat.

Thibodeau's weapon went silent as Guiver pushed through the front door. She stood battle gallant, an unwavering force in the alien onslaught and Tsia couldn't help but stare. Maybe it was the way combat had changed her, maybe it was her weird tastes but as she stood there staring at the legendary soldier Dr. Tsia couldn't help but find the Major stunningly beautiful, even more so than at rest aboard the ship. Everybody looked better in their element and this was undoubtedly Guiver's

They secured the elevator and piled in, riding the metal shaft upwards. When the doors opened so did their rifles. Guiver and Thibodeau were the first out of the elevator's cabin, their energy rounds quickly felling the grey-skin that patrolled the roof-level. It took two minutes to check the floor and clear it of what few grey-skins remained.

"We're clear!" Reid broadcasted as the final husk was killed. Guiver glanced at the MS and gave him a nod. "Thibodeau and Keiser – secure the entrances. Tsia: to the guns. Everybody else: ammo up."

Clay and Campbell each slung the big guns on their back and grabbed their main weapons. They had to rendezvous with the remainder of Bungee inside Windfall Tower. They bolted through the pedway and down the stairs to the street below. They had four blocks to cross to get to the tower, four blocks that now were most likely crawling with infantry. A military force could hold up in a sentry building for days if needed, out on the street was a completely different matter.

They walked quietly, scanning each street and alleyway as they moved. Husks were everywhere but oddly enough they were not moving to the tower but instead they were moving away. Clay looked back at Campbell. "The hell they doing?"

"Regrouping," he whispered. "It'll take a strong frontal assault to pierce through those defences."

The roar of an engine caught the AS's ear and she turned to their origin. A pair of HEF jeeps, being driven by husk infantry, sped past them. A smile crossed Clay lips. "I just found us a ride."

Allana Guiver paced nervously as she waited. She didn't do well with just standing around. She was used to waiting, it was nearly military tradition – hurry up and wait – but she didn't enjoy it. When there was something to shoot, there were few better at it then her. But when the situation called for science, Guiver was useless. At one time she wondered if she should learn the science but quickly decided against it. Each person only had a small amount of free time in their lives and each person had to choose what to spend that free time on. While others chose to spend it studying topics they loved, she spent it hopping from one woman's lap to another. It wasn't that she didn't respect the sciences and those who studied it, she respected anybody who could do something that she couldn't, it was more that Allana knew she was out of her element when it came to the sciences and decided to spend her time at something she was very talented in.

"How mu—"

"So help me God, Major, if you finish that sentence I will put a bolt in you myself," an infuriated Tsia interrupted. "Asking me every thirteen seconds will not make me go faster."

Tsia grumbled to herself as she quickly typed on the sentry gun's console. She'd worked on systems similar to the sentry's before, multi-linking systems with a highly complex UI, but the system on the Pherca moon was steps above anything else. The moon used a fully automated sentry gun system that operated on a seven level sensor system strengthened with a HEF friend or foe codec encryption. Yet as long as the basic coding was the same then she had a starting point. She still had layers upon layers of system to pour through before she could discover the source of the Viatos block.

"Ma'am, we have an incoming message." Reid's voice pulled her attention. Communications were being jammed all across the moon; anything short of single kilometre was coming up with static. "It's coming from the starport."

Paick Starport, named after former *Avalon* Prime Minister James L. Paick, was one of the few strategic places not taken by the Viatos, with air superiority they didn't need to. Any ship that tried to leave would have hell fall upon them from the patrolling diamond fighters.

"This is the C.S.S *Casino Royale*," the voice came over the intercoms. Tsia was too deep in thought to notice Reid transferring the transmissions. The voice, a desperate man, pleaded to the heavens. "We are busting at the seams, we need to take off."

The C.S.S *Casino Royale* was a freighter. Reid didn't need to look it up, he knew by the name. All HEF ships were named after elements of the Earth that was. All HEF freighters were named after classic books.

"Is Newshound giving us this?" Guiver asked. Reid just shook his head. "Can we reply?"

"This is broadcasting across the moon but all transmissions are still being jammed. The only reason we can hear this is because the Viatos want us to." Reid said, his head shaking ever slightly. "We can't say a thing; all we can do is listen."

"Jesus, they're going to make an example of them." The thought just hung in the air. "See if we can get Newshound."

Tsia returned to the sentry's system as Reid worked. His fingers bounced off the air as his thumbed twitched and danced. Combat specs could be used by eye movements and blinks but for the more complicated commands he needed to use his fingers and thumbs over a holographic keyboard visible only through the glasses themselves. Reid called out over the military frequencies, channel by channel, as he searched for the reporter.

"Got her."

"Newshound this is Bungee Actual," Guiver screamed into her handheld radio. "We need to talk to the *Casino Royale*. They cannot take off."

"I've been trying. I can't get through," Sera anxiously replied.

"This is the C.S.S *Casino Royale*," the desperate man called out. "I'm requesting any air support in the area. We need to get the hell out of here."

The ships transmission faded out as Guiver yelled over the radio. Tsia didn't like being helpless and obviously neither did the Major.

"We're through," Reid triumphantly affirmed, "Go ahead."

"*Casino Royale* this is Bungee Actual. Do not take off, I repeat, do not take off." Her voice was stern and commanding but dripped with desperation.

"I'm full up, Actual, I need to take off."

"The guns are down. You have no cover."

"The starport is filling up. We need to get them off planet. I have six hundred souls aboard. I'm taking off."

Guiver yelled into the radio, over and over, begging for them to stop but the ship never replied. Instead the line went quiet. Guiver ran to the roof's edge and looked out over the city. In the distance she could see the *Casino Royale* moving towards the sky, its engines burning brightly as it propelled it through the atmosphere.

"Doc, those guns?" Tsia shook her head. She was nowhere close.

The sky sparkled as the diamond fighter descended on the carrier like a swarm of locust. The sky lit up as each alien fighter opened fire.

"Mayday, mayday. We're under fire." The radio came alive. "We're under fire and we need assistan—oh god! They've hit the thrusters. Mayday! Anybody in the area we need help."

Guiver angrily clenched her fist. The diamond fighters flew past and spun around and returned for a second attack. "They've hit the second engine. We're going down. Mayday!"

With the engines gone the ship fell to gravity and plummeted to the ground, crashing into the city streets in a ball of flame. Like a second sun the explosion lit up dimming sky. With the Pherca sun setting shadows had begun to creep up on the city, the *Royale*'s explosion had sent them scurrying back, even just momentarily.

"That was your final warning." A hollow voice echoed over the radio, "any ship that tries to take off will receive the same fate."

Six hundred souls.

Six hundred souls.

That number rolled through her mind over and over and each time it infuriated her more, enraging her to the point that she only saw red. With a roar Guiver pitched the handheld radio off the roof, watching it fall to the street below.

Six hundred souls.

She put her hands on the rail and stared down at the street below. She tried to tell herself she was doing all she could but somehow it was proving fruitless. All she saw was red and all she had was anger. What the hell was she doing here? Here in this future, on this moon, on this mission? She was a relic from a different era, an artifact better suited in a museum then a battlefield.

"What's the order, madam?" Guiver glanced back at the French marine. Thibodeau stood there staring at her, looking to her for leadership. They all were. Those she'd known for only a week to those she'd met no more than an hour ago. They all just stood there look to her.

"We follow the plan."She straightened up and approached the squad. "We'll wait for Clay and Campbell then we push forward. Ensemble will stay here and get the guns up while the rest of us make for the starport. That," she said with a point to crash, "is not happening again."

"Two vehicles approaching," Gregory called out. "It's Campbell and Clay."

Gregory dragged his fingers over the black jeep with a smile. "Oh man, I love these things." The medic was more than excited; he was downright giddy. "This is a v-Tol 487. This is the HEF ground-force heavy duty all-terrain jeep." It was a land based vehicle with four thick tires, reinforced plating and a mounted gun all in a nice green colour. "And I even like the colour."

Guiver's eyes darted from the young medic, Asian descent with black hair and quirky smile, to the jeep. It looked very similar to the jeeps she was used to, four wheels, five seats, a mounted gun and piss and vinegar built into the steel, but with that futuristic look that set it apart. She smiled at it. She'd always liked a sturdy Jeep. Nothing bested a Jeep, especially not a Land Rover. Why go for the British knock-off when the original would do?

"Why is there blood all over the interior of this one?" The medic asked, "is this husk blood?"

Clay just shrugged. "It didn't want to let go of the jeep. So we had to convince it."

"Good work. Let's mount up and get out of here." She glanced back at Thibodeau and Tsia. "You two going to be okay here?"

"Oui. I am setting up mines to protect the building's perimeter," the AS explained. "We'll have the building locked down and protected by proximity turrets. It will take an army to get to us, madam. What about you? You got enough gear?"

Guiver nodded. They loaded the two vehicles with as many mines, explosives, ammo and gun as possible. She knew she needed them if she planned on holding the starport for any length of time.

Reid spoke up and started assigning seats. "I know the city so I'll take lead car. Keiser and Clay, you're with me. Everybody else you're with the major."

Clay gave the medic a surprised look as they passed each other. "Never took you for a gear-head, Sal. What gives?"

"I'm not; I just met my wife in the front seats of one of these." He smirked. "Made my daughter in the back seat." The two burst out laughing and bumped fists.

"Stow it.' Ried said. "I'm driving. Keiser you have shotgun and Clay, you're on the big gun."

"I wouldn't have it any other way," she said as she climbed on.

Guiver climbed onto the rear jeep's gun and cocked the weapon. "Campbell: stow the sniper and take passenger seat. Gregory: hand him your rifle and take the wheel."

The six marines fell silent, the sounds of weapons being checked and occasional ready were the only sounds heard. LS Gregory powered up the jeep and linked in the Bungee spec network. Guiver's glasses blinked twice then came alive with a flurry of new information. Both jeeps were marked as friendly, the distance between the two flashing occasionally as well as the fuel level of both, a new vehicle-possible route and, sensing that she was the gunner, the ammo level and barrel temperature of the mounted gun. Even her ear pieces began to shift in her ear, emitting a low buzz that would dampen the damaging effect of the mounted gun deafening bang. With a final blink the jeep's designated codename appeared.

"Mako this is Grizzly Actual," Guiver called out. "You good to go?"

"Roger that."

"Then. let's ride."

CHAPTER EIGHTEEN
Pherca Moon Invasion +10:37 hours

The marine woke up slowly, his body knowing nothing but pain. He found himself on a concrete floor. He was in a room with dozens of bodies. All of them were human and most were HEF military. Some of them were marines, just like him, but most were navy. Sprinkled amongst the gaggle of unconscious bodies was the odd private military goon. He winced as he climbed to his feet, his eyes watching the door. He slowly moved from body to body, checking for a pulse and trying to waking up those who were still alive. Yet despite his shakes and a slaps they wouldn't budge. They were all alive but but out cold.

As much as he hated leaving them here he had to get himself clear, to get reinforcements and come back to save them. He crouch by the door and examined the lock-pad. He gave the keys a couple pushed but got nothing in return. Tempting fate he gave the door a push and smiled as it separated from the frame. These were electronic door with accompanying locks, if both were down so to was the power. The marine exited the room and quietly crept through the hallways. He was in an office building, abandoned by the human populace. He needed to find out where he was. He spotted two husks standing by another room, sentries of some sort, and look around for a weapon. With no traditional weapon in sight the marine whimpered slightly as all he could find was a splintered plank of wood. He crouched down and steadied his breathing. He had the element of surprise, they hadn't yet heard him – or so he hoped – but there was still two of them and only one of him. He'd had to be swift and silent because he wouldn't get a second chance.

Like lightning he struck, slamming his shoulder into the leftmost husk, forcing it to topple to the ground, and spun on the right-most, stabbing his splintered piece wood deep into the husk's neck. The dull-eyed creature gurgled as it crumpled to the floor. The marine turned back to the left-most husk and lunged, his foot catching the alien's face as it desperately scrambled to its feet. The grey body fell back to the floor. The marine grabbed the creature by the head and with a violent twist snapped the alien's neck. He let go of the body and ducked into the second room, suddenly understanding for why they stood guard. Lying in a couple of haphazard piles were dozen of HEF weapons, vest, and miscellaneous gear.

With a devious smirk he grabbed the first vest he found and pulled it over his torso, pulling the side-straps tight. He examined the small pile of combat-specs but wasn't surprised when he found them each either with a broken arm, shattered glass or fractured circuitry. Combat-specs were standard for every HEF marine and PMC soldiers, but one or two solid hits and they busted, let alone suffering through an explosion.

Explosion. The fire, the heat and the pain; memories of each echoed through his brain and his body. How did he survive the explosion when hundreds of others didn't? His head hurt at the thought. Pain seemed to ripple through his head only to bounce off of his skull and continued on a new path. He winced as he tried to put the thought out of his mind. How he survived was a mystery for another day. He took several deeps breathes and felt relived as the pain started to diminish.

He fished through the handhelds, one by one, until he found one - that despite its cracked screen - still worked. He booted it up and thumbed through the screens as he looked for the map. Normally he'd route directions to combat-spec, it saved the hassle of constantly pulling out the handheld to re-check your position especially in a firefight, but without one he needed constant access to his map. He padded his vest with his palm and smiled as his hand felt a familiar shape. God bless the marines. They trained their grunts to fight the same way, to move the same way and to pack their gear the same way. He pulled a roll of tape from his bag and quickly wrapped tape around the handheld and his arm. The device was taped to the inside of his right wrist. It was going to be a bitch to get off but he wouldn't have to worry about that if he was dead. Better a bitch then a body.

Next were the weapons. He grabbed a pistol, checked the ammo and slid it into his holster. He pocketed as much ammo as possible, and then some, before doing the same with the rifles. Next was a knife and grenades. He found the blade easily, sliding it into its appropriate sheath, but couldn't find a single grenade. The more he thought about it the more it made sense. An explosion would cause the grenades to detonate as well....

The heat, the fire, the pain – he remembered it all. Pain returned to his head as he remembered the feeling of the world around him crumbling atop of him and he recalled giving up and letting the black overtake him. How did he survive? Why would the grey-skins just scoop him up? Once again he tried to control his breathing until the pain lessened.

He looked back to the room. No explosives; as a marine he required a great deal of explosives to make himself feel comfortable. Without them he just felt – empty. He had to improvise. The marine scooped up a few extra rifle mags and laid them before him. With is his newly acquired knife he gently stabbed it into the tip of the rifle magazines. He stuck it in at an angle then pried the knife back like a lever. The blade sunk in about three centimetres before the small metal covering snapped off. He put the broken mag down and picked up another, repeating the process on the second mag and eventually a third.

It was a trick that every police officer, sailor and

spy knew but nobody was ever officially taught. It was the worst kept secret passed down from person to person. It was a secret taught to him by his marine sergeant and one he'd taught to his subordinates. The secret was that any magazine, for any weapon, was little more than a grenade. If you ignite a power-pack or magazine it would detonate; the stronger the gun the bigger the explosion. It was first discovered the hard way when an older generation power-pack magazine was accidentally hit in storage room by a misfiring gun. The pack exploded and took half the police station with it. Since then precautions had been created. Magazine manufacturers built a small metal covering on the top of the power-pack. It still allowed for a steady flow of energy into weapons without allowing an overflow to cause an accidental detonation.

He had just removed those protective coverings and now had three new grenades. He carefully slid them into his rear-vest pockets and scooped up his rifle. He quietly moved to the door and leaned out into the hallways; still silent. He ducked backed in and looked at his wrist. He punched in his destination and watched as the screen spun and shifted as it calculated the best route. It was time to go to work.

"Contact: to our left." Guiver's body reacted immediately as she thrust her body to the right, forcing the mounted gun to aim left. The targeting reticle on her spec locked onto the husks and highlighted each with a red box. "We have nearby friendlies."

"Get our boys out of there. Engage hostile." Guiver yelled. Anything else she said, or any reply, was lost beneath the roar of the twin v-Tols' mounted guns. The high-powered rounds ripped through the surprised husks before they could react, tearing through their chest and clear into whatever lay behind them. Three seconds later the Viatos platoon lay dead on the street. The gun ran silent, their barrels still spinning but no longer firing, and Guiver barked her orders. Ried and Gregory each stayed behind their respected steering wheel. Clay and Guiver kept their mounted-guns pointed at the street. Keiser and Campbell climbed out of the v-Tols and entered the now silent building. Guiver heard muffled cries. Moments later she heard the reassuring words coming out. Campbell and Keiser emerged with two other men in tow. They were dressed in black and had a symbol on their shoulders she wasn't familiar with. "Who are you?"

"Specialist Matthew Stark and Senior Specialist Anthony Hughes;" the senior of the two replied crisply. "Blackwell Security. Who are you?"

"Major Allana Guiver," She explained, "ED...er... HEF. What the hell is Blackwell Security?"

"They're a private security owned by Universal Crops Growth," Keiser explained quickly. "UCG grows food on moons and planets across the galaxy for the HEF, Avalon and the fleet. BS is their private military." Guiver raised an eyebrow. Keiser knew that way too quickly. He shrugged. "They've been head-hunting me."

"It's just you two?" The two men gave a distressing nod and Guiver could guess why. Get in, take rear but keep your rifles ready. We're making for the starport."

With everyone secured, the twin v-Tols roared to life and barrelled down the street. Guiver glanced to the sky randomly as they drove, her eyes catching the swarms of diamond-fighters spinning and circling as they patrolled the sky. If Ensemble didn't get the guns online this mission was going to end horribly. The moment they tried to power up any of the bigger ships the fighters would descend on them like a swarm of killer bees. Everything was hinging on the civilian.

"Grizzly Actual this is Mako Actual." Guiver responded with a go-ahead click. "We're coming up on the destination."

Guiver double-clicked her radio, a signal for I understand, and switched channels. "Newshound, this is Bungee Actual."

"Go ahead, Bungee."

"We're inbound on your location. We're riding in on vehicles. Requesting you put out the welcome mat,"

"Roger that. Sending you coordinates now; see you in a few. Newshound out."

Paick Starport reminded Guiver of the JFK airport back on the Earth that was. It was massive building, miles upon miles in length and had dozens of terminals.

Gregory steered Grizzly to follow Mako as Reid changed directions. The pair turned toward a massive set of hangar doors, Guiver's glasses instantly picked out three gunmen from the shadows, highlighting each with a red box. Guns were trained on them as they approached. The doors pulled apart, opening the hangar doors like a cave of wonder before Ali Baba, and the v-Tols drove in. The massive hangar, one used to store starfighters, was empty save for hundreds of random boxes and fifty armed men and women. Guiver could tell from a glance that while some were trained, most weren't marines, sailors or private military.

"Drop your weapons and stand down," an armed man ordered. Guiver released the mounted gun and stepped down from the jeep, her rifle still hanging from her chest. The man, a HEF sub-lieutenant, stared at her with his rifle. "Drop it!"

"Who's in charge?" She asked slowly.

"I am," a second voice called out. An older man, a full fledged lieutenant, pushed through the ranks as he approached her. Walking steps behind him was a stunning blond woman. "Lt. Kenny Holm. Who are you?"

That was the question wasn't it? She wasn't Major Allana Guiver of the EDI, the EDI dissolved centuries ago. She wasn't Major Allana of the HEF navy or the HEF marines, neither branch held the rank Major in their structure, but on her docket, the one they reactivated when she was thawed listed Major as her rank. This left one, albeit unorthodox, solution.

"I am Major Allana Guiver." She explained, "I'm the ranking member of the HEF army."

She felt the volley of confused stares aimed at her but she ignored them. Sub-Lieutenant Jeffery Quentin spoke up. "Um, ma'am, there isn't an HEF arm....wait did you say that you're Major Allana Guiver?"

"Yes I did and as of right now I have created the HEF army," she boldly said. It was almost unexplainable but the moment those words left her lips she suddenly felt better then she had in a very long time. It shouldn't have meant that much but to say she was part of the army, to have those four letters define her again felt...right. "And our first mission is to get these civilians off this planet. Now lieutenant I need you and Newshound to explain the situation."

"I'm Newshound." The blonde woman stepped forward with an offered hand. "I'm Sarah Gamble, reporter for KMH News." Allana took the hand and firmly shook it.

Guiver looked around the room and eyed the fifty armed men. "Is this is? Nobody else made it?"

"Any civilian that didn't want to pick-up a weapon was ushered into the starships outside." Lt. Holm explained.

"And we have about twenty tied up and locked in a back room." Allana raised an eyebrow. "They turned on the military populace, drew weapon and opened fire while others tried to sabotage what few defences we had."

"Sympathizers?" Holm just nodded. Allana looked back over the nearly empty hanger. "How did this happen? How did your military structure fall so quickly?"

"We're still piecing that together," Sarah explained, "but it looks like sympathizers turned on our high ranking officers."

"I worked for the marine regiment stationed here," Holm explained. "The marine Commander was attacked by his steward. The kid flipped out and put a knife through his neck."

"Killed by the OS that brings him lunch," Campbell winced. "That's harsh."

"Similar stories are popping up across the moon. The city's mayor died when his driver steered his car into a tree at 100 km/hour. The moon's Captain was locked in an office which was one of the first targets in the bombings. The head-sentry technician was pushed off one of the gun towers by his own 2IC."

The three looked to Guiver for a reaction but she had none. "So an alien race, that nobody knew existed a week ago, has supporters and sleeper agents? They obviously have a lot of money backing them." The three stared at her in shock. "What? What did I say?"

"Ma'am," Cambell said quietly as he approached. "Murders are not as common as they were for you. Almost nobody kills for money anymore. Hell, almost nobody kills anymore." Allana looked at her sniper in disbelief. He started to explain. "After we lost the Earth that was, and our numbers were a fraction of what they used to be our values shifted. Call it a survival instinct or call it a priority change but what used to seem like a good reason to kill another human no longer does."

"You're saying murder doesn't exist anymore?"

"I'm saying it is very, very rare. Man does not kill man," Campbell said. "It took us loosing close to a billion people but we aren't big on murder anymore."

Allana didn't know how to respond. Human guns didn't kill humans and now humans didn't even murder. She wasn't objecting to how humans had evolved, she was just surprised. Her race was quite adept at murder. Yet the more she thought about it, the more it made sense. Prior to the Second World War, Japan was known as a brutal and vicious military power. Then the US dropped Fat Man and Little Boy. The war ended, Japan surrendered and the nation's priorities shifted. The Japanese people forever renounced war as a sovereign right and instead aspired to an international peace based on justice and order. Those words were even written into their constitution. Guiver didn't know exactly how it had happened but somehow Japan's history had echoed through time, its message falling upon the ears a new generation.

Amazing as it was, this new development changed things; it changed everything. If murder was not common place then what made these people kill? What turned loyal sailors into alien loyalist and sleeper agents?

"Lieutenant: Assign five men to accompany my medic. I want him to give those sympathizers a once over. The rest of you are with me."

"Hold on," Quentin said loudly. "Are we going to just blow by the fact that she just called herself Major Allana Guiver?"

"I didn't call myself that," Guiver sternly said. "My parents called me Allana and the military called me Major. This isn't a trick and this isn't a game. I am *that* Major Allana Guiver."

"Trust me," Campbell said. "I was there when we pulled her out of cryo-sleep. She beat the shit out of me."

Holt and Quentin looked at each other in disbelief. A shocked murmur rippled through the fifty armed men and women. Nobody spoke because nobody knew what to say. Holt was the first to break the silence.

"You expect us to follow you because you have a famous name? You claim you're from an army that doesn't exist and you're already separating our forces for something dumb like examining the prisoners." Quentin asked. He glanced over at Lt. Holm. "Sir, I suggest--"

"I expect you follow me because I outrank you. Army or not I'm a Major and that's equivalent to Lieutenant-Commander in navy speak. So zip your lip, listen up and do what I say." Guiver turned to the room of fifty, "That goes for everybody here. I'm the highest ranking officer here so I'm taking charge. We will hold this starport and we won't let a single grey-skinned husk past that door.

We are getting these civilians off this moon and there is not a damn thing that those aliens can do about it."

The moment the words left her lips the moment she realized where she was. Fate was a cruel mistress. Even here, centuries in the future, fate had brought her back to Kiron Port. It was a different time, a different celestial body, a different name and even a different alien threat, but this was still Kiron Port.

Her and fate needed to have a serious talk.

The sound of an explosion ripped Tsia from her panel and Thibodeau from her screens. The doctor looked up as the marine grabbed a sniper rifle and ran to the edge. From high atop the Windfall Tower AS Thibodeau looked down at the street below, her rifle's scope magnifying her sight. She saw a squad of husks, of what once numbered five, that now numbered two. One of the grey-skinned triggered a mine, laid out by Bungee before their departure and vanished in the explosion that also took two others. Thibodeau lined up her scope and squeezed the trigger. With a bang that echoed through the streets her rifle fired, taking with it the skull of a standing husk. She readjusted the rifle and aimed at the last remaining husk. Its eyes glowed green but it didn't try to go for cover or open fire, it just stood there staring at the building, studying every detail, as a second shot ripped through its chest.

"If they had time to radio back," she called out as she scanned the remainder of the street, "then they'll know were here. Depèche toi with that program."

Dr. Bristol Tsia scowled as she worked. Why did people keep telling her that? She knew she had to hurry, she was hurrying, why did they think she wasn't? It was one of many reasons that Tsia preferred working with spooks instead of military; spooks were patient and realistic. The military wanted everything now.

She was getting close, the jamming tech the Viatos had installed was complex but she was unravelling it quickly. This job would be nothing for Hera'sun, she would be through this by now. She just had to try her best to do Hera'sun proud. Tsia glanced up at the clock. Bungee had made contact twenty minutes ago; they were at Paick Starport and were busy securing it. Allana's work was going to be for nothing if she couldn't get the gun wo--- there it was, there was the cipher. The tech was encoded by a cipher, an insanely complex code that made the already insanely complex program more so by encoding it. With the cipher in place things were finally started to make sense.

"What are you cleared on?" Thibodeau asked.

"Everything but I'm shit with a sniper rifle."

"Très bien. Give me your pistol." Bristol handed the marine her pistol. Thibodeau reloaded the handgun with a fresh magazine before handing it back.

"Holster it," she ordered. The doctor obeyed; only half paying attention as she continued working. The AS placed a handheld SMG, and a dozen fully loaded mags, on the desk beside her. "That's your main weapon."

A properly manned sentry tower could hold-out against a massive numbering force. The tower had a hole in its wall and Ensemble had not near enough man-power. They were two people defending their position against what could be dozens of husks. The building provided a great amount of cover and protection but she still needed to optimize her make-shift foxhole. The marine went about the room, placing assault rifles and ammunition at different points across the room. She place three by the front door, two by the unused desk that was acting as cover, one by the security screens and accompanied each with several grenades. By the ledge she returned her sniper rifle and placed with it several replacement magazines and a thumper. With firearms everywhere the two women would always have a weapon no-more than an arm's reach away.

"Drink this." Thibodeau handed the doctor an energy drink. She looked the can and frowned.

"You know these things only last like three or four hours. An energy crash is the last thing I need right now."

"If we're still on the planet in four hours then we're beyond screwed." The French marine explained. "I need you at full so drink up, cul sec."

Tsia just blinked. She really couldn't fault that logic. She popped the top and was greeted by a fizzy hiss. She lifted the can to her lips and started to drink. The sound of a second explosion filled the air. Thibodeau glanced at her security screen, the images captured by cameras all through the tower and its surrounding buildings. She saw the image of husks marching without fear into the makeshift minefield.

"They're here," she barked as she bolted for her sniper rifle. "We won't have long---."

"Yeah, yeah. I know." Bristol grumbled, "Hurry up."

Able Seamen Tanya Clay stood behind the v-Tol mounted gun and stared out at the street below. Bungee and all of its newest additions had spent the better part of the last hour preparing their defences. Guiver didn't let anything go to waste. She used whatever supplies and tools available to them and whatever ever the stalwart fifty had combined with the arsenal they brought with them from the tower to best secure their position. They laid claymores outside on the street, they positioned Campbell and the long gunners on a high sturdy perch and lined the doors with anybody who could hold a rifle. It was Clay's suggestion, however, to use the actual tools found in the warehouse to remove the guns from back of the v-Tols and bolt them to the second-story floor. They now looked out over the street and would fire from an elevated position. It would provide an advantage and Clay loved an advantage.

The mounted guns were mounted for a reason, they were freaking heavy. Every bone in her body sung out as she leaned on the gun. Lifting them up the stairs had required six bodies apiece and even then they still were heavy as sin. Her body hurt like hell and had no problem reminding her of that fact. Clay was used to pain; it was part of her life. Most people despised pained and did what they could to avoid it, Clay was different. Clay went looking for pain. It wasn't that she wanted to be hurt or that she liked the pain it was just that pain was the aftermath of the life she choice.

Clay was an adrenalin junkie. She liked excitement; she craved it. She was obsessed with the thrill that came when her life was on the line, when she risked death and when she was pushed past her limits. To the marine nothing beat the adrenalin rush and like a junky she did whatever she could to get her fix. It's why she went skydiving, it's why she base jumped, it's why she became a ship jumper and it's why she decided to become a marine three years ago.

She craved excitement but pain always had a way of hitching a ride.

But in moments like these, the quiet between firefight, she felt her body coming down. She stood up and shook her body, slapping her face on one cheek then the other. She took a deep breath and looked across the hallway at Specialist Stark manning the other gun. Matthew Stark reminded her of her brother, grizzled, hard and always enduring. He waved her over.

"You okay?" She nodded. "Here I have something to help keep you focused." With a smirk he reached into his pouch and handed her a flask. She didn't drink on the job but somehow, at what could easily be her last stand, it seemed fitting. She unscrewed the cap and took a swig.

Her eye lit up and her body sang out only this time in happiness. Any semblence of her brother vansihed as she felt a sudden burst of affection for Specialist Stark; hell, she felt like she could kiss him. There was only one thing in this world she loved more than her firearm and that was scotch.

God she loved scotch and this was very good scotch.

"Thanks," she smirked. "But don't drink too much. I need you lucid."

Stark gave her a seductive wink, "No worries, you've got my full attention."

Leading Seaman Sal Gregory waved over the Major. "I just finished my check. They all seem more or less healthy. Some have battle scars and twin neck punctures, I'm guessing defensive wounds, but aside from a couple bolt burns, most of them are injury free. This leaves us with one important question."

"What do we do with them?" Allana finished. The medic just nodded. "I don't like the idea of them on a civilian ship, who knows how far they're willing to go to support the Viatos."

"They could sacrifice themselves to take down a ship," Gregory suggested.

"Exactly, and I don't want to pull men away from the door. We're stretched way too thin as it is." This left one solution and not one she was overly comfortable with. "We'll play it by ear," Gregory raised an eye at the weird expression. "But as it stands now we leave them here."

"Ma'am, I...I don't like it."

"Neither do I but they choose their side and I rather not unleash loyalists into the *Avalon*," Allana explained. Her conscience argued with her decision, they could be brainwashed and she was robbing them the chance to be cured, but they came here knowing they could save everybody. They had to save who they could and she wasn't risking innocent lives for corrupted ones.

"Contact!" The radio cut through the moral dilemma. Campbell called out from his perch. "I see a small squad approaching – five husks."

Guiver clicked her comms open. "Snipers: drop them. We're not wasting valuable mines for miniscule foot-traffic." The air filled with rapid rifle shots and then silence. Allana walked into the main room and called out as loud as she could. "All hands: get ready, they know we're here."

CHAPTER NINETEEN
Pherca Moon Invasion +12:22 hours

Leading Seamen Devin Campbell kept his scope on the horizon. From atop the roof he could see the approaching Viatos forces, marching in their direction. He was on the roof of a nearby building, connected to the starport by a series of flimsy planks. Guiver had put three snipers on the roof as her eyes-in-the-sky. Accompanying him was Senior Specialist Anthony Hughes and Kev Hazeltine, one of the Stalwart Fifty. Accompanying them were six more of the fifty. They were led by Sub-Lieutenant Jeffery Quentin and each armed with assault rifles and a pair of thumpers. Their job was to wait until the husks passed beneath them and then fire down from above; their job was to mow them down.

Guiver had set-up their defence nicely. She forced everybody into one side of the hanger, and demolished the wall between them. The Major wanted everybody on the right end so she could dictate from where the husks would come from. They wouldn't approach from behind, there was nothing there. Paick Starport was on the edge of Nova Kingston, the very edge, and beyond the hangars were the runways. Beyond them were spiralling mountains with peaks jetting up into the clouds. When Nova Kingston was being designed it was done so to maximize farming space. To do this, city engineers pressed the starport as close to the mountains as safely possible. In the eyes of the military and the developers, and most of the inhabitants, the mountains signalled the edge of the Pherca moon's useable surface.

With the divider in place and the mountains behind them, the Viatos ground forces only had one viable direction to approach from, one that passed beneath the gaze of tall building lined up on either side of them. It was an inevitable bottleneck. Sadly with the wall collapsed and the mountains where they were, Bungee, and its newest additions, had no method of retreat save for the ships and that was only an option if Tsia fixed the guns.

"Contact: 700 meters," a voice cried out over the comms. Campbell stared down his scope. The W-78 Timberwold anti-personnel sniper rifle, the HEF standard, had an effective range of 1500 meters but without a kilometer long line of sight its user was limited to whatever he could see. For Campbell and his roof-perched snipers, their line of sight was approximately only 700 meters, 723 if he wanted to be specific. It wasn't anything to laugh at; the standard assault rifle peaked out at 300 meters. Being able to hit a target a full 400 meters before they could effectively hit you was always a blessing. The only frightening factor was that 400 meters was not that great of a distance. On the Earth that was, the record for the 400 meter dash was 43.18 seconds. That didn't give the snipers lot of time.

Campbell lined up his scope with the nearest husk, one of easily a couple hundred, and kept his rifle firm as Quinton's voice come over their comms. "The green eyes are the dangerous ones. They move faster, quicker and have better aim but their only ever seems to be a limited number of them. When one dies another grey-eye becomes green.

"Campbell: You're going to target the green-eyes while the rest of the snipers take down the grey-eyes." Campbell was the better of the three snipers; it made sense to give him the tougher-targets. Campbell glanced up from his scope and looked at the Sub-Lt. that stood beside him. He gave Quinton a quizzical look as the officer cut the comms. "Guiver and I were talking and I have a theory. I think the green-eyes jump from body to body. I want to see what happens if we start cutting off their escape bodies." He shrugged at the last few words. He had nothing better to call it then escape bodies. "If it doesn't affect anything we'll go back to targeting green first."

It was a hell of a time to test a theory but it made as much sense as anything else had today. Campbell returned to his scope and stared down the street. The husks were moving forward, almost in parade formation. "I've got no green-eyes in the front line." Campbell whispered.

"Then take whatever you can until you do." He replied. Quinton opened up the comms. "Bungee Actual we're good to go; permission to fire?"

On the hanger's second floor was a small table. It was set-up by a street facing window. Allana sat at the desk with a sniper rifle cradled in her arms. The bipod legs rested on the table as the butt of the rifle was nuzzled into her shoulder. Guiver's eye was pressed to the scope. Where Hazeltine and Hughes would be shooting from the left and Campbell from the right, her rifle was aimed out a window and directly down the center at the oncoming Viatos mass.

Standing beside her was Marco Nelor, one of the Fifty, with binoculars in his hand and acting as her spotter. He wasn't HEF or one of the PMGs, he was just a home-grown farm boy with guts, a gun and enough bravery to fight for what he believes in. He reminded her of a TV stereotype: fresh face, dark hair, thin and with a toned body from years of hard labour. He seemed nervous around her, stammering each time she spoke, but he was eager to help wherever her could.

On the first floor, Lt. Holm stood by the door with the remainder of Bungee and the Stalwart Fifty. The hangar doors were thick, as they'd learned while cutting makeshift gun ports from the steel, and could withstand quite a few hits from military grade weapons. It was the snipers, the mowers and the mounted gun's duty to stop as many husks from hitting the door as possible.

The Major clicked open her comm. "Doors: Hold fire until they reach the 300 range. Mowers: hold fire until they're beneath you. Mounted: Wait for the fireworks." The mounted guns could effectively reach the full 700 meters but Guiver had a surprise set up at the 600 mark. "Snipers: Take them down."

The street erupted in sniper fire, rapid bangs barely having time to echo as the next one drowned it out. From within her scope Allana could see the front line of husks drop one by one from sniper fire, her own rifle kicking back as she dropped grey-skin after grey-skin, but the husks didn't stop. The alien infantry pushed forward, ignoring the fallen like one would road-kill on a rural highway. They moved onwards, the rear ranks using the vanguard as shields. They reminded her of Spartans moving in a phalanx formation. Each warrior worked together and used their shields to deflect spears and arrows. The only major difference being the Spartans used actual shields and in lieu of other Spartans.

The husks picked up speed and pushed onwards, crossing the 675 mark. They hadn't fired a single shot. Allana moved from husk to husk, looking at of their eyes before putting a bolt between them. None of the husks had awakened, as she called it, or carried the green-eyes, as Quinton referred it. They were just sending wave after wave of grey-eyed grey-skins to their slaughter. Allana dropped another husk with the squeeze of her finger; she ejected her empty mag and replaced it with a fresh one. Seconds later she was staring back down her scope dropping the first husk to come into sight.

"They've hit 615 mark," Marco stammered. The snipers could pick them off at the 700 mark as could the mounted guns. The mowers, high atop the building roofs, and those on the door would hit anything at the 300 mark. The 400 was laced with proximity claymores to slow them down, but at the 600 mark was Allan's little surprise. Six hundred meters from the hangar door were twelve blocks of plastic explosive, covered by small piles of dirt, all wired to a single detonator held by Lt. Holm.

"Holm: when they hit 545 flip the switch." Guiver watch as the husk mass pushed across the 600 mark. She wanted to take as many of those grey-skinned bastards as she could with this surprise and unlike the proximity claymores - which detonated upon contact and would only be effective against the front line and those unlucky enough to beside them - if they waited for the middle of the mass, or until there were a larger number over it, it would rip through them all. "Now!"

The lieutenant flipped the switched and pressed down on the detonator. The plastic explosive erupted in balls of fire, dirt, bodies and red mist. Despite their dire circumstances Guiver couldn't help but smile. Clay let out a whoop of excitement and yelled as loud as she could. "Light'em up!"

With a deafening roar the two mounted guns came to life, their high powered bolt traveling at over 900 m/s as they ripped through the vanguard and up the husk mass. The husk bolted at top speed, each grey-skin moving as the exact same speed as one beside it. It was unreal. Guiver had seen a platoon run at full speed; she'd done it herself. They started out as one but they quickly staggered as the quicker took point and the slower fell behind. No two human ran the same speed let alone several hundred but the husk did. Each grey-skin stayed the same distance apart the entire run as they did the moment they started. No husk was faster or slower than any other. Their customized phalanx formation never fell apart as they sprinted, it just moved at a faster speed.

The front line raised their plank-rifles as they ran, the formation crossing the 500 mark within seconds, and started firing. Guiver assumed they were out of effective range of their weapons but effective range meant just that, the greatest range at which the weapon was still effectively efficient. Although unlikely, they could still hit something. This was another military manoeuvre Guiver was familiar with: pray and spray.

"Snipers: take the rear." Guiver, and the rest of the snipers, were no longer aiming at the front ranks of the mass, they left that to the sheer might and power of the mounted guns. Instead they used their greater range and started picking off targets in the back. Allana forced herself to fire faster and faster. Her plan had been going flawlessly but that was before the enemy returned fire. Everything changed when the bad-guys started shooting back.

"Câlice osti!" Thibodeau cursed as the last proximity mine detonated, taking with it only a single husk. The mines had proved to be less effective then she'd hoped. Once they knew the front entrance was guarded by mines they sent husk after husk into the field to root them out, sacrificing single troops at a time so that the others could safely pass. For the first time since Bungee left Thibodeau was glad that Guiver had taken the claymores instead of the simple mines. When a claymore exploded it fired shrapnel in a 60° arc and was meant for taking out large groups, her mines weren't fragmentation mines. They just exploded in a ball of flame taking with it anyone close enough to suffer. At least with Guiver the claymores could prove useful. She scowled as she stared down her sniper scope. The husks, now with clear passage, were bolting for the front door. Dozens were charging the building. Thibodeau clutched her rifle and fired down on the street below, catching husk after husk with blaster bolts, but for every Viatos husk she dropped, two entered the tower by the main door and god only knew how many entered by the rear hole they made earlier.

"Merde!" She switched to her thumper and leaned over the edge. With a loud echoing thump the grenade launcher fired a blast to the ground below. It erupted in a ball of energy tossing the now limp husk forms across the street. Thibodeau didn't give them a chance to regroup, she just fired a second time and a third, both blast exploding and taking several husks with them. Not all the husks were dead, some were broken or crippled but broken couldn't fight which meant broken was just as good as dead.

The French marine bolted for her security screen, dropping her thumper by the desk as she passed. Her fingers danced across the keys as the screen started to move and flicker. She could see the husk throughout the building storming their way up to her. The elevator was disabled; it was the first thing she did, which meant they were forced to take the stairs.

A screen flashed red as an internal turret locked onto a husk and opened fired. The proximity turrets were exactly as they sounded, turrets that once set-up and programmed, would automatically fire on anything that entered its range. Most marine squads had carried one or two portable versions but the ones in Windfall Tower were built it the building's frame. They hid in walls, floors and ceilings until activated, then they poured bolt after bolt into whatever came near. The Tower's turrets were all linked into the security screens and Thibodeau could watch every kill and gauge their distance.

Thibodeau felt a small sense of relief that none of the husks had made it to her floor yet. They were being held at bay by the turrets a dozen floors lower. The turrets wouldn't hold them for long. All it would take would be a lucky shot or a well placed grenade or rocket and the device was useless. They weren't meant to fight the wars for the soldiers, they were meant to be yet another weapon in their arsenal.

The sound of gunfire echoing over the city forced the marine into a run. From the sound and the constant echo what he was hearing wasn't a small skirmish; it was a full-on battle. The marine clutched his rifle tight against his chest as his legs pushed him forward. It was like basic training or battle school, all those morning he spent running with a rifle in his hand. They made every marine run like that, day in and out, to prepare them for battle, for moments just like these. His PO used to scream that nothing was more important to a marine then running. God, he hated it when that Petty Officer turned out to be right. It was worse than when every child grew up and realized that their parents were right and worse, that their parents actually knew what they were talking about.

The sounds of footsteps forced the marine to a stop. He pressed his body against the nearest wall and crept along it. He peered around the corner and spotted a platoon of husks approaching from down the street. They were the reinforcements; the alien infantry were strengthening their position. He had a chance to cut them down, to kill them here and affect the battle he was missing. It wouldn't be a big effect, the platoon numbered only twelve, but every husk he killed here meant one less for the others to fight.

He crouched by the corner and he pulled two

magazines from his vest. They were his make-shift grenades. He slid both across the pavement, both in the eventual path of the running platoon. Then he waited. It took only second until they reached his ambush; those grey-skins were fast on their feet. With a short burst from his rifle the marine fired into the first magazine and watched as it exploded. A second burst of gunfire ignited the second and the marine sprung from his cover. The two balls of fire quickly killed seven of them, his rifle roaring to life as he dropped two more. The marine's rifle seemed never to stop, the small pauses in gunfire almost unrecognizable by most. His weapon fire quickly dropped the remaining three. As the last Viatos body hit the pavement the marine slowly spun, checking each direction for hidden husks. If they weren't here they soon would be. He glanced once more at the alien corpses and felt a twinge of regret. Why did so many have to die? Confusion swept over the marine. Why did he care about the Viatos?

A wave of pain assaulted his head. The marine winced. He put the thought out of his mind as he tried to control his breathing. The pain lessened and the marine tried to regroup his thoughts. He glanced at the inside of his right wrist, his eyes falling on the handheld taped to his arm. According to the map he was closer to his destination then he thought. With two final breaths he took off running, pulling his rifle back against his chest.

Nothing was more important to a marine then running.

The Viatos gunfire crashed against the hangar door and the second floor walls. As each bolt connected it made a metallic ding, one that sounded like an eerie musical note. As the thousands of bolts crashed in rapid succession the doors dinged like an evil carnival ride blinking and singing its spine-chilling song into the darkness. The alien assault was little more than a scratch, their weapon fire harmlessly crashing against the steel, but the sound it made was terrifying. Even the most hardened soldier pulled away from the door at the sound. Holm jolted back, his eyes wide in shock and his heartbeat racing in surprise. He tightened his grip on his rifle and stepped forward, leading the others.

"Keep it together," he ordered, unsure if he was trying to convince them or himself.

He slid the barrel of his rifle through the make-shift gun port and stared outside. The gun ports were little holes, 30 cm2 squares, cut into the steel with a blow torch. They gave the shooter a steady porch, a view of the outside battle and nearly complete cover from the incoming fire. Holm stared out at the oncoming onslaught. The husk horde still moved in their make-shift phalanx and the mounted gun still mowed them down and they approached, but for each one that died another mindlessly stepped up.

"Back to the door!" Reid bellowed in his deepest instructional voice. It was up to him and Keiser to keep the Stalwart in place and fighting. He moved from person-to-person, ushering them back to their portholes. "Take all the fear and hate and just hold onto it for couple moments longer. Let it build up and bubble beneath you because very soon you'll get a chance to fill every one of those grey-skinned bastards with weapon's fire. That's when you let your anger out and that's when you'll show them just how pissed off you really are."

Reid glanced at his medic, Gregory anxiously gripping his weapon as he wait, and caught his gaze. Sal just nodded. The two had been through a lot together in their years as marines and both knew what the other was thinking. Reid truly wanted to unleash his anger into the alien bastards, but as Sal knew, he just prayed he lived long enough to have the chance.

Guiver looked down her scope as her rifle barrel moved up the horde, snapping off a bolt whenever her sights fell upon a set of eyes. Hazeltine and Hughes were dropping any grey-eyes they found while Campbell hunted out the green-eyed husks. She, however, was looking for something completely different.

"I...um....I've got it, sir...I...er...I mean, ma'am," Marco stammered. "I...er...they're in the back."

She spun her scope to the very back and smirk as her eyes fell on the form of the commanders. She'd seen them earlier when they led a platoon through the streets. They were seven foot tall blue skin humanoid aliens dressed in armour power-suits with a dome helmet. These aliens were clearly in charge, a superior race perhaps, and the husks listened to their every command. Three of the blue-skins commanders stood in back gesturing with their hands as they talked. Allana lined her sights on the middle commander, one with a small yellow stripe down its armour, and gave her trigger a squeeze. The bolt passed the entire length of the battlefield and smashed squarely into the creature's chest. Its right shoulder snapped back but the Commander didn't fall; it barely even moved.

Allana's eyes widened in fear; were these creatures were un-killable? She fired thrice more to find out, each bolt crashing into the yellow-striped Commander. Each struck with the same force as the last, like high-speed baseball slamming against a wall, and while a single shot did little damage, three in quick succession contained enough force to knock the creature off its armoured feet and squarely on it blue-skinned alien ass.

The two other commanders dove for cover as the yellow-striped lay on the ground yelling into its comms. The couldn't hear the commander, she could barely hear her own comms over the roar of the twin mounted guns, but Allana could see its lip's move. The Major eyed the other two, safely hidden, and smirked. Diving for cover meant they feared the incoming gunfire. If they feared the bolts then that meant the bolts could kill them. They weren't invincible but their armour was tough. Her scope returned to the fallen commander, the alien climbing back to its feet and pointing at her, and she lined up for a seco----.

A pair of hands grabbed her shoulders, yanked her from the chair and pulled her to the ground. She crashed down hard, landing on top of the farmer's boy.

"Sniper!" A small red block appeared on Clay's specs highlighting the sniper in the far building. The husk sniper lay before a window, safely tucked away in the far building and aimed down the battlefield like Guiver had. Clay shifted aim with her mounted and whooped loudly as she opened fire. The high powered rounds ripped through the wall and recklessly split the sniper into tiny shreds.

Guiver rolled off the farm boy and looked at the wall behind, noticing the blaster hole it now sported where her head should have been. She looked over at the kid and smiled. "You just saved my life."

"I saw....um...one of those aiming light dot things,ma'am." He stammered, "Their bad right?"

She just nodded. "I owe you one."

"Well...um...ma'am. You could um...." He mindlessly rubbed his shoulder as he stumbled through his words, "You could join me for dinner after this is done."

Allana gave the kid a stunned look. Someone had been watching the wrong type of war films. "Wrong place, wrong time," she explained as she moved to her rifle, "and definitely the wrong tree there, pup."

Thibodeau stood before her security screens and frowned as the husks moved further upwards. The turrets' kills number was high but the Viatos seemed to have a near endless supply of husks to throw at her.

There were many events today that were surprising in the least, a new alien race presenting itself, war breaking out on the Pherca moon and Thibodeau finding herself baby-sitting a spook, but the husks marshaling their forces to take the Windfall Tower's security room wasn't; their numbers only reassured the marine she was in the right place. The Viatos defence, as it stood during the briefing, was based on disabling the sentry guns and maintaining aerial dominance. If Tsia could reactivate the guns the tide of this battle would drastically shift and the husks would do everything to stop that from happening.

The husks were only three floors below her, their safety buffer quickly vanishing. Thibodeau's screen blinked rapidly as another turret sprung to life at the husks' proximity. The bolts slammed into the first grey-skin and clear into the second. The two fell as the turret riddled the third. Thibodeau watched as one after another the husk stormed the turret-guarded room. Each would get two steps in, fire two shots at the turret and receive four in their chest, fall over and make way for the next husk behind it; then they repeated. She knew what they were attempting to do – and they were succeeding –, they were chipping away at the turret shot by shot but she'd never seen a military to sacrifice their own forces for something so trivial as a turret. The Viatos, however, were unlike anything she'd seen. "Mon dieu!"

Tsia looked back from her console and gave the

French woman a look of concern. "Are we in trouble?"

"Not yet," Thibodeau said with a shake of her head, clutching her rifle like a security blanket. "But soon."

CHAPTER TWENTY
Pherca Moon Invasion +12:42 hours

Captain Cantor sat in her ready room staring at the clock for what seemed like the trillionth time. Bungee had roughly two hours left, two hours before ---. They had two hours.

It used to be much easier for her, to sit safely in the ship miles above a planet or moon, while the marines risked their lives. It used to worry her, she'd be inhuman if it hadn't, but not like it did now. There, safely secured in warp, she was a bundle of nerves. Her hands twitched, she went through bouts of hyperventilation and the ship readiness reports. She had been trying to read the same report for the last hour and a half but it still went unregistered by her brain.

The door opened and Commander Somers walked in. The XO took one look at his Captain and shook his head. "Jesus, ma'am," he muttered, "Agrima; have you gotten any sleep? You were running on empty before Bungee launched."

"If they don't sleep I don't." She just shook her

head. It was a noble sentiment but it was also a very stupid one. "I got maybe an hour tops."

Somers moved to the couch. Sitting in the centre was a curled black mass of fur and attitude. He reached down to shove Cinders out of the way but decided better of it when the cat raised it head and stared at him with flattened ears. It was the look a mother gave after catching their mischievous son holding a hammer and smiling It was the look a teacher gave a student after seeing him come to show-and-tell with a mysterious moving box. It was a look that said *what the hell do you think you're doing*? Somers coughed nervously and resigned to sitting in the uncomfortable chair instead. Cinders the cat, the true ruler aboard the *Mojave*, lowered his head back into his curled mass content in his dominance.

"Last scan just came in." She had her crew scanning the Pherca moon to find out what forces the Viatos had there, it started off scanning once an hour but as the time carried on her scans increased. "A second Viatos ship has arrived, a corvette at best."

They were back to two-on-one.

"We've gotten most damage repaired but we'll probably need a refit very soon." He looked up from his handheld. "Although if we're at war I don't know when that will be."

"How are our armaments?"

"The energy cells are holding firm, we're down a pair of aft cannons but we're working on them." He answered, "and we blew our chaff load. I don't know about going back in, ma'am. We do--."

"I don't want to hear it," she snapped. "As long as they're still alive I'll go in after them. I will not--."

"Incoming ship!" Cantor was on her feet, her hat back on her head, before the words had fully come through the comms. Somers, struggling to keep up, followed his Captain as she emerged onto the bridge.

If she was in normal space, Cantor's first reaction would have been to call for shields and to spin up the guns but in the warp, a space outside of space, weapons were useless. No known weapons could be fired in warp.

"Report!"

"There's a ship barrelling through warp, ma'am. Holy hell, they're booking it," Morrison dictated in amazement. "Coming into scanning range." Cantor waited patiently, despite her urge to throttle the man until he spoke. "It's HEF: she's the *Rwanda*"

The *Rwanda*? How the hell did that make it here? Cantor nodded to the comms officer and flashed the transmission onto her screen. A large man appeared on screen decked in the same clothes she wore. "Salut, mon amie."

"Captain Matthias De-Serres," She said with a relived smile. "How the hell did you get here so fast? You weren't due for another three hours and what are you doing with the *Rwanda*?"

As long as she'd known De-Serres he had been MI: military intelligence. He was the military tactician, the one who devised plans, formulated attacks and sent spooks out on missions. He wasn't a ship captain.

"I am only along for the ride, madam," he grinned. De-Serres was a bigger guy, lovable and caring but ruthless when it came to his job. He was cunning and devious and with the strength of a fleet behind him would strike at the enemies of the HEF with crippling results. He was the nicest-deadliest man she ever knew. "Captain Ferrell Dumont is at the helm."

Dumont was a dark-skinned warrior, fearless and eager. Deep within her soul Cantor felt a small chill, an unsettling chill. If the HEF had those two paired off then no good could come of it. For a fraction of a moment she almost felt sorry for the Viatos. "You're still avoiding my question. How did you make such good time?"

"That is classified, ma cherie," De-Serres said with a chuckle and a wink. "But let's just say she's had some new improvements."

De-Serres was one of the true blue French. Born from a French line the he claimed dated back to the Earth that was. Fact or fiction, he was here and he had more guns then she did. "Is it just you and I?"

"The *Cairo* is leading two more ships. They'll be here within the hour," De-Serres just smiled. "More of mes petits ameliorations. I need a situation report; things are developing and we need to know what the plan is."

Campbell snapped off another bolt, collapsing the skull of an unlucky husk, and ejected his mag.

He dropped behind cover as he quickly reloaded his Timberwolf. Campbell had kept his scope moving through the horde, searching for the green-eye husks, yet the further he looked the more he began to worry. The green-eyes were the power-house of the Viatos ground forces, the elite troops in a horde of remarkable soldiers, but they were nowhere to be found. In this last stand at Paick Starport the elite were nowhere to be seen. Either they thought this battle wasn't the crucial pivot point that Bungee and the Stalwart did or the other shoe hadn't dropped yet.

The husks pushed forward, crossing the 460 mark, as their rifles flared to life, slamming the hanger doors with a flurry of energy bolts. None of this made any sense. They were just wasting ammunition, their bolts doing little to no damage and they were sacrificing husks by the dozens in order to gain meaningless ground. This wasn't war; this was noth----.

Then the Viatos guns went silent.

Campbell spun up, his rifle snapping down onto the field and he stared in wonderment. The husks had stopped cold, forty meter shy of the claymores, as had their rifles. The husks were split down the line, their ranks staggered, as half of the grey-skins aimed at the left row of building and the others aimed at the right. With a uniformly hollow thud a flurry of Viatos propelled grenades emerged from the formation, arched in the air and, after succumbing to the powerful forces of gravity, plummeted down onto the building roofs, exploding on contact.

Then the husks scattered.

Like cockroaches scattering to a sudden light the husks scampered in every which direction, the phalanx formation instantly dissolving. Dozens bolted for a building, left or right, and pressed themselves against the wall and opened fire on the opposite side. Several platoons dropped to one knee and propelled volley after volley of grenade at the hangar before they were gunned down while three grey-skins bolted forward, each triggering a different proximity sensor, and vanished in a sea of shrapnel and steel metal balls.

Future claymores – or, present, she kept reminding herself - barely differed from those in Guiver's time. They were anti-personnel mines that fired shrapnel and small metal ball in a 60º arc. The term anti-personnel, at least in her day, meant that the mines were never intended to kill, instead just injure them requiring a logistical increase, normally medical, support required by enemy forces. But as steel balls rocketed forward, ripping through the husks' grey skin, bones and spine like a rock through paper, she'd realized that even in the future the term anti-personnel meant exactly the same as it used to and so did to the vague definition of injure.

Guiver cursed as three mines vanished, a fraction of their potential used, and cursed again as the sound of rifle fire emerged from the frightened rooftop mowers. They were firing too soon and giving away their hidden position; this wasn't part of the plan.

No plan survived contact with the enemy.

"Fuck it!" She cursed, "Light 'em, Holm." With a deafening roar the hangar violently shook. She had been expecting the roar of gunfire not the roar of an explosion and the feel of an earthqua—moonquake. "What the bloody hell?"

A pair of diamond fighters zoomed past the building, the roar of their engines trailing them second later. They were being bombed by the Viatos air-support. Guiver pointed to the starfighter and gave Clay a determined look, like a farmer letting the dog off the leash to defend the homestead. "Take them out."

Clay smirked and angled her mounted upwards, Stark following suit, and let loose a loud, psychotic cackle as she unloaded round after round into the air. The twin diamond fighters circled in the air, spinning as they avoided gunfire, and flew back toward the hangar for a second run. Stark jolted his aim rapidly as he struggled to hit the left diamond with a single bolt but Clay held a steadier aim, most of her bolts still zooming past the spinning and dodging fighter, and a bust of five bolts slammed into its side. The typically smooth fighters suddenly jerked upwards and kicked in their afterburners, fleeing into the sky.

Guiver raised another eyebrow. What military held no qualms about sending hundreds of soldiers to die but panicked the moment one of their starfighters took even the most superficial damage?

Lt. Kenny Holm held his rifle firmly as the weapon vibrated with each shot fired. He stood, along with the rest of the door's guardians, with a rifle, pressed against his shoulder, firing through their port holes. The Stalwart gunfire tore through the husk that bolted for the hangar, using the small but safe path created by others. One by one they fell before them, most within 300 meters of the door, but few had punched through only to fall only two meters before the door.

Sarah Gamble heard the echo of the gunshots as she rushed for the door, her arms full of more ammunition. She dumped in a pile before the door guardians. She doubled over, panting for air, as she tried to figure out what to do next. Her handheld, in conjunction with her reporter equipment, was scanning the air for jammed transmissions and would signal her if she got anything. Like she had with Bungee and others she could cut through the alien jamming and pass along data. She'd learned how to work through a media block during the Kobold Unification. She was a war journalist back then, something she thought she'd left behind, and had to learn how to break both the Kobold and HEF jams if she wanted to broadcast and get paid. Seeing little else to do, Sarah bolted for the ammo cache and scooped up more, taking it with her as she moved for the second floor. She'd barely reached the stairs when her comms channel exploded with transmissions.

The noise was sudden and startled her, the ammo dropping to the floor in a loud clang. She thumbed her volume down and pulled free her handheld. Her system hadn't pulled free another signal; this one came in on its own. She rapidly shifted channels, one after another, to find each was just like the first, filled with a storm of calls. The alien signal jam was down.

"This is Northboat. We're under fire."

"They're closing in."

"I..umm...I'm Jack Hart. Those aliens have killed my military. Help, I need help."

"Mayday: Brisk Raker is down. They're taking hostages."

"They just slaughtered fifty human civilians. Dear God."

Sarah looked over at the door and caught the eyes of Lt. Holm and MS. Reid. Both had the same look on their faces. Each of them had heard the transmissions, the radio cries. Each of them knew the carnage that was happening. The alien signal jam was down and the truth was pouring out. Tens of thhousands more were on the moon, military and civilian, and they all needed help.

Doctor Bristol Tsia blinked twice. It had just vanished. The signal jam had been there a second ago, it had been combating her code manipulation, but then suddenly it was gone. She'd hit it with a makeshift program meant to rips through useless code; it had been a stall technique. It wasn't meant to work but it had. HEF marines and civilians could communicate across the moon; they could contact any ship circling around;

they could communicate with *Avalon*. She jammed on the keys as she digitally dove for the guns. They were clean of any infection. All that remained was for the guns to reboot. She'd done it.

The rapid cracks of an assault rifle pulled her from her self-congratulations and focused her attention on the doorway. Thibodeau stood by the open door firing into the hallways. "You done yet?"

"More or less." Tsia replied as she grabbed her SMG and bolted for the door. "They here?"

"Oui!" The two women crouched by the door and stared into the hallways. The husks poured from the stairwell and bolted towards them. "Kill 'em all."

The pair of weapons roared to life as they filled the hall with a flurry of blaster fire. The first wave dropped to the floor, their bodies sprung dozens of new holes, and the second approached. The women opened fire again and filled the next wave much like they did the first. Then the third emerged.

Tsia bit her lip as she fired. They couldn't hold out forever.

The marine moved carefully as he entered the tower through a makeshift hole. Somebody had really wanted to enter this building, so much so that they went as far as to blow a hole in the wall. He shrugged, to no one in particular, and moved inwards, reaching the main hallway. His assault rifle snapped to life as his eyes fell on the errant husk and then again as two more responded to the sound. With three down the marine made for the stairwell. He kicked opened the door and stepped inside. He glanced up and groaned.

That was a lot of steps.

His battle-school Petty Officer would be laughing at this. Clutching his rifle close to his chest the marine took a deep breath and bolted up the stairs.

The echo of raining hell filled the ears of Senior Specialist Anthony Hughes as he killed from a distance. The mowers, the three on his side, were firing down at the mass below them with reckless abandon. The battle hadn't gone as planned - which battle did? - but they were improvising. With another hasty, albeit well placed round Hugh tore the neck out from another soulless husk and moved to the next.

It had been seven months since he'd held a sniper rifle let alone fired one, ever since he'd enlisted with Blackwell Security he hadn't needed to pick one up, but when that lady, the one with the famous name, asked for anybody with skill using a sniper rifle he stepped up. He traded his assault rifle for a sniper and climbed to the third floor, out the window and onto the rooftop. He hadn't minded giving them his assault rifle, it wasn't even his. He wasn't attached to it. Who got attached to an assault rifle?

Had they tried to take Catalina away he would've made a fuss.

Catalina was his Heisenberg 7-CS pistol. He

purchased a stock model and then started modifying it. He gave it a 3-dot sights, a national match slide, a bevelled magazine well, competition trigger, polished feed ramp, checkered front strap and mainspring housing for more positive grip, a delta hammer and a relief-cut trigger guard for higher grip. It also featured a permanently-disengaged grip safety, a controversial modification. This was his baby.

A burst of husk fire came from his left, it sounded closer than the others. Hughes looked left and reacted. Husks were on the roof; green-eyed husks. They'd just killed two of the mowers and levelled their weapon at the other sniper. In a burst the sniper - Kev Hazeltine – ceased to exist. Hughes pushed away from his rifle, its size a hindrance for close battles like these, and summoned Catalina to his hand.

His girl rang out thrice, punching through the first green-eye's skull, before hungrily looking for another. She rang out twice more and took down another with twin holes in its neck. Hughes glimpsed to the side, his eyes spotting the large metallic power box that lay on the roof, and bolted; Catalina's song granting her lover the cover he needed as he called out over comms. "Green eyes are on the roof!"

Hughes slid behind the metallic cover as his girl's song ended with a click. In a swift motion he ejected the magazine and quickly fed her another clip. He peeked over the steel barrier. Three husks opened fire as they pushed up on his right side. He raised Catalina and let her sing once more, her national match slide snapping back with each note. Nobody sang like his Catalina.

There used to be six. His mind raced: three on his right and two dead; that left one remaining. They were trying to flank him on his left.

As Catalina sang on the right side Hughes reached to the back of his belt and wrapped his fingers around Gabriela. If Catalina was his lover then Gabriela was his mistress, his tawdry affair best kept to dark corners and seedy motels.

Gabriela was a smaller pistol, a Trillium-9s. It was a 7-round pistol stainless steel slide and trigger guard, commander hammer, machined rear site, wolf springs and trigger action job all meticulously preformed by him and him alone.

Catalina sang out over his right as Gabriela snuck over to the left. If the green-eyed husk were to try and flank him from his left then he would let Gabriela have words with them. Catalina was a singer. Gabriela was not. She was a dictator; she told you how it was going to be. Hughes listened for the silent husk, for any sound to give him away. A small metallic clang gave Hughes a smile; the husk was about to lunge. With a sudden burst Hughes leaped to the left, out from behind his cover, and let Gabriela bark twice. Her orders barked only to darkness. Before Hughes stood not a soul, alien or otherwise; his mind raced. Had he miscounted or miscalculated? Another sound pulled his attention upwards.

His eyes went wide as he saw a green-eyed husk leaping upward with its plank rifle aimed down at the roof. The barrel lit up, briefly, as the rifle fired a grenade downwards.

"Green eyes are on the roof!" Campbell pulled his rifle back and aimed along his roof. His eyes lay on the husk, with glowing green-eyes, approaching them.

"Move back!" He yelled as he squeezed the trigger twice. The head of the nearest husks vanished in a burst of red and Campbell aimed for the second. Another shot ripped through the creature's chest. "Get off the roof!"

Two green-eyes charged Campbell as a third dropped to prone and started taking pot-shots. Campbell turned and ran, his feet bouncing over the flimsy plank that linked the two rooftops with little regard of his own safety. As his feet both hit sturdy roof, he spun around and gave the wood a firm kick, pushing it off the roof and tumbling down to the street below. He smirked, turning back to the hangar, but froze as his body went numb.

Campbell dropped to his knees as the smell of burning flesh filled his nose. The scream of Quentin seemed to drift off as did the sounds of war and gunfire. He barely felt the firm grip of the Sub-Lt. grabbing his arms and pulling him inside.

Ordinary Seamen Leif Keiser bolted up the left stairs towards the third floor. Reid ordered him up there after

Hughes cry filled the comms. The green-eyes had made it to the roofs. It made sense as he ran, this was an obvious ambush and the husks knew it. So they marched their endless hordes right up the line as a distraction while the Special Forces did the rest.

A small boom from the right told him that somebody had detonated the right window. When Bungee was setting up their ambush they put a small ripcord explosive under the third floor windows. If the roofs became compromised they just had to pull that cord and the small incendiary would demolish the window much like Guiver had the middle wall. It wouldn't block the husk from passage for good but it would hold them off for a bit.

Keiser reached the window and peered out, not believe what his eyes saw. A husk, green-eyed, leapt over a metallic power box and fired a rocket propelled grenade downwards at Hughes. When the grenade exploded the PMG vanished in a dust of red and tongues of flames but the blast propelled the husk into the air, reaching greater heights and distances than he'd ever seen from a grey-skin – green eyes or not –, and it soared through the sky landing delicately before the left window.

Keiser wanted to be impressed and he wanted to be scared all at the same time but instead he just pulled the trigger. His rifle roared to life and ripped shreds of flesh from the rocket-jumping husk. Keiser shifted his aim and fired again, dropping two more before they had the chance to respond. The OS pulled his weapon back inside, dodging fire from the last husk and grabbed the cord. With a violent pull the explosive triggered and seconds later the window was gone, replaced by rubble.

CHAPTER TWENTY-ONE
Pherca Moon Invasion +13:22 hours

"Is he going to be ok?" Quentin asked. LS Gregory knelt by Campbell as he examined the sniper's wound. He tore away the clothes and tried to get a good look.

Sal couldn't get a good look. Campbell was alive, barely, but he didn't know for how much longer. The wound was on the back, very close to the spine, and he needed to get a clear look to see if there was any permanent damage. He pulled a scalpel from his vest and started to peel back the burst flesh as he dug deeper into the LS's back. If the weapon fire nicked a nerve then Campbell could be paralysed for the rest of his life.

"You okay? You don't look so good either." Sal looked at the officer. Quentin and just waved him off. "Then get on the door. I'll take care of him."

Quentin nodded, grabbed his rifle off the floor, and bolted for the door. He took an empty porthole and started firing. The claymores, all but gone, had ripped through some troops but most that had fallen by the door had done so by Stalwart gunfire. Lt. Holm looked over at him and nodded. The two continued firing.

"Contact: 800 mark."

"What now,"Holm muttered. He looked down the street, past the dead bodies that littered the street, and spotted five v-Tols jeeps revving down the street, each driven by a green-eyed husk. His eyes narrowed. Three of the v-Tols held the standard mounted machine gun on their back but two were armed with something different. "Rocket launchers!"

"Clay!" Guiver only had to say her name. The AS shifted her mounted and opened fire. Her mounted gun, running dangerously low of ammo, tore into the nearest rocket v-Tols. The forward tire blew and the jeep became lopsided, but it didn't stop. Clay pumped dozens of rounds into its engine, but it didn't stop, and finally the last dozen into the rear hitting with it the gas tanks. The v-Tol erupted in a ball of fire.

Clay turned to the next rocket-jeep but heard only a click from her gun. "Out! Stark take him out."

"I can't. The other two are acting as cover."

"I'll get him." Guiver stared down her scope as she tried to steady her shot. She snapped off two shots but both flew by harmlessly. She steadied her aim and lined up a third. With a bang the rifle fired, the bolt cross the street's entirety and embedding itself deep into the rocket-jeep's driver. The green-eye faded and the body jerked as it chocked on the last drops of life. The jeep turned sharply and flipped over.

The remaining three v-Tols sped towards the hangar

as fast as they could go. The door guardians jumped back as the three crashed into the steel door at once. The jeep crumpled on impact, folding in on itself like a hand becoming a fist.

"Well that was dumb," Holm muttered as he slowly moved closer. The crash had done little real damage. It damaged the frame, but some serious dents in the door, and ruined the paintjob but the door still stood and the Stalwart still stood strong. He peered out. The three husk drivers were alive, their eyes still glowing green, but their bodies were broken and mangled. Yet unlike the other broken husk, these three acted differently then Holm had ever seen. Normally a husk died in a revolting manner, choking on fluids or bleeding out, but these three did neither of them, instead their bodies began to hum and their veins turned bright red and glowed brighter by the second. It reminded Holm of a military detonation device that once the two liquid combined they'd explo----.

"Get back!"

For the second time in as many hours the hangar trembled, shaken by the force of an explosion. The three husk drivers had detonated their bodies, taking with them the three crashed v–Tols and igniting every dead husk body that lay by the door. The husks weren't mindlessly charging they door, they were packing in as many explosives as possible.

The burst had rippled throughout the hangar, tossing the second floor occupants from their feet.

Marco, Stark and Hughes were pitched against the far wall but Clay had been pitched through it. The drywall had been strained to its limit with the impact of the first three but when Clay's form slammed against it, it gave. Clay body smashed down to the floor below and she groaned loudly. She could feel the pain as she tried to breathe, cracked rib – maybe two, and her head felt dizzy and weak: she had a concussion.

Clay was used to pain; it was part of her life. But in times like this she really shone. Despite the broken body and fractured perspective, her body called out for energy. It began to take effect immediately; she could feel the familiar jolt of energy surging through her body, the addictive feeling of invincibility and the rush that came with it.

My name is Able Seaman Tanya Clay, she thought to herself, I am an adrenalin addict and damn it if I don't love it.

She looked up and scanned her surroundings, her new-found energy goading her on. The door was torn open by the blast and the members of Bungee and Stalwart were tossed around like discarded trash. She rushed to her nearest teammate, Keiser, and helped him up. The young OS, wobbly from the blast, thanked her, grabbed his gun and bolted for the door. She moved to another and then a third, helping each of them up before moving on.

"More v-Tols." Clay bounded over to the door. Keiser and the few other back on the feet were crouched and firing from behind whatever wreckage they could find. She glanced out and saw two more HEF v-Tols, driven by green-eyed husks, screeching as they drifted around the far corner and barrelling towards them.

Reality seemed to slow down for Clay. The hangar door was gone, the remaining mounted gun on the second floor was silent and there was nothing to stop the stolen jeeps. They would plow right into the hangar and that would be game over for Bungee. She searched the room for a thumper, a claymore or anything that could stop a jeep. All she saw were the jeeps they'd driven here.

The Mako.

This was a dumb idea. She bolted for the Mako and leaped into the driver chair like a stunt driver. She pulled what remaining plastic explosives she had and pressed it against the dashboard as she revved the engine to life. With a squeal of her own tires, she gunned the jeep forward and sped out of the hanger. She drove head first for the oncoming v-Tols. This was going to be the ultimate thrill; the ultimate hit of adrenalin. She didn't hate to admit it but driving headlong into another jeep only to detonate both in a ball of fire had her more excited than ever before. In the last few seconds before doing something crazy a conventional brain, mainly the portion that houses and operates the common sense and self-preservation functions, would light up and scream as loud as it could. Clay's didn't; Clay's brain just edged her on.

She gripped the steering wheel tightly as the jeep bounced over the fallen husks and torn rubble. She lined up her jeep, flipped on the cruise-control and bailed. She leapt from the jeep and tucked into a roll. She painfully bounced along the street. The two jeeps collided, the steel crumbling on impact and transformed into a bright ball of flame as Clay detonated the plastic.

Clay lay on the ground, her body numb from the pain, but she still laughed. It started out a small chuckle but quickly became an exhausted and victorious guffaw, one that sounded like she was a tired action star who'd just killed the final boss.

"My name is Able Seaman Tanya Clay!" She bellowed loudly between laughs, "and today is going to be hard to top!"

Her laugh died when she saw the commander walk onto the street. The armoured blue-skin brazenly marched down the street. The grey-eyed husks formed up before him. Once more like a parade formation they pushed forward, the phalanx reborn, as they marched towards the hangar door. With the mounted guns silent and the only gunfire coming from the few who stood by the door, the platoon marched unopposed. Clay scrambled to her feet, her body singing that familiar tune and bolted. She limped for the hangar.

The commander pulled a weapon from his back, it wasn't a plank-rifle like the ones used by the grey-skins it was a rifle that looked similar in design to a human weapon. The Commander cocked the rifle and held it in an identical fashion, cradled in his arms. He narrowed his eyes. He glanced down at the wrist-device; a handheld built into his gauntlet and spoke softly. The microphones in his helmet picked-up his words and reacted to his commands. The suit shifted, the front armour pressing together tightly as the suit's legs shifted for velocity.

With a burst of speed the commander dashed forward, slamming into Keiser and barrelling into the hangar. The commander's rifle roared to life, ripping through the Stalwart and turned toward the Lieutenant. Holm fired against the commander's reinforced front but with little effect. The commander shot forward and gripped the Holm by the neck with a single hand. The suit shifted again, amplifying his strength tenfold, and made hoisting Holm into the air a simple task. The blue-skinned stared at the human officer. He marvelled at the human's bid for life, the way it kicked its legs and clawed with its hands. heir fight was impressive, commendable even, but it was pointless. With a twist of his wrist the Commander snapped Holm's neck and savoured in the satisfying crack. The human's body went limp. The Commander pivoted and pitched the corpse into a surprised MS Reid. The two bodies collided and both crumpled to the ground. The commander eyes narrowed as he stared at the rest of the human populace.

Quentin's jaw dropped. He stood there staring, like everybody else, at how easily it had killed Holm. It wasn't a struggle or a fight; it was little more than snapping a twig. Rage seethed through his body. He was never one for temper but as his eyes narrowed on the murderous alien one suddenly appeared. He tightened his trigger finger and his rifle flared to life.

The bolts collided with the armour with little effect. The alien dashed toward Quentin, his legs shifting for speed, and struck him in the chest with his open palm. The blow sent the HEF officer flying backwards into the air. The command pivoted, pushing off his right foot as he changed directions and sprinted at Marco Nelor. The farm boy tried to dodge but found his feet not quick enough. The butt of the alien rifle collided with his skull and sent him skipping across the ground like a stone.

The commander came to halt as a propelled grenade collided with his chest. The impact rocked him, like hitting steel with steel, and dropped him to one knee. His HUD flashed warnings before his pale eyes. He glanced to the second floor stares, his sensors zooming in and scowled. Slowly moving down the stairs was a female human armed with a HEF thumper. He climbed to his feet, his legs shifting once more for speed but a second grenade slammed against him followed by a third.

"Secure the door."

The rest of the humans scrambled about, obeying Guiver without question. The commander eyed her, ignoring the increasing number of warning flashing before him. A small hiss of air pulled his attention to the growing crack in his dome helmet. She'd compromised his suit; that arrogant human sevla.

She ditched the thumper, the dreaded click revealing it uselessness and bolted down the stairs. As her foot hit floor her pistol jumped to her hand. She lifted it before her and quickly squeezed. Shot after shot rang from the handheld gun, the first two colliding with his helmet. He wiped his warning from his screen and climbed back to his feet. Shifting his legs again he braced for another burst of speed but so had this woman. Her aim dropped, from his chest and head, to the joint mechanism that enhanced his legs. Her gun rang out continuously as bolt after bolt of human fire ripped into the side of his left knee. A busted leg joint wasn't crippling but as he sprung forward with full speed only to have the speed robbed from his a mere second later, he tripped over his own legs and crashed to the ground. The commander pushed himself to a knee. The female's gunfire returned to his dome helmet, the crack growing with each bolt until the weapon signalled his relief with a loud click.

Guiver dropped the weapon and sprinted forward, leaping at him as she got close. She wrapped her hands around the back of the dome and used it as leverage to pull her forward, slamming her knee through the dome and into his face. The blow knocked him back on his ass, the third time shed caused that to him. She straddled his body and quickly punched his face, over and over. His suit reassembled for strength and he jabbed Guiver's side, knocking her off of him and sending her to the floor.

Guiver winced as she picked her body up off the floor. The blue-skins had enhanced strength. Augments; their suits were like the augmented humans she fought before war broke out. They did it with bio-implants and genetic surgery; these blue-skins did it with power suits. Either way the same rules applied. Don't get hit and kill them quickly.

The alien ripped off his busted dome with a scowl and tossed it aside. He climbed to his feet as his suit shifted again, the panels on his neck moving and changing as they reassembled themselves. He opened his mouth. "You're not like the rest, female. You have conviction and skill."

"All you need to know is that I will kill you," Guiver promised as she drew her knife. The pair was only half a dozen paces away from each other. "Even if I have to rip that your suit off of you, inch by inch."

"What is your name, female?"

"Major Allana Guiver." She shouldn't have been talking to him, she knew that, but her body felt numb from that last punch. She needed the moment to recover. "What about you, blue-balls?"

"Field Warden Voldl of the *Geval Haut*." The suit shifted again. "What is *Major*? Your ranks have not this designation."

They knew HEF ranks, they had men on the inside and they were able to take out a moon's military structure. They were prepared for this war.

The sounds of the sentry guns coming online echoed

through the city, dozens of gun activating at once, and was followed by the unmistakable sound of exploding ships. Ensemble had succeeded and the guns were shooting the diamond-fighters from the sky.

"Give it up, Voldl," she demanded. "We won."

"You don't have the moon," he taunted. He drew a punching dagger, a curved blade that ran across his knuckles and slipped it on his right hand. "Others may make it off the surface, Major, but I will make you sure do not."

He moved first, his right arm shooting out twice with blade-thrusts. His left arm darting out the moment the right retracted. He was trying to snag her. Guiver shifted right, ducking beneath his snag, and fired her own punch into the side of the alien's assumed torso. Her fist collided with the armour and she instantly regretted the punch. It felt like punching something dense but soft to the touch, like fur-covered steel. She raised her arm to block the next strike, regretting that as much as the first as her arm went numb from the alien strike, and grabbed his shoulder. She struck with her knee, her joint striking over and over into his side. She shifted her grasp, sensing his inevitable escape, and slammed her elbow into his face. He stumbled back, impressed with her skill, but had only a heartbeat's reprieve as she lunged forward with a stab of her blade. His arms shifted, calling upon the speed that remained in his limbs, gripped her arm with both of his and pulled her over his shoulder. His suit shifted again, sacrificing speed for strength mid throw, and tossed her.

"Bungee this is Crow Actual. We're here to provide cover for the escaping ships; start sending them up."

As the words came across her comms a great weight felt instantly lifted from Sarah shoulders. She replied a confirmation and began contacting the civilian ships one after another. The Crows were a wing of HEF starfighters and with them as escorts the civilian ships could clear the Viatos screen. The roar of high-powered engines rushed in like a wave. The ships had their engines warmed up and ready to bolt when the notice came. They had been impatiently idling.

Sarah glanced at what was left of the door. The husks were pushing through and what few remained of both Bungee and the Stalwart were desperately trying to hold them back. "This is News---."Now wasn't the time to explain her sudden codename. Now was the time to lie.

"This is Bungee Actual. Requesting some form of air support. The husks are pushing through and we cannot hold them off."

"Peregrine Five here. I'm on it," a female voice replied. "Seven and Four, you're with me. Commencing burning dog-shit run."

Sarah wanted to groan, military people were often rude and crass and when it came to maturity they rarely measured higher than a thirteen year-old, but if a dramatic rescue came with crude humour then she'd take it. Beggars couldn't be choosers.

Three HEF fighters zoomed past, leaving a trail of jellied liquid in their wake. The liquid rained down on the street below, igniting as it fell. It engulfed the entire stretch, and anything unlucky enough to be caught in it, in three lines of brightly burning flames. The husks didn't scream or shout, they just marched forward, ignoring the napalm that rapidly burned their flesh. They marched and fought as the skin off their back burned away, as the circuitry embedded throughout their bodies melted away and until the very legs that held their bodies dissolved until they could support them no more. The husks burned to nothing, vanishing in a column of flame. But never did they speak a single word.

Sarah glanced down at the hangar, at what remained of Bungee and Stalwart finishing off the husks. To the side Guiver and the commander continued their savage brawl. Before the Kobold War, Sarah was amazed how fighting and battles never seemed like they did in films. When two beings fought, they didn't move like a dance using coordinated strike and flashy dodges. It was a brutal struggle that used inhumane strike and borderline torturous holds. There was nothing pretty about a fight.

She aimed her pistol at the brawl, her sights moving as quickly as they were, but she couldn't get a clear shot. She lowered her weapon, resigning Guiver to her own fate. She turned to the remaining few that guarded the door. She snapped off a pair of rounds into a burning husk's head and bolted over.

"Reid," she bellowed as she ran. "Get'em to the *Great Expectations*. We're getting the hell out of here."

CHAPTER TWENTY-TWO
Pherca Moon Invasion +14:05 hours

The marine pulled his head back as Viatos gunfire riddled the stairs. He breathed heavily and cursed loudly. Running up the stairs was hard enough, fourteen floors at fifteen steps a floor meant he had climbed 210 steps. Dodging dodge enemy fire just made it worse. His chest ached, his arms felt limp and his adrenalin was running dangerously low but he pushed forward. He popped out from the protective cover and let a burst of three rounds loose. Two collided with the railing, leaving only a burn mark on the steel, while the third found a home deep in the husk's eye.

The marine dashed up the next series of stairs, firing as he moved. He reached the next landing and elbow tackled the second husk into the wall. He hooked the butt of his assault rifle behind the stunned grey-skin's neck and with solid pull force the creature off the wall and down the stairs, it's limbs making a snapping sound that echoed through the empty stairwell. The third husk swung with its plank-rifle, a close-quarters attack for their kind, but if they could use their rifles as melee weapons so to could he. The marine's hands shifted as he swung his rifle upwards, using the barrel to block the swinging weapon. His arm shook as weapon met weapon but he ignored it as his legs bolted into action. His right leg shot forth and planted a low side-kick into the husk's left knee. As the marine's right leg returned his left shot up, striking the same place as before with a forward sidekick. Both kicks, moving at lightning speed, caused the alien leg to buckle leaving the grey-skinned face vulnerable for a final strike. The marine retracted his left leg, only partially, and swung it around planting the final whip kick to the alien's face. The creature crumpled to the ground. The marine flipped his rifle downward, squeezed off a round into its head and pushed onwards.

A Savate three-kick combo; it never failed him.

Thibodeau cursed in French as her rifle click. She pulled away from the door and hid behind the wall. She tossed her rifle to the ground, it was completely out of am, and pulled a grenade from her vest. The husks had breached the hall and were closing on the sentry room's door. "Get back, mon dieu."

Thibodeau pulled the pin, tossed it into the hall, grabbed Tsia by the shoulder and bolted for the desk. The two ladies vaulted over the upended table as the grenade exploded. Thibodeau grabbed a shotgun, one of the final remaining weapons and cocked it. She popped up and aimed at the security room's door. Her shotgun roared to life as the first husk marched in.

"Pigeon, where the hell are you?" Tsia bellowed into her comms. The plan said that the moment the guns were back on that Cole would return with the shuttle and extract them. They hadn't seen the shuttle; they hadn't even heard a single world from it. "Pigeon!

Tsia popped up from cover and fired what little ammo she had left for the SMG. Her mind raced as bolt after bolt barrelled forward, calculating the worst.

I'm going to die here, on this planet; on this fucking moon. She thought, *and I'm terrified. I'm fucking terrified.*

The sentry guns were on and civilians were escaping. It should have made her feel better, it should have given her some meaning to her death, but it didn't and for that she felt guilty. And there it was, she figured, the true difference between a spook and a marine. She was going to die saving the day and she fucking hated it. A marine would have revelled in it a death like that. They were born and bred to die for their ship.

Her SMG clicked and she just dropped it. She pulled free the pistol from her waist. Each pistol clip had twelve shots; she had three clips in total; she only had thirty-six rounds. In Guiver's day a soldier or spook would save the last two rounds for them, one for Thibodeau and one for her, but that didn't work anymore. Human guns didn't kill humans.

It might work on her though, she wasn't exactly human.

She'd long expected that human weapons would

kill her; her physical biology was different enough that the careful modification that the HEF had put into their weapons, the mods to render them nigh useless against humans, would prove ineffective against her. If things got bad – worse - then she could test her theory and take her own life but she couldn't she leave Thibodeau here to suffer on her own.

"Ensemble this is Pigeon: coming in hot. I've got three on my tail," Tsia smiled in relief at Cole's voice.

"This is Raven Niner coming to assist. Let's clear the way, boys," a new voice replied.

Tsia whooped. She directed Cole to the Security room's ledge for an extract. They couldn't get to the roof or the ground so they'd have to make an awkward exi--.

A grenade bounced into the room and exploded, pitching both women against the wall. Tsia hit first and felt the air scamper from her lungs like rats from a sinking ship. She dropped to the ground and gasped for oxygen. Thibodeau hit second.She dropped to the ground with her faculties' intact. She spun back to her feet, rifle in hand and found herself staring down the barrels of nine husk weapons. Thibodeau dropped her gun and raised her hands. The husks, with their glowing green eyes, didn't speak. The Viatos, with their weapons raised, stared at the pair.

"Disarm or be eliminated," a husk demanded. It spoke perfect English with a hollow voice that seemed to echo itself.

"Va te faire foutre, trouduc," Thibodeau snapped as

she tossed her weapons to the ground.

"You continue to struggle," the husk continued. "Despite that we are the cleansing grasp here to raise you from perdition. You and your kind will do well to accept your fate."

"Nique ta mere!" she responded again. The doctor threw her pistol on the ground. Tsia didn't know any French but somehow she figured that what Thibodeau had just said was neither kind nor pleasant.

"On your knees, hands above your heads." The two ladies obeyed, reluctantly dropping down.

The sound of steel sliding across steel caught Thibodeau's ear. She glanced down as a rifle magazine slid into the room. Thibodeau threw herself over Tsia and closed her eyes. Two seconds later a burst of gunfire collided with the energy pack. The magazine exploded. The marine bolted into room, firing while moving.

He dropped the husk directly before him with two shots to the neck and moved counter-clockwise. He placed a bolt between the eyes of the second husk and ventilated the third with a burst of three. Thibodeau bolted across the room, sliding across the floor as she grabbed the shotgun. She aimed at the nearest husk and fired. The energy shell took most of the husk's face with it. The two marines fired over and over, never stopping until the last husk fell.

The marine moved to the ledge. He glanced out at the hovering shuttle and waved it in. When he turned back to face them Thibodeau gasped. Tsia glanced up.

The marine was badly injured. His body was bruised and cut, his clothes torn and burned but the worst was his face. He looked to have blond hair and blue eyes, and was once a decent looking man, but the left side of his face was dark red and covered in pink bubbles. The marine had recently been in a fire or an explosion and barely survived. Yet despite the injuries, Tsia still recognized him.

"Branford?" she nervously asked. "Is that you? Dear lord."

Petty Officer Marcus Branford gave the civilian doctor a small nod as the shuttle lowered and the rear-hatch opened. "Grab your gear; we're going home."

Guiver's body quickly spun as she fired a powerful rear-kick squarely into the Voldl's chest. The commander stumbled backwards. Guiver hopped from one foot to another and followed up with a spinning whip kick that snapped across the blue-skinned face. With each punch and kick she threw, the alien could take and seven more just like it. The suit was a military marvel. It adapted to what its wearer needs, alternating between strength and speed with little difficulty, all while providing more than adequate protection. She, on the other hand, had nothing save for her vest, her wits and whatever upgrades the *Spellsong* had given her. With every punch she could feel them; in fact she'd been feeling them all day. She could aim better, shoot faster and even in a scrape like this she was punching harder, striking quicker and just plain being all around tougher. It wasn't like she had been augmented, her body was still her own but it was working at peak efficiency. She was at the peak of human fitness. She didn't tire, she didn't slow and she didn't weaken. With every broken knuckle, torn flesh and cracked rib she felt stronger. The more she fought the better she felt.

Guiver blocked another punch, the pain almost non-existent now, and fired back two of her own, slicing at his face with the edge of her knife. He winced at the cut, muttering a foreign curse, but kept on fighting. He shifted his weight, adjusted his arms for strength, and fired a devastating punch. It should have forced her back or knocked her chin clear off her face, but it did neither. Instead she curled her torso sideways, avoiding the punch, stepped into the commander footing and snapped with her elbow. He tried to pull back; he tried to move but as the firm human elbow smashed against his face his footing faulted as he staggered over her feet. Guiver grabbed the extended arm, snatching it before he could recoil it, and twisted upwards, leaving his underarm exposed. With a scream and a stab Guiver buried her knife deep into the alien's armpit and twisted.

Voldl snorted as his legs gave out and he crumbled to the floor like a fallen tower. Guiver panted as she stood over the body. She wanted to spit on him but found no saliva available, instead she stood over him and bled.

"We are your salvation," he muttered. "We are here to cut free the cancerous heart of humanity, to pull you up from perdition."

"Your people still might, who knows." she replied, "But I can be certain you won't live to see it happen."

"What are you, Major? What makes you different than the rest of these space-faring vagabonds?"

She pressed her foot into Voldl's chest and knelt down. She pulled the knife free. "I'm a solider; I'm the last soldier. And where I come from a soldier is a hellva lot tougher then the navy."

"Your people have no army," he scoffed. "Why cling to an extinct ideal?"

Major Allana Guiver couldn't help but smile, despite the pain and the agony, despite the war going on around her; she couldn't help but let a grin escape on her broken and bruised lips. She knew why she clung to the army and she knew why she could never let it go. It was part of her, it always had been and it always would be. It wasn't all she was or who she was but it was a part of what she was. In the days before the first Great War, before the founding of the EDI she had been a member of the Canadian Forces, a part of the Canadian Army and a proud member of the Princess Patricia's Canadian Light Infantry. The PPCLI didn't have an official motto, they never needed one, but they did have two unofficial ones. There was *First in the Field*, a throwback to the First World War where the PPCLI were the first Canadian units deployed. The second unofficial motto felt a lot more relevant. "Once a Patricia, always a Patricia."

And with that she buried the blade deep in the

Commander's neck. She watched him die, like he was the sacrifice that secured her future, like his death was the final and irremovable stamp in figuring out her new identity in this uncertain future but the truth was she just wanted to make sure he was dead.

Satisfied at his passing she withdrew her blade, sheathed it, and took from him the curved punching dagger he wore. She looked up and saw Sarah rushing over to her.

"Guiver! We've got--." She recoiled a bit, staring at the horrid sight that was Allana's face. "Holy fuck, you look like shit. Never mind, get up. We're getting out of here on the *Great Expectations*."

Guiver looked around. She saw Reid and Clay approaching quickly, a handful of the Stalwart and Quentin and Keiser carrying Campbell's. She couldn't see Gregory or Stark and Marco just lay on the floor, fifty meters away in the same spot he had been since he'd been struck down.

"Where are..."

"They're on the GE." Sarah replied, cutting off the Najor's pain filled inquiry. "They've been bringing the injured there so Gregory and others can treat them."

Guiver looked out onto the runway as ship after ship, accompanied by the brave pilots of Crow wing, rocketed to the stars taking with them as many of the innocents as they could carry. The moon would still belong to the Viatos but every life that got off this rock made the mission worth it.

"Radio Ensemble and tell them to meet us in the stars." Guiver recoil at the pain as she climbed to her feet, nearly dropping back down to the floor. Sarah grabbed her arms and helped her up. Clay handed her a discarded assault rifle. The Major checked the weapon and cocked it. "We're talking the *Great Expectation* and getting the hell out of here." Clay and Sarah both nodded in agreement and what few remained moved for the waiting ship.

Then the *Great Expectation* blew up.

CHAPTER TWENTY-THREE
Pherca Moon Invasion +14:35 hours

As Crow wing escorted the civilian freighters up the remaining HEF wings, Peregrine, Raven and Kites, circled the Pherca sky gunning down any diamond fighter they could get a lock on. Every starfighter wing of the HEF was named after a bird from the Earth that was, the only exception being Special Forces squadrons. The four wings descended from the stars like a swarm of their namesake, plummeting at great speeds and killing their prey before they knew what was happening.

Three squads of diamond fighter - nine fighters in total - bolted for the hangar, looking to blow any civilian ship out of the sky before they left orbit. Three diamonds were shot out of the sky by the Peregrine wall and three by Kite weapons. One diamond was forced to retreat by enemy fire but two ships made it past. Two ships made it over the hangar. Using whatever remaining payload they had in reserve, the twin diamond fighters hit the *Great Expectation* with everything. It was the final freighter left on the moon and the Viatos couldn't let it escape. They dumped everything they had into the ship and watched it explode.

Sarah Gamble just stared in disbelief. Gregory, Stark and the hundreds of others burned before her eyes and all she could do was stare. Keiser bolted for the ship; he needed to help, to do something but was quickly grabbed by Quentin and Reid. There was nothing he, or anyone, could do and they all knew it.

"Well, we're boned," Clay muttered.

Guiver screamed. As loud as she could and at the top of her lung she yelled. She started with *damn it* and *crap* before rotating into every curse word she knew, stringing them together in one long continuous Hiroshima-size nuclear weapon of profanity. She used words too colourful for sailors, construction workers and rappers. She used words that she normally found offensive. She even used extinct curse words, phrases and prose that the remainder of Bungee and the Stalwart had never heard before. Eventually the thawed Major ran out of words and simply screamed.

As quickly as her outburst came it vanished. Guiver stood there, panting heavily as her mind raced. She flipped open her comms and started to broadcast.

"*Mojave* this is Bungee Actual. Do you read?" She said calmly.

"This is *Mojave* Actual," Cantor's voice replied, "Thank God you wern't on the *Great Expectation*."

"What is the sit-rep of our boys?"

"All wings are retreating. We've got dozens of hostile

warps. We're booking it out of here as soon as you touch in with us."

"Where is Pigeon and Ensemble?"

Silence. Moments later Cantor's voice returned. "Pigeon is five minutes out from touching down with us. They have Ensemble aboard. What is your ETA?"

"We...." She paused. "We can't make it *Mojave*. We're stuck here. Last ride out went up in flames."

Silence.

"What's the plan then Bungee?"

Guiver looked back at the group. "We'll resist and we'll fight. This war is just beginning."

"Good hunting, Bungee." Cantor replied. "We'll see on the other side. I'm...I'm sorry."

"To hell with this," Sub-Lieutenant Cole voice cried over the comms. "Circling back now."

"Negative Pigeon," Guiver yelled. "Do not turn around."

"I... sshshshs can't... shshhshs." Guiver's face seethed in rage. Cole was making static noises with his mouth. "Can't hear you.... shshsh.... going through a tunnel.... shshshshs..... I.... er.... ah.... purple elephant."

Guiver screamed. She started once again with *damn it* and *crap* before rotating into every curse word she knew, stringing them together in one long continuous Nagasaki-size nuclear weapon of profanity. Just as before, as quickly as her outburst came it vanished. Guiver stood there, panting heavily. Not only was this maneuver beyond stupid and not only was he putting

Thibodeau and Tsia in needless danger but the shuttle couldn't hold them all. Someone would have to stay back.

"I'm not going, ma'am." Reid spoke first. Guiver's eyes snapped at him and glared. She wouldn't let any of her men stay behind instead of her. She opened her mouth to speak but Reid cut her off. "You didn't hear what I did over the radio, ma'am. We weren't the only ones. There are hundreds more soldiers out there, lost and alone. They need to be organized and they need to fight."

"We can do that," Quentin added. "You said it yourself. The war is just beginning. We become the rebellion, the stalwart few fighting for freedom."

"Soldiers are scattered," Sarah finished. "We unite them and we fight. By the time you get back, the moon will be ours. All you'll have to do is sweep up the mess."

Guiver looked around. Six of the original Stalwart were nodding, they were joining the rebellion as well. "Fine, then we all stay and we all fight."

"You're really her aren't you?" Quentin asked. "You're really *the* Major Allana Guiver; the one from the first war, from Kiron Port?" She nodded. He laughed. "You're like humanity's personal Excalibur, rising from the water to save the Avalon in it's time of need. You're here for a reason and fighting for just this little moon isn't it. There is a whole war going on that you need to be a part of. You go be you, be the hero and we'll do our best to make you proud back here."

"I..."

"Sorry, ma'am," Quentin said. "You don't get a say. We're staying and you're not. We will be the rebellion, *your* rebellion. You go make us proud out there and we'll make you proud down here."

Quentin snapped to attention. His right hand crisply snapped to the side of his skull. He saluted the legend. Ried quickly followed suit. Sarah and the remaining civilians, despite not being military, did the same.

"It was an honour, ma'am." Reid said.

"No," Allana said as she saluted back. "The honour is mine."

Guiver watched as Clay and Keiser carried Campbell onto the shuttle. A few Stalwart climbed on after. Guiver stepped onto Cole's shuttle and stared at Branford. A sense of relief cross her face. Scars or not, she was happy to see him alive. She just gave him a nod and glanced at the dead husk lying on the floor. "The hell is that?"

"A gift for Doc Mallory," Tsia replied. Allana nodded. It made sense but as she eyed the corspe she secretly hopped that Tsia was *never* her secret santa.

"Get us out of here."

Captain Matthias De-Serres held a command screen and watched the data unfold. The fleet ripped free from warp and swarmed the Viatos ships. The *Rwanda* and the *Cairo* unloaded an unprecedented amount of damage upon the alien ships. It was different watching a battle unfold from aboard ship then back home on the *Avalon*. There was a sense of urgency and risk that he rarely experienced. To him war was numbers, plain and simple.

His screen flashed and Captain Cantor appeared before him. He flashed his trademark smile, one that had wooed many a women before.

"We have our priority target secured," she reported. "We're making for the gate. We have to get our secondary target then we're heading home."

"Roger that, *Mojave*; safe travels." The call ended. He thumbed the data to Captain Dumont.

"Get our birds onboard," Gumont barked. "And give the Mojave cover. She's bolting for the gate." De-Serres watched silently. Scanners showed multiple Viatos ships inbound; they were quickly going to be outnumbered.

"*Mojave* clear." De-Serres rapidly typed on his command screen. With the *Mojave Desert* gone, and their priority target with them, he was free to launch Operation: Avalanche.

Allana Guiver felt numb and she enjoyed it. It wasn't the numbness she'd felt a week earlier, a numbness of the world around her and the world she was no longer apart of, she was literally numb. Doc Mallory, the blessed woman she was, had pumped her so full of pain-killers that movie and TV actors, assuming they still partook in anything they could find, would be impressed. Her body hurt or so she was told. It needed to heal but at this moment she couldn't feel it. Add in a good night's sleep and she'd be right as rain. Her mind paused, was that a saying that still existed in human culture? How did a culture stuck on space ships even know what rain was?

Guiver sank back in the Cantor's ready-room couch and let the cushions slowly consume her. Cantor called her name and Guiver snapped back to reality to find everybody in the room staring at her. She blinked in confusion. The last she looked it had just been Cantor and her. Now there was also Somers, Morrison, Mallory and Tsia. Guiver glanced down and noticed that her lap had been claimed and conquered by a black mess of feline fur. She quickly apologized but had it waved off by the Captain. Tsia bit back on a chuckle.

It had been four hours since the *Mojave Desert* had departed from the Pherca moon. They were on-route to re-claim the *Spellsong*. A great deal had happened in a very short amount of time. Mallory's medic examined each injured member while the doctor herself performed an autopsy on the husk corpse. The moon's escaped ships rocketed back to HEF space and first news of the Viatos strategy reached the Avalon to civilian and military alike. Humanity was at war again and everybody knew it. But the most distressing change of them all, in Allana's opinion, concerned her face appearing over every human media channel in the verse.

The moment they broke orbit thousands of pictures and videos hit the future-interweb-airways. Much like in her time each handheld could snap a picture and record video and thousands of handhelds had digitally snapped an image or video of her, rifle in hand, fighting on the line. There was even a video of her standing before the Stalwart edging them forth with a motivational declaration.

"We will hold this starport and we won't let a single grey-skinned husk past that door. We are getting these civilians off this moon and there is not a damn thing that those aliens can do about it." She was a goddamned sound-byte, again.

It didn't take long for the media to piece together who she was, the legendary Major Allana Guiver had returned. The media was currently bombarding the HEF with demands for the truth. Was she a clone? Was this a trick? How could the Allana Guiver be fighting on the Pherca Moon?

God, she thought, *I really hope I'm not a clone. My life is fucked up as it is.*

Allana never thought herself newsworthy or that her legacy would last this long. Hell, she never expected to have a legacy. But according to Bristol she was popular history, she was up there with General George Patton from WWII, General Asa Baird from the great Arau Pau war and Admiral Lawrence Leir from the Kobold Unification. Children loved to write about her for school and movie companies wanted to make movies about her. Bristol explained that she was two-parts bad-ass, two-parts hero and one-part mystery. Records about her suddenly stopped after the post-Kiron Port events.

She vanished and nobody knew to where or why? There was little else people loved more than a celebrity mystery. People speculated about her as much as they did about Samurai Squad. That was an element Guiver understood. Back in her day people couldn't help but speculate about the final days of Osama bin Laden, SEAL Team Six or the assassination of the augment leader Rachael Higson and the unknown team that took her out.

Gone were her wishes to be a regular civilian and to lead a quiet life. War had once again robbed her of her plans. At least this time she could blame the media for some of it. It was her right as a senior citizen to complain about the media. It was her right as a senior citizen to complain aout whatever she wanted.

Cantor asked about the crew's health. Acting Sub-Lieutenant Brea Mallory started with Guiver and moved down the list. "What of PO Branford?" Guiver interjected.

"He has several cuts and bruises, numerous torn knuckles and a twin neck punctures, probably defence wounds, but none of that matters compared to his face," she reported. "Forty-Seven percent of the left side of his face is covered by second degree burns. I've given him a couple dermal-sheets to help repair his face and I've pulled him off active-duty."

"We still need him, Brea," Somers said. "We need every hand we've got to reclaim the *Spellsong*."

"I've given him a dermal sheet to help repair his

face. While I don't suggest it, he could potentially be up in a couple hours. I can't promise anything, sir, but once we've got the *Spellsong* I have to pull him off active duty for at least a month."

"I understand," Somers said. "It does give us some holes in our roster. I need everybody I can until we can get the Spellsong back and rendezvous *Avalon*."

"We have new bodies on the ship," Cantor said. "Put them to work. There are no free rides on my ship, especially now."

"Yes, ma'am."

Cantor turned back to Dr. Mallory. "Tell me about the alien body."

Mallory explained her autopsy finds. She started with a long, lengthy wave of medical jargon but stopped, after just five minutes, as she noticed all the confused stares. She sighed and restarted.

"The husks are not the Viatos, they are their grown soldiers. I think the blue skins are the Viatos," she explained in laymen's terms. "This husk is three weeks old, best I can figure it they were grown this way. They're not clones or biologically grown experiments, they are literally what we call them: Husks. They have no real brain, at least not like we would classify them. They essentially have a computer program guiding them, albeit a complex one. They operate by set parameters. It's like a flow chart. Do I see a hostile? If yes then proceed to contact directives and follow commands, else then repeat patrol protocol.

"They are, for lack of a better word, grown with their guns and augments attached. Their weapons are powered by their hearts and once they run out of energy or ammo they will melt away. I suspect each husk lasts just less than thirty days."

That explained their disregard for husk life. They grew them like weeds, sent them out to fight and grew new ones to replace those they lost. It still didn't explain their difference when their eyes changed.

"They have bio-circuitry that acts as radios, transmitters and a powerful one that works as a receiver." Mallory continued, "I check with Hera'sun and she says it's far beyond anything needed for simple comms chatter or wireless updates. According to Hera'sun it's wierd to overwrite their computer-brain."

"To make them self-destruct," Morrison added.

"That doesn't need anywhere near the amount of incoming data that this is built for. This receive can receive a godly high amount of data and a lot faster than most of our ship systems can."

Allana blinked her eyes rapidly as she tried to focus but despite her best attempts her mind kept wandering. The pain-killers would only be in her system for an hour more, so the doc had told her, but until then her mind was being weird. She thought of the cat in her lap being chased by a dog around the ship until both leapt from the air-lock and landed in the middle of an EDI base during the Arau Pau war. The cat vanished and the dog was guiding an EDI solider around the base's perimeter sniffing for explosives. Allana rubbed her forehead. The meds were kicking her ass, making her mind jump from topic to topic without logic holding her back. The dog suddenly lay down and the base shifted to the EDI recreation room. The dog was having his ear scratched by his handler as both man and dog watched the other soldiers sit before a TV, each with a controller in their hands, as they fought each other in the digital realms of combat.

Allana sat up, her back straighten up and her eyes went wide. The cat glared in discontent as her movement. Didn't this human know how much of a privilege it was to be his chair?

"It's a god damn video game." The room looked at her once more. "It's a god damned first person shooter." It suddenly made sense. Everything the husks did made sense. "Do you guys have video games?"

"Yeah, why?"

"Back in my day we had war games where you played soldiers. You took the soldiers perspective and you shot things. They were very popular and even become a sport of sorts. You couldn't learn war from them because there were no consequences."

"We have similar things," Somers replied, "My son loves those gun-killing games. He sits there all day killing people......" His head tilted as the XO suddenly understood.

"The grey-eyed husk is a video game's non-player character," Allana explained. "And the green eyes are when a controller, or a player, starts a game."

"So anytime we saw a green-eye, somebody had just taken control of that body from some remote location," Mallory finished. "That explains the massive receiver built into their bodies."

That one fact explained the Viatos. It explained why none of the husks seemed invested like the humans were, they weren't risking their lives. They were just playing a character. It explained their erratic moves. Ever race created advanced infantry tactics in an effort to keep their infantry alive longer. The Viatos didn't have conventional tactics because there wasn't the same need to preserve their lives. If a green-eye died, it re-spawned in another body. It explained the sudden jump in skill when their eyes shifted colour, players were always better then the AI. It also explained the insane moves they pulled like the one Keiser told her. Who fired a grenade downward at an enemy mid-jump? Nobody would save for a gamer trying to pull off a rocket-jump.

Whoever these Viatos were they had turned war into a video game.

CHAPTER TWENTY-FOUR
Pherca Moon Invasion +20:33 hours

Allana Guiver felt pain and she preferred it that way. The painkiller had worn off and her full faculties had returned. While being numb felt better at the time, feeling pain felt more real. Allana stepped onto the shuttle and plopped down into the first seat she could find. Bristol climbed on after her, followed by Clay and Branford. Guiver couldn't help but marvel at the vast improvement that Branford's face had taken. Doc Mallory explained that his treatment was a dermal sheet directly to the face that fed medicine and other future stuff to heal and regenerate the tissue in his face. It all sounded like mumbo-jumbo to her but whatever he had wore on his face for the last five hours had transformed his gruesome face from the horror it had been to the lesser-horror it was now.

The *Mojave* was about to pull out of warp to rendezvous with the Monastica ships *Lionasa* and *Ktrshic*. Hera'sun requested that Allana be introduced to the captains of the two ships, she was an important figure in their religion and the gesture would be greatly appreciated by her people. Cantor agreed and Allana nervously said yes.

Branford and Clay both checked the SMGs that hung from their slings. They were dressed in tactical gear with a vest and helmet but Allana was not. This was a diplomatic mission for her, she didn't need a weapon. Allana climbed to her feet and moved to the cockpit. She smiled at Cole and he offered her a seat in the co-pilot chair.

"There's another game on tonight, ma'am" he offered as she plopped down. "You in?"

She gave him a smile and nodded. "Question for you, I'm entitled to a weapon right?"

Cole nodded. "All officers, on any mission, are entitled to at least a pistol. It's military doctrine. Branford not tell you that?" Guiver shook her head. Cole reached down to the console between them and punched in a seven key code. The top slid off with a buzz and revealed three pistols resting within. "Weird. Every shuttle has a couple upfront. Take one, just give it back. They belong here for emergencies."

Guiver thanked him and withdrew a holstered pistol. She cleared the weapon, reloaded it and cocked it before returning it to its holster. She clipped the holster to her belt and changed the conversation. The two chatted, even as the corvette tore back into reality. Cole exited the Mojave and flew out among the stars. Allana stared at the three ships before them, the *Spellsong* and the two

Monastica ships. The ships were alien in every sense of the word. They belonged to another race, Allana knew next to nothing about them and they looked unlike anything she had seen before. To the Major they looked like a slightly curled finger with a ring, a size to big, resting squarely in the middle of the hull. According to Hera'sun the ring was the focal point of the ship. It provided greater weapons and engines. The hull had its own engines and guns but the ring provided an extra punch. When a Monastica ship needed more fire-power the ring slid to the bow and spun like a revolver and fired blast after blast. If it needed more speed it slid to the back and acted like the after-burners on a starfighter. Resting in the middle, as both did now, gave the ship a nice balance of both.

Cole steered the shuttle towards the *Spellsong* as per the Monastica request. They wanted to meet on their holy symbol. Minutes later Cole docked on the divine ship and opened the back hatch. Allana clapped her friend on the shoulder and stumbled into the rear. The four exited into the hangar. Tsia and Branford had seen the ship before and marched inward but Clay hovered by the shuttle as she marvelled at its size and style. Guiver found herself looking at something much different. The hangar seemed to come alive as she stepped aboard, light suddenly turned on and different system started to hum, but despite all the activity the hangar was empty. There was no waiting party or Monastica shuttles. There was no Monastica anywhere. The ship was empty.

"Weapons up," she snapped as her hand dropped to her pistol, unclipping the snap. "Something's not right."

Branford's head dropped in disappointment. "You're too smart for your own good, Major."

Before Allana could give a confused reply the PO spun and slammed his elbow squarely into Bristol's throat. The doctor made a noise that sounded like a cross between a gag and a snort and then dropped to her knees as her lungs begged for air. Branford's SMG roared to life, plugging Clay with three rounds in the chest, which slammed her against the shuttle door and dropped her to the floor. Branford fired at Allana as the Major dove out of the way. A lucky bolt clipped her shoulder and her body screamed. Every inch of Guiver's body burned with agony, her head screeching in anguish akin to a powerful migraine. Allana wanted to scream but for the first few moments found her voice unresponsive.

The doors opened and six grey-skinned husks, with green-glowing eyes, marched in with their planks levelled. Allana fought the pain, ignoring it like she had all those years she'd spent in the tube and slowly raised her pistol. The barrel shook as she fought her own body. Every bone and nerve wanted to curl up and pass out, the desired effect of the human energy weapon, but she wouldn't allow it.

"Don't do it, Major," Branford ordered as he pressed his SMG to Bristol's head, "or I put a bolt through her skull."

"But human guns don't kill humans," she said, her voice returning in a raspy form.

"But this bitch isn't exactly a purebred is she?" he taunted. "My bolt will burn through her pretty little head and spill everything out on the floor below. Now unless you want another dead doctor on your hands I suggest you drop the gun and get your ass over here. The husks want you and this ship."

Allana dropped her gun and slowly climbed to her feet. "Why? Why help them Marcus? They killed your fellow marines. They killed Winters."

"They're not the enemy. They're the few that will save us. They'll cut out the cancerous heart of humanity and --"

"Raise us from perdition. Yeah, I've heard that. They've radicalized you, Marcus. They are not the salvation. They are going to make us extinct."

A pair of bolts shot out from the shuttle. Two more followed and another two after that. Cole stood in the shuttle's rear, a pistol in each hand, firing as quickly as he could. His first two dropped a pair of husk and his following four made the rest scatter. Clay winced and fired from the ground. Her SMG riddled the closest husk as Guiver pulled a 180 and dove for her discarded pistol. She scooped it up, spun back again and fired twice into a charging husk. She looked for Tsia and Branford and spotted the PO dragging her out of the hanger as six more husk poured in.

"Get in," Cole yelled. "We're out of here."

Allana cursed, grabbed Clay, and dragged her in. Cole closed the door, secured it and bolted for the cockpit. Cole slide into his chair and reached for the guns first. The shuttle's weapons roared and punched a hole in the *Spellsong's* hull. With a roar of the engine Cole flew the shuttle out of the *Spellsong*, the remaining husks following them as the vacuum of space pulled them out of the ship's hangar.

Guiver grabbed the comms and opened the channel. "The *Spellsong* is compromised. Husks have control of the Spellsong."

Cantor cursed. "How the hell did that happen?"

She never got her answer as space lit up with the rainbow colours of warp and two Viatos ships poured out. They opened fire and stopping the *Mojave* from intercepting them. The Viatos dove for the *Spellsong*. They flew in close to the vessel, skimming the hull and latched onto it as they passed. With the alien ship in toe the Viatos ship tore a second tear in reality and vanished into warp.

The *Spellsong* was gone and they were two days away from the nearest Trent-gate. It took seven minutes for Cole to get the shuttle back aboard the *Mojave* and three minutes for Guiver to move from the docking bay to the bridge. She stormed into the room with a heavy pant.

"Where are they?" she barked.

"They're in the warp. We can't track them," Somers updated as Cantor spoke to command screen. Agrima had a channel open to both Monastica Captains and all three were quickly speaking. "What the hell happened on your end?

"Branford has switched sides. He set a trap to hand me over to the husks but now he's got Doctor Tsia." Guiver stared at the stars as she caught her breath. "They keep referring to humanity's cancerous heart. What are they talking about?"

"Cancerous: no clue. Heart of Humanity: That's the Avalon."

"So we go to the *Avalon* and stop them," Guiver snapped.

"We can't. We're two days away from the nearest gate. They're gone."

Allana kicked the nearest console and swore loudly. She couldn't do this, not again. She couldn't lose her. She'd lost too much for one lifetime and she couldn't handle anymore.

"Sir, I have an anomaly," Hera'sun called out. Somers crossed the bridge and knelt by the Monastica's station. "The Viatos dragged the *Spellsong* into warp but as it vanished from reality it seemed to leave by a pair of...droppings."

Hera'sun brought the object onto her center screen and zoomed in. They were large circular shells floating through space. They looked like escape pods but without portholes.

"Anybody in there?" The XO asked

"No life-support, no engines, transmitters or even

space for a person," she explained. "It's not hollow; it's filled to the brim with circuitry."

"A bomb?"

"No explosives," Hera'sun paused. "The tech is more advanced but it looks like the same compilation of a trent-gate; it's giving the same energy reading as one as well."

Somers blinked. Trent-gates were huge but these pods were each only slightly bigger then a car. "The ship was compromised by the husks. Why would they eject a gate-pod?"

"Before it left the *Spellsong* seemed to be emitting strange energy readings. It was communicating with something and different systems across the ships randomly started to activate. I've seen this only once before." Hera'sun spun her chair around and pointed at the Major. "I saw it when I escorted her aboard the divine ship. I think the two of them are connected; the divine presence and its avatar."

"You're saying that the ship made sure Guiver could follow it?" The Monastica nodded, whispering a small prayer. "Then we can go after it. Start working on the pod, figure it out."

"Excellent. I'll start getting a team together," Guiver exclaimed.

"No." Both looked over at Cantor. The captain clipped her command screen to her chair and stood up. "I just finished talking to the two other captains and we all agree. It's too dangerous to try and retake the

Spellsong. We have to destroy it."

Hera'sun's body froze. The words ripped through her chest and tore at her alien heart. "But we can't," she pleaded.

"We can't leave it in the Viatos hands," Cantor explained. "I'm sorry but tech that advanced could allow them to rip a hole through humans, Monastica, Kobolds and anything else brave enough to challenge them. The *Ktrshic* captain suggested it."

Priest-Captain Yven'lun; he was a respected captain and dedicated priest among her people. His mission, the *Ktrshic*'s mission, wasn't one of exploration like most others but one to provide support and religious guidance to the Monastica fleet. Every ship in the fleet had its own priest aboard but for the strongest guidance or the most important of religious undertaking the fleet sought out the small handful of Priest-Captains. In the space faring culture like their own, the religious powers travelled to their people. If the holy man thought destruction as the only recourse left to prevent the *Spellsong* from desecration then, as much as it pained Hera'sun, destruction it was.

"Tsia is aboard that ship," Allana snapped. "We can't let her die."

"Stand down, Major," Cantor ordered, using a tone she'd hadn't found available in years. "I don't want to see her die any more then you do but I cannot risk you or anyone else for the sake of one person."

Guiver didn't know what to do. She wanted to flip

out, to rip the naval officer from head to toe and to tell her that the army didn't leave anybody behind. She wanted to slug the older woman and take command of the ship but none of that would get Tsia back. Instead she stormed off the bridge.

Back in her quarters Allana plopped her tired, yet angry, body onto her bed and screamed. She didn't curse and she didn't yell words, she just let out a burst of noise. They were going to destroy the *Spellsong* and she was pissed and devastated all at once. Ignoring the fact that the *Spellsong* had been her home for four hundred years the ship held the last bits of Tenuvah aboard it. Her VR glasses only worked if the Spellsong was in range and still in one piece. When the alien ship exploded in the midnight of space she was going to lose not just one doctor, but both. In one single explosion Tenuvah and Bristol would vanish.

Allana grabbed the glasses off her dresser and placed them on her eyes, praying that she was still in range. The world melted away and was quickly replaced with the base on Kiron Port. Tenuvah stood before a docking door with the love of her life, Allana Guiver, trapped on the other side.

"What are you doing Tenuvah? Let me out!" Allana screamed, jamming the keypad over and over, each press getting a depressing error beep. She gave up, resorting to smashing her fist against the steel, tears rolling down her cheeks. "Let me out. Don't do this to me."

"Get on the ship and get out of here." Tenuvah's

pistol dropped from her hand. She pressed her hand on the transparent steel. "I need you to live; I need you to continue being the wonderful woman that you always are. You have a new life; don't waste it wishing for what can't be. I love you babe, I always will."

Then like static on a screen, she vanished, taking with her all of Kirion Port. Allana dropped to the floor, what little there was in the endless white world, and hugged her legs. She buried her face in between knees and cried. She heard footsteps approaching, each step echoing on forever. She didn't need to look up, there was only one person left to talk to, only one person left to give her advice. In times like these it was him, it was *always* him. He'd never speak but his expressions spoke novels.

She looked up and saw the silent visage of Master Corporal Christian Tribal. He knelt before her and made eye contact. To most people his face never seemed to change, it always held the same solemn look, but that wasn't true. Those who knew him, like her and her battalion, could spot the subtle nuances in his face and knew that each spoke volumes. Their eyes didn't move or budge, they didn't dart around or try to signal others using a secret code; they simply stared at each other, blinking as needed. Yet somehow they each knew.

"Major." It was one word and it would be the only one he'd say. He offered her his hand and hoisted her to her feet. He handed her a pistol.

She gripped the weapon and cocked it. "Let's go be

big damn heroes."

"Blessed be, I got it working." Somers glanced over at Cantor and got a nod.

"Send our allies what you found and take us out. We're leaving without the Monastica ships." Cantor said, "They'll catch up. Communications: Start broadcasting our location to all nearby ally ships. I want people to be able to find us."

The pod began to spin and glow, the circuits flashing rapidly as the device quickly built up energy. In an explosion of rainbow colours the pod exploded, leaving a temporary tear into warp in its place.

Cantor marvelled at the device. It was a one-shot gate. Ingenious.

The *Mojave*'s sub-lights roared to light as the ship flew through the tear and entered warp space.

Guiver pulled off her glasses, slipping them into her front pocket, and grabbed her green bag. She plopped it down on her desk, quickly unzipped it and fished through its contents until her fingers came across the familiar cold steel. She withdrew the pistol and pulled back on the slide. It was a pistol, not an energy pistol but a good old-fashioned bullet-shooting-gun pistol; it was *her* pistol. The moment she stepped on the *Avalon* her new life became real. Out in the black there was still desbelief. Once she stepped on the big boat this life became her life. She'd be an upstanding future-girl.

She'd use future weapons and never again kill another human being and she was fine with that. But as she slid the twelve-round clip into the pistol, thinking about the next time she saw Branford, she smiled at a single realization.

She was still a long ways away from the *Avalon*.

The armoury doors opened and Allana stormed inside. The young marine working the station, a young man whose name she could remember at the moment, glance up at her.

"Um...ma'am you're no---." His lips, temporarily, snapped shut as she held up her gun. She didn't aim it at him, she simply held it up so he could see it. "That's not an energy pistol. Is that a slugthrower?"

Slug thrower; a cute futuristic name.

"I need weapons. Are you going to stop me?"

"No, ma'am." He snapped. "But...I....need authorization to open the cage for you."

She pointed her gun at the cage's lock and squeezed the trigger. A loud bang, followed by the metallic clang, filled the room as the lock-panel shattered. She pulled open the door and grabbed a tactical vest, throwing it over her shoulders. Her vision became blocked, for only a second, as she put on the vest, pulling down over her face, but when her vision returned she found four new bodies in the room, each staring at her.

It was Clay, Thibodeau, Keiser and Doc Mallory.

"What do you want?" Allana sternly asked.

"We're here to help you," Clay smirked.

"I'm here to talk you out of it," Mallory clarified. "This is a stupid plan."

Guiver, ignoring the doctor, glanced at Clay and shook her head. "The marines will have all of your asses for this. Your careers will be over."

"We'd be scared if we were marines, ma'am," Keiser interjected as he stepped forward and grabbed the vests, handing them out one by one. "But if I recall, you assigned each of us all to the HEF Army."

"That's what I remember." Clay smirked as she pulled on hers.

"Private Lief Keiser reporting for duty," he said with a sharp salute.

"Private Tanya Clay reporting as requested."

Their excuse would never hold up in a military court marshal but she was still glad to have them both. Guiver looked at Thibodeau. Unlike the other two she wasn't there when Guiver made her ridiculous and grand statement. She had no flimsy excuse.

Thibodeau just shrugged and pulled on her vest. "J'aime une bonne bagarre."

Before she could respond with a snide remark or a touching nod a devastating pain shot up left-side. Guiver grunted and dropped to the floor, plummeting to her knees. She could feel a pair of invisible claws, from some heinous creature, ripping into her back, squeezing her body and pinning her down. Guiver knew there was nothing there, she knew that this was a phantom pain of some sort, but she could feel it. Mallory rushed over to help but stopped mid-way as the Major violently flailed her arms.

Let go of me!

She twitched again and felt the left-claw release her. She shook her right side and twitched again, the invisible right-claw letting go as well. Guiver dropped to the floor, the pain vanishing, and breathed heavily.

Free!

"We have the *Spellsong* in sight." Cantor grabbed her screen and pulled up the data. She had been in warp for little more than an hour, burning every engine they had, as they chased the Viatos ships. Even with the extra luggage they moved through warp with such grace. It was pure luck alone that allowed them to catch up to the stolen ship, Cantor hazarded to guess how far ahead the Viatos would be without it.

"She's breaking free?" Cantor bolted to her feet and watched on the main screen. The *Spellsong*, for some unknown reason, began to violently shake and twitch, the sides flailing about until it broke free of the alien grapples. With no engines to combat the warp currents, the ships veered downwards, crashing against the dimension walls, and tore back through into reality.

"Get us out, now!" Cantor couldn't explain it but she wasn't looking a gift horse in the mouth. The *Mojave* tore out of space, returning to the realm of reality and veered towards the drifting *Spellsong*.

Guiver yelled as Doc Mallory jammed a thick needle into the soldier's shoulder. The needle, a medical examination device, sent three electric jolts throughout her body. "You just happened to be carrying a medical needle?"

"I'm a doctor. It's my job," Mallory snapped back as she withdrew the needle. She looked down at her handheld. "It's your nano-bots, they've reactivated. Don't do this, Allana. You're not well and I don't know what effect the Spellsong is going to have on you."

"I have to," Guiver replied between grunts, forcing herself back to her feet. "I can't let Tsia die for me. So either get on with the *physically trying to stop me* or get out of my way; I also have a job to do."

Mallory eyed the Major before cursing and grabbing a rifle. "Go, but I'm coming with you. Somebody's got to look after you."

Thibodeau handed out the rifles as Clay handed out the ammunition and gear. The French marine handed the Major a rifle and nodded for the door. The five of them exited the armoury and moved for the hangar.

Thibodeau pulled up alongside Guiver. "How are we getting off this ship?"

"I'll steal a ship and steal a pilot," Allana explained as they entered the hangar "And then I..."

Her voice trailed off as she saw the shuttle ready and waiting. The door was open and the engine was running; this ship was ready to fly. Allana climbed in and moved to the cockpit. Cole sat in the pilot's chair with his legs up on the dashboard and his thumbs eagerly tapping along his handheld. "What took you so long, ma'am?"

"What are you doing?"

"You need a pilot and I happen to be the one that likes you the most." He pulled his feet of and spun towards the controls. "Sit down and buckle up. We're punching out of here."

Allana smirked; this almost felt like home. "How are we getting out of here? Cantor's not going to just open the doors."

"You didn't have a plan at all, did you?" Guiver shook her head. Cole laughed as he tapped on the handheld. "Good thing you have me. You see Cantor, Somers and Branford were assigned to the *Mojave* because they were the best; this was a reward for them. Then there were people like me. Some of us are here because we're being punished."

The *Mojave Desert* circled in space as their guns warmed up. The *Spellsong* was directly in their sights. Cantor expected that the ship could take a few hits; she just hoped she had enough fire-power at her disposal to sink the alien bird. With the go ahead from tactical Cantor rose from her chair, taking her standard combat-stand and raised her arm to signal the attack.

"Hangar door is open." Her head snapped over at her XO. "A shuttle just launched. Who the hell gave them permission?"

The Captain cursed quietly. Cole; the kid was too

good at what he did. This changed plans. One casualty was acceptable, horrifying as it was, but six, including Guiver herself, was not.

"Helm: take us around. Tactical: Open fire the moment the Viatos show themselves. Comms: Do not, and I mean not, let our beacon go offline. This isn't a hit and run anymore, we're in a death fight." She looked back the main screen. "All hands: battle stations."

The shuttle docked and the rear hatch opened. It was the same shuttle they had docked in earlier, when the Viatos ambushed them only this time the hole had mysteriously been repaired. Guiver was first off the shuttle, her boots hitting the alien deck with a thud as her rifle roared to life at the incoming wave of husks. The grey-skins fell and Allana pushed inwards, the marines not far behind. With each step Allana took into the *Spellsong* the stronger a feeling grew within her. A shiver ran through her spine and her fingers tingled. With each step the ship became clearer in her mind, memories of the ship's layout flooding her brain. The ship was reacting to her and her to it.

She pressed her body against the hangar door and waited for the others, only seconds behind, to catch up. Her mind maintained a razor focus, never once straying to the consequences of her action. Instead all she thought about was pushing inwards and saving Bristol.

Doctor Bristol Tsia.

The ships schematics flashed before her eyes and

suddenly she knew. She knew where Branford was holding her. Guiver opened hangar door and urged her team left down a hallway.

Mallory watched at Guiver moved without hesitation. lay, Keiser and Thibodeau had all seen her in action, the doctor had not. Guiver knew exactly what she was doing; she knew how to lead a team and always seemed to know where the husks were before anybody else did. She'd have her rifle up and firing before the rest of them even laid eyes on the ugly grey-skins. She'd fire down an empty hallway and the bolt would hit the husk square in the head just as it turned the corner.

Guiver pulled the squad to a halt at a set of metallic double doors. A shiver ran through the Major's body as she looked back at the four of them. "I'm going forward. Clay: go left and shoot in a wide arc. Keiser: Go right and keep low. Thibodeau: They have snipers on the elevated walkways. Go 11 o'clock, 2 o'clock and then back to 10. Mallory: Husks behind in you fifteen seconds. Check?"

The three marines confirmed while Mallory stood there slightly confused. None of her orders made sense. She was a doctor not a marine but even she knew that her breach method was sloppy. It provided no cover or protection but before she could say anything the Major moved. Without anyone touching a panel the double doors sprung opened and Guiver and her marines bolted inwards.

Clay went left and fired, her wide angle catching a broadly spaced out husk formation. Keiser went right and kept low. He saw husks behind a series of elevated alien crates that provided cover solely from the knee up. He aimed downward, crouching as he ran, and fired bursts through each of their legs. Thibodeau had her rifle aimed at the walkways and saw the snipers. They ran to the edge, looking for a clear shot, and got there at different times. The husk at 11 o'clock hit the edge first and found a bolt between his eyes, the one at 2 o'clock got there second and died to a bolt through the neck, and the third sniper, the one at 10 o'clock, got there third only to find a burst of rifle bolts waiting for him.

Mallory just stared. The entire room was cleared, without breaching and without explosives, and it took ten seconds; thirteen max.

She heard the door open from behind her. Mallory spun to find three husks approaching from the rear, bolting up the hallways. The doctor squeezed burst after burst into surprised husks and each hit the floor before they were even halfway near her.

Correction: clearing the room took exactly fifteen seconds.

Clay let out a whoop and Keiser boasted a bold look on his young face. Mallory wasn't nearly as impressed, she was worried. "How did you do that? How did you know exactly where everybody was?"

Guiver stared at her hand in surprise. "I can feel it." She enlightened, "I can feel the ship, I can feel everybody in it and I can feel all of its systems." Guiver closed her eyes, her face scrunching as she grunted.

"What's wrong?"

"Nothing; I just shut off the air to twelve different rooms." Allana explained as her eyes opened, her chest panting. "I can affect the ship it just takes a lot of concentration."

She pointed at the double door and they slammed shut instantly. "Doors are easy, it's the bigger systems that hard to grasp. It's like trying to get that word that just on the tip of your tongue." Without a hint of warning the ship violently shook, Guiver screamed and then dropped to the floor.

"The *Spellsong* is taking hits." Morrison called out as the *Mojave* flew past the alien ship, using it as cover from the Viatos.

"Cut cannon power by 50%," Cantor ordered. With less power the cannons could fire twice as often but with less punch. "And start splitting up our weapon's fire. One cannon per hostile."

Somers bolted over to the helmsmen and leaned over his station. "Start taking evasive manoeuvres. Every thirty second duck behind the *Spellsong*; it'll give us some breathing room."

The *Mojave*'s gun fired rapidly, the ship bolts crashing against the alien shield, as the ship rocketed out from behind the *Spellsong*. Their weapons could deal a punch if Morrison could target all guns on one hostile but Cantor needed to keep both occupied. If she constantly bombarded both with energy bolts neither could launch their diamond fighters. The *Mojave* didn't have any starfighters to combat the diamond.

"Incoming warp." Cantor stomach tightened, knotting up as the expectation of the worst. "It the Monastica ships."

Cantor found herself sighing loudly. They were up a creek already, she didn't know what she would have done if more Viatos had shown up.

"Morrison: pick a ship and target it with all guns." Cantor snapped, "Somers: tell the *Lionasa* and the *Ktrshic* to target the other ship. Inform them of the change and tell them we protect the *Spellsong* at all cost."

The two Monastica ships came about, their center ring firmly lock in the ship's rear, and targeted all guns onto the lead Viatos ship. Their armadillo ships glimmered as waves of energy rippled from bow to stern and into the center ring. The two rings began to spin as they moved up the hull, past the center mark and locked on the bow. The spin picked up speed as the ring's forward guns emerged from their gun ports and opened fire.

Guiver climbed back to her feet, the pain nothing more than a faint lingering ache. "The ship took fire;" she panted. "And I felt it. I felt every ache."

"We have to hurry up" Mallory explained. "Sustaining this level of stress would be impossible for the healthiest of bodies and you're damaged goods already."

"I love it when a pretty woman thinks about my body," Guiver grunted, forcing a joke. Mallory opened her mouth to speak but found herself speechless. Despite her orientation being the opposite of Guiver's, there was a certain appeal of being flirted with by the legendary soldier.

"We're almost there," Guiver said.

The major led them through the ship, past a galley, past two alien bathrooms and past numerous officer quarters. Twice they encounter husk patrols but none made a difference. One became trapped behind fire doors with a wave of Allana's hand while the other found the gravity in their room suddenly shut-off. The squad stopped at a random door and Allana felt another shiver run through her body. "She's in here."

Branford nervously paced. Allana was on the ship and she was punching her way here. He couldn't help but snicker. Hell hath no fury like a woman scorned; words to live by. His handheld beep and he gave it a glance.

"My Saviour," he began, turning to the highest ranking husk. "The anomaly's at the door."

"Prepare for combat," the husk barked. It didn't need to use words, they could communicate without speaking in these bodies, but Branford knew they spoke for his behalf. Thirty husks scrambled to take position, some dropped to one knee as other moved for the front door.

"Back-up," Branford barked, correcting them. "They'll breach the wall with an explosive and storm the room. The further back we are the better." He pointed to a series of C-shaped consoles that were attached to the far walls. "Get near those. They'll provide cover and distance."

The husk paused. Their glowing eyes blinked and then did as they were told. Branford had learned the truth about the husks. Each was a vessel for the Viatos' divine power. He assumed that the blinking green eyes were the choirs granting permission. The husks pressed against the electronic consoles and aimed at the door.

Let's see you deal with this one bitch, Branford thought smugly. *Somebody is about to get a brutal surprise.*

Then the consoles exploded. They erupted first in sparks, twinkling like the *Avalon Day* fireworks and then they exploded in a massive ball of fire, taking over half of the husks with them. The door sprung opened and Allana stormed in with Thibodeau, Keiser, the doctor and the bitch from Black Helo. Allana's rifle spastically jumped, firing bolts seemingly at random. At first Branford thought she'd lost it but as he spent a second watching he realized it was quite the opposite. Her aim wasn't spastic, it was insanely precise. She was firing with accuracy beyond what would be humanly possible.

Branford raised his SMG and fired a burst directly at her, his aim nearly as accurate as hers, but what should have been a bullseye – three bullseyes – became a clear miss as she suddenly, and at the last second, twitched out of the way, causing the bolts to sail past her. Branford cursed and dashed for the back room. The prisoner was there and better yet he could ambush the Major when she came after him. Branford entered the room and stood by the door, his SMG raised high. The moment she stepped in he'd slam the butt of his rifle deep into her skull. She wouldn't have time to react.

Branford mind raced as he waited. The way she fired, it was unbelievable. Was she always that good? Had he been fooling himself this entire time. The way she moved, it was like she knew where everybody was with but a single glance. Was she it? What she the true savior?

His brain erupted in pain.

No. The Viatos were humanity's savior. They knew the cancer that existed and they knew how to remove it. His faith was with the Viatos. Question not the Viatos; question not your faith.

The door open and Branford struck but instead of a satisfying steel-to-skull crunch he heard only the steel-on-steel grind as the Major blocked with her own weapon. But how?

Allana struck fast, kicking at his knee, twisting his arms with her weapon and shoving him back with a powerful push. He stumbled back, recovering his footing just in time to see Allana charging at him. She struck with her knee, nailing him in the chest. Using the barrel of her rifle, she slapped his gun downwards. She shifted her grip and reversed the weapon, slapping the butt of the weapon into the left side of Branford's face. The PO screamed a blood curdling cry of mindboggling pain as the hard-as-steel butt of the weapon slapped the burnt half of his face. His left leg buckled, his body dropping to the floor, but Allana gave him no pity. She arched back and struck again, once more putting the butt of the assault rifle into the burnt side of his face. His other leg buckled and he crumpled.

Allana let go of her rifle, the sling catching it as it fell, and drew her futuristic energy pistol. She aimed the barrel centimetres away from the facial burns and pulled the trigger. The bolt crashed into his face and burned through his skin. An energy bolt, under normal circumstances, would put every nerve of your body on alert and make each of them burn in agony. A bolt directly to the surface of a second degree burn caused enough pain to make any man or woman seriously contemplate death.

Guiver squeezed the trigger once more.

"I should put a bolt through your skull and kill you right here," she said as his screaming died down. "But I can't can I? Human guns don't kill humans."

"Welcome....to.....the....future," he spat

Allana dropped her energy pistol. She reached around to the back of her belt, to the rear holster, and pulled free her pistol; her good old fashion pistol. She levelled it at Branford's head and pulled back the hammer. "It's a good thing I'm an old fashioned girl."

She pulled the trigger.

CHAPTER TWENTY-FIVE
Pherca Moon Invasion +23:13 hours

Captain Cantor gave a silent whoop as the lead Viatos ship disassembled under the combined might of the *Lionasa* and the *Ktrshic*. She watched as each of the little pieces ignited their engines and vanished into the warp through dozens of small personal tears. The rear ship had succumb to a similar fate, albeit by the Mojave's weapon, moments earlier. Cantor moved to her chair. The battle was over and she could sit down.

"Warp signatures."

"They're running, I know."

"Negative, ma'am." Hera'sun explained. "I mean they are indeed running but I have incoming Viatos. Three are tearing through right now and five more are on their way."

Cantor froze midway between stand and sit. Eight Viatos ships? She pushed herself back up and took her combat stand. "Any reply from the beacon?"

"No, ma'am."

"Morrison: target the first thing that comes out.

Somers: make sure our Monastica friends are doing the same. Comms: get me Major Guiver and send it to my screen."

Cantor held her command screen and waited. Second later she heard the Major voice. "This is..... crap.....no codename. Um....this is Avatar." Perhaps it was time to accept what fate had for her.

"Two hostile ships are down, three more have just shown up and five more are on their way. Get out of there, now!"

"Roger that *Mojave*. Avatar - out."

Allana looked at Tsia's unconscious body. She was strapped down to some sort of examination table. The Major frowned and focused.

Release her.

The restraining straps unbuckled and retracted back into the table. Guiver kept her concentration firm on the table.

Wake her up.

A jolt of electricity shot through Tsia's body and forced her awake. Tsia sat up with a jolt, her heart racing as adrenalin coursed through her veins. Guiver approached her, removing the rifle from around her neck, and helped the doctor to her feet.

Tsia wrapped her arms around the Major and gave her a powerful kiss.

It was the kind of kiss that could change a person's view on the world. It was passionate and thrilling, exciting and erotic and unlike anything Allana had kissed in a long, long time. She felt the sweat drip down Bristol's alluring lips, the salty and wet taste and the feeling of the remnant electricity flowing through Bristol's body and into hers. Allana broke the kiss, much to both of their chagrin, and handed her the rifle. "Let's go."

"Is that a slugthrower?"

The pair regrouped with the rest of the team. "Eight Viatos ships inbound. Time to hoof it."

With nothing but her old fashioned pistol in her hand, Allana led the way. She could still feel the other platoons of husks aboard the *Spellsong* but none dared to challenge her. Why bother when Allana would soon be trapped. The Viatos would destroy the *Mojave*, the *Lionasa* and the *Ktrshic* and then Allana would have nowhere else to go.

Allana stopped at the hangar door and opened it up with her mind. "Get to the shuttle."

One by one she watched her squad - her friends - move from the hallway into the hangar. As Tsia, limping in the rear, passed into the hangar Allana mentally willed the door shut. Tsia spun around to find steel separating her from the Major. She moved to open the door but Allana willed it not to budge.

"What are you doing?" Tsia yelled.

Allana clicked on her comms. "Cole. I can't make it to you. Get out of here."

"What? What happened?"

"I'm trapped by a door."

"Oh to hell with this. I'll blast op--."

"Denver; No,"She snapped. Her voice softened as she pleaded. "Please. Get them out of here."

Silence.

"You don't want to come back do you?" he asked.

Allana stared through the door's porthole. Brisol was devastated. She was lividly slamming her fist against the door. It was always doctors.

"I was willing to die to save one girl." She said softly, "I have to do the same for another. If she's going down then I'm going down with her."

"I can't talk you out of it can I, ma'am?"

"Goodbye, Denver."

Allana watched as Thibodeau grabbed the civilian and dragged her off. Another girl whose life she just saved, another doctor she tricked behind a door for her own good and another girl who hated her for it.

She had a type.

A burst of pain shot through her body as one thought flooded the Major's mind.

The Bridge.

The *Mojave* shook as alien fire riddled its shields. Each blast tore a chunk of the shield's power, the barrier draining faster than water from a busted bucket. Each of the three allied ships was desperately fighting to stay alive against the Viatos.

"Shuttle incoming."

"Open the hangar and get them aboard. Give them covering fire," Cantor barked. "Is there a Trent-gate nearby?"

Somers just shook his head.

"Radio the Monastica ship. It's time to run."

"Incoming warp."

Space lit as five Viatos ships tore into reality. The five new ships poured out, taking up points around the HEF ship and its allies. Cantor cursed loudly. "Ma'am, We have a message."

Cantor pointed to the big screen. The face of a blue skinned alien appeared. "Power-down your weapons or be destroyed." Cantor reluctantly nodded at Morrison. The tactical officer thumbed off the power and watched as the guns ran silent. "Very good, now stand by. We will discuss your surrender momentarily."

Cantor plopped down in her chair. They were outnumbered, outgunned and they had nowhere left to run. The battle was over and they had lost.

Allana stepped onto the *Spellsong*'s bridge "Tenuvah!" She bellowed, screaming at the top of her lungs. She screamed over and over until her throat became horse. "Where are you?"

The rest of the *Spellsong* looked unmistakably alien but the bridge looked human. It had the standard stations, communications, tactical, science station and helms. It had the XO's chair, a giant view screen and the standard captain's chair.

The captain chair suddenly lit up from the base, strands of light moving up the chair like a glowing tree. Allana never claimed she was a genius but in a room of dark and silent stations the one glowing chair seemed like an obvious hint. She marched over and carefully eased her body into the chair. She pulled the VR glasses from her front pocket and carefully placed it over her face. The world didn't dissolve instead she found herself exactly where she was, on the *Spellsong* bridge, but standing before was Tenuvah.

"Hello, Anna."

"Ten!" Allana smiled. "I'm here, just like you wanted me to be. I'm done fighting and I'm here, with you."

Tenuvah leaned down and pressed her lips against Allana's. The pair kissed and Allana felt happy. The doctor pulled away, delicately stroking the soldier's face. "You're friends are going to die. You need to save them. You need to keep fighting."

"I can't; I can't do it anymore," she whispered.

"You have to. You are Allana Guiver. There is nobody else who can do what you do, babe. Humanity needs you and you need them." The view screen flickered and space outside the *Spellsong* flashed before her eyes. The *Mojave* and the two Monastic ships were trapped and surrounded by the Viatos ships, lead by a Viatos battleship. "They can't run or fight. They are going to die unless you help them."

"One last time," she whispered. "One last time;

what do I do?"

"You're our captain. Tell us to take battle stations."

"All hands:" Allana said uncertainly. "Battle stations?"

Her glasses flashed rapidly as terabytes of information poured into her head while flickers of light hit each station as the equipment hummed to life. Holograms took form, one per station, and each sat down.

"Communications online, ma'am. We are five in the bush," Allana blinked. Manning communications was the energetic bowler wearing Corporal Jamie Diswal.

"That's not a saying," she muttered disbelieving her eyes.

"Helms operational, my Major." The familiar Russian accent interjected. Allana looked at the form of Sergeant Piotr Budian eagerly working away.

Allana looked over at tactical to see the silent Master Corporal Christian Tribal tapping away. He looked back at her and nodded, returning to his work. She looked at Tenevah as she sauntered over, her rear bouncing slightly, to the science station. "Ready when you are, babe."

"Na without meh ye not," The gruff Highlander boasted as he plopped himself down in the XO chair. "This goona be some rammy lass. I be dreich if I be missing tha."

This was her crew, her team, her family. With them by her side she could do anything, she'd done it before and she'd do it again. "Ok, let's do this."

"Wait!" Everybody turned towards Budain. The Russian Sergeant smiled. "I think Tribal wants to say something."

The silent sniper looked up from tactical and flipped Budain the bird and everybody laughed. Guiver smiled. She was home.

"Let's go be heroes."

"Charging weapons!" Morrison screamed.

Cantor's eyes went wide as the biggest Viatos ship, the battleship, exploded as a beam weapon tore through its hull. It didn't disassemble like every other encounter; it just exploded like a regular ship. Cantor grabbed her command screen. The weapon's fire had come from the *Spellsong*. A second beam ripped through a second ship causing it to explode as well.

The big screen flickered and Allana face suddenly appeared upon it. "You better not be sitting down, *Mojave* Actual. This fight ain over. Get back in the fight! I'll cover you." Allana looked away from the camera. "Helms: Put us between them and the Viatos."

The screen flickered and Allana was gone.

"What the hell is she still doing there?" A stunned Somers asked. "And who is she talking to?"

"Doesn't matter," Cantor decided. She rose from her chair. "Morrison: Fire at will."

"With pleasure, ma'am." Cantor watched as the *Spellsong*, operating on her own power for the first time, moved forward as it provided cover.

"Those were our freebies weren't they?" Allana asked. Tribal just nodded. The main beam weapon would have won this easily but the Silians didn't allow that.

Who were the Silians?

Allana forced herself to focus, to push the new information from the forefront of her brain, and to worry about the battle.

"Ten: scan the Viatos and adapt to their weapons." Three purple lights appeared in the night sky together in a triangle and moved over the nearest Viatos destroyer. When the lights were finished the *Spellsong*'s hull began to shift, changing to adapt to modern weapons. New guns emerged, similar to what the HEF fired but as strong as a Viatos blast, and opened fire.

The Silians believed in equality.

"Comms: contact all Viatos ships and tell them to surrender," she ordered against her better judgement.

"They just told you to shove it, boss lady." Diswal laughed.

"I was hoping they'd say that. Tribal: hit them with fucking everything. I want all of their attention on me."

"Ye frein need ta be runnin'. Let's getta a hole for them while we thol,." McCree winked. "We cun take a punch."

"Good. Get them a gate," she ordered. "Tribal and Budian: make us the biggest target you can. This ball is all about me."

"We'll make you the prettiest princess, my Major."

Bolts and cannon blasts crashed against the *Spellsong*, each blast ripping through the shields and damaging the hull. Guiver stared out at the battle, watching the battle unfold. Space battles weren't her thing; she preferred the face-to-face fight. Cantor could keep the space skirmish.

"We got'er lass. We cun open 'er gate at yer comman'." Allana nodded.

"Diswal: open a line to all three." The screen flickered and a three-way split screen appeared before her. "I'm opening a gate. Get out of here. I'll cover you." She cut the comms before any of them could object. She looked at Tenuvah and frowned.

"You know what you have to do, Allana."

She had to self-destruct the ship. The Viatos couldn't get the *Spellsong* and now that all of space knew it existed they couldn't let it drift either. It was too powerful.

The Silians would rather die than upset the balance.

"Activate self-destruct sequence." The bridge flashed red and a countdown began ticking down, Allana's death clock.

"We'll that'er be aboot that'," Brian laughed. He stood up, came to attention and saluted the Major. She saluted back. "Ye gimme a hee'va rummy. I be dying happy and fu'."

"You're drunk?" Allana said with a laugh.

He shrugged. "Whit's a body tae dae?" And with that he vanished.

Master Warrant Officer Brian McCree.

"It's been a blast, boss lady. I wouldn't change it

for the world," Jamie laughed. He stood up, came to attention and saluted the Major. She saluted back.

"You died in battle, kid," Allana apologised.

"Meh. It's better to have love and lost then to have gotten the worm."

"That not a saying."

"It is now." He tipped his hat and vanished.

Corporal Jamie Diswal.

"It is nigh time I say goodbye, my Major." Piotr said. He stood up, came to attention and saluted the Major. She saluted back.

"I'm sorry I couldn't be what you wanted me to be."

"I died fighting by the woman I love and became famous for it. Grigori Rasputin has nothing on me." He began to hum a *very* old song, changing the world for his own benefit. "Bah! Bah! Bah! Budian! Russia's greatest love machine." Then he and his music faded away.

Sergeant Piotr Budian.

The sniper was next. He stood up, came to attention and saluted the Major. She saluted back. The two locked eyes and stared each other down until finally he spoke. "Major." Then he vanished.

Master Corporal Christian Tribal.

"Guiver's Battalion," she said softly, finally getting the goodbyes she wanted so long ago. "You are dismissed."

Tenuvah walked over to her and gently touched the soldier's shoulder. "It's time for you to go, babe."

"I know." Allana smiled. "I finally get to be with

you."

"No, no you don't. You have to go fight. You need to do what you do best. You need to go be the big damn hero and save humanity. That's why you were frozen, that's why your here. That why the Silians chose you."

Silians. The name rattled around in her since the glasses dumped a terabyte of data into her. "Who the hell are the Silians?"

"They were *the* advanced race. Take every movie cliché and they were it. They looked after our universe. They protected us until we got big and they made sure things stayed sane. They never used weapons stronger then what any culture had and they always planned for the worst."

"So what do they want with me?"

"You're their plan for the worst."

"I don't want to be," Allana admitted. "I'm tired of being Plan B. I want to settle down and live my life."

"You will, I promise," Ten said. "You just have a long way to go to get there.

Allana sighed, "light-years to go before I sleep."

"Maybe in a different life we could have been perfect for each other. Maybe everything would've worked out and we could've been happy together. I wish that's how it was now, I really do," Tenuvah smiled. "But we can't keep going on like this. You need to move on. You'll never forget me, you'll never replace me but you can't live with a ghost forever. You have new friends and new family. You need to live your new life."

Tenuvah leaned in and gave Allana one final kiss. "I love you."

"I love you too," Allana replied. "You always were my Perfect Ten."

"I hate that name."

"I know."

"This is my final gift, Anna; your second chance." Tenuvah said. Then she vanished.

Doctor Tenuvah Sheppard, MD.

A beam of light dowsed Allana, blinding her momentarily. When her sight returned Tenuvah and the *Spellsong* were nowhere to be seen. Allana looked around to find that she was standing aboard the bridge of the *Mojave Desert*. A very confused Captain and crew just stared at her. Allana glanced at the view-screen just in time to see the *Spellsong* exploded taking the remaining Viatos with her.

Tenuvah's final gift was to transport her off the ship.

"Major?" Cantor asked. "Um...where did you come from?"

"I take it you don't have transporter technology?" Cantor shook her head. "It's still just a feverish dream of sci-fi writers?" Cantor nodded.

Allana rubbed her chin and shrugged. "Then I know about as much as you do."

"This is horrible," Hera'sun cried out. Allana turned towards the alien and opened her mouth to apologize for the destruction of the *Spellsong*. The alien never gave her the chance. "Teleporters are possible. This means

Nurem'sun was right." She shook her head. "There will be no living with him now."

Allana grabbed her green bag and plopped it down on her bed. She unzipped it and grabbed her old pistol. She ejected the mag and cleared the barrel. She dropped the weapon into the bag. She opened up her front pocket and carefully withdrew the VR glasses. With a delicate touch she tucked them into the brim of the bowler hat and smiled. She'd never forget and she'd never replace them but she couldn't live with ghosts. She had a new life, it seemed a lot like the old one – battle after battle – but it was hers.

A knock at the door pulled her attention away from her bag. Bristol stood in the doorway. "Hey."

"Cole claimed the rec-room big screen for that dismal sport of his but he asked if you wanted to join him," Allana smiled. Her new life also had space hockey.

"You don't like it?" Allana asked.

"Sticks, pucks and nets. What's the point?" She paused and eyed Allana's eager face. "You already love it don't you?"

"Wait until I find the right team to root for," the Major laughed. "I have to be careful though, I need to find Space-Senators or Space-Oilers. I can't be cheering for Space-Habs or Space-Leafs. That'd just be wrong."

"I literally have no clue what you're talking about.

FROM THE AUTHOR

A wise man once told me that no man writes a book alone. Then he asked for my spare change. On that day I learned two things: I'm only where I am today because of friends and family and that wisdom doesn't pay the bills like it used it.

A lot has changed in my life but my friends haven't. Thanks to Cliff, Lenny, Matt, Jay, Mr. DeYoung, Chelsea, Kayla and Megan. You have always pushed me forward and never shied away from telling me to "Fix it! Fix it!"

To the Gentle Girls (seriously, is that name still a thing?). You have all been there for me and helped in ways I never thought possible. Thanks MM, CL, CM, KF, KC and of course the other MM.

To my family; you are my biggest supporters and critics and somehow that works!

To my Mom: I wouldn't be here without you. Seriously. Not at All. I love you and thanks.

A very special thanks goes to the following:

Bowser and the Princess: you helped me un-forget Basic Training and re-taught me the military way. You also kept me from going bankrupt.

Megan: You turned a decent character into a fully fledged one. Thanks Ms. Editor.

Blondie Bear and the Munchkin: I never thought that this Humpty Dumpty could be put back together again but you two did it!

Ken: Nobody pushed harder to see the Viatos attack then you. That's not suspicious at all. SYMPATHIZER! I think I need to check your neck for twin punctures. Thanks!

To my wife Val: Re-Read the dedication.

And to the High Emperor Zid:

ALL HAIL!!

WHAT'S WORSE THEN BEING STUCK IN A VIDEO GAME AND NOT BEING ABLE TO LOG OUT?

My name is Rake and I'm stuck in a MMO. It wouldn't be so bad if I was in my max level main but I'm not. I'm stuck as my level 1 Rogue. I'm stuck in my bank alt.

Now I'm running for my life, I'm fighting to stay alive and I'm trying to figure out how the hell to get out of here.

Where's a GM when you need one?

HELP!

BEING STUCK IN YOUR BANK ALT!

Vörissa's Catalyst

—ONLINE—

Patch 1.01: New Game+
Patch 1.02: Escort Mission
Patch 1.03: Corpse Run
Patch 1.04: In Another Castle
Patch 1.05: Silent Protagonist

In this new series by Award Winning author Larry Gent, we dive in the action and mystery of the *Stuck Online* genre.

Follow Rake and Co. as they fight in a harsh digital world. If they're smart they'll keep their lives. If their lucky they'll keep their sanity and if they're both, they just may find a way to log out.

MIDNIGHT READING PUBLISHING

ABOUT THE
AUTHOR

Larry Gent is a is a bottomless well of knowlegde on historical wars in worlds that are, sadly, fictional.

Larry is a enthusatic gamer whose dream as a child was to be either a detective or a TARDIS Repair Man (it's like a VCR repair man except you just see the ending of the movie first). He got into writing to give back to the worlds he's enjoyed so much from.

A Perth, Ontario native, he lives in both Ottawa and Halifax where he works as a freelance writer and full-time dreamer. He lives with his wife Valérie and his owner Zid the cat.

Website: Larrygent.com
Twitter: @42webs